Artful
Lies

D1344467

30131 05712544 2

LONDON BOROUGH OF BARNET

Artful
Lies

JODI ELLEN MALPAS

ORION

First published in Great Britain in 2020 by Orion Books,
an imprint of The Orion Publishing Group Ltd
Carmelite House, 50 Victoria Embankment,
London EC4Y 0DZ

An Hachette UK company

3 5 7 9 10 8 6 4

Copyright © Jodi Ellen Malpas 2020

The moral right of Jodi Ellen Malpas to be identified as
the author of this work has been asserted in accordance with
the Copyright, Designs and Patents Act of 1988.

All rights reserved. No part of this publication may be
reproduced, stored in a retrieval system, or transmitted
in any form or by any means, electronic, mechanical,
photocopying, recording, or otherwise, without the
prior permission of both the copyright owner and the
above publisher of this book.

All the characters in this book are fictitious, and any resemblance to
actual persons, living or dead, is purely coincidental.

A CIP catalogue record for this book is
available from the British Library.

ISBN (Mass Market Paperback) 978 1 4091 9750 8
ISBN (eBook) 978 1 4091 9751 5

Typeset by Input Data Services Ltd, Somerset

Printed in Great Britain by Clays Ltd, Elcograf S.p.A.

MIX
Paper from
responsible sources
FSC® C104740

www.orionbooks.co.uk

For my husband

Chapter 1

I never imagined I'd really do this. I never dared to consider leaving my mum behind in our small village of Helston, but after years of battling guilt and grief, I've finally made it here, to London, where I've always wanted to be. Maybe a few years too late and *definitely* under shitty circumstances, but I've made it.

Mum will be fine. It's what I've told myself repeatedly since I boarded the train. Her bright smile felt forced, her wave seemed hesitant, and her voice was shaking with emotion when she held me tightly and told me to show London what I'm made of. But I'm not sure what I'm made of. I'm yet to find out.

Mum will be fine. Mum will be fine. Mum will be fine.

I'd probably be more certain if Dad was there with her.

My father was a very traditional man. He owned a small antiques store, most of the stock worth peanuts. He used to say that the monetary value was of little importance – that more opulent art and antiques were more trouble than they were worth. I didn't agree with him, though I learned over the years not to get into a debate over that. Many called my father eccentric. They were right. He was a character for sure, spent all his time lost in the mountains of junk he called his treasure, his spectacles resting on the end of his nose as he inspected, polished, or restored whatever piece he'd recently acquired. Mum used to call his shop Steptoe's Yard. I used to call it *the office.*

I certainly inherited my father's fascination of all things old, although I have always been drawn to the richer and more historical end of the art and antiquing spectrum. The more rarefied and desirable pieces. The real treasures of this world, not the dilapidated junk my father seemed to find. I'd aced my A levels, was sailing through a history degree at university, and was all set to chase my dream . . . and then Dad passed away. A brain tumour was diagnosed one week, the next he was gone. There was nothing to be done. There was also no time to come to terms with it before he was confined to his bed where he rapidly deteriorated to nothing. He was skin and bones. Half the man we knew. Mum was devastated. I was in shock. Dad was gone.

And so it was. My future was sealed. I sacrificed my dreams of venturing off into the big, wide world to keep Dad's memory alive and his precious store open. The natural progression, I guess you could call it. It didn't feel very natural to me. While Dad's treasure held a certain fondness in my heart, it wasn't the level of history I dreamed of exploring. But Mum needed me.

Now he's been gone five years. I've spent the best part of my twenties immersed in dust and struggling to keep my father's business afloat, dreaming of history beyond my family legacy. Like Sotheby's and fine antiques. Like auction houses and historical masters of art. Like the tons of books on treasure I've immersed myself in. It was all suddenly out of reach. Guilt, grief, and a heavy sense of responsibility kept me in Helston. I felt suffocated. Unfulfilled. Dad's business struggled more each day, and my sense of purpose was crumbling with it. And then there was a breaking point. The point when I realised I was worth more than I was settling for – both professionally and personally. It was the moment when I walked in on my boyfriend and my best friend tearing each other's clothes off.

I didn't scream. I didn't collapse to my knees in despair. My heart simply didn't have the energy to beat faster. I turned and walked away, my mind focused on my next move, as David chased after me and Amy sloped off quietly. My next move didn't involve either of them. In that moment, I realised that I owed it to myself to chase my dreams, and with Mum's blessing and encouragement, I was ready to do exactly that.

So here I am in London, the busiest and most grand city within my reach. I can't afford to go back to university to finish my degree, but I'm prepared to start at the bottom and work my way up. I need to get some money behind me and pick up where I left off all those years ago.

I can do this. I'm where I am supposed to be.

I look at the photograph in my hand, the one I always carry on me. It's of me and Dad. His arm is draped loosely around my shoulders, my long, red hair tangled in his fingers, and my face is screwed up on a laugh from his fierce grip. He never liked letting go of me. 'I'm in big, scary London, Dad,' I say to the picture. 'Wish me luck.' I tuck it away in my purse and take a deep breath.

The sun is warm on my face, and I'm smiling as I scurry along with my fellow Londoners down Regent Street. I'm in the smartest clothes I could find in my wardrobe – a black skirt that I fear is on the short side for an interview, but it will have to do, a white blouse with a cute black and white polka-dot scarf, and a black mac. My toes are pinching in my high-heeled shoes, but I don't care. I'm jobless, friendless, and I have a limited amount of cash. Surprisingly, none of these things are making me stressed, but it does mean nailing my interview today is essential. The job market is sparse. There are never many openings in the art and antiques world at the best of times, but the market is particularly dry at the moment. My only other option isn't even an option yet – not until the agency confirms the rumours are true. There are whispers of a very appealing position coming to the market, but until those whispers are confirmed, the agency can't tell me anything more. So I really do need to nail today's interview. I can't depend on an option that might not even be an option. I'll only survive another month before the rent is due on my flat in south London. *Flat?* I smile to myself. Two rooms hardly qualify as a flat. Everything – the bedroom, the kitchen, the lounge, the dining area – is in one room. The other room is a poky bathroom. But it's mine. It's a start.

I reach the end of the street and stand by the side of the road, glancing around before looking down at my watch. I have fifteen minutes to find my way to the address I have noted down, and I've no clue which direction I should be heading in. I retrieve the directions I was sent, but they don't make any sense, so I grab my phone and bring up Google Maps. Except I don't have an internet connection, and it's all I can do not to throw the damn thing at a wall when I realise why. I have no data allowance left.

'Shit,' I curse to myself, diving in front of a businessman. 'Excuse me, could you tell me where Bond—' I'm barged aside on a frustrated scowl without a word of apology as he steams past me. 'Nice,' I mutter, straightening myself. 'Oh, could you help me, please?' I intercept a smartly dressed lady, but she just waves a mobile phone in my face before taking it back to her ear and hurrying away. 'Great.' I assess the many people dodging my immobile state as I stand in the middle of the pavement like a clown. 'Welcome to London,' I sigh, my shoulders dropping.

I cross the road and cheer when I see a map on the corner. It takes me a few seconds to figure out where I am, another few to find my destination, and only a nanosecond to realise it's going to take me more than fifteen minutes to walk it. Or hobble. My feet are throbbing. Today's interview is for an amazing position – personal assistant to a curator at an auction house. It's perfect. I can't be late.

I dive into the road and wave my arm in the air like a madwoman, searching for an available cab amid the sea of black cars. The indicator of one starts blinking, and it cuts across the traffic, pulling up to the kerb beside me.

Stepping off the pavement, I reach for the door handle, but that's as far as I get. 'Oh,' I cry, as something crashes into my side, knocking me off balance. I stagger, losing my footing on the edge of the kerb, the damn heels that have crippled me all morning dictating my fate. The ground comes towards my face too fast for my brain to catch up and feed any instructions to my hands, which are refusing to come up and save me. *Goddamn it.*

Accepting the inevitable, I clench my eyes shut and wait for the paving slab to meet my face.

But it doesn't.

There's no thud, no pain, no yelp.

Warmth engulfs me, gathering me into a safe bundle and hauling me gently up, saving me from my imminent fall. There *is* a thud, there's impact, but my landing is soft, and I'm still vertical. My arms are gathered in front of me, trapped between my chest and something firm. And the smell. Oh, Jesus, the smell. An inherently masculine smell, leather and spice and something lemony. It saturates my nose, makes my head spin.

'Careful,' a man whispers, gently setting me down.

My eyes remain locked on his throat – a throat that's dusted with even, dark stubble. I should be thanking him. I should be straightening myself out. I should be getting in that cab before I'm late for my interview. But no matter how much I yell at myself on the inside to snap out of it, nothing on the outside is functioning. The roar of London around me is nothing but a muffled white noise.

I clutch my bag to my chest like a protective shield as I peek up. His hair is mousy brown, cut neatly and close to his head at the sides, but longer on top, set with what I know would have been a rough muss of wax-coated fingers. Hazel eyes with flecks of green are shining at me from behind thick-rimmed glasses that rest perfectly on his perfect nose. His eyes, framed with long lashes, are heavy and angelic, almost feminine, and look at me with a lazy, almost amused stare. Jesus, it's all I can do not to step closer and study them. He looks familiar, and I cock my head, wondering where I could have seen him before. I'm being silly. I've been cooped up in Helston for most of my life. I couldn't possibly know him.

My eyes drop like stones when I realise I'm staring, landing on some smart grey trousers. His stance widens, like he's aware of the observation he's under and has decided to showcase it in its best light. The material is pulling on his thighs a little from his hands filling his pockets. He has sturdy thighs. Strong thighs. Rugby-player thighs.

I cough my throat clear. 'Excuse me,' I say, taking hold of the cab's door handle. But he moves fast, sweeping past me and jumping into the cab. *My* cab. 'Hey,' I say indignantly, my arm jarring as I lose my grip of the handle when he pulls the door shut behind him. I step back in shock. He doesn't even look at me, doesn't even acknowledge that he's left me stranded on the kerbside. What I do see, though, is a broad back beneath a grey blazer and a navy scarf wrapped loosely around his neck. And then, when he settles in the seat, I catch sight of his profile. I'm rendered pathetic again for a second. He has the most perfect profile of any man I've ever seen.

I shake myself from my inappropriate observations. This wanker just stole my cab – an arsehole move that wipes out the fact that he saved me from my fall in the first place. Or that he's a gorgeous son of a bitch. I will him to look at me so I can toss him an evil look, but the bastard evades my eyes and the cab pulls away before I can yank the door open and hurl a load of abuse at him.

Stunned and irritated, I stand on the kerb with my mouth open, staring at the rear of the cab driving away. He slowly turns his head and looks out of the back window. The cab might already be fifty-odd feet away, but I definitely see the slow formation of a smug smile.

'You arsehole,' I breathe, and stare for far too long until the cab gets lost among the other traffic. 'Shit.' I pull myself together.

My eyes shoot across the road, my arm flying into the air once more, but I don't get lucky again. Every cab sails right past.

Taking a deep breath, I shake my head as I reach down and remove my heels. I don't have the time or freedom to be bothered by what I'm about to do. 'Excuse me,' I sing as I rush down the street in my bare feet, weaving and dodging everyone in my path. My legs work fast, and despite drawing a few frowns from the pedestrians jumping from my path, I focus on making it to my interview on time.

But I'm not on time.

I land outside the grand building at quarter past ten after taking too many wrong turns. My face is damp, my long, red hair is in my eyes, and my cheeks are probably pinker than usual. I must look a mess.

Holding the side of the wall, I slip on my shoes then take a risky peek at my reflection in the window. 'Bollocks.' My fears are confirmed. I look like I've been dragged through a hedge backwards. My brown eyes are watery, my mascara running. Hardly fitting for an elite auction house.

I spend the next five minutes straightening myself out, which now makes me a full twenty minutes late. If I wasn't so desperate for the job, I wouldn't be so cheeky as to present myself at reception and reel off my excuses. But I *am* desperate. I really need this job. And I really, *really* want it. This particular London auction house – Parsonson's – is renowned for dealing in only the most famous and collectible pieces. It's everything I've ever dreamed of.

Okay, Eleanor. You can turn this around. Smile. Stand tall. Let's do this.

My phone starts ringing, and I growl my frustration as I dive into my bag. My ex-boyfriend's name on the screen adds to my already frazzled nerves. 'Go away, David,' I mutter, rejecting the call before turning off my phone. I said everything I had to say while he chased after me yanking his boxers on. Which was a basic *fuck off.* Hasn't he got the message yet?

Throwing David out of my mind, I focus on the task at hand: getting myself a job. Removing my mac and straightening my shoulders, I push my way through the glass revolving door into the reception area. I immediately feel out of place. It's clinical, with only a curved white desk that blends into the white floor and walls, and four white leather couches are positioned to form a square. It's also silent, but my tentative footsteps, click-ing loudly on the marble floor, soon break the quiet, drawing the attention of a pristine woman behind the desk.

She looks over her glasses at me and smiles, warming the chilly atmosphere. 'Good morning,' she greets, standing from her chair.

'Hi.' I surreptitiously pull my blouse into place, conscious that my attire is too drab, and this place is anything but. 'I have an interview. I was told to ask for Shelley Peters.'

'Ah, Mr Timms's secretary. You are?'

'Eleanor Cole.'

'Yes, I have you on our system.' She reaches for a clipboard and passes it over the high desk, and I relax a little, relieved that she hasn't mentioned my lateness. 'Sign in here, please.'

I take the pen and scribble down my name before pushing it back across the desk. 'Thank you.'

'You're welcome. Take the lift to the seventh floor.'

Smiling my thanks, I make my way over to the lifts, press the call button, and take the time while I'm waiting to restore my equilibrium. When the doors open, I step inside, and I'm whisked up to the seventh floor where I discover that the minimal theme is uniform throughout the building. With the exception of a few plants, this space is just as sparse and cold. 'Hello,' I say as I reach the receptionist's desk.

A lady looks up, not a hint of friendliness on her pointed features. 'I assume you are Eleanor Cole,' she snaps, tossing a file to the side of her desk.

I tense under her disdainful look and straighten my cheerful face. 'Yes.' I have a feeling that even if I told this woman I'd been run over and had dragged myself out of hospital to get here, it would be of no concern to her, never mind some rude arsehole stealing my cab. 'I'm sorry for—'

'Let's not waste any more of each other's time. Mr Timms is a very punctual man. You're over twenty minutes late.'

'It's just—'

'The dog was run over? Your train derailed?'

'No, it's—'

'Mr Timms has moved on to the next candidate, who, by the way, has qualifications.'

'But I believe I have working, practical knowledge to rival any other candidate,' I argue. My CV was something to be proud of when I'd finished it, even if it was missing some important things ... like qualifications. With a lack of those, I had to be creative. I wrote pages and pages of words, touching on everything I know. Which is a lot. It must have caught my potential employer's attention, since I got this interview. Or *did* have it.

'It's irrelevant now,' she mutters. 'Thank you for your time. Goodbye.' A well-manicured hand picks up the phone. 'Good morning, Parsonson's.'

I step away from the desk, well aware I'll get nowhere challenging her. And, actually, I'm certain I wouldn't want to work here even if I was destitute.

As I slowly walk to the lift, I ignore the cold hard fact that I *am* pretty much destitute, and this job could be the difference between keeping my new home and pursuing my dream, or returning to Helston a failure. My reality is suddenly all too real as I enter the lift and fall back down to earth with it. *The cab-thieving bastard.*

After offering the nicer receptionist a tight smile as I slip past her desk, I enter the revolving door and use my waning strength to push it around. I'm feeling a little lost and defeated, walking with no sense of where I'm heading.

What will I do now? I guess it's back to square— the door jars and I crash straight into it, ricocheting off the glass with an almighty bang and dropping my bag. 'Goddamn it.' I blink my vision clear, taking my hand to my knee and rubbing away the stab of pain before I crouch and start gathering up the contents of my bag. Could this day get any worse?

I'm still crouching when I take a peek to the left, then the right, seeing I'm imprisoned on both sides by glass. It's only when I stand and brush my red mane from my face that I notice him.

A man.

A man wearing a grey blazer, trapped on the other side of the revolving door. My eyes flip up to see an insanely handsome face as he reaches to his neck and pulls at something.

A scarf.

A navy scarf.

Realisation sucker-punches me in the face.

His grey blazer, the scarf, his ridiculously good looks, and those shining hazel eyes.

Where are the thick-rimmed glasses? As if he's read my mind, they appear, lifting slowly to his face, but he doesn't put them on. He puts one arm of his glasses to his mouth and slips it between his teeth, and my eyes follow it the whole way.

Cab thief.

And now job thief too.

My gasp of breath steams the glass in front of me, my eyes shooting to his. His mouth stretches into a grin, his lazy eyes sparkling. He remembers me. I want to give him a piece of my mind, but I find myself clamming up instead. He's the reason I'm wandering out of here feeling dejected. Or *was* feeling dejected. Now I don't know what I'm feeling. Awe? Attraction? He must be a wizard, or something equally magical, because I feel like I'm under a spell. My mind is reeling off plenty of instructions, but they're fading to nothing before I can act on them. 'You.' My pathetic accusation tumbles from my lips on a mere whisper.

'Me,' he confirms, as he cocks his head, looking me up and down as he slips on his thick-rimmed Ray-Bans. 'Okay there?'

'Yes.' My reply comes out on a breeze of air, and when I should probably be pushing my way out of the revolving door, I find my eyes feasting on his striking face instead.

'You going to stay there all day?' he asks, a hint of humour in his tone. He puts his hands in his pockets and gets comfortable in his standing position. He's flawless, even if he's a rude arsehole. 'Well?' he asks as I nibble on my bottom lip, my hand tentatively lifting to the glass of the door as I rummage through my mind for words.

And suddenly I have one.

'Twat,' I mumble, feeling my awe leave me and irritation find me. 'Thanks to you, I missed—' Something collides with my back, and I'm suddenly moving forwards. 'Hey.' I dig my heels in, leaning back, trying to stop him from turning the door. I'm no match for him. I narrow my eyes on him as he continues pushing. 'Having fun?' I ask.

He gives me a small but wolfish smirk. 'The greatest.'

I'm spat out of the revolving door, but not on to the street. I'm back in the reception of the auction house again. Frowning, I pivot to look beyond the glass on to the street. He's standing there, his smirk gone, his eyes low and dark. For the love of all things gorgeous, he belongs in an art gallery.

His hand comes up, reaching towards me, and my eyes finally give up their focus on his stunning face. He pulls at something that's trapped in the door.

Something black with white polka dots.

I gasp and reach up to my neck to feel for my scarf. It's not there. My eyes snap to his again, finding more sparkles of mischief as he slowly winds the material of my polka-dot scarf around his fist. Oh good God, he has something of mine, which means I need to talk my legs into moving so I can get it from him.

Shit, this is ridiculous.

I barely lift a foot off the floor before my intention to claim back my scarf is halted. He lifts it to his nose and watches me as he inhales deeply. The muscles between my thighs go into spasm. I burn up. I can't move. But I can talk. Just. 'My scarf, please.'

He starts taking slow steps backwards, keeping my scarf where it is for a few moments before he slowly lowers it, revealing a smile that could floor every woman in a ten-mile radius. 'Payment for saving you.'

What? Saving me? I'm jobless because of him. The man is delusional. And too fucking hot for his own good. I swallow and close my eyes, trying to gather my patience. It takes far longer than I'd like, and when I finally open them, ready to take on this annoying idiot, he's gone.

Air hits my lungs and burns them, and my hand goes to my chest when the rate of my heartbeat suddenly registers. It's frantic, wild, fighting within the constraints of my chest.

What on earth?

I push my way round the door and land on the street. He's nowhere to be seen. My hand goes to my neck again, just to check my scarf isn't there, just to check I didn't imagine what just happened. My neck is bare. If my pulse wasn't thudding in my veins, I would think I'd dreamed that.

Payment for saving you.

I laugh under my breath and start taking slow, tentative steps towards the main road.

No, arsehole, you didn't save me. You ruined my fucking day.

Chapter 2

I let myself into the communal door of my building, just as I hang up to my mum. She seemed well – positive, actually. It was lovely to hear but difficult to match. I fed her a load of rubbish, told her my first interview went great and I expect to hear from them. I couldn't tell her the truth.

I take the stairs to my first-floor flat slowly, feeling a little weary, but liking the sense of belonging that grows as I come closer to my front door, despite the limited furniture and personal effects. I've slowly formed a home that's something close to cosy – and it really is cosy – but I'm bordering on skint as a result.

Slipping my key into the lock, I push the door open and drop my bags before kicking off my heels on a sigh. The part of me that knows my dad wasn't all too fond of me venturing into the daunting world of the antiquity business wonders, stupidly, whether he's influencing all this bad luck. Trying to get me back to Helston to run his junk shop. I wince. 'I didn't mean that, Dad.'

My mobile rings, and I retrieve it from my bag, groaning when I see the number of the estate agent I've hired to sell my dad's shop. 'Hello.' I drop down on to my couch.

'Miss Cole, Edwin Smith here from Smith and Partners.'

'Hi, Edwin. Any news for me?'

'Well, you see, we've had plenty of people through the door, but, frankly, Miss Cole, potential buyers are struggling to see past the junk that's piled ceiling high.'

My blood heats, his statement cutting deep. 'Junk?' I ask, not bothering to tame the insult in my tone, and ignoring the fact that I constantly refer to my father's treasure as junk.

There's a slight pause before he speaks again. 'The stock,' he says diplomatically. 'I think it would benefit everyone if it was cleared from the shop. Buyers will see the amazing potential without ... *the stock* cluttering the generous space. And you'll get your sale far quicker. I'm working in your best interest, Miss Cole,' Edwin adds. 'It's been on the market for over a month with no bites. Alternatively, we could revise the asking price.'

'Not an option,' I reply without hesitation. What we'll get for Dad's store will barely cover the mortgage on the place. Mum needs relieving of the financial strain.

I sigh. 'I'll make arrangements to have the shop cleared,' I assure him, knowing deep down he's right. The shop looks like a scrapyard at best, but the thought of brutally sifting through the many eclectic things my father hoarded over the years fills me with dread. My guilt for abandoning his business to chase my dreams still lingers. It's a daily battle to stop it from overwhelming my efforts to move on. Going back to Helston to face his shop again will only make that battle harder. I let out a little laugh. Yes, because everything is going so well here in London.

'Thank you, Miss Cole.' Edwin hangs up, and I put my head in my hands for a few despondent moments before a light rap on the door pulls my attention back up. I'm frowning as I wander to the door and pull it open.

'Hi.' A voice hits me before I can see who's standing in the corridor. A woman. She's smiling brightly, her blond bob styled perfectly.

'Hello.' I cock my head questioningly.

'I heard you come in. Thought I'd introduce myself. I'm Lucy.' Her hand comes towards me. 'Lucy Bason. I moved in the week before you. I live across the hall.'

I take her hand. 'I'm Eleanor.'

My new neighbour's bubbly presence is hard not to smile at. 'Are you from around here?' she asks.

'No.' I shake my head, thinking I feel like a fish out of water, and I probably look like one, too. 'I come from the West Country.'

'Oh,' she sings, delighted. 'I'm new in town, too.'

'How are you finding it?'

She rolls her eyes. It's a small gesture, but her tired expression makes me feel better. She looks like she's struggling as well.

'Tough,' she admits, enhancing my relief. At least I'm not the only one. 'But I got a job today at an accounting firm, so I guess it isn't all bad.'

My relief is shot down in flames. She has a job. That's more than I have. 'Congratulations.'

'Thanks.' She smiles, but it quickly falls into a frown. 'You okay?'

I sigh, giving up on the chirpy act. Today has been a challenge. 'I had an interview. It was a total fail.' I avoid why, unable to muster the strength to go into details.

'Oh.' Lucy deflates with me. 'That's too bad.'

'It's fine.' I wave a hand dismissively. 'The job wasn't really for me.' A lie. It was right up my street, and I'm feeling a little bitter about it. 'There's potentially another position coming up very soon. Fingers crossed.'

'What's meant for you won't go by you.'

I smile as I step back and open the door wider. 'I'm sorry, would you like to come in?'

'Sure.' She smiles brightly, drawing one from me too, and bursts into my flat.

'Can I get you a drink?' I ask. 'I have wine.'

'Oooh, I'd love a glass.' She bounces across the room and drops her skinny arse on to the small couch. She's so slim. I take a peek over my shoulder to my curvy arse and frown. No amount of exercise can reduce it.

I pour two glasses and hand one to Lucy as I take a seat next to her. 'Nice to meet you.' I toast the air, and Lucy laughs, following suit before we both swig and let out collective sighs, laughing and falling back on to the couch. 'Why does it seem like you've had a day like I have?' I ask. She got a job. Surely she's delighted.

Lucy snorts. 'My morning was amazing. I got a job and went shopping to celebrate. My afternoon, not so much.'

'Why?'

'Both my parents showed up.'

'Is that a bad thing?' I'd love for both of my parents to just *show up*. Sadness washes over me, and I spend a few too many moments accepting that *that* will never happen. Dad, of course, is no longer with us and I'd be surprised if I could ever get my mum to leave the stifling confines of Helston to come and visit me.

Lucy drops her head to the side and looks at me tiredly. 'It is when they're trying to drag me back to the sticks.'

'The sticks?'

'The back of beyond. The deepest depths of the English countryside, where my only friends were pigs and fucking cows.'

I laugh. 'Why do they want to drag you home?'

'The natural progression.' She sighs, taking another sip of her wine. 'I'm destined to take over the family business, but I'd rather shove nails in my eyes.'

'I get it,' I reply quietly, sipping thoughtfully. She feels trapped, and I can totally relate to that.

'There's a big scary world out there,' she continues, 'and I want in.'

I smile, thinking Lucy and I could be great friends. Her circumstances might be different, but we're so similar in our situation.

'How about you? What brings you to London?'

'An ex-boyfriend who I never want to see again.' I smile tightly when she cringes, probably reading between the lines and reaching the right conclusion. 'But above everything, like you, I want in to that big scary world, full of possibilities.'

'Good for you.' She clinks my glass. 'How did your parents react to you flying the nest?'

'My father passed away.' Lucy's face drops, but I smile, trying to ease her obvious discomfort. 'The natural progression thing, I get that. I ran his business after he died. A little antique store. I use the word "antique" loosely.' I laugh, seeing his face in my mind, concentrating as he talked me through what he was doing to an old clock when I was a little girl. Back then, I had no desire to venture far from my parents or the tiny antique store that seemed huge when I was a child. It was only when I started studying history, got lost in the hundreds of books at my library and gained a broader knowledge of the words 'antique' and 'art' that I saw beyond Dad's idea of history. Now the hours, days, months, and years of reading, studying, and dreaming, seem like a stupid waste of my time. 'I love history,' I say quietly. 'Just stuff with a bit more history than Dad managed to find.'

Lucy smiles sadly. 'How did he die?'

'Brain tumour. By the time they diagnosed it, it was too late.'

'Oh, Eleanor, that's terrible.'

I nod in silent agreement. I've drowned in the sympathy my father's sudden death brought. Not a day went past without someone in my small village passing on their condolences, until I was certain there wasn't anyone left to feel sorry for us. I was wrong. The looks, the whispers, the awkward silence that descended whenever I walked into a shop and people clocked me. It all became too much. It made the urge to flee Helston stronger, but the guilt was equally as strong. I couldn't leave Mum. I couldn't leave the shop. I couldn't leave my boyfriend.

'And the boyfriend?' Lucy asks tentatively.

I jump up off the couch, keen to put this conversation to rest. 'He drifted away from me and drifted closer to my best friend,' I say bluntly, showing no emotion at all as I head into the kitchen. Grief makes you blind. And somehow, even though Amy 'meant nothing', she and David are still in orbit together. I know because my mother has mentioned seeing them together around town. So why the fuck is the bastard still calling me?

Snatching up the wine, I top up my glass. 'More?' I ask.

Downing the rest of her glass, Lucy holds it up to me. 'Pour on,' she orders, making me grin.

Perfect. I tip the remaining contents of the bottle into her glass.

A few hours later, we're staring at three empty bottles. Having demolished the first bottle of wine within minutes, Lucy hotfooted it across the hall to her flat and grabbed anything alcoholic – which happened to be a bottle of red and some cheap sparkling stuff. We've really mixed it up, and our drunkenness is evidence. I haven't eaten or showered, and my red hair is bunched messily in a huge knot on my head.

We've talked for England. We've covered every topic imaginable, put the world to rights, and laughed our way through it all. Lucy and I are now firm friends. We're also prancing around my apartment to Whitney Houston's 'I'm Every Woman' like a pair of overexcited, slightly sad, single nutjobs.

'We should go out this weekend,' Lucy sings. 'Oh my God, we should totally paint the town red.' She falls on to the couch and attempts to sit up while holding up her half-full glass so not to spill it. And fails. 'Oopsie.' She laughs, deciding to neck it before rolling off the couch on to the floor. 'I think I'm a bit pissed.' She hiccups and scrambles to her feet, swaying on the spot. 'You, Eleanor Cole' – she points her glass at me, hiccupping again – 'are a bad influence.' *Hiccup.* She wipes her mouth with the back of her hand and spends a while trying to focus on me. 'I feel a bit sick.' She starts circling her tummy with her palm, her face going a little green.

'Oh no, you're not going to throw up, are you?' I sober up in a second, the thought of my new rug being decorated with Lucy's vomit helping me along. I take her elbow and guide her to the bathroom. 'Put your head over the loo.'

She collapses in front of the toilet, her head dangling life-lessly as she groans. 'Ohhhh Godddd, I'm gonna . . .' She jerks and throws up, grabbing the seat of the toilet while I try to hold back her hair. My face wrinkles in distaste as the smell wafts up and pollutes the air.

'All right?' I ask, transferring her blond hair into one hand so I can pinch my nose with the other. 'Water?'

'Shit, I haven't spewed on alcohol since university,' she mum-bles, her arse plonking to the floor clumsily. She rubs her palms on her cheeks. 'Yes, please, water.'

'I'll get some,' I tell her, rushing to the kitchen. I'm back a few seconds later, smiling as she glugs the lot back, gasping before collapsing to her back, dropping the glass to the floor.

'Come on. Up you get.'

'Just leave me,' she slurs. 'I'll be fine here.'

'You can get in my bed.' I use all of my might to heave her up, looking out the bathroom door to assess exactly how far I need to drag her. I calculate roughly eight metres. Doable. 'Just don't vomit in my bed,' I beg, cringing at the potent stink of Lucy's sick creeping out of the bathroom behind me.

I practically carry her across my apartment and let her col-lapse on my bed like a sack of spuds. I don't need to worry about tucking her in. She grabs my quilt and rolls over, taking it with her.

'Perfect,' I sigh, standing back and glancing around my new home, wondering where the hell I'm going to sleep. 'It's you and me,' I say to the couch, taking the fake-fur throw from the base of my bed.

After flushing the loo, squirting nearly an entire bottle of bleach down it, and emptying a can of air freshener, I flop on the sofa and snuggle down. And when I hear a cute murmur and a few snorts, I can't help but smile at the ceiling. I might be jobless, but it seems I'm not friendless any more.

Welcome to London indeed.

Chapter 3

One of the things I love most about London is the readily available coffee. Back home, there were no bustling coffee houses. But here, every corner I turn presents the opportunity to have one, and I'm going to indulge in it.

As I push my way through the door of a coffee house the next day, I find it buzzing with activity, and I inhale the rich smell of coffee beans, letting the air stream out with my order. 'Medium flat white, please.'

'Drink in?'

'Takeout.' I juggle my phone and my purse to retrieve a fiver, sliding it across the counter as I check my emails after getting more data this morning, hoping the job agency has sent through some potential positions. It's all I can do not to screech my delight when I see an email for a *rare and exciting opportunity*. The whispers were true. 'Oh my God,' I breathe, frantically reading through the information. They're offering me an interview at three o'clock today. That's only an hour away. 'There's nothing like a bit of notice.' But then I'm frowning at my screen. They're not in a position to disclose the company name at this present time? 'What?' I question my phone. Why? So I have no idea who I'm dealing with? I read on, being advised to look for a sign that says 'The Haven' once I arrive at the address given, before it gives me a rundown of the position, at the same time telling me that the firm is established and renowned in art and antiques. 'Then tell me the damn name of the company,' I mutter, as I tap out a reply, accepting the interview anyway.

It's not like I have the luxury of options. There aren't companies throwing job offers at my feet.

I dial my mum, needing to hear her voice, not that I can tell her how miserably everything is going.

'Eleanor,' she says, so happy to take my call. My despondency fades a little, and, grabbing my coffee, I spin around, set to walk and talk, but as I turn I'm met with something I became all too familiar with yesterday.

Something navy wrapped loosely around a stubbled throat.

What the hell?

My coffee cup starts to shake, like the slight flutter of my heart has travelled down my arm to my hand, making it vibrate, and my phone sits limply at my ear as my mother repeats her *hello* a few times.

Him.

Cab thief.

Scarf thief.

Job thief.

The gorgeous, angel-eyed specimen.

'I'll call you back, Mum,' I squeak, letting my phone slide down my cheek. I faintly hear her 'okay' before I end the call and slip my phone into my mac pocket. And that's all I can achieve in the movement stakes right now. What is it with this guy? Three encounters in two days? London is huge. My gaze lifts, being pulled up without instruction, until my eyes find and root themselves on his lovely hazel orbs.

His handsome face breaks into a grin. 'You shouldn't have cut your call short on my account.'

'I didn't,' I mumble, taking my eyes from his before they haul me under his spell.

'We should stop meeting like this.' He reaches over my shoulder to hand the barista a note. His voice. Good God, his voice. It's stupid, but the only way I seem to be able to semi-function in the presence of this man is by keeping my eyes off him.

So I do just that, glancing around the coffee house. 'Are you following me?' I ask, switching my coffee into my other hand in the hope that movement might lessen my quivers.

'Don't flatter yourself, princess. I'm simply getting a coffee.'

Princess? 'I am *not* a princess. And where's my scarf?'

'What scarf?'

His question flattens my sass, and I suck in a shot of air, my eyes flying to his. I'm not sure if it's because of shock, or that they're simply greedy for more of him. He's smirking. 'The one you stole from me,' I remind him, my head tilting, trying to read him. He's smug.

On a shake of his head and a feigned confused look, he glances up to the sky. 'I don't recall.'

I laugh sarcastically. I'm in no mood for his games. Not today. He ruined my day yesterday, wrecked my chances of getting my dream job, and I'm not letting events repeat themselves today. 'Have a nice day,' I say tightly, turning and walking away.

'What are you reading?' he asks, pulling me to a stop. I look down at my bag, seeing the book I'm currently lost in poking out. '*Miller's Antiques Encyclopedia*.'

He nods, approvingly. 'The bible of the antiques world?'

'Yes.' I frown, studying him, thinking how familiar he is again. 'Do I know you?'

'You wish.'

Oh, the cocky bastard. I'm about to put him straight, but he steps towards to me, stamping out my intention with his closeness. My body locks up, I lose all sensible thought, and my words abandon me. He takes his coffee and walks closer to me. I'd move, but I'm too busy trying to keep my composure. He drops his mouth to my ear, and my eyes clench shut, my lungs going heavy, challenging my breathing. 'I would ask you to dinner,' he whispers provocatively, clearly aiming to sound sexy as fucking hell. It works. Despite my irritation at this man, I'm trembling in my heels, pulsing down below, and I'm really quite annoyed about it. 'But I'm inclined to avoid women with stalking tendencies.' He breaks away, turns, and saunters out, leaving me with my mouth hanging open.

'I am not—' My mind empties, distracted by his award-worthy arse as he strides away.

I exhale on a gush of air as I relieve my burning lungs. And before I know it, I'm going after him, not prepared to be left in a flummoxed state once again. Oh no. He's done it twice to me already. Not this time. And besides, who said I'd accept his invitation, anyway?

'Hey,' I yell, rushing across the coffee house, nearly taking out a pensioner on my way. 'Sorry,' I say, breaking out into the fresh air. I see his back in the distance and march after him. 'Let's get one thing straight.' I'm walking on his heels, my legs working fast to keep up with his long strides. 'I am not stalking you. I'd say it's more *you* stalking *me*.'

'If it makes you feel better, princess.' He tosses the words over his shoulder in the most annoyingly cool fashion.

Who the hell does he think he is?

'And for the record, I wouldn't have dinner with you.'

'Okay, then.' He strides away, but I keep on his tail, an irritated frown on my face.

'You're not my type,' I say, and he laughs, though he doesn't stop or look back.

'I'm *every* woman's type.'

My face twists. I can't argue with that. Even now, as I pathetically chase him down the street to argue my immunity to him, there are women at every turn staring at him. 'Not mine,' I say, if only to win back some dignity.

'Okay. Not yours.' He takes a sip of his coffee, smiling around the cup.

Oh my God, he's infuriating. 'Don't walk away from me.' I grab his arm, pulling him to a halt. The feel of him renders me stupid for a moment, and I'm catapulted back to yesterday when he saved me from my fall and caged me in his arms.

I release my hold of him like he's caught fire, an electric shock piercing my heart. *Oh my God.* He turns slowly, revealing a face framed with high, surprised eyebrows. Did he feel that? He looks down at his arm, studying the spot I just touched, before looking back at me. I drop my stare to the ground, like I can hide from him or something. I can't hold our eye contact any more. I feel like he's reading my mind. The aftermath of our contact is still burning me. I realise these are inappropriate thoughts, given the man is a perfect stranger, but it's impossible to think clearly when he's so close. Lord, I bet he's an animal in bed. Everything tells me so. The powerful legs, strong arms, tall physique. He works out, and I bet he gives many women a good workout from time to time, too. And he's confident. Definitely too confident. The fact that I'm thinking all of this – and not the mystery of him appearing out of nowhere on three occasions – should be worrying. I may have been kept captive in my hometown by guilt for my adult life, but I know a bad boy when I see one. This man has womaniser written all over his gorgeous face. In thick, black marker.

My gaze is rooted to his thighs, my teeth nibbling on the inside of my mouth as I let my mind wander to dangerous places. And then I'm frowning when I consider that I assume them to be dangerous places. Why not wild and exciting? I laugh on the inside, damning my suppressed life. I definitely do *not* need dangerous. But maybe I do need fun.

My eyes find his again. He's watching me closely. Very closely. And his cheeky smile is nowhere to be seen. It gives me a few moments to consider my previous thought.

Dangerous.

'What are you staring at?' I ask, shifting under his heavy stare.

'I'm thinking I might change my habits and take a stalker out for dinner after all.'

I laugh again, and this time it's genuine. 'You are the cockiest man I've ever met.'

'And you have the most beautiful red hair I've ever seen.' He reaches for my hair and plays with a lock while I remain still, my breathing going to shit. His eyes flick to mine. 'We're obviously a match made in heaven.'

'Behave.' I flick his hand away, feeling my cheeks heat and my mind go off on a tangent, wondering about his bedroom skills once again. Shit, I'm deprived. 'I need to go.' I smile sweetly. 'I'd say it was a pleasure, but—'

'You wouldn't know.' He winks. 'But if you ever want to find out . . .'

'I really don't.' It's the biggest lie I've ever told. 'Goodbye.'

'Shouldn't we shake hands?' He tosses his coffee cup in a nearby bin and extends his arm, and I eye it with caution, trying to brace myself to make contact. It takes way more mental preparation than it should.

I place my hand in his and immediately feel fire blazing through my veins. 'Nice to meet you.'

'Wasn't it just,' he says, his face straight.

I snatch my hand back and scoot past him, my movement rushed and clumsy, causing me to knock his arm.

More fire. Fuck, welcome to London indeed. I breathe in deeply, fighting to compose myself.

I'm not sure what happens next.

I'm moving too fast to comprehend it. 'Oh.' I blink repeatedly as my back is pushed into something rough.

A brick wall.

And something hard pressed against my front.

A body.

His body.

My breathing has accelerated to breathy gasps. His face is close to mine. Nose to nose. I'm tense, rigid, nailed to the wall behind me, his palms flat against it on either side of my head.

His eyes are roaming my entire face, and I push myself back against the bricks in a vain attempt to escape the heat of his body.

But he moves in closer, not holding me against my will, but making it pretty impossible for me to escape. My heart is thundering so hard, he must feel it. But it's not fright that's the cause of my immobility or heaving chest. It's something else – something I'm not particularly comfortable with. 'What are you doing?' I whisper. I've never felt lust so strong or bold, and it's knocking all sense from me.

He frowns a little, moving back. 'I believe this might be foreplay.'

Fucking hell.

My lips part to allow some air into my burning lungs. What the hell do I say to that? 'Or it could be considered assault,' I counter, tossing my own cup in the bin, too. 'Depends on how you look at it.' Assault? What a laugh. I'm aching everywhere, but I'm not about to admit it to this cocky arsehole. I bet women fall at his feet daily. I'm not going to be one of them.

I pad my feet into the concrete, just to check I'm still standing, as he holds my eyes, his forehead a map of lines. He slowly inches nearer again, his mouth coming closer to mine, his breath tickling my skin. I can feel myself falling under his spell, but before I give in to the pull of the lips he's brandishing, I come to my senses and slam my hands into his chest, pushing him away. 'Excuse me, but I have no time for holier-than-thou twats,' I retort indignantly.

'Ouch.' He laughs a little, pulling the lapels of his jacket in, but that frown is still there. 'Then how about you stop following me?'

'I'm not bloody following you,' I breathe, exasperated.

'Sure you're not.' He turns on his expensive brogues and walks off. 'See you around, princess.'

'I hope not,' I yell to his back. *That arse.* It brings tears to my eyes. *Bastard.*

I feel bemused, hot, lustful, embarrassed, mystified ... annoyed. 'Such a twat,' I say to myself, quickly checking the time. 'Shit.'

My thoughts realign in a heartbeat. If he's made me late for this interview, too, I will most definitely be stalking him ... so I can wring his fucking neck.

I dash off in the opposite direction, waving my arm frantically for a cab. At least I know Mr *I believe this might be foreplay* won't be taking *this* cab.

I've never met such a conceited wanker.

Chapter 4

First impressions. They really do count, and what I'm staring at right now doesn't bode well for my interview. An alleyway. There's an iron door guarding the entrance with an old metal sign with 'The Haven' above it.

The Haven? 'Hardly,' I say quietly. *But beggars can't be choosers.*

I ring the buzzer on the keypad next to the door and wait.

And wait.

And wait.

I ring it again, this time holding it down for a few seconds so the irritating shrill stretches out, making me wince. There are a few crackles then a huff of displeasure. 'Patience is a virtue,' a woman's voice snaps, making me step back. 'How can I help?'

I inch forwards, putting my mouth closer to the intercom. 'Hi, I'm looking for The Haven.'

'You've found it.'

'I have an interview today. Arranged through the agency.'

'Your name?'

'Eleanor Cole.'

'Push the door.'

'Excuse me?'

'The door, dear. Push it.'

I stare at the intercom. Never have I heard the word *dear* said with such snark. I can almost hear her eyes rolling. A shift of metal snaps my attention from the intercom to the door, and I gingerly reach out and give it a little push. It opens, revealing an alleyway that doesn't seem to have an end. Or a light. Despite being slightly wary, I cross the threshold, trying to adjust to the dark. There's a smell of damp brick walls, making my nose wrinkle in distaste. It reminds me of my father's workshop – old and neglected. The familiar smell dashes my enthusiasm further as I slowly edge forwards. I don't know where I'm heading or what I'll find once I make it there. *If* I make it there. I've moved five paces and still can't see any signs of life at the end. It's eerily silent.

Bang!

'Shit.' I fly around, startled, my heart rate rocketing, the sound of the door crashing closed echoing around me, trapping me within the confines of the brick tunnel. My hands start grappling at the wall, feeling their way across the bricks in an attempt to get me back to the door. The ground beneath my heels is rocky, my shoes not coping with the uneven surface, making me trip and stumble.

It's a few frantic moments, but I finally make it back to the door, and it takes just two solid tugs on the handle for me to conclude I'm going nowhere except further into the black hole. 'Fabulous.' I have two options. I can stand here in the dark and rot, because it doesn't seem like anyone is rushing to greet me. Or I can risk breaking an ankle while attempting to make it to the end of this black hole to nowhere, because it seems the only way I'm getting out of here is by finding someone who can let me out.

I feel my way down the alleyway again, tentatively putting down each foot before settling my whole weight on it. This is ridiculous. Has every interview candidate endured these conditions? 'Some light would be handy,' I grumble, hearing a repeat of my words when the echo travels into the black distance ahead of me. 'Phone!' I blurt out, blindly feeling in my bag for it. Why didn't I think of that sooner?

But the second I lay my hand on my mobile, light floods the

pit of darkness. My hands instinctively come up to shield my eyes from the sudden glare.

'There you are, dear.' It's that voice again, except this time there's no trace of irritation, only warmth.

I blink repeatedly, trying to find my focus, and when the black blobs finally dissolve from my vision, I see a face that matches the voice perfectly. The voice belongs to a small and round woman, aged at least seventy, and the short curls sprayed into position on her head are violet. Once I can bring myself to rip my eyes away from her wild-coloured hair, I let my gaze drop to find her dressed just how I would have guessed. A mid-length skirt, a two-piece matching blouse and cardigan, and to round the look off perfectly, a string of pearls draped around her neck.

'Hello,' I say cautiously. She defies the unnerving circumstances and environment that I've found myself in. She's all cute and cuddly. This place is anything but.

'You made it halfway, dear,' she tells me. 'I'll escort you the remaining distance.' She gives me a little jiggle of her head, an indication for me to follow, before she turns and leads the way. I rush to catch up with her, watching my feet on the uneven cobbles as I go. 'The name's Mrs Potts, dear.' She marches on, and I smile to myself at the fitting name. 'We'll have a chat over a cuppa.'

'A chat?'

'Oh.' She laughs, waving a hand indifferently. 'I'm sorry. We're supposed to call it an interview, aren't we? A bit formal for my liking.'

'Formal?'

'Yes.'

'How long have you worked here?'

'Forty-three years, dear.'

My eyes widen and my heart plummets. Everything so far suggests I'm walking into an interview for a job that'll be no more beneficial to my dream career than running my dead father's dead business. I wince at my stray thoughts. 'That's some service,' I murmur.

'I'm part of the furniture, me.' She takes a sharp right, and I follow, glancing around, regardless of there still being nothing but brick walls closing me in. 'He'll need a wrench to turf me out.'

'He?' I ask.

'Yes, dear. The boss.'

My eyebrows rise, my face contorting into something I can only imagine looks like bewilderment. If she's seventy-odd and has worked here for forty-three years, how old is the boss? 'What's the name of the company, if you don't mind me asking?'

She halts abruptly and swings around, regarding me with interest. It makes me back up slightly. Her head tilts to the side. It makes me nervous for reasons I can't fathom. She's an old lady. She seems perfectly harmless. 'That will be disclosed to the winning candidate.'

My lips press together as I frantically search my brain for an appropriate response. I can't find one. 'Oh.' What is this, the magic circle? Every second longer I spend in this cold, damp alley with this unexpected old lady is increasing my anxiety, and, I've got to admit, my curiosity too.

She turns and trots off, and I glance over my shoulder, wondering whether I should leave. 'Do you have a nervous disposition, dear?'

I turn back to find she's stopped again and is watching me closely. 'Why?'

'You look ready to bolt.'

'Not at all,' I lie through my teeth.

'That's good.' Off she goes again, and I follow. 'Because, you see, the boss, he's a little . . .' She pauses. I can't see her face, but I can tell by the slight cock of her head that she's thinking how best to word it. 'Difficult,' she finishes, leaving me even more worried. Difficult? 'Here we are.' She swipes a card through a metal keypad on the wall. Security? Okay, so that's a step up from my father's store. Putting some weight behind her, she pushes the door open.

And I nearly fall over. 'Bloody hell,' I splutter, looking around me in shock.

'Now then, dear.' She looks at me disapprovingly. 'Is there really any need for such language?'

'I'm sorry. Just a bit of a surprise, that's all.' I've stepped into another dimension. Left behind me are the damp brick walls and stale smell. Now, I could be standing in the Garden of Eden. We're in a cobbled courtyard, with a horseshoe-shaped brick building surrounding us and a stone fountain positioned centrally, trickling a peaceful sound of water over the edges. Iron railings form balconies on the first level of each of the three walls, and luscious greenery climbs the brickwork. It's beautiful and so very unexpected. It doesn't look like any type of business is run from here. I want to live here. I want to swing open those balcony doors in the morning and drink in the fresh air, let the voile curtains billow around me while I stretch and let the sun warm my vitamin D-deprived face. You would never know that the madness of London existed beyond the walls of this idyllic place.

'Welcome to The Haven, dear. This way.' Mrs Potts seems oblivious to my awe. 'We'll chat—' Her lips purse as she pushes her way through one side of a giant wooden double door. 'We'll conduct the interview in here.'

I enter the huge room, trying to hold on to my surprise once more. I fail. 'Wow.' I walk aimlessly into the centre of the area, gazing at the ceiling that stretches up at least two floors. Tapestries cascade down the bare brick walls, and the most beautiful pieces of furniture grace the colossal space. Sideboards, desks, chairs, tables, cabinets . . .

It's all haphazard. There's no uniformity or organisation to the room. Cabinets displaying vases, lamps, and ornamental pieces are scattered across the floor space, and paintings are propped up in every available space, covered in protective sheeting. It's organised chaos. It's a treasure chest: Aladdin's cave. Pandora's Box . . .

Nothing like my father's store.

'Oh my God,' I tear my awestruck eyes from the endless beautiful pieces and allow them to rest on Mrs Potts.

She smiles at my wonder and heads towards a door, leaving me slowly turning and drinking in the space again. 'I'll pop the kettle on. Won't be a moment.'

I begin to wander, weaving through the pathways between the endless items of furniture, soaking up the sheer beauty of it all. My fingertips lightly glide over various surfaces as I pass them. I'm smiling, too. The history in this room is almost alive. It's strange to admit it, but it's like I can almost hear the antiques. It's as if they're all talking to me, keen for me to centre my attention on each and every one of them and let them blow my mind with their stories. Problem is, I wouldn't know where to start. There are things I recognise, things I've studied. Famous pieces. I stop in the middle of the room and breathe in deeply, letting the air in my lungs leave on a happy exhale. This is more like it. This is what I imagined when I watched my dad pour his energy into restoring worthless pieces of junk, when I've lost myself in books. I shake my head in wonder. 'But where am I?' I ask quietly as my eyes take another greedy circuit of the room, lifting slightly once I've pivoted a full three-sixty degrees.

What I see when I look up has me stepping forwards, trying to focus. Towards the back of the giant space it breaks into two levels, a glass wall dropping from the vaulted ceiling to meet a mezzanine floor. It's like a giant glass box keeping watch over the grand room.

My eyes travel the width of glass, fascinated by the clean lines in such an old, worldly, sumptuous room. But the flow of my drifting gaze falters when something catches my eye, and I squint, trying to zero into the blackness beyond the glass.

A chill spikes my skin. There's someone watching me, I can clearly see an outline of a body. I step forwards, drawn in closer by the shadow, but then the silhouette slowly fades to nothing, dissipating like a puff of steam, like it was never there. Frowning to myself, I cock my head thoughtfully, staring into the blackness.

'Tea,' Mrs Potts says from behind, startling me. I swing around, finding her ambling towards me with a tray in her hand loaded with a teapot and some china cups decorated in a floral pattern.

She indicates a couple of large leather captain-style chairs, sets the tray down on a side table, and sits down, the chair creaking under the strain of her round frame. 'It won't give,' she says, a light flash of a smile on her face. 'They don't make furniture like this these days.' She pats the matching chair next to hers. 'Take a seat.'

I gingerly lower myself to the chair, brushing down my skirt. I feel dowdy and out of place among such valuable treasures.

Mrs Potts hums happily as she serves the tea, giving me a traditional teacup and saucer. I accept and smile my thanks. 'Drink up, dear.'

So I do, feeling awkward under her watchful eyes travelling back and forth with the cup as it journeys to and from my mouth. I awkwardly make my way through half my tea before softly placing the china cup on the matching saucer.

'Wonderful.' She looks truly delighted as she takes the fine china from my grasp and sets it aside. 'Show me your hands.'

I hesitate, frowning, but she smiles warmly to encourage me, and I slowly extend my arms, watching while she runs observant eyes over my hands. 'Very steady,' she muses, taking a gentle hold. 'No shaking.'

I smile nervously. Is she going to read my palm or something?

Or produce tarot cards? 'Why would I shake?' I ask.

'Nerves,' she confirms. 'We can't have butterfingers around all these fine pieces.'

'I can imagine.'

'We only deal in the finest, dear.'

'You have many beautiful things.' It's a million miles away from what I'm used to, and I'm alive with the potential of working with these wonderful antiques. I want to work here. If I saw the cab thief now, I might kiss him instead of slapping him. I can see myself lost among these treasured artefacts of history. I'm suddenly buzzing, full of enthusiasm. I *have* to nail this.

Mrs Potts releases my hands and casts a proud eye around the room. 'That we do. Now, how are your archiving skills?'

'You mean filing?'

'Chronologically, yes.'

'Very good,' I confirm, because they are. I expect there will be a few more files here than my father had, but I'm ready for the challenge. 'My father's records go back decades. They were a shambles before I rebuilt his filing system.'

She smiles. 'Your telephone manners?'

'I'm very diplomatic.'

'That's good. We deal with the top auction houses – Sotheby's, Bonhams, not to mention our clients who are mostly English aristocracy. We need to be polite.'

Sotheby's? Bonhams? I could scream my excitement. Mrs Potts's head cocks, and I know she's thinking about my earlier outburst when I couldn't see a damn thing in that dark alley.

'I'm very polite.' *When I'm not trapped in a pitch-black hole with no escape.*

'Indeed. Now, how broad is your knowledge?' She casts her arm around the room, and my eyes follow, taking it all in again.

This is a test. My chance to impress. 'Well, over there is a pencil portrait of Francis of Lorraine. He was the Duke of

Guise. I believe François Clouet was commissioned by the duke himself.' I smile when Mrs Potts nods, eyes bright. 'And that over there next to Anne Boleyn's necklace' – oh my fucking days, it's her actual necklace – 'is a solid gold statue of King Tutankhamun. Or King Tutankhaten, before he changed his religion. It weighs sixty pounds, and I believe it was lost in history until an American named Professor Limmington unearthed it on an expedition in Cairo in 1845.' I'm almost breathless, because this room is truly mind-blowing. 'And I know that *that* over there is a rare example of a Louis the fourteenth chair.'

'With original gilding,' Mrs Potts adds, smiling.

'With original gilding.'

She chuckles and returns to her pad. 'Organisation skills?'

'Brilliant.'

She waves her chubby hand through the air again, laughing. 'That'll make him happy.'

'Him?'

'The boss, dear. Keep up.' She's out of her chair and walking across the room, my eyes following her path before glancing up at the glass wall that's guarding the room. Prickles are pitter-pattering across my skin. It's the oddest sensation. 'Confidence in handling comes through years of experience,' she continues, pulling my attention back to her. 'But you have a nice steady hand, so you're off to a good start.'

'I worked in my father's antique shop for years,' I say, avoiding the fact that my dad's treasure could never compare to what I'm surrounded by now. I also avoid the pang of guilt that stabs me. It might not have been treasure on this scale, but it was still treasure to my dad.

'How lovely.' Mrs Potts chuckles, slipping some white gloves on before opening a cabinet and picking up an intricately patterned Ming vase. She then proceeds to juggle it between her hands like it's a ball. I straighten my back, nervous at the sight of such a rare piece being handled so cavalierly. She places it down and twirls it to the right, smiling at it fondly for a few moments while I look on. 'Now then.' She marches over to me and hands me another pair of gloves. 'Pick it up, dear.' She nods towards the Ming vase.

I accept the gloves and approach the vase nervously, concerned the pressure will throw my confidence. I get the feeling that the care of these treasures is more important than any knowledge I might have in the antique department. So, I pull up my big girl knickers, put on the gloves, and take hold of the vase with both hands.

I turn to present the treasure to Mrs Potts. 'It's stunning.'

She smiles brightly. 'Of course it is. It was made for the Qianlong Emperor.' She inclines her head, like I should know that.

I didn't, but I know who the Qianlong Emperor is. 'Oh my God.' I'm holding something close to three hundred years old.

'It's worth one point two million.'

'What?' My hands instantly start to shake, and Mrs Potts flies to me at a speed that defies her round body *and* her age.

'I'll take that.' She swipes it from my hands, leaving me to grab a nearby heavily carved Elizabethan sideboard to steady myself.

'One point two million?' I blurt, watching her tucking it away safely in the cabinet. Holy shit, I've underestimated how far removed this is from my father's business. I think the most he ever achieved for a piece that he spent two months lovingly restoring was a grand. A thousand pounds for nine weeks' work. But 1.2 million? Yes, my knowledge is broad, but the value of pieces hasn't been something I've much cared for, just the history. The responsibility and pressure of dealing with them, handling them, is something I've grossly underestimated.

'Yes, dear.' She turns disapproving eyes on to me. 'Maybe your handling skills aren't so great, after all.'

I sag internally, aware I may have just cocked up my interview. 'I'm sorry.'

An impish grin appears, surprising me, and her already rosy cheeks gain more colour, clashing with her violet curls. 'We can work on your fumbling fingers, dear.'

'We can?'

'Certainly.' She indicates the white gloves, so I quickly take them off and hand them over. She drops them on to the nearby table and is off again. 'This way, dear.'

I'm in pursuit, but I'm far more cautious as I dip and weave through the maze of antiques. 'Where are we going?'

'To meet Mr H.' She swipes a card before she pushes through a huge wooden door, the creaking echoing loudly around me. Mr H. The boss? Difficult Mr H. 'Just down here, dear.'

Following Mrs Potts's steps, we pass door after door, the corridor walls lined with paintings that blow my mind. I spot a Dalí, a Raphael, a Rembrandt. 'Fuck,' I whisper, eyes wide. And then a stone staircase curving to the right grabs my attention. My head turns as we pass, my gaze rooted on the point where the stairs disappear around the corner into darkness.

'That's out of bounds,' Mrs Potts says, snapping my attention back to her. 'Never venture that way.'

I want to ask why. There are so many things I want to ask, but she's quickly pointing out more. 'At the very end of this corridor is Mr H's private suite.'

'He lives here?'

'Yes, dear.'

'And you?'

'Oh, I have myself a nice bungalow up west. Lived there for fifty years. It's too big for just me, mind, but I couldn't bring myself to sell it after I lost my Ernie ten years ago.'

'Oh, I'm sorry for your loss.'

'Very sweet of you, dear.' We come to a halt outside some intricately carved double doors, and Mrs Potts yanks on a brass bell hanging to the right. I take in the detailed engravings on the wooden doors. The first thing I notice is two people, both naked. Then I spot a tree and an oversized engraving of an apple. 'The Garden of Eden?' I ask, stepping forwards to get a better look. It's beautiful, so detailed and intricate.

'Stunning, don't you think?'

'It really is.' I reach up and run my fingertip over the face of Eve. I've never seen anything like it. 'And purple heart too.' It's a notoriously difficult wood to carve, so the creator of this masterpiece must have been beyond talented and patient.

'Come in,' a gruff voice calls, and I snatch back my hand.

'After you, dear.' Mrs Potts pushes one of the doors open, and I look to her, nervous. 'Go on.'

I'm reluctant, though I don't know why, and when I slowly convince my heels to take me forward, past the doorway, my mouth drops open. 'Bloody hell,' I whisper, slapping my hand over my mouth the moment the words pass my lips.

'Language, dear,' Mrs Potts scolds, pushing my lower back to encourage me forwards. This place just keeps on giving and giving. Three of the four walls are made up of floor-to-ceiling bookcases, all bursting at the seams with books, all old, judging by the smell. It's too much, but my eyes take in more and more and more.

Two chesterfield couches reside proudly opposite each other with an old trunk positioned in the middle, and at the end of the room there are huge sash bay windows, dressed in luscious heavy gold drapes that pool to the floor.

And between them, a desk.

And what a desk. The king of desks. Solid. Sturdy. An absolutely beautifully engraved double pedestal piece. My bottom lip slips between my teeth as I consider how many people have sat at that desk. Or *who* has sat at that desk. It looks like a replica of the famous Theodore Roosevelt desk that was saved from the 1929 fire at the White House.

I'm so rapt by the beautiful piece – its story seeping from the well-oiled dark wood – that I miss the fact that there's actually someone sitting at the desk.

Someone concealed behind a broadsheet.

'Mr H,' Mrs Potts sings, wandering over to the curtains and tweaking the tie-backs. 'This is Eleanor Cole. You asked to meet her.'

The paper rustles, and I watch on a held breath as it's folded slowly before my eyes, revealing the occupant of this amazing office.

I smile, taken aback. He's wearing a bottle-green shirt with a brown tie to match his tweed jacket, and his head is topped with a thick silver mop, combed neatly to the side. He's a looker now – at what, mid-eighties? – so he must have been a stunner in his day. He has one of those warm, friendly faces that make you feel like you've known them for years.

'Good afternoon, Miss Cole.' He looks over the top of his spectacles at me as he places his newspaper on the desk.

'Good afternoon, Mr ... H,' I reply politely, following Mrs Potts's lead. I resist the urge to curtsey. I feel like I'm in the company of royalty, with my surroundings, his attire, his posh accent. He could be a duke or a lord.

'Your CV was very impressive, how you spoke so passionately about this world.' The old man pushes his paper to the side of the desk.

I blush a little. 'Thank you.' I'm still in the dark and a bit taken aback by this interview process, but I really, *really* want this job.

'We could do with some help for Mrs Potts,' he continues. 'She isn't getting any younger.' Chuckling, he rests back in his captain's chair, a big smile on his face.

I hear Mrs Potts tittering from across the room, and I look over to find her rolling her eyes as she makes her way to Mr H. She unhooks a walking stick from a coat stand to the side of the desk. Even his walking aid looks like an antique, all shiny and gold.

'Eleanor is quite something, Donald,' Mrs Potts says. 'I think she'll fit in well.' She thrusts his walking stick at him, and I go all warm and fuzzy inside. She thinks I'll fit in well, which is great because I do, too.

Mr H's face immediately bunches in disgust at the walking stick being waved under his nose. It's plain to see he's a proud man, and needing a walking aid clearly frustrates him. My dad would have been exactly the same, had he made it to Mr H's ripe old age.

'Bossy boots,' he mutters, accepting the cane and pushing away from the desk in his chair. I nearly laugh out loud when he flicks me a wink. Difficult? From what I've seen, which, granted, isn't much, he seems wonderful. I already love him. 'Do you consider yourself honest, loyal, and trustworthy?' he asks me.

'Very.' I nod.

'And how can you prove that?'

'Well . . .' I fade off, trying to figure the best approach. 'Mr H, I could give you many examples of my loyalty and trustworthiness, but you would never know if I was telling you what I think you want to hear. I can't provide references because I've only ever worked for my father in his antique store. The only way to win your trust is to prove myself. If you'll allow me.'

He smiles, bright and happy. 'I agree, Eleanor. I don't believe in references, anyway. The proof is in the pudding.'

I watch Mr H struggle to his feet, using the cane and Mrs Potts for support. 'It's time for your medication, old man,' she says, winking at me.

'Yes, yes,' Mr H grumbles, flipping her a half-scowl, though I detect playfulness there, and Mrs Potts smacking his arm lightly confirms it. He checks the time on his pocket watch – a lovely gold piece, which I suspect is solid. 'You're not far behind me, Dorothy. And just you remember who is boss.'

She slaps his arm again and this time they both chuckle as Mrs Potts ambles alongside an unstable Mr H. I smile, admiring the clear fondness between the employer and employee. I remember how Mrs Potts said she had worked here for decades. The thought makes me nervous, I'll never live up to Mrs Potts. She is leaving me some big boots to fill, and she fits right in. I can only hope I can, too. If I get the job. *Please, let me get the job.*

I start to follow them when Mrs Potts swings around, just as they reach the door. 'Take a seat, dear. Won't be a moment.' She nods past me, and I turn to see an old leather chair facing the magnificent desk.

'You want me to wait here?' I ask, but before I can find her again, the door slams and I'm alone in this big, plush office. 'I'll take that as a yes, then.' I shrug to myself and wander over to the chair, resting my bottom on the edge, not wanting to get too comfortable, and being unable to anyway. My tight skirt won't allow it. I shuffle and tug at the hem.

Then I wait.

And wait.

And wait some more.

A good five minutes pass before I turn in my chair to find the door. There's silence, not a sound from beyond, nothing to suggest that Mr H is on his way back. How long does it take to give him his meds? My shoulders drop a little as I relax, and I cast my eyes around the office, drinking in the opulence again, before my gaze lands back on the door. I start to nibble my lip, wondering at what point I should go in search of them. I don't know, so I swivel back around to get comfy, prepared to wait a little longer.

And jump a mile. 'Jesus,' I gasp, flying back in my chair when I'm confronted by a man sitting opposite me. My hand instinctively shoots to my chest and applies pressure to dull the sudden, excessive thumping of my heart. It's going hell for leather as I stare at the man before me.

No!

Him.

Cab thief.

Scarf thief.

What the fuck?

Is he a hallucination? Lord knows, I've been relentlessly – and futilely – blocking the mental images of him from my mind.

'Well, would you Adam and Eve it?' he says quietly. His eyebrows are slightly raised behind his glasses, showing curiosity mixed with a little shock. He's real. He's definitely real. Where the hell did he come from? He's just sitting there, reclined in Mr H's captain's chair, his left ankle resting on his right knee as he lightly brushes the index finger of his left hand back and forth across his top lip, watching me closely. I don't know what it is about him, but he strips me of the ability to think clearly, to speak fluently, to move without looking like I'm jerking.

I make a desperate attempt to compose myself by removing my palm from my chest and coughing, shifting in my chair. On the inside, I'm in all kinds of chaos. My frantic mind is reeling. Where the fuck did he come from? *Who* the fuck is he?

'What are you doing here?' I breathe.

'I could ask you the same question,' he says on a disbelieving laugh. 'There I am, minding my own business in my apartment, and I look down at my grand hall and see *you* standing there.' He scowls. 'Juggling with one of my priceless Ming vases, I might add.'

I blush bright red, cringing. But something he said finally registers in my bewildered mind. He pouts, looking adorable, all boyishly handsome. He knows what's just slammed into my mind. '*Your* grand hall?' I ask, coming over even hotter.

'*My* grand hall,' he repeats, confirming my fears.

Oh my days. 'Your grand hall?' I question again, because I

can think of nothing else to say. He nods slowly. This is his business? I point over my shoulder to the door. 'But the old man? Mr H?'

He gives me a cunning smirk. It's the cheekiest expression, and it's making my pulse quicken. His dimple. It's deep and flings his conceitedness into the realms of adorable. Adorably annoying. 'My grandfather.'

'Oh,' I whisper, stunned.

He leans over the desk, coming closer, keeping his eyes on me. It makes me sit back, pushing myself into the chair. 'I think The Fates are definitely trying to tell us something.' His words are quiet but crisp and clear, and my eyes drag across his exquisite face, absorbing every tiny detail. My skin is tingling, my tongue is thick in my mouth, and my nose has taken a hit of his unique leathery, lemony scent from his closeness.

Oh . . . fucking . . . hell.

'I don't believe in fate,' I murmur, remaining motionless under his intense focus, despite getting hotter and hotter.

He draws too many unwanted reactions from me, irritation being only one in a long list of more pleasurable but forbidden effects he has on me. I start fidgeting in my chair again, glancing away.

'Struggling to keep it together?' he asks, encouraging my gaze back to his. Then his eyes zone in on my lips, and he falls into a bit of a trance. I watch him for a moment, fascinated by his thoughtfulness. 'Me too,' he eventually murmurs, flicking those lovely hazel eyes back to mine.

He's struggling? With what?

'Are you familiar with the Hunt Corporation?' he asks casually.

'Of course.' I laugh. Everyone who knows anything about antiques knows of the prestigious firm. They're the most famous dealers in arts and antiques in the world.

'Well . . .' He clears his throat, making a long, drawn-out

affair of it. Then he deadpans. Totally serious. His hand comes towards me, but I pull away, wary. I've shaken that hand, not two hours ago. Touching it again would be monumentally stupid. 'Pleasure to meet you,' he says on a whisper of breath. 'The name's Becker Hunt.'

I go dizzy, realisation smacking me in the face.

He grins, seeing that the penny has finally dropped. 'I'll be your new boss . . .' His eyes root on my lips. 'Possibly.'

Chapter 5

My eyes are wide and my mouth agape. I'm not sure how long I remain silent and useless before him, but when his declaration finally worms its way past my shock, I wince, I cringe, I slap myself all over the fancy office. And I do this while Becker Hunt watches me, amusement splashed across his irritatingly handsome face. The Hunt Corporation. Mr H is Mr Hunt Senior, the old boy who isn't seen in public any more. And Becker? Oh Jesus, Becker Hunt, the grandson. This delicious bastard before me has run the company since his grandad retired. I knew he looked familiar. I've seen him in magazine after magazine, with various women draped all over him. He's notorious. A playboy. How did I – a student of art and antiques – not realise? I know why. I was too bamboozled by a potent dose of lust mixed with a few dashes of irritation. Not to mention that the photos I've seen of him do him *no* justice. No justice at all. I'm sitting in the offices of the Hunt Corporation. I should be dizzy with excitement, but I'm not. I'm mortified.

My head drops back, and I click my neck as I look up at the ceiling, praying for some guidance. I called the MD of the Hunt Corporation a holier-than-thou twat. What have I done? It takes a few uncomfortable seconds for me to accept that nothing is getting me out of this horrific situation, especially with a job, unless I grovel. Apologise. I squirm at the mere thought.

I chew my lip as I look at him. He quirks a sexy eyebrow. And I just know he wants that apology.

Difficult? Mrs Potts called the boss difficult. I'm more inclined to use *arrogant*, though I detect there's a playful edge to Becker Hunt. I've had first-hand experience of that playful edge. And the cockiness. I shrink on the inside, once again hearing my words as I shoved him away outside the cafe and called him a holier-than-thou twat.

But what was I supposed to do? I quickly sprint through my options before I dive in with an apology he doesn't deserve. Do I really need this job? Yes, no thanks to him for nicking my cab yesterday, and more than I need to remove these stilettos from my achy feet. Do I want this job more than I want to slap his arrogant face? I purse my lips. That's debatable. Can I keep my mouth shut during my working day? Be professional? Yes ... if I get the job. I have more self-control than I'm giving myself credit for. And speaking of self-control, will my damn body ever stop trembling when he's close? Can I repel him? Get on with my job? I'm not sure. But the main question, the question that overrides all that have come before, is whether I'm going to be given the opportunity to try.

Damn it. I hate to admit it, but I'm at the mercy of this god-like man. I don't like it, not one little bit, but I'm not about to cut off my nose to spite my face. I want this job. I *need* this job. My rent is due soon, and there's no other job like this out there. Plus, this is a foot in the door of a world I've dreamed about being in for ever, and after being immersed in the wonder of it all, I'm desperate for more. This is the Hunt Corporation, for Christ's sake. This is an insanely rare opportunity. I'm not going to let Becker Hunt ruin my hopefully flourishing career. And I *fit* here. Mrs Potts thinks it, and I think it too. For the first time ever, I feel like I truly belong.

It's time to grovel. It's time to prove that I'm the girl he needs. Professionally, of course.

I take a deep breath. 'I apologise,' I whisper, so quietly I barely hear it myself, yet the slight cock of an eyebrow tells me he heard it perfectly.

He gets up and saunters around the desk, taking a seat in the chair next to me. 'I'm sorry, what did you say?'

I suddenly have an overwhelming urge to punch him in his smug, beautiful face. He's going to milk my apology for what it's worth. Bring it on, Hunt. 'I apologise,' I say louder, and smile, trying to eliminate the sarcastic expression from my face.

He leans forwards, invading my personal space. 'Come again,' he whispers. It's all I can do not to throttle him. Or kiss the lips he's flaunting like a juicy bone to a ravenous dog.

My eyes close, and I breathe in deeply. I shouldn't have. My nose has just been reminded of his delightful manly scent. 'I'm sorry for calling you a holier-than-thou twat, Mr Hunt,' I say, loud and clear, telling myself not to flip out if he asks me to repeat myself again. This is the Hunt Corporation, I remind myself. The elite of the elite.

'No need to apologise.'

My lids flutter open, and I find him standing over me. Then his palms meet the arms of my chair and he dips, leaning down and caging me in. I freeze and hold my breath as his face comes closer and closer until his mouth is at my ear. I've never felt so vulnerable in my life. Or lustful. Or annoyed.

'I really am a holier-than-thou twat,' he murmurs in my ear.

My breath catches in my throat and he moves away from me, leaving me a pile of want in the leather chair.

'I didn't particularly want to hire anyone, but Mrs Potts needs help. You'll do.' He nods – all formal – turns, and starts to leave.

I'll do? I bolt up in my chair. 'You're offering me the job?'

He slows to a stop and turns around, looking at me quietly for a few moments. His mouth drops open to speak, but then closes again when he seems to think carefully about something. He appears uncharacteristically uncertain, his lovely eyes dancing across my face, a frown in place. I tilt my head, a little in interest, a little in impatience. 'Do you want it?' he asks.

This should be a stupid question, given we're discussing a position at the Hunt Corporation – a place many would give their right arm to work for. But we're also talking about me being in close proximity to this divine, albeit infuriating, man on a daily basis. 'Yes,' I answer without much thought, because it really doesn't take much thought. I don't even know what the salary is, or any of the package details.

'Then it's yours.' He turns and walks away, just as Mrs Potts comes flying through the door. Her alarmed face takes in my flustered form, before she turns to Becker Hunt. I follow her line of sight, finding him resting his hands in his trouser pockets, relaxed in his standing pose. He's exuding cockiness. And masculinity. And sex.

'Afternoon, Dorothy,' he says cheerfully.

'You promised to let me handle this,' she seethes, clearly not afraid to unleash her temper on her boss. 'Becker Hunt, you infuriate me.'

I'm stunned at the anger rolling off Mrs Potts.

'Calm your britches,' Becker huffs, his long legs eating up the distance between them. He pauses next to a riled Mrs Potts, but he doesn't look at her. 'Don't worry' – he sniffs, pushing his glasses up the bridge of his nose, exuding coolness as he rolls his broad shoulders – 'I haven't bitten her.' I'm treated to his perfect profile as he turns his eyes down on to the short, old lady. 'Yet,' he adds, before crossing the threshold and disappearing down the corridor. 'She starts tomorrow.'

I gasp.

Mrs Potts gasps.

Yet?

Oh . . . shit.

'Well,' Mrs Potts fumes, slamming the door behind him. I watch her faff with her string of pearls, getting all worked up. 'Damn man is a rogue.'

I feel I should calm her fussing hands that are now frantically dusting down her front, but I'm still pretty useless. 'Are you okay?' I manage to say, before realising my fingers are clawed into the arms of the chair. I release them and flex, allowing the blood to circulate again.

'I'm sorry, Eleanor.' She shakes her head in despair and makes her way over to me. I can't help but smile when she offers me her wrinkled old hand, like she suspects I need help to my feet after what I've just encountered. She's right. My legs feel like jelly.

'Difficult?' I ask as I take her offering and stand, pulling my skirt down as I do.

She almost laughs, but I can tell that her fizzing anger prevents it. Taking a deep breath, she sighs. 'He just can't help himself.' She opens the door and gestures for me to exit, which I do on a nervous smile, wondering if I'm going to be given any more than that. I know I can't ask. It isn't my place. 'This way, dear.'

We pass the curved staircase again, and my damn curious eyes drift up the stone steps.

'Out of bounds,' Mrs Potts says sternly, not even looking back to see where I'm looking. I realise now why. That's his apartment up there, where he stood and watched me in his grand hall. I mentally slap myself for fleetingly wondering what he must have thought seeing me here. 'Here we are.' Mrs Potts ushers me through another doorway, and I find myself in an enormous traditionally appointed kitchen, with an old-fashioned range cooker and a grand old table and huge, solid wooden chairs in the middle. 'I'll make tea. Take a seat, dear.' She fills a kettle and pops it on the gas stove.

I head to the table and sit down, then watch Mrs Potts as she faffs around the kitchen. I jump a mile when something wet touches my leg, smacking my knee on the underside of the table as I do. 'Ouch. Bloody hell, what is that?' I jump up and scamper back, frightened out of my skin.

'Language, dear,' Mrs Potts says, giving me a disapproving glower. Completely composed, she approaches and crouches, looking under the table and extending her hand. 'Come on, boy,' she coaxes gently.

I frown and bend to see under the table, and it's only a few moments until a wet nose appears. 'Aw, look.' I join Mrs Potts in her crouched position as a big furry beast emerges.

'Meet Winston,' she says, a proud edge to her tone.

'He's so cute.'

'And nervous. You have to gain his trust.' Mrs Potts scratches his ears roughly, and I laugh as he nuzzles into her hand, grumbling deeply as he does. 'He's Becker's best friend.'

Best friend? His best friend is a dog? 'A British bulldog?'

'Yes, dear.'

I put my hand out and Winston sniffs tentatively, clearly unsure of me. 'Hey, Winston,' I say quietly, moving my hand up to his ears. He recoils a little, unsure, but soon edges forwards again. It takes a few minutes of gentle coaxing, but he eventually allows me to scratch his ears, then a few minutes later, he's right up close and rolling on to his back, paws in the air. I laugh and give his belly a rub.

'He likes you.' Mrs Potts sounds surprised. 'You're privileged. He doesn't like many people.' My gaze lifts with her as she stands. 'That's enough, boy. In your bed.'

Winston displays his displeasure with a few more grumbles before rolling his big body back on to his paws and trotting across the kitchen, curling up in his bed.

I smile and take my seat as Mrs Potts returns to preparing the tea. 'Becker is very picky about who he has around his treasure. So far, that means no one,' Mrs Potts states matter-of-factly. 'But he knows I haven't got a lot of gas left in my tank. We've needed someone for a long time, but he's categorically refused. It's a family business, you see. And the Hunts have always been very private about their business dealings.' The kettle starts to whistle loudly, and she grabs a tea towel before removing it from the stove and filling the china teapot. 'I'm so relieved Becker has finally accepted we need help. And now that he's met you, I suppose we can commence business.'

I don't think it's a good idea to share the fact that I've already had the pleasure of meeting Becker Hunt.

Mrs Potts sighs. 'But I fear a girl as pretty as you might not be a good idea.'

'I'm not pretty.' It's out before I can stop it, sounding desperate.

Mrs Potts frowns at me. 'Really, Eleanor? That red hair and those big brown eyes are men magnets. Not to mention that curvy bottom you're sporting.'

I restrain myself from looking over my shoulder to said bottom. After all, it's not like I haven't seen it a million times in the mirror or squeezed it into dozens of pairs of jeans. I get my arse from my mother. And her narrow waist. Does Becker Hunt like pretty redheads with peachy arses? I don't know, but I need to convince Mrs Potts that I don't like cocky, arsehole men. 'I've heard he's a womaniser,' I state tentatively, wanting her to understand that I know all about Becker Hunt's reputation. What I don't want her to know is that I've experienced his womanising ways first hand. He's suggestive, tempting, and has the power of seduction down to a fine art. And he manages to be a total prick during the process. It defies reason that he should have such an effect on me, and I hate him for it.

'Donald, that's old Mr H, Becker's grandfather, calls him spirited,' Mrs Potts says wistfully, taking a sip of her tea.

I snort. I can't help it, and she shoots her eyes to mine. 'Sorry,' I say.

Her lips curve. 'Becker can be a charmer when he wants to be.'

I don't see him as charming, not in the least. I see him as an arrogant pig. A philanderer. Any female with a brain cell should see that.

'That man sends every woman he meets dizzy with those godforsaken good looks that he's inherited from his grandfather.' Mrs Potts confirms it. I'm not alone. I was dizzy, too. 'He's a maverick. A rogue. A player. Seduces women for fun. Honestly, he has a problem. It's unhealthy.' She looks past me thoughtfully for a few moments before returning serious eyes to me. 'But he's the best dealer out there. He gets that from the long line of Hunt men. Although I dare say he might just be the best of them all. His parents would be proud.' She takes a sip of her tea, and I follow suit, intrigued. His parents. That was headline news. His mother was tragically killed in a car accident many years ago, and his father was found dead in Rome a few years later after a mugging gone wrong. Becker Hunt has had his fair share of tragedy.

Mrs Potts snaps back to the room, as do I. 'Anyway, he's assured me he'll behave and let you get on with your job,' she tells me. 'He knows I need the help, and he needs to make sure he keeps his' – her lips purse – '*ways* under control. You'll become immune in time.'

My brow wrinkles. 'Immune?' I place my cup down, and she reaches over the table and squeezes my hand.

'To Becker,' she says. 'I have every faith you can keep things professional, dear. It's so exciting to have someone new at The Haven.'

Professional. I can do that. And now I'm determined to resist the man at all costs. I want this job more than I want him. I quickly rewind. I don't want him at all. He might be the most handsome man I've ever laid eyes on, and he might send my pulse racing, but Becker Hunt isn't the kind of man to whom any woman should give the time of day. Why so many do is beyond me. God knows what doors could be opened for me because of working here. My mind is on the job and nothing else, and I plan on keeping it that way.

'I can keep things professional,' I say to myself, glancing at the door when it opens. In walks a young chap, all preppy with wild spikes atop his head, pulling a huge briefcase behind him. He looks flustered.

'I'm here,' he sings.

'Ah, Percy.' Mrs Potts hurries over and grabs his cheeks, squeezing while he grins. 'You're a good boy.'

Percy laps up the praise being showered on him. 'I try my best, Mrs Potts.'

'Percy takes care of all the fancy technology at The Haven,' Mrs Potts says, turning to me. 'He's going to fix you up with a security card so you can access all the rooms.'

Percy heaves his case from the floor and carts it over to me, grunting as he hauls it on to the table. He looks at me with a mild smile on his face. 'Eleanor, I believe?' he muses, flipping the catches and popping the lid.

I nod, craning my neck, my eyes following his skinny fingers into the case. There's no paperwork or files, just a mass of chrome boxes with buttons and levers. He takes a card from his pocket and starts swiping and scanning it, before handing it across the table to me. 'Voilà,' he says.

I reach forward to take it, but Mrs Potts swoops in and snatches it from Percy's hand. 'I'll take that. Until your contract is signed, anyway.'

Percy slams his case shut and takes a hanky from his inside pocket, dabbing at his forehead. 'He finally agreed to some help?' he asks, looking to Mrs Potts.

'It's about time.'

Percy starts chuckling, a silly goofy laugh. He's a total geek, but completely adorable with it. 'Well, I can understand his reluctance. You're inviting whoever you hire into the Hunt family, after all.'

'Hmm,' Mrs Potts muses, glancing across to me. She smiles when she catches my eye. 'Like Eleanor has said, trust can only be built.'

I smile in return, so determined to gain their trust. This place is wonderful and loaded with priceless treasures. It's beyond a dream job.

Percy pulls his case off the table, grunting when it tugs his shoulder down sharply. Then he looks at me. 'Good luck.' He smiles a knowing smile, and I read between the lines. Percy doesn't only mean in building their trust. He means with the sinful man who heads up the Hunt Corporation.

'I won't need it.' I smile right back.

I'm exhausted by the time I get home. But so damn happy. The plan, according to Mrs Potts, and one I'm quite content with, is to get stuck right in. So I start tomorrow. Apparently, I'll learn in time to know exactly what's needed and when. She told me it's how she survived, until she became indispensable. I want to be indispensable. I might have felt completely overwhelmed, but the feel of The Haven, the endless gorgeous artefacts, the warmth, the odd sense of belonging that engulfed me throughout the rest of my day, has made me determined to make it work. I was totally engrossed in the catalogues that Mrs Potts showed me in one of the offices, all from various exhibits across the globe, some going back decades. Page after page of antiques with pictures, histories, facts, and figures. I recognised many of the items, got excited when I could predict what certain passages of information would say. She'd been most impressed. I was like an enchanted child. The desire to fill my mind with the information in front me was almost too much to cope with, especially the unfamiliar stuff. I was hungry for it, reading and storing it in every corner of my mind. I was in heaven.

After showering and falling into bed, I do something utterly stupid. I google Becker Hunt. And I hate what I see. Becker.

Everywhere. With a different woman on his arm in each picture. Some casual photographs, like him getting out of a car or walking into a restaurant, and some posed, like at private VIP galas or auction houses. He looks handsome in the snaps, yes, but in the flesh he's really something to behold. My face screws up in disgust at my wayward thoughts, and I snap my laptop shut, depriving my eyes of the gorgeous man who graces the screen. I need to keep my head down and learn the job.

After calling Mum and sharing my good news, I snuggle down with a contented smile. I'm not only keen to get to sleep because I'm knackered, but I also want tomorrow to come sooner so I can immerse myself in the tranquillity and enthralling dealings of The Haven again.

Chapter 6

The next day, after signing my employment contract with the biggest smile, I'm given the grand tour of The Haven by a very proud Mrs Potts. I swear, the place is a never-ending labyrinth of priceless, gorgeous works of art.

'This is the showing room, dear,' she says, ushering me through an old stable door that leads off the courtyard. 'It's where we display pieces for viewings.'

I breach the threshold and smile at the stark space that's free from any furniture or wall hangings. All that's contained within the room is an easel to hold paintings and a tall glass cabinet, where I'm guessing pots, vases, or other similar artefacts would be placed within. It's the most naked space I've seen so far in The Haven. It's easy to know why – it's so when pieces are showcased, that's all there is to focus on in the room.

'And now I'll show you the library.' Mrs Potts is off across the cobbles, heading to the doorway that leads into the Grand Hall. I follow eagerly, and when we enter the hall that's cluttered with treasures from every era you could imagine, I'm instantly warmed through again – the smell, the sight, the feeling that can only be achieved in a room full of Old Masters and valuable pieces.

Something comes to me as we're weaving through the priceless art and antiques. 'Mrs Potts, there must be millions of pounds' worth of treasure in here,' I say, keeping up with her shuffling body. 'Isn't security an issue?' Yes, I've seen the security keypads, but the doors and walls protecting this space are hardly Fort Knox.

Mrs Potts chuckles under her breath, like I've told a joke. It makes me feel silly, though I don't know why. It's a perfectly sensible question. 'Trust me, dear. No one is getting into The Haven, let alone the Grand Hall.'

I frown, thinking the Hunt Corporation might be being a little blasé about security, but I don't press, because the huge glass wall that keeps watch over the Grand Hall grips my attention. I look up to complete darkness, my imagination running wild. Now I know it was him lurking in the shadows yesterday, watching me. The prickles that crept across my skin as I stared up at the glass match the same kind of tingling that I've experienced each and every time I've encountered Becker Hunt. And, on cue, a shudder glides down my spine. Is he there now, watching me?

My mind is off on a tangent as I vaguely note Mrs Potts swiping her card. I shake my mind clear as I follow her, and we're swiftly heading down the corridor, passing the collection of beautiful framed pictures – watercolours, pencil drawings, oils – one of which I recognise instantly. 'John Constable,' I observe, gazing at it as we pass. By the slight tilt of her head, I can tell she's impressed.

We approach that alluring staircase, and I force my eyes forward, refusing to give in to the overwhelming temptation to peek up to the dark space. Thankfully, Mrs Potts drops a gear in pace until she's beside me, distracting me, like she can sense my inner battle. She smiles. 'We keep all the client files in the library. They've become jumbled up over the years.'

I return her smile, grateful for her intervention. 'Are there many?'

She laughs. 'Just a few. Here we are.' She indicates for me to open it, so I swipe my card as I gaze up at the wooden doors that stretch to the ceiling.

'Done,' I say, taking the handle. The doors are solid and heavy, so I have to physically put all my weight against them to push them open.

'The library,' Mrs Potts declares.

'Oh my goodness,' I breathe as I step over the threshold, in awe as my eyes scan the room. I wander into the centre and spend a few moments taking it all in, slowly pivoting. There are no windows, leaving every wall adorned in floor-to-ceiling bookcases, all built in a rich, dark wood. The room must be forty-feet high, similar to the Grand Hall, and there's a gold balcony circling halfway up with ladders leading to various sections. There's not an empty space, every shelf is loaded with books, binders, files. And the smell. I breathe in hundreds of years' worth of history from the pages surrounding me as I look up, seeing an intricately carved cornice framing the ceiling, and within it, a mosaic of millions of pieces of broken tiles, forming a stunning picture. 'Heaven and hell,' I whisper to myself, rapt by the illustration adorning the ceiling.

'Good and bad,' Mrs Potts replies, standing patiently by, allowing me to absorb the magnificence of the room. I could be a while. I'm spellbound.

The extravagance isn't the only thing that blows my mind. I bet the wealth of information found on these shelves couldn't be read in a lifetime. Possibly not even ten lifetimes.

'More or less every morsel of history the Hunt Corporation has amassed in over two hundred years of trading, dear,' she says fondly. 'Every client we've had, deal we've made, sale we've agreed to, item we've sold, as well as hundreds of antique reference books to boot.' She smiles at my flabbergasted face. 'Not to mention travel guides, map books, and encyclopaedias.'

It's making my head spin in the best possible way. 'It's wonderful.'

'I'll leave you to have a look around, dear. Mr H needs his medication.' She whips her duster out and gives the gold handle of the door a quick dust. 'The client files are on the far wall, dear. Top and bottom.' She indicates to one of the ladders. 'The reference books are over there.' She points across the room. 'You'll find your way around soon enough.' Mrs Potts disappears out the door, leaving me alone in the immense, quiet space.

I spend a good five minutes inspecting the room before I make my way to the far wall. As I near, the spines of the books become clear, and I'm soon close enough to read the text. Record books. They're deep red in colour, with gold type, and they're labelled alphabetically with years in brackets. I reach forward and select one, slowly sliding it out. The title reads: K (1961–1964)

Opening the cover carefully, I become immediately engrossed in the pages, my eyes scanning and absorbing the information while I stand at the foot of the towering bookcase. There's a page for each deal, every detail imaginable neatly scrolled in black ink. The client's name, address, interests, even a photograph of them – some posed, some caught in a moment. The pictures are all black and white, too, and the attire the figures wear is indicative of the date on the spine. Then there are the pieces bought, the value, the price paid – all figures that blow my mind.

I glance across the page and see a familiar face. 'JFK,' I gasp, running a finger down the picture of him laughing in the Oval Office. 'Incredible.' I force myself to snap the book closed and replace it on the shelf. The Hunt Corporation's dealings have always been cloak-and-dagger. And seeing what I'm seeing now – the values, the people, the insanely famous treasures – it's not such a mystery as to why.

Peering to my right, I spot one of the gold ladders leading to the balcony that circles the room. I can't resist. Kicking my heels off, I pull my hair into a messy ponytail before clasping each side of the ladder. Then I slowly and carefully climb to the top, and I soon find myself walking around the circumference of the room on the gold balcony. I glance down, surprised by how high I am. I reach up and rest my touch on the spines as I continue, the consistent mild rise and fall of the tips of my fingers over the books creating a quiet, relaxing thrum.

I loop the room twice before stopping at a shelf in the far corner and picking out a book. 'Treasures from the Ming Dynasty. You're on the wrong shelf,' I say to myself, my head shaking in wonder at the picture adorning the cover. It's the vase I nearly dropped during my interview, looking even more spectacular with strategic lighting directed on to it. This is another world, a world I never guessed would be this amazing – and the longer I spend in it, the more fascinating and intriguing it becomes. I tuck the book under my arm and take the ladder back down to put it in its correct place.

Stepping off the bottom rung with the book under my arm, I slip my feet back into my heels and make my way over to the other side of the library where a wealth of reference books are kept. Slotting it into place, I run my eyes across the length of books, so damn fascinated by it all. I've read hundreds of books on antiques, some general and some specific, but seeing this makes me feel like I've only scratched the surface. I reach up to pull out a textbook on Roman treasures, but pause, my hand hovering in the air, when I feel tingles pitter-patter across my skin. I try to shrug them off, scowling at the shelves before me. The tingles only intensify. Goddamn it. I slowly peek over my shoulder to see what I knew I would.

Becker Hunt is standing across the library, his shoulder resting on a bookcase, watching me quietly. I quickly look away before my eyes take the opportunity to drink him in, focusing on the book I was about to browse and pulling it free, flicking through the pages.

'You found the library,' he says quietly, his voice smooth and low.

I keep my attention forward. 'Mrs Potts left me to explore while she gives Mr H his meds.' Those damn goose bumps won't shift, no matter how much I beg them to.

'Do you like it?' he asks, his voice still quiet.

'I love it.' I don't hesitate. I'm in my element, and if he's been standing there watching me for a while – and I just know he has – then he'll have seen my awe as clear as day. It's magnificent, and not even my disdain for my new boss will make me say otherwise. He's clearly proud of it. He has every right to be.

'I'm glad,' he says, making my fingers pause as I turn a page. My eyes strain, wanting to look over my shoulder at him, but I stubbornly deny them the glorious sight and continue perusing the reference book. Then I hear him inhale, and what he's going to say next is suddenly all I can think about. 'I'm feeling a whole lot of *Beauty and the Beast* going on here,' he says.

My eyes shoot up from the book, my breath undeniably hitching. I just hope he didn't hear it. 'Strange reference.' I force stability into my tone.

'Maybe,' he replies, his voice getting louder. Oh God, he's coming over. 'Maybe not.'

Instinct has my feet kicking into action and walking me around the circumference of the room, my face buried in the book. 'Did you need something?' I ask casually but attentively. After all, he's my boss.

My eyes look up involuntarily, and I immediately damn them to hell and back. Shit, how can such a cocky arsehole look so sinfully delectable? He's suited and booted, his glasses perched on his perfect nose, his mousy hair a perfect ruffled mess. And stubble. *Gah!* I force my eyes back down.

'I'm due to fly to South America,' Becker says. 'I need you to sort flights and accommodation.' He walks over and hands a file to me. 'All the details for my trip are in here, as well as the computer login. Dorothy isn't great with technology, hence the paper file. Percy's set you up an email. Contact him if you need help.'

It takes way longer than it should for me to reach for the file, and when I do, my hands are visibly shaking. He's going away? This is good. Very good. 'I'll see to it.'

'And get me the files on Antonio Alice.' His hand brushes mine as he withdraws, and I gulp, shaking my head and my thoughts into line.

'The painter?'

'Correct. I'm not sure how long I'll be gone. Just book seven nights for the meantime until I have a better idea on how the deal will pan out.'

'Okay.'

'And research Mason Cox, while you're at it. I want everything you can find on him.'

I look up on a frown. 'I'm sorry, that name isn't familiar to me.'

'Why not?'

I come over a little hot, scanning my mind for anything that'll clue me in. Shit, have I screwed up? Should I know Mason Cox? I feel the heat in my cheeks begin to rise, my brain not helping me out.

Becker grins. 'Don't sweat it, princess.' He turns and struts away, and I have to force my eyes upwards so they don't take in his lovely arse. 'He's a small-time dealer sniffing around. No one knows him. His details are in that file.'

I clench my jaw. The wanker. 'I'll get it done,' I answer tightly, holding up the file.

'Thanks.' He opens the door but pauses. 'Oh, and Eleanor?'

'Yes?'

Looking over his shoulder, his face deadpans. 'Be quick about it.' He winks and then exits.

I breathe in deeply and call Becker Hunt every insulting name that comes to mind. 'Twat,' I mutter, opening the file he handed me. I hope this deal takes months.

Chapter 7

It's my third week in the job. Lucy and I have spent endless nights together, drinking wine, watching rom-coms, and talking until our tongues ache. She's a true gem, the sturdiest friend I've ever had in my twenty-eight years. With both of us employed and loving it, we've enjoyed a few messy nights on the town, as well as a few well-deserved shopping trips. Life in London is finally becoming what I always hoped, my dreams have been realised.

I've continued to ignore calls and texts from my ex-boyfriend and my ex-best friend. Ignoring them is becoming easier by the week. David wants to see me. Wants to make things right. What an idiot. He is a distant memory. And an unfaithful fucking arsehole.

I've made it a point to call Mum at least every other day, and each time she's sounded better, happy to hear how I'm getting on. The only thing hanging over my head is the chore of getting my arse home to sort out Dad's shop. The urgency to see to it is even less now that things are working out here. I'm happy. Content. Going home could upset all that. It could reignite my guilt for abandoning my father's beloved store. It could also have me bumping into people I never want to see again. So, I've been putting it off.

Becker Hunt hasn't been around, his South American deal taking longer than expected, and for that I'm grateful. I'm getting used to The Haven's routine without any annoyingly lovely/irritating distractions. Our contact has been limited to phone calls and emails, which is great because I don't have to look at him. It hasn't stopped him from trying to get a rise out of me on our calls, though. He's intolerable, but I've worked hard to let it slide. In fact, I think I'm becoming immune to him. His sheer presence, even from the other side of the world, is potent, so I've focused on fulfilling what's expected of me quickly and with as little interaction as possible. Becker Hunt commands attention. I'm getting closer to being able to give him that attention without fighting constantly to rein in my uncontrollable, *unreasonable* attraction. Yes, I'm becoming immune. Even to his constant innuendoes and fierce need to try and rile me. It seems that Becker Hunt absolutely loves winding me up.

One thing I've learned in my time at The Haven is that there is no dress code. There's no need for office attire, so today I've opted for some beige capri pants and a fitted white shirt. I can't bring myself to revert to the flats that always graced my feet back home, so my toes are still pinching in my heels as I feel my way down the dark alleyway, counting in my head. I smile when the lights fire up, despite it hurting my eyes.

After negotiating the cobblestones a little further, I swipe my card and break free of the alley, entering the tranquil courtyard of The Haven. I can't help it; I sigh and breathe it all in, closing my eyes on a satisfied smile. Yes, I love it here. Everything about it. I'm relatively free to immerse myself in the history I've only ever had the pleasure of reading about. I'm talking to art dealers across the globe, famed auction houses, and learning new things every day. It's my own personal heaven.

'Morning, princess.'

I jump, my eyes snapping open. 'Jesus.'

Becker's perfect eyebrow hitches at my surprise.

'Don't do that,' I yell, making him recoil and pout a little. It's an adorable pout, accompanied by something else in his eyes. It's mischief, which worries me. My mouth snaps shut. Professional. Be professional. Where's he come from, anyway?

I haven't arranged his return journey from South America. 'You arranged your own travel?' I ask.

'Thought I'd surprise you. Did you miss me?'

Oh, I can feel that irritation beginning to bubble – I'm vehemently ignoring my awe. 'Excuse me,' I breathe calmly, knowing the importance of escaping before my greedy eyes get the opportunity to remind me of his beauty, or his lovely nose, or his short messy hair, or his broad shoulders, or his hazel eyes, or his . . .

I step forward a pace, keeping my eyes at my feet, hoping he'll take the hint and get out of my way. It's a few moments of waiting until I accept he isn't going to, so I move to the left. And so does he.

'I'm told you're settling in well,' he says, but I still refuse to look at him.

'Yes, very well, thank you,' I answer, giving myself a cheer for my professionalism. Then I move to the right. And so does he.

'Good,' he says quietly. 'Very good.'

Biting my lip, desperately wrestling off the urge to take a quick peek at him, I step to the right again. And so does he. 'Excuse me.' It takes everything in me to maintain my strength. He's like a magnet to my eyes. Nothing as stunning as him should be ignored. Immune? I laugh to myself. I don't think that's possible.

It's a long, long while, but I eventually see his smart brogues shift.

'My lady,' he says quietly.

Damn it. I chance a peek up at him as I scoot past, catching the signs of a cheeky smirk. And, *shit*, if my eyes don't sprint over his entire face as I continue past, and then down his tall frame.

'I look better naked,' he says, all low and sexy. That soon breaks my trance, and I swing away, outraged, marching on.

'I don't plan on finding out,' I mutter under my breath, and he laughs, telling me I didn't voice my promise quietly enough. I stop, turning to face him. 'You know, I'm pretty sure I could make a complaint to HR about sexual harassment.'

He grins. 'I *am* HR. What's your complaint?'

I narrow my eyes. 'You're not funny.'

'Then why are you fighting to hold back your grin?'

My lips purse. Damn him. 'Are you going to continually try to get a rise out of me?'

'A rise?' He peeks down at his groin area, and then glances back up, his grin now mild. 'Too late.'

My eyes naturally drop to his groin, and he chuckles as he turns and saunters away. My head cocks in admiration, his lovely backside my focus. It really is a sight to behold, his sexy swagger executed to a T.

'Stop looking at my arse,' he shouts over his shoulder.

I cringe. Holy shit, I need to find some control. He's my boss, for Christ's sake. 'I was doing no such thing.'

'You know,' he calls, 'I'm pretty sure I could make a complaint to HR.'

'What's your complaint?' I ask on a frown.

'That you're undressing me with your eyes.' He doesn't entertain me with another glimpse of his lovely face, just carries casually on his way, disappearing through the large doors into the Grand Hall.

Oh my God, he's impossible.

'Morning, dear.' Mrs Potts's friendly tone cuts through my aggravation, and I turn around to find her with a watering can in her hand.

'Morning,' I chirp, feeling all kinds of guilty for being caught in the act – the act of total feebleness. I straighten myself out and walk over to her as she rains water over the beds of flowers edging the fountain. 'How are you, Mrs Potts?'

She drops the can and dusts off her hands. 'Tickety-boo,' she says quietly, running suspicious eyes all over my face. 'Becker's home.'

I avoid eye contact *and* that statement. 'I'll be in the library,' I say, avoiding any further observations she might make, like my observation of Becker Hunt looking sinfully tasty. 'I have some calls to make and lots to detail for Christie's.' I take off, rolling my shoulders and talking some reason into myself. Work. Focus on work.

My feet move fast to get me to the library, and after heaving the door closed, I rest my back against it and look up to the depiction of Heaven and Hell, laughing to myself at the irony. 'Very apt,' I say as I head for the couch to drop my bag. I only make it halfway when the phone on the coffee table starts to ring. I change course and take the call.

'Hello, the Hunt Corporation, Eleanor speaking.'

'Oh, hello.' The lady's voice is surprised. 'I was expecting Becker to answer.'

'You've come through to the library,' I tell her, looking down at the phone and seeing the various buttons labelled for different rooms within The Haven. I notice the one labelled 'office' is illuminated. 'He appears to be on a call.'

'I'm sorry,' the lady says. 'Who am I speaking to?'

'Eleanor.'

'The new recruit?'

'That's me.'

'Oh, how lovely.' She sounds surprised. 'I just have a question. Maybe you can help?'

'I'll try. Who's calling?'

'Paula. Becker and I—' She stalls for a beat. 'We work closely together.'

I'm immediately, and quite unreasonably, wondering how close is *close*? Work? They're on first-name terms. Every other client or associate is referred to by their surname. 'How can I help you?' I ask, pushing my professionalism to the front of my mind and my wondering to the back.

'Is he free tomorrow?'

I stare down at the receiver, a little flabbergasted. 'I'm not sure.' I'm not organising his personal life. Wait. Is part of my job organising his personal life?

'Okay. Get him to call me, if you don't mind.'

I do. 'Certainly.' This is probably a stupid question, but I literally have to ask. 'Does he have your number?'

'Of course.'

Of course. 'Right. I'll ask him to call you back. Goodbye.' The receiver leaves my ear, but she goes on, prompting me to take it back.

'I bet it's interesting working with Becker.'

Something tells me by *interesting* she's not referring to the insane amount of gorgeous pieces of art and antiques I'm surrounded by, but maybe the gorgeous man. Is she testing the waters? Sussing me out? 'Interesting indeed.' I give her a little something to think about. I have no right to, obviously, and part of me is wondering why I'm being rather hostile, even if I sound perfectly polite.

I hear her hum. It's a thoughtful hum. 'Well, if you could get him to give me a call that would be great.'

'Certainly.' I hang up, noticing Becker's office phone is no longer engaged. I purse my lips. I'll tell him later. Pivoting, I head back towards the couch, but I don't make it very far.

Because something is in my way.

Something hard.

And I walk right into it. I yelp as I bounce back, blinking repeatedly. The sudden sensation of warmth on my upper arm momentarily freezes me in position, before I'm quickly batting him away. 'I'm fine,' I blurt, ducking past him. 'You need to stop appearing from nowhere.'

'I like surprising you.' There's humour lacing the edges of his words, telling me that adorable lopsided grin will be fixed in place, yet I don't give in to the enticement of it, centring my focus forward.

I gather the files I need and park myself on the couch, crossing one leg over the other, turning my attention on my task so I have something to focus on, other than him. 'You don't surprise me, you make me jump,' I say, hearing the even beats of his footsteps getting closer.

His long legs bend, bringing those thighs into clear view as he lowers to the couch beside me. 'What are you doing?'

'Putting together the details for the new lots going to auction next week.'

He peers at the book in my hands. 'Ah, the Quahog pearl brooch. Gorgeous, isn't it?'

I smile at the picture of the stunning piece of jewellery. 'And rare. The stone, I mean.'

'Tell me about it.'

I look up on a frown. 'What?'

'The brooch. What can you tell me about it?'

I cock my head on a small smile, curious. Surely he knows all about it? He nods encouragingly. I shrug to myself. Maybe he's testing me. 'It dates back to the early eighteen hundreds.'

'Eighteen twenty-five,' he says quietly. 'Go on.'

'It's a rare purple Quahog pearl.'

His smile makes my stomach flip. 'One of a kind?'

'Probably.'

He drapes his arm across the back of the sofa, getting comfortable. 'Definitely,' he replies quietly. 'It's fifteen millimetres in diameter. One sold five years ago measuring in at fourteen millimetres in diameter. This one right here will take the record.'

'Wow,' I breathe, my eyes roaming his otherworldly face. But something else is calling my attention right now, and it has more to do with his knowledge and expertise. This language – all things art and antiques – is one I've never spoken with anyone. It's slightly more dangerous territory, if I'm honest.

I blink myself back to life. 'You know, pearls are highly prized in Japan. You should consider selling this at an auction house there.'

'I'm happy for you to arrange that.' He swallows and seems to shake himself back to reality, too, and I quickly return my attention to the file in my hands.

'Someone named Paula called,' I blurt out, glancing at him from the corner of my eye, gauging his reaction. Nothing. 'She asked if you're free tomorrow.'

'I'll call her.'

My teeth clench. Jesus, Eleanor. 'I noticed the Rembrandt has a hairline crack in the frame. I wondered whether you'd like me to have it looked at.'

'Yes. I'll send you the details of the restorer I use.'

'Thank you.' I continue to flick through the pages of the file until I'm almost at the back. He's silent. Soon I'll have no pages left to turn.

I peek out the corner of my eye again and find him gazing at me intently. He moves closer. 'Do you like working here, princess?'

'I love it,' I admit. 'The treasures. How things so ancient haven't lost their beauty. It blows my mind.'

He smiles. It's faint, but so bright. 'Any particular favourites?'

That's impossible to say. There are too many. 'I love your desk.'

His head cocks. 'It's a sturdy desk.'

My eyes drop to his lips. 'Sturdy,' I mimic quietly. 'Yes, it looks very sturdy.'

He's silent for a moment, then his lips part, preparing to speak. 'I really love hearing you talk about my treasure. I know I'm your boss and all, but it turns me on like nothing else.'

'Are we in the realms of sexual harassment again, Mr Hunt?' I breathe.

74

'I don't know. Do you feel harassed?'

'No. More intimidated.'

'By me? Why?'

'You're a little challenging.'

He smiles. *God, please, don't smile at me. I might dive forward and kiss you.*

'You're quite challenging yourself, Miss Cole.'

'I like keeping you on your toes.'

'Oh, you're doing a very good job of that. Among other things.'

Don't ask. 'Like?' *Goddamn me.*

'Like,' he whispers, 'disarming me constantly with your sass. It's . . . very attractive. If you didn't work for me, I can't promise I wouldn't have had you on my *sturdy* desk by now.'

I try not to allow my eyes to go round in shock. I try. And nosedive. What on earth am I doing? I shouldn't be encouraging him. Bantering with him. Imagining kissing him.

I gulp and go to speak, to put him in his place politely but firmly. But a palm rests over my mouth before I can get the words out. I freeze, his flesh hot against me, and resort to taking deep inhales through my nose to load my lungs with much-needed air. He comes closer still, keeping his palm exactly where it is. I could push it away if I wanted to. But I can't.

Our eyes lock.

My heart rate accelerates.

And I'm deathly still.

He stops when his perfect nose is only a hair's breadth away from mine, his eyes darkening, revealing . . . something. Craving. He isn't playing now.

Oh shit. Shit, shit, shit, shit.

Placing his other palm over my breastbone, he narrows his eyes a little, like he could be mad with me. 'Your heart's rivalling mine in the pounding department.'

Oh Jesus, Lord above. I don't speak, I don't argue, because his hand is hindering my ability to talk. And it's in this moment I re-evaluate my definition of the word *charming*. I've always thought someone charming was agreeable. Friendly. Charismatic. I now understand that you can add captivating, enticing, and tempting to that list, too. Becker Hunt is all of those things. His intentions might not be charming – whatever those intentions are – but his pure sex appeal, his otherworldly boyish good looks, and the god-like physique that I just know is hidden under his fine clothes, all are.

My boss is the epitome of sexy.

He knows it, and, worst of all, he knows *I* think it, too.

I remain still, determined not to be the one to break the connection. I'm not weak. I can match him in the self-assurance department. I'm not going to be one of the hundreds of drooling women falling at his feet. Becker Hunt has met his match. I don't know where it comes from, maybe my love of the job I want to keep, but I find the strength I need and close the distance between us until our noses touch. I know his face so well by now, that if I could see it all, he'd have a slight crease on his forehead from his frown.

I reach up and take his hand, gently pulling it down from my mouth. He doesn't stop me. There's sexual tension sizzling between us, cracking and sparking. It makes me draw a deep, self-controlled breath before I give in to it. Before Becker Hunt wins and proves what we both know: I'm more enthralled by him than I am irritated. But what about him? Is this just a game to him?

My eyes can't resist a brief glimpse of his mouth. His lips are slightly parted. I could kiss them right now. Get an answer to my question. But I don't swoop in. I'm not breaking. I like it here. I'm staying, and I won't be distracted by his attempts to . . . well, distract me. Mrs Potts is right. *Focus on the job.* He really can't help himself, so *I* will have to help *him*.

I lift my eyes. 'If you'll excuse me.' I pull away and shut the book with an ear-piercing crack, getting a small thrill when his shoulders jerk – something he tries and fails to disguise. I hold his eyes. 'You're keeping me from my work, Mr Hunt.'

He watches me with his penetrating stare for a few moments. I don't shy away. I mustn't show weakness. Then he clears his throat, pulling back like he's been burnt. 'I have a meeting in my office. Bring me tea for two.' He stands, straightening out his suit and raking a hand through his tousled hair. He's flustered. Well, isn't that a novelty.

'Yes, sir,' I answer swiftly and clearly, placing the book on a nearby coffee table.

'And don't call me sir,' he snaps, striding off and yanking the huge door open like it's weightless. He slams it behind him, creating a deafening sound that rings in my ears long after he's gone.

'Jesus.' I exhale, relaxing my strung-out muscles. That was way harder than it should have been. But I did it. I showed him. Take that, Becker Hunt. I will not break.

When I'm sure my legs can hold me up, which takes way too long for my liking, I head to the kitchen to fetch tea for two, as per his curt order.

'Hello, dear.' Mrs Potts shuts the fridge as I enter and places a chicken on the counter. 'How are you getting on?'

'Mr Hunt would like tea for his meeting.'

The instant worry that passes across her old features amuses me. 'I'll take it,' she says, crossing the kitchen and pulling a teapot down from the shelf of an ancient wooden cabinet.

I join her and take the teapot from her grasp. 'Mrs Potts, I can handle it.'

She eyes me doubtfully on a disbelieving huff. 'The tea, or Becker?' She attempts to reclaim the teapot, but I pull it away and give her a raised brow.

'Both. He employed me to take the pressure off you. To relieve you.'

'Yes, but—'

'I'm immune.' That's not true at all, but I've certainly reached an epic milestone. 'Mrs Potts, I can see you have your hands full with Mr H. Please, let me help.' I need to prove I can do this, to Mrs Potts *and* to myself.

It doesn't take her long to relent, though I can tell it's reluctantly. 'Have it your way, but don't come crying to me when he breaks your heart.' She's off across the kitchen again.

Breaks my heart? 'Let's not get carried away, Mrs Potts.' I laugh, opening the cupboards to find what I need. 'My heart is perfectly safe.' It's my treacherous senses that are the problem here. No living, breathing woman could be unaffected by Becker Hunt.

She scoffs and dumps the chicken in a tray, then proceeds to cover it in tinfoil. 'That's what they all say.'

'You have no need to worry,' I assure her. Yes, he's annoyingly attractive and probably hot in bed, but I know, beyond all things I know, that Becker Hunt isn't the kind of man I could fall in love with. He's too self-obsessed and conceited. He's too in love with himself. And I definitely love my job too much. I know what true heartbreak is. I felt it as I said goodbye to my dad five years ago. I felt it when I turned from betrayal and left for London. This job? *This* is everything. I'm beginning to love *me*, and that's what will keep my heart intact against Becker Hunt.

My tea for two is complete, the silver tray looking fit for royalty. I leave Mrs Potts hacking away at a pile of potatoes and make my way to Becker's luxurious office, tray across my palms, my back straight. It takes a bit of awkward negotiating of the tray, but I finally balance it on a raised knee and ring the brass bell.

'Come in.'

His demand is clipped. He's pissed off. This knowledge fills me with unreasonable satisfaction as I push the handle down with my elbow and enter the room, kicking the door closed lightly with my heel. I spend a few moments reacquainting myself with his office, pulling up when I see a new addition. An amazing new addition to the regal space in the form of a huge grandfather clock. Not just huge. It's massive, and when I look closely, I see the clock face is a stunning replica of the Shepherd Gate Clock.

'Anytime soon.' Becker's sarcastic comment yanks me from my admiration of his new piece.

'Tea,' I announce, braving his eyes and smiling sweetly. 'Where would you like it, Mr Hunt?'

His scowl travels across the room like lightning and smacks me in the face. 'Desk,' he orders, keeping narrowed eyes on me as I saunter over and slide it in front of him.

'There,' I say casually. 'Right on your *sturdy* desk.' What the fuck am I doing? I peek up at him to see his mouth hanging slightly open. He's shocked. I don't blame him. I'm shocked with myself. I'm deplorable, playing him at his own game. But I can't help it. He just pushes my buttons. I smile, almost in apology, and his eyes close briefly. He's gathering himself.

I wander across the room and indicate to the clock. 'It's stunning.'

Becker loses all irritation in a heartbeat and smiles, standing and joining me. I make a metal note that when Becker is in a bad mood, I simply need to talk about his treasures. 'Isn't it?' His hand reaches forward, and he glides a light fingertip over the face. 'You know it?'

'Of course.' I rip my eyes away from his finger caressing the clock and smile up at his face. 'It's an amazing replica.'

'Indeed.' Becker's hazel eyes become heavier, lazier, and I quickly recall what he said in the library. I turn him on more when I talk about his treasure. That could be a real issue, since The Haven is drowning in it and I love talking about it. I clear my thoughts and glance away. 'I'll leave you to your meeting.' I pass him, brushing against his arm, and squeeze my eyes closed, ignoring his quiet intake of breath.

He coughs. 'Yes, you're dismissed.'

Dismissed? It takes every crumb of my willpower not to turn and cuff him around his beautiful head. Oh, I've really got under his skin. Good. So now he's going for plain arsehole? Because I rebuffed him? Such a child. 'Will there be anything else?'

'I said you're dismissed.' He shoos me away with a wave of his hand through the air, riling me further. But I maintain my self-control and turn away from him slowly, adopting something shamefully close to his sexy swagger as I slink away.

Taking the handle of the door lightly, I pull it open and perform a slow turn as I exit and pull it closed behind me, just catching a glimpse of Becker Hunt's face before the door comes between us. He was looking at my arse. I want to smile my satisfaction, but I know I'm dancing on dangerous ground. *Very* dangerous ground.

I wander back to the library and swipe my card to let myself in. I shouldn't be goading him, but he's easier to handle when he's being a difficult, arrogant cock, rather than a smouldering, tempting cock. I feel like I've gained a bit of control. Or am I kidding myself?

I call to make arrangements with the restorer, and I'm surprised when the guy who answers calls me by my name with no introduction. Maybe Becker's told him about me, like he must have told that Paula, whoever she is. Who is she? I stop my conjecturing right there. That part of his business isn't my business.

After agreeing on a time for the painting to be collected, I hang up and make my way to a ladder, but the phone on the table rings again and I rush back across the library to answer. I'm working up a sweat, all this to-ing and fro-ing. 'Hello.'

'There's a file labelled (W) 2010–2015,' Becker mumbles. 'Third shelf up on the fifth case clockwise from the door. Bring me it.' He hangs up, leaving me with my mouth agape and the phone dangling limply in my hand.

'Such a twat,' I grumble, my earlier coolness drowned out by his expert tosser-like behaviour. I slam the phone down and stomp to the specified shelf, quickly locating the correct file before stomping back to his office. I wish he'd piss off back to South America.

I use the brief time it takes to get there to cool my simmering temper, and I only ring the bell when I'm sure it's under control.

'Come in.'

Plastering an over-the-top smile on my face, I push my way into his office. I feel his eyes on me in an instant. Burning eyes. 'Your file.' I hold it up on my way to him, clocking another man seated at Becker's desk, his back to me. 'Good afternoon, sir,' I greet politely, watching as the man slowly turns to face me.

'Hello . . . Miss?'

I falter in my stride, a bit taken aback. His grey-flecked hair suggests a middle-aged gent, but his friendly face and warm brown eyes put him nearer the mid-thirties. He's handsome in an unconventional way, with a prominent Roman nose and very square jaw. 'Eleanor,' I exhale my name, placing the file blindly on Becker's desk and offering my hand.

'Miss Eleanor?' He smiles and takes my hand.

'Eleanor Cole,' I clarify, letting him do all the shaking.

'I'm Brent Wilson. So, you're Becker's new assistant?'

Assistant? 'Well, I—'

'She's on trial,' Becker butts in, rounding his desk to meet us on the other side. 'Her future at the Hunt Corporation is yet to be determined.'

I throw him a shocked look. Is it? Why? Because I'm not giving him what he wants, he might now start making my life a misery to get rid of me? He's sorely mistaken. I refuse to let him get under my skin. And where are his morals? He knows Mrs Potts is coming to depend on me, even if he hasn't. It's no secret that Becker was reluctant to hire outside help. Would he really let his bruised ego get in the way of giving Mrs Potts the respite she needs?

'Well,' Brent pipes up, 'if you don't want her, Hunt, I'll gladly take her on.'

It doesn't matter that this Brent bloke is being a chauvinistic pig, talking about me like I'm not here, or like I'm a piece of meat to bargain over. No, it doesn't matter because the animosity that's leaping from Becker's prowling frame is overriding any need I have to jump all over Brent's sexist arse. And anyway, he's quite cute. I open my mouth to thank him for the offer but get cut off yet again when Becker takes my elbow and tugs me away.

'She's looking promising,' he grumbles.

I swing disbelieving eyes up to him, which he totally ignores. 'I am?' I can't help myself. So now I'm promising?

His lovely lips purse as he casts me a brief, cautious glance. 'You're dismissed,' he grunts, physically leading me to the door.

I glance over my shoulder as my feet work fast to keep up with Becker, smiling suggestively at Brent. I can't even find the decency to be ashamed of myself. I shrug Becker off and straighten myself out. 'Can I get you anything else, Mr Hunt?' I ask, cocking my head questioningly.

His jaw ticks wildly as daggers shoot from his fiery eyes. 'No,' he whispers. 'Just the information I requested earlier.'

'I'll have it ready by the end of the day.'

'This sounds a bit cloak-and-dagger.' Brent laughs.

'You know the Hunt Corporation,' Becker says, face straight, his stare fixed on me.

'Don't I just,' Brent replies thoughtfully. I can feel his eyes on me, too, as I bow my head and hold my boss's eyes as I pass him, brushing his jacket sleeve. It wasn't intentional. He hisses, but I manage to control my reaction to the jolt of electricity that attacks me from our contact. Or was that simply angry vibes emanating from him? Regardless, it's stolen my breath, and I fight to get it back as I leave his office.

'Wait.'

I pull to a sharp halt and turn, finding Brent coming towards me. My eyes flit between him and Becker standing motionless and wide-eyed by the door, a frown creeping its way on to my forehead. 'Yes?' I say.

'Please, allow me to take you for dinner sometime,' Brent says softly, reaching into his inside pocket and pulling out a card. He holds it out to me, and my hand lifts slowly to take it. But he doesn't let go. 'Call me?'

Our arms remain suspended between our bodies, while Becker bristles at the side, probably giddy with annoyance that there is absolutely nothing he can say to dismiss Brent's offer. This is my personal life, and he has no control over that. 'I'd love to.' I sound confident and gracious, though on the inside I'm wondering why I accepted so easily. I don't know this guy, *and* I'm supposed to be sworn off men.

Becker has now moved from bristling to physical twitching. I can feel it. Sense it.

'Excellent,' Brent says. 'I'll look forward to it.'

He finally releases the card, and I back away, glancing at Becker as I do. He's swallowing repeatedly, his eyes darting around his office until they eventually land on mine. The world stops rotating on its axis, but my head spins wildly to make up for it.

'Goodbye,' I say quietly, continuing to back away, unable to rip my stare from the vacant expression on Becker's face. He twitches slightly, and I can see with perfect clarity that he's suddenly back in the room. Where was he? He looks to Brent, then to me, before he snaps to life, grabbing the door and practically slamming it in my face.

I stand on the other side for a few moments, bringing the card to my mouth and chewing the corner thoughtfully.

Is my boss jealous? This revelation wreaks havoc on my increasingly knotted mind.

Chapter 8

It's the end of my first month at the Hunt Corporation, yet I feel like I've been here for years. I've spent endless days immersed in the library, losing myself in the abundance of books that grace the shelves, and I've familiarised myself with the unique filing system.

I've answered Becker Hunt's every demand, and he's certainly been demanding, from finding files to making calls; from providing information, to cross-referencing a few pieces. His orders are always short, snappy, and curt, and he's hardly looked at me since Brent asked me to dinner last week. His abruptness, and the fact he's obviously avoiding me, has suited me just fine. Immunity is easier with minimal contact.

Now I'm curled up on one of the leather chesterfields in The Haven's library after giving myself a few minutes respite. It's been non-stop this week.

Mrs Potts pokes her head around the door, her violet bomb of a hairstyle glowing vividly. 'It's gone six, Eleanor.' She smiles at the pile of books stacked next to me on the couch.

'It has?' I ask, glancing down at my watch.

'Time melts away at The Haven, dear.' She smiles warmly. 'I'll be in the kitchen.'

'Okay,' I say as she slips out. I unravel my body from the couch, feeling a little stiff, but a quick stretch of my arms above my head soon sorts me out, before I put the books in their rightful places.

My phone rings, and I answer as I make my way to the kitchen. 'Hello?'

'Eleanor?'

I pull to a stop, not recognising the voice. 'Yes?'

'Brent Wilson.'

'Oh, Brent.' I cringe. I never called him about that dinner. To be honest, I threw his card in my bag and didn't think much more about it. Someone else stole my thoughts for the rest of that day, and I've spent most of my time battling to keep Becker Hunt in a safe part of my brain. Like the professional part. Besides, I'm off men. A few more emails from my ex begging to see me reminded me of that. 'Hi,' I squeak.

'I thought I'd see if you're available for dinner this evening?'

'Well, I'm . . .' I grapple with myself to find a reasonable explanation to decline. 'Wait. How'd you get my number?'

'If a man wants something, he'll find it,' he answers smoothly. 'So, dinner?'

'Brent, it's really very kind of you to offer, but . . .' I turn on the spot, willing some more words to follow – words that'll be tactful, rather than a flat refusal. I'm really not interested in dinner, with him or *anyone*.

As I glance up, something catches my eye down the corridor, and I find myself taking a step back. Becker is standing outside his office, watching me. He has a scowl in place. He's been listening to my call? Something comes over me – something childish and silly. 'I'd love to, Brent,' I say, my eyes fixed on Becker's. His jaw starts to tick. 'I'm just finishing work.'

'Great. I'll meet you at The Wolseley at eight.'

'See you then.' I disconnect the call, wilting under Becker's fierce expression for a good few seconds before he drags his eyes away and turns, disappearing back into his office. I bite my lip and start walking backwards, my eyes rooted on the engraved door until I reach the bathroom. I feel like I just leapt back on to dangerous ground. What game am I playing?

After I've used the loo and collected my bag and coat, I head for the kitchen. 'Eleanor.' Old Mr H is sitting at the table when I enter, and Mrs Potts is sliding a roast beef dinner towards him. 'Come and tell me how you are.' He taps the seat next to him. 'Still enjoying it here?'

'Absolutely, yes.' That's the understatement of the century.

'And your mum. Is she okay?'

I smile fondly; I appreciate that he asks. He does most days since I told him she's back home and missing me terribly, though happy I'm finally doing what I really love. 'She's good, thank you, Mr H.'

'Super.' He smiles brightly. I want him to be *my* grandad. Becker Hunt might be all kinds of difficult, but his grandad, Mrs Potts, and even Winston, more than make up for that. I've become so fond of them.

'Eat up,' Mrs Potts demands, pointing to Mr H's knife and fork that are laid neatly on the table.

'Yes, yes,' he grumbles moodily, scooping them up and looking at me expectantly. 'Would you like some supper? Dorothy makes a mean roast.'

I glance over to Mrs Potts, who's rolling her eyes. 'Thank you, Mr H, but I have a date this evening. I need to go home and get myself ready.'

'A date, you say?' He jiggles suggestive eyebrows, making me laugh.

'I'll see you out,' Mrs Potts says.

'Thank you. Have a good evening, Mr H.'

He forks a piece of beef and waves it in the air, rolling his eyes. 'Yes, I'll be partying and falling into bed in the early hours, don't you worry.'

'Those days are gone, Donald.' Mrs Potts laughs, gesturing the way.

He takes a mouthful and chews. 'Whoever the lucky man is, I hope he treats you like a lady.'

'I'm sure he will,' I say, following Mrs Potts out of the kitchen. We make it only a few paces when we're hit by a loud screech that bounces off the walls around us. 'What the hell was that?' I ask, looking around, startled.

'Lord Almighty,' Mrs Potts mutters, taking my arm. 'Nothing, dear. Let's be going.'

I can do no more than follow, looking over my shoulder, but then I hear it again, this time louder. 'There,' I say, pulling her to a stop. 'There it is again.' It sounds like a cat's being strangled.

'It's nothing, Eleanor,' she insists, making me frown.

'It doesn't sound like nothing to me.'

'It really—'

'Oh, Becker. You dirty boy.' The high-pitched voice stabs at my back, and I swing around, despite Mrs Potts's best efforts to pull me on. I'm horrified by what I see. A woman falling out of Becker's office half-naked, her modesty covered only by frilly satin underwear. 'Come get me, tiger.'

Tiger? My face screws up. I hate her. Why do I hate her? I toss the question aside quickly, afraid of the answer. Is this the woman I took the call from? Paula?

I know what I'm going to see next, and as much as I know it's going to make my eyes bleed, I can't seem to force my legs to carry me away. Mrs Potts is determinedly tugging on my arm, yet I remain in place, waiting for the inevitable. The brazen hussy steps back until her back meets the wall, then she holds a finger up and motions for him to come to her while she licks her lips seductively.

I'm prepared. I'm prepared. I'm prepared.

He appears.

Bare-chested.

I'm not prepared.

I swallow hard. Good God, there are no words. He's an Adonis.

My eyes yell at me when I force them away, but I soon give

them what they want and look at him again. Why am I doing this to myself? I'm beginning to hate this man. He irritates me, makes my blood boil with rage, and those things should make him unattractive. But they don't. If anything, it's making him even more enticing. I just don't get it. I'm done with pricks. And Becker Hunt is the king of pricks.

I torture myself further by watching as he moves in slowly until his hard body is pressed up against her super-skinny frame, pinning her to the wall. He's going to kiss her, and the distressed ache I feel completely muddles my mind. I should be cheering her on, thankful he clearly has someone else to occupy himself with. I should feel lucky to have escaped his so-called *charm*.

But I don't feel lucky. I feel sick with jealousy. Quite frankly, I'm prepared to pull her off him by her hair. What's got into me? I need to remove myself from this god-awful situation, but just as I've convinced my dead muscles to help me do that, I see him pause right before his lips meet hers. His profile is perfect, and I manage to blank out the women, who's a whisker away from his face, and relish in it. Then he slowly turns towards me.

And I stop breathing.

His hazel eyes are serious. 'Enjoy your date,' he growls, a hint of a salacious smile gracing his perfect mouth. Then he roughly grabs the woman's arm and drags her towards the curved stone staircase to his apartment.

My teeth grind and my jaw aches from being clenched. The absolute, first-class, total and complete arsehole. I should slap his face.

But . . .

Oh my God. I see something.

Something monumental, something that's knocked me sideways, more so than the unreasonable hurt I'm feeling. I'm distracted from my unwarranted wounded feelings by the biggest tattoo I've ever seen, which spans Becker's back.

I step forwards to get a better look, but I can't make it out, can't fathom the design; he's too far away. It's just shadows of grey ink, but it's alive and swelling on his broad back. Riveted. I'm absolutely riveted by the revelation. A tattoo. Not just a tattoo, but an enormous piece of art.

When he reaches the foot of the staircase, he pushes Tiger Bird up and looks back at me. My lip involuntarily curls. Then he disappears up the stairs, and the last thing I hear before a door slams is the sound of a highly excited scream. Then silence. Then the hurt surges through me like a hurricane. That was all for my benefit. And it fucking stings like hell.

'Oh dear,' Mrs Potts says quietly, yanking me back to the here and now. 'Oh dear, dear, dear.'

I shake my head on a disbelieving, quiet laugh, and muster all my strength to face Mrs Potts and appear fine when I'm far from it. He's humiliated me. I fucking hate him. 'Good night, Mrs Potts.' I pass her quickly before I confirm what I know she's thinking, if I haven't already.

The fresh air hits me like a brick when I make it to the courtyard, and though the alleyway is perfectly lit, I'm blindly following the path that'll lead me to the outside world – a world that is far more appealing right now than the wickedness than resides in The Haven. I'm in no mood for a date, but the alternative is sitting at home and torturing my mind with constant reruns and flashbacks of Becker Hunt pushing that woman up against a wall. A woman, I admit, I stupidly wish was me. I've never been at once so attracted and repulsed by a man. It's fucking with my head. Everything else is going so smoothly, my new life exactly where I want it to be. Screwing with that now would be monumentally foolish of me.

Becker Hunt does things to me – things I've never encountered before – and although he delivered one stinger of a proverbial slap to my face, I know it was tactical, if only to prove to himself that I would be bothered by it.

And he succeeded.

I'm delusional if I try to convince myself he didn't notice the hurt I tried so hard to hide. Totally delusional. He's playing dirty because I rejected him. Because I accepted a date with Brent Wilson. Becker Hunt isn't used to rejection, and he clearly doesn't like it. I only received Brent's call ten minutes ago, and then spent a few minutes in the kitchen with Mr H and Mrs Potts. Was his *she-tiger* already in his office? She must have been.

And God, do I feel like a fool now.

Chapter 9

I'm pushing my way through my front door when Lucy comes barrelling out of her flat, all dressed up.

'Hey,' she sings at me, but her chipper face fades when she notices my moody expression. 'What's up?'

'He's an arsehole,' I spit, unable to hold it in any longer. I've declared it repeatedly to myself time and time again, but that's nowhere near as satisfying as saying it out loud to someone else – someone besides him – and since I'm unable to do that, because he's my boss, then I'll have to find other outlets for my frustration. Lucy is the only other person I know in London, with the exception of Mr H and Mrs Potts and I can't very well vent my vexations with them. They think I'm immune.

Lucy steps back, furrowing her brow. 'Who?'

'The twat I work for.' I drag my tired body into my flat, hearing Lucy's heels following me. I can sense her curiosity. I've told her the job is going great, because it is. I never mentioned the sinfully good-looking arsehole that I work for because he was irrelevant. That choice of silence is going to change now.

It all comes spilling out. 'I never told you, because it didn't seem to matter,' I mutter moodily. 'But my boss; he's hot. Tall, angel eyes, perfectly straight nose, delicious body, deadly handsome.'

'Oh?'

'Yes,' I grumble, throwing my bag down on the sofa. 'He's also an arrogant prick, a womaniser, and—'

'And you fancy the pants off him.'

I gasp in disgust. 'I do not. He fancies himself too much.'

She laughs and plonks her arse on the couch. 'What's he done to piss you off so much?'

'Everything,' I grunt. She doesn't need to know the finer details, how I encountered him before I went for the interview at the Hunt Corporation, how the sexual attraction is so potent it sends me dizzy. Nor does she need to know about the stupid back-and-forth game we seem to be playing. Or the fact that he just made my eyes bleed at the sight of his naked chest and the woman he had pinned to the wall. Oh God, she really does need to know all of that. So it all comes out. The lot. Every tiny detail, from beginning to end, and the whole time I'm talking, Lucy's mouth opens wider and wider until her chin is skimming the floor.

'Fucking hell,' she breathes, wide-eyed, which is exactly the reaction I expected. Then I do something I promised I wouldn't do again. I grab my laptop and open Google.

'What are you doing?' she asks.

I type in his name, pull up images, and turn the screen to Lucy. I don't need to say any more. That jaw she's just picked up? It crashes to the floor again. 'Sweet baby Jesus.' She grabs the screen and thrusts her face up close. 'I know his face.'

I laugh. 'He's a playboy extraordinaire.'

'And he's your boss?' She looks at me incredulously.

'Yes. He owns the Hunt Corporation. I knew he was familiar when I first bumped into him.'

'Well, I wouldn't mind looking at *this* all day.'

The traitor. 'He's an arsehole,' I remind her. 'Look.' I point to image after image, all of Becker with a different woman on his arm. My face screws up.

Lucy doesn't clock my distress. 'Fuck me, he looks steaming hot in glasses.'

'Lucy,' I cry, slamming the laptop. 'He's playing a game. He won't win. He doesn't care if I quit. He didn't even want to employ anyone in the first place, and I'm pretty sure he only hired me because he sees me as a challenge. He went to kiss me, I rejected him, and he didn't like it.'

She dives across the couch and hugs me fiercely. I'm caught off guard, but I return her embrace. 'You are so strong,' she says, making my brows meet in the middle. 'I can't say I'm made of the same stuff.'

I pull free and watch as she guiltily drops her eyes. 'Who?' I ask, tilting my head in warning, ensuring she knows I want every detail and there will be consequences if I don't get it.

'A guy at work.' She sighs deeply, toying with a bit of thread hanging off her dress. 'His name's Mark. I suspect he's a player, and I know I don't need that kind of shit, but he asked me out and I said no, and then he asked someone else out, and now I've wound up with a date called *Roland* in a silly fit of revenge.'

I catch it all but focus in on one thing and one thing alone. 'Roland?' I ask on a laugh.

She nods tiredly. 'I know. Says it all, doesn't it? He's a junior accountant from floor three.'

'Oh God, who would call their kid Roland?'

'Um, Roland's mother?'

I fall back in fits of hysterics, imagining what Roland looks like. 'Tell me he's hot,' I demand, hoping for a redeeming quality.

'Not as hot as Mark.'

I straighten my lips, my laughter disappearing as I ponder the fact that we're in the same boat. We're both going to dinner with men to prove a point to other men. And what is the point, exactly? That we're idiots? 'Why do you think Mark's a player?'

'There's a rumour flying around the office. Something about him and a girl from floor eighteen getting it on in the printer room.'

'Oh . . .' I purse my lips and Lucy nods, rolling her eyes.

'Have you asked him if it's true?'

'No way. He'll think I care.'

'You do,' I say on a laugh.

'He doesn't need to know that.'

I smile to myself. She's so cool. 'Well, I'm going out for dinner tonight, too.' I head for my wardrobe, which, sadly, I reach in only three paces. 'Help me decide what to wear.'

'Dinner with who?' She joins me, eyeing my wardrobe dubiously.

'Brent. He's a client of my arsehole boss.' I frown to myself. 'At least, I assume he is.' It was never actually mentioned what their association was.

'Brent who?'

'I don't know.' I reach into the back of my mind. 'Wilson.'

'Brent Wilson?' Lucy shrieks, making me jump. '*The* Brent Wilson?'

I frown. 'I don't know. Who's *the* Brent Wilson?'

'Silver fox, mid-thirties, kind of a big nose, but still quite handsome?'

'Yeah.'

'Fucking hell, Eleanor. Where have you been? Hiding under a rock?' She reaches into my wardrobe and yanks out a nude dress. 'He's a millionaire. Fucking loaded. Houses here, New York, Paris, Mali-fucking-bu. Holy shit, you could be a kept woman.' She thrusts the dress back into my wardrobe on a disgusted snort, then rifles through the rest of the hangers. 'This could work, I suppose.'

I take the midnight-blue long-sleeved bodycon dress and hold it up against me, failing to match Lucy's excitement. So he's stinking rich. Clearly this should thrill me, but the sensible part of my brain is reminding me that I'm going on this date on principle. 'You suppose?'

'Well, we'll dress it up with some chunky jewellery.' She grins. 'I bet the arsehole was delighted.'

I shrug. 'How stupid would I be to get involved with my boss?' I can't believe I've asked it out loud. I don't need it confirmed.

'I think exceptions can be made when your boss looks like that.' She points to my laptop.

I slap her hand down. 'It was a rhetorical question, Lucy.'

'Where are you meeting Brent?'

'The Wolseley at eight.'

She grins. 'The Wolseley, eh?'

I roll my eyes and head for the shower. 'I take it The Wolseley is posh.'

'Yep. I'm heading that way, though to a far less desirable haunt on Leicester Square. My date's a cheapskate. I'll wait for you.'

I step into the bathroom and crank on the shower. 'So, what does *the* Brent Wilson do?' I ask as I strip down.

'Hotels,' Lucy says. 'Shit-loads of them in every major city. The Statons.'

'Fuck.' I shove my head around the door. 'I know them.'

'Who doesn't?' Lucy gazes at me, worried. 'You look tired.'

'Tough day at work,' I admit, stepping into the shower and closing the door behind me.

'Tough day controlling the urge to jump the arsehole?'

I scowl at the steam-filled air. I'm not even dignifying that with a reply.

I leave Lucy at the Tube station after getting a pep talk, not that I need one. I know what I'm doing, and I can't find the will to stop myself. Not after his little performance in the corridor of The Haven earlier. My self-respect seems to have vanished into thin air since I clapped eyes on the charming Becker Hunt.

Strutting into The Wolseley, swaying my curvy arse like a pendulum, I cast my eyes around, refusing to allow my nerves to get the better of me. I saw Becker's reaction when Brent got a little friendly with me in his office last week, and I also saw his face when I took Brent's call and accepted his dinner invitation earlier. Just the knowledge that Becker knows I'm out with Brent is fuelling me, and – *unreasonably* – I cannot wait to go to work tomorrow and remind him by slipping it neatly into conversation. I've already decided that however tonight turns out – massive fail or a pleasant first date – Becker is going to get an enhanced version of the latter. I'm about to have the best night of my life.

'Madam?'

I look up and meet the stare of a lady standing before a wooden podium. 'Hi, I'm meeting Mr Wilson.'

Her whole being lights up before my eyes, then she coughs and makes an obviously bad job of composing herself. 'Certainly, madam.' She steps out from behind her stand and gestures to the left. 'Mr Wilson has arrived already. Let me show you to your table.'

I follow her lead, absorbing the happy chatter that's filling the grand space. Her reaction to Brent's name only increases my smugness. It doesn't matter that I promised myself no involvement with men. I can make an exception for a millionaire. A smile breaks across my face, just as I catch the eye of Brent across the room. He matches my expression, rising from his chair to greet me.

'Eleanor,' he says as I approach, putting both hands out to me as he lets his gaze travel up and down my body. 'You look beautiful.'

I take his hands and let him kiss both my cheeks. 'Thank you.'

His lips linger for a brief moment, his hands increasing their grip. 'I took the liberty of ordering drinks.' He breaks away and pulls a chair out, gesturing for me to take a seat.

A glass of champagne is handed to me before Brent sits and claims his own fizz, holding it up on a smile.

'Are we celebrating?' I ask, chinking the side of his glass.

He raises his eyebrows suggestively and takes his glass to his lips. 'I'm having dinner with a beautiful woman. I'd say that's something to celebrate, wouldn't you?' He tips his glass slowly, watching me as I glance away and shift a little in my seat. 'I'm glad you agreed to have dinner with me.' Brent's declaration pulls my attention back to him, and I finally allow myself to take him all in. His brown eyes seem warmer and his grey hair greyer. His square jaw also seems squarer.

'So am I,' I reply, smiling.

'But I can't help but wonder if your acceptance was because you really wanted to have dinner with me' – he watches me closely, and I cringe, knowing what words are going to pass his lips next – 'or whether there's a bit of one-upmanship going on between you and the charming Becker Hunt.'

I cringe even further. There's that word again. *Charming*. 'Mr Wilson, there's really nothing very charming about my boss.' I give myself a little pat on the back for two reasons. One, because I sound confident, and two, because I referred to the arrogant swine as my boss. Let it be clear that *that's* the only way I see Becker Hunt. Almost like forbidden fruit, which he is, and not only because he's my boss.

The pleased smile that spreads across Brent's face fills me with satisfaction. He believes me, which is good, because I'm speaking nothing but the truth. 'Many would disagree.' He takes another sip of his champagne.

'Many must be stupid, then.'

Brent almost spits his drink out, his chuckle turning into a proper belly laugh. He quickly puts aside his glass as I look on, bemused, then grabs his napkin and pats at his mouth. 'I apologise.'

'No need,' I assure him, polishing off my own glass and placing it on the table. A waitress is by my side a second later, and my glass is refilled. I smile my thanks.

'You have fire in your belly to match the vivid red of your beautiful hair.' Brent reclaims his drink and tips it towards my head, like he's toasting my red hair. 'I like that.' He takes a sip, keeping his eyes on me. 'I like *you*, Eleanor. Smart. Ambitious.'

That's it. I can't hold it off any more. I blush, severing our eye contact and muttering my thanks. If we're going to talk *charming*, this guy is nailing it. It's been a long time since I've been romanced by a man, and I'm unsure whether to be un-comfortable or flattered.

I'm immensely grateful when the waiter hands me a menu, saving me from catching fire under the heat of my own cheeks.

'I recommend the lobster cocktail,' Brent says. 'And the Pimm's sorbet with champagne drizzle is a must.' He smiles warmly.

'Then I'll have that,' I reply quickly, placing my menu down. 'And for mains?'

'You choose.' I gesture towards his menu. 'You clearly have impeccable taste.'

He releases a light shot of laughter and places his menu down, shifting in his chair slightly as he glances away. I watch him, interested by his reaction to my easy acceptance. Should I have declined and made my own choice? Does he like a woman with her own mind? I *do* have my own mind. I'm just struggling to think clearly right now. He's coming on strong, and I'm not sure how I feel about it.

I'm still mentally assessing my approach to this date a few moments later, still observing Brent as he brings his eyes back to mine. 'Eleanor,' he says quietly. 'I desire the finer things in life.'

I sit back in my chair. 'Really?'

'Yes, really,' he replies quickly and confidently before sig-nalling for a waiter, leaving me wondering what the hell that means. I remain quiet while he reels off our order, asking for more champagne and giving very specific instructions of how he'd like our steaks cooked. He doesn't check how I might like mine. But then, I did tell him to choose on my behalf. So, I let him do his thing. He's cool, exudes confidence, and commands respect.

We chat casually for a while, and it's really rather pleasant. 'So, you have a chain of hotels?' I ask as the waiter tops up my champagne glass. He starts chuckling under his breath. 'Have I said something funny?'

'Not at all.'

'Then why are you laughing?'

'I apologise.' Taking his glass, he tips it to his mouth while watching me over the rim. I do the same, matching his cool string of movements. 'It's just, well, I love your indifference.'

'You do?' I ask, unsure of how I'm supposed to interpret that. Am I supposed to be gushing and swooning all over him? Is that the usual protocol for his dates? Damn me and my rusty dating etiquette.

'It assures me you're not after my millions.'

My mouth drops open, just as the waiter places something before me. 'Enjoy, madam.'

'Thanks,' I reply, keeping my eyes on Brent as he plunges his fork into his lobster salad. 'How do you know that for sure?' I can't help myself. I could be a gold digger. His obvious confidence that I'm not almost makes me want to prove him wrong, stupid as it may sound.

'I've encountered many women, Eleanor.' He slips his fork past his lips and chews slowly. 'I like to think myself a master at figuring them out.'

'You do, do you?'

'I do,' he replies, looking at his salad and mixing it with his fork. 'For example, I know you really only accepted my offer to dinner to piss off your boss.' He glances up, clearly searching for my reaction to his conclusion. He won't be disappointed. I'm squirming all over the restaurant, now mixing my own lobster salad.

'Not at all,' I retort quietly, hating that he's figured out *this* woman. Damn. There are a million things I could say, anything to assure him my intentions were nothing of the sort, but I'd be lying, and he'd know it.

'Of course,' he says. 'But I'm looking forward to showing you that you've made the right choice. You won't even remember Becker Hunt's name after a night with me.'

He's watching me closely. Holy shit, did he just say that? 'He's my boss. It starts and ends there. He doesn't feature in my thinking space beyond that.'

'Glad to hear it.' He smirks, popping another chunk of lobster into his mouth. He chews slowly and swallows. 'So, tell me what you get up to at the notorious Hunt Corporation.'

'I . . .' My words dry up, and I think for a moment. 'Mr Hunt is very private when it comes to his business.'

'Yes, he's known for playing his cards very close to his chest.'

If he knows that, why did he ask? Am I being tested? And if so, why? 'Then you should know I won't divulge anything work-related to anyone outside the Hunt Corporation.'

He smiles. 'Loyal, too. You really are a catch for Becker Hunt.'

I'm not sure how to interpret that. 'I love my job. I'd like to keep it. Besides, it wouldn't be very professional of me, or legal, for that matter, to talk about my boss's company.'

He nods, thoughtful, as his eyes hold mine. Good God, he's watching me way too closely. I need a timeout.

'Excuse me while I use the bathroom.' I stand, placing my napkin on the table. Brent's quick to follow suit, rounding the table to pull out my chair. 'Thank you,' I mutter before scurrying through the tables and down the stairs, falling into the ladies' in a flustered state. 'Christ,' I breathe, running my clammy hands under the cold tap while I take in my flushed cheeks. They nearly match my hair. I make a vain attempt to straighten myself out. My plans to meet his confidence have been spectacularly dashed by my pathetic bunk from the table. I never stopped to think about whether Brent would question why I'm here. Yes, I find him attractive, but there's a much deeper, and really rather silly reason why I'm here. Becker-Fucking-Hunt. I cease my intended direction of thought before it runs away with me and focus on my situation. Brent has made his attraction clear. Why can't I just go with this? Have some fun? Get my boss out of my head?

On a sharp, satisfied nod of my head, I square my shoulders and make my way back to the restaurant.

My steak is waiting for me when I arrive, and Brent is sitting patiently, sipping his drink. 'Okay?' he asks as he stands and pulls out my chair.

I take my seat and take a deep breath. 'Yes, thank you.' I let him place my napkin across my lap and take his chair before I collect my cutlery. 'This looks delicious.'

'I'm glad you think so. Please, lead the way.'

I smile in response to his gentlemanly manners and push my knife into the meat. It slices easily, and the moment it passes my lips, I sigh, sinking my teeth into the succulent steak.

'Good?'

'Hmm.' I chew slowly to savour the taste. 'Very good.'

'Tell me about yourself, Eleanor.'

'I moved to London just over a month ago. New start.'

'New start?' He nods. 'No better place to make a fresh start.'

'Have you lived in London all your life?'

'Yes. My great-grandfather emigrated from America in the early nineteen hundreds and established the family business soon after arriving.'

'From America?' I ask, surprised.

He smiles fondly. 'Yes. He met my great-grandmother only a day after being in London. Love at first sight.'

'Very romantic.'

'Tell me about it. They had my grandfather a year later, and the rest is history. Everything I know, I learned from my dad, and he learned from my grandfather and so on. They were very shrewd businessmen.'

'Were?'

'My grandfather passed away twenty years ago. My father has been gone for five.'

'I've lost my father, too.' I surprise myself with my willingness to share, but it only seems right since Brent is being so open. 'He also died five years ago.'

'I'm so sorry.'

I shrug on a smile. 'Live for today, right?'

'Right,' he confirms quietly, seeming to drift off into a day-dream for a few moments while I look on. 'Jesus, I'm hardly wooing you, am I?' Brent laughs. 'How's your steak?'

'Amazing,' I answer honestly, focusing my attention on my plate and taking another mouthful. Silence falls again, except this time it stays for considerably longer while we both eat, him obviously distracted, me wondering why. It's beginning to get slightly awkward when his phone rings and he stands, placing his napkin on the table. 'I'm so sorry. Please, excuse me. I need to take this.'

I nod and set my knife and fork down, watching as he strolls through the restaurant towards the bathroom, his phone at his ear.

I move back when the waiter approaches, giving him clear access to my empty plate. 'Was everything okay with your meal, madam?'

'Perfect, thank you.'

'Dessert menu?'

'Oh, Mr Wilson mentioned some Pimm's and champagne thingy.'

The waiter winces at my uncouth reference to what is likely a ridiculously expensive dessert. 'Pimm's sorbet with champagne drizzle, madam?'

I cringe, embarrassed, as my phone dings. 'Yes, please.'

Sighing to myself as the waiter leaves, I open the text message as I sip my champagne. It's Lucy.

Roland is wild!

A burst of laughter flies from my mouth, sending spurts of champagne with it. I can sense Lucy's sarcasm from a simple text, and I imagine her utterly bored out of her poor mind. Grabbing the napkin, I dab at my mouth as I reply.

Mine has hit a rocky patch. x

I click send, looking up to see if Brent's on his way back as I casually sip my champagne. Then I'm coughing all over again, except this time I nearly fall off my chair, too.

My date is nowhere to be seen.

But Becker Hunt is.

And he's sitting opposite me in Brent Wilson's chair.

Chapter 10

My back sticks to my seat like superglue. He's relaxed, holding a tumbler lightly in his grasp, his elbow resting on the arm, and he's smirking at me.

All casual.

All sexy.

All . . . irritating as hell.

'Evening,' he says, his head cocking a little in amusement. He finds my shock funny? I should be used to him appearing out of thin air by now. 'How's the date going?'

'Amazing.' My one-word, over-exaggerated answer comes out of nowhere. It makes his head cock further, and I fight back the tell-tale burn in my cheeks.

'Really?' he muses, taking a sip of his drink and rolling the liquid around his mouth before he swallows. 'Because it didn't look like riveting conversation from where I was standing.'

'Where were you standing?' I ask, taking a quick peek around the restaurant, conscious of Brent's return.

'At the bar.'

I return my eyes to Becker. 'Why are you here?'

He pouts and waves a hand dismissively through the air. 'Just wanted to tell you that I need you at work by eight tomorrow morning. I have a meeting with one of the curators at Christie's at nine. I need the file on the sixteenth-century Spanish tapestry on my desk before I leave.'

My eyes bug. 'Are you for real?' The cheeky bastard. 'Text me. Call me. Don't stalk me on a date.'

'I was passing.'

'Sure you were.' I laugh, having another peek around the restaurant. 'How did you know we were here?'

'He brings all his women here.'

'Right,' I spit, frustrated, still scanning the space around me. I'm not naïve. It's clear that Brent Wilson has enjoyed his fair share of women. How do these two know each other? Maybe I should have asked Brent that.

'And I'm very real, Eleanor.'

My eyes shoot to Becker, and I damn my skin type for being so pale it gives away even the slightest flush. It's not slight now, though. I'm burning up with a mixture of anger at his nerve, and lust that I hate not being able to control. I don't have time to argue with him, although there's nothing more I'd love to do than tell him where to shove his eight o'clock start. I need him gone before Brent gets back. 'Fine, I'll see you then. Goodbye.'

His eyebrows jump up, a smile pulling at the corners of his lovely mouth. 'Trying to get rid of me?'

I lean forward. 'Yes,' I hiss, outraged by the level he's stooping to. 'This is my personal time. Go make some woman scream in delight, *tiger*.' I regret my words instantly, but it's too late to retract them.

His face breaks out into a full-blown, blinding smile. 'Jealous?'

'No.' I sit back in my chair, desperate to escape the cocky bastard's smugness.

A plate is placed in front of me, and I look up to find the waiter with a deadpan face. 'Your Pimm's and champagne *thingy*, madam,' he says flatly.

Becker lets out a burst of laughter, but I'm too uncomfortable to be bothered by the waiter's dry wit. 'Thank you,' I say, watching as he places another serving in front of Becker, frowning as he does.

'Sir?' Becker totally ignores the question in the waiter's tone, pulling the plate towards him.

'Cheers, chap.' He winks across the table at me before taking his spoon. Or Brent's spoon.

'Don't you dare,' I whisper-hiss as he plunges it into the ball of sorbet. 'Becker, don't you—'

It's too late. He ignores me and wraps his lips around the spoon, keeping his laughing hazel eyes on me. 'Hmm.' He licks his lips slowly. 'Champagne.'

I close my eyes and flop back in my chair, taking a deep breath while resisting the urge to pick up my own spoon and beat him around the head with it. 'I can't believe you just did that.'

'Believe it, princess.'

'Don't call me princess.' I growl, my patience drained. He's the most infuriating man I've ever met. 'And why the hell do you keep calling me that?'

He smirks. 'Why, does it grate on you?'

There you go. *That's* why he calls me such an annoying pet name. 'Please, just go.' I'm zapped of energy to take him on. 'My *date* will be back any minute.'

'Too late,' he whispers, standing and looking over my shoulder. 'Sorry, this might be a little awkward.' He's not sorry at all. This was all part of his plan, the wanker.

Every muscle in my body tenses as I watch Becker slap a huge, insincere smile on his face and hold his hand out. 'Brent, fancy seeing you here.' He's being sarcastic, of course, because he's just told me that Brent Wilson brings all his women here. God, what was I thinking coming on this date? I'm really not ready to venture into the dating world again. The aftermath of David's betrayal still stings, and I certainly don't ever want to be *one of many* women in a man's life. I've been sidetracked and blinded by my fierce need to poke back at Becker Hunt. And my plan's failed spectacularly, anyway.

I'm wasting my time playing his stupid games.

I'm better than this.

I'm cut short from mentally beating myself up when Brent's hand appears in my field of vision. 'Hunt.' He's not growling, but he's pretty damn close. Something tells me these two guys barely manage to rub along for business purposes, because the animosity bouncing between them is almost tangible.

Their handshake is brief, both men clearly trying to put on a show for my benefit. What a waste. I might be dying a thousand deaths, but I know rivalry when it's being shoved in my face. They despise each other.

'I hope you're taking care of *my* staff.' The emphasis on *my* doesn't escape my date's notice. Or mine, for that matter.

'I'm a gentleman, Hunt,' Brent says on a smile, as if to put it out there subtly that he thinks Becker isn't. I inwardly laugh. He's right. 'Eleanor is a catch. I can see why you'd want to keep her.'

A hint of worry travels across my boss's face before he forces a smile. 'She fits in very well.' He performs a ridiculously over-the-top bow, gesturing towards Brent's seat for him to take. 'I'll leave you to your date.' He flicks me a smile, before returning his attention to Brent, who's lowering to his chair, frowning at his dessert.

My lips purse, and I glance to Becker, cringing. He's backing away, amused. 'Tastes good,' he says, cocky as can be, before turning on his expensive brogues and swaggering his way out of the restaurant.

My eyes fix firmly on his tight arse, encased in lovely thigh-hugging grey trousers. His back is covered in a crisp white shirt, but all I see in my mind's eye is that tattoo. That amazing tattoo. Then I go back to his arse. Oh, that fucking arse. It makes me want to cry. I follow it all the way out, only returning my attention to the table once it's out of sight.

And then I'm quickly brought back down to earth, where I'm in a restaurant on a date with a man who's just had half his dessert scoffed by my wayward, infuriating boss. I want to die. Right now. Awkward comes nowhere close. I'm biting the inside of my lip while Brent continues to frown at his half-eaten champagne and Pimm's thingy. I don't know what to say, so when my phone bleeps, I jump at the opportunity to distract myself while Brent comes to terms with the fact that Becker Hunt infiltrated his date *and* his pudding. I open the text.

Stop looking at my arse x

I feel the heat build in my veins, feel the frustration and anger grip me. He can't bulldoze his way into my private time. I try to stop myself. Really, I do. 'Twat,' I seethe at my phone, slamming it on the table in a temper. Eight o'clock start? I snort to myself. He can go swivel. If this is an attempt to ruin my date, hamper my fun because I need an early night for an early start, then he's sorely mistaken. I swipe up my champagne and down the lot.

'I assume you're not referring to me.' Brent reaches over and tops up my champagne, smiling.

I feel terrible. 'No, of course not. He really rubs me up the wrong way. I'm so sorry about that.'

'Don't be.' He pushes his mutilated dessert aside, a distasteful look on his face. 'Becker Hunt rubs up many people the wrong way.'

'Including you?'

He laughs. 'How did you guess?'

'You seemed friendly at The Haven.' Now seems like a good a time as any to figure out what the deal is between them.

'Hmm.' He rests back in his chair. 'I have a certain fondness for beautiful things, and Hunt has a bad habit of acquiring the beautiful things that I want.'

I nod thoughtfully, warily, wondering whether Becker makes a point of acquiring things Brent wants. It wouldn't surprise me. He's a dirty player. I can attest to that myself, and now I'm wondering if he's the same in business. You can't be the best without being a little ruthless. 'What is it that you want?'

He smirks. 'Are we talking business or pleasure?'

'Business,' I confirm without hesitation. Becker has a habit of obtaining things that Brent wants? Is that why Brent invited me to dinner? Am I a tool for revenge? I close my eyes, sigh, and rise from the table. Oh my days, I'm so stupid. I'm a piece of meat. A pawn. I'm not getting involved in their pissing contest. I'm worth more than these arseholes deserve. I need to keep my head down and do my job. 'Thank you for a lovely evening,' I say, tucking my chair under the table and collecting my phone and bag.

Brent stands swiftly, his forehead wrinkled in confusion. 'You're leaving?'

I can't believe what I'm about to say and, worst of all, that I genuinely mean it. 'I need to be at work for eight.' I'm not giving Becker any reason to mark my card, no matter how much it physically pains me.

'Oh.' He seems to deflate before my eyes, but whether this is because he's genuinely disappointed, or because he's down a point to Becker Hunt, I don't know. I'm Becker's employee, after all, and Brent's date has not only been hijacked by someone he clearly holds in contempt, but has also been cut short. 'One more drink can't hurt, surely?' he asks hopefully.

'No, really. But thank you.' I step away from the table, keen to escape and slap myself all over Piccadilly in disgrace.

'Another time, perhaps?'

'Perhaps,' I murmur, before turning on my heels and fleeing, hating the feeling of despondency that's beginning to wash over me.

I've been sucked in and played. Been made a fool of.

By both men.

This isn't what I came to London for. I'm not a toy, and I refuse to be treated like one.

The game is over.

Chapter 11

I don't arrive at The Haven in the morning at eight. No, I arrive at seven thirty after a crap night's sleep. I navigate the dark alley with ease, and even predict the exact moment the lights spring to life. It brings a smile to my face, and once I emerge into the lush surroundings of the courtyard, I remember why I love it here. I spot Mrs Potts watering the colourful beds around the fountain.

'Your working hours are nine to five,' she says, placing the watering can down and dusting off her hands on her apron.

'Mr Hunt has a meeting at Christie's at nine. I need to get him the file on the Spanish tapestry before he leaves.'

'And he couldn't get it himself?'

I just shrug, with a lack of anything else to do or say.

Mrs Potts sighs. 'I apologise, dear. The man is a menace.'

'It's okay. I couldn't sleep, anyway.'

She raises curious grey eyebrows at me, reminding me that Mrs Potts knows I had a date last night. 'Oh, I see.' A slight blush creeps across her cheeks.

'Oh, no.' I laugh, quick to put her right. 'I was home by nine thirty, tucked up in bed.'

Her blush recedes, being replaced with curiosity. God, what would she say if she knew what happened last night? Come to think of it, what would she say if she knew my date was Brent Wilson? I decide it's best not to tell. Besides, it's done. No more dates.

'I'll be in the library.'

'That's fine, dear. Help yourself to tea in the kitchen.' I hold up my empty Starbucks cup, showing I have no need for tea, and she smiles. 'I need to get Donald up and at 'em.' Mrs Potts moseys off across the courtyard, and I head for the Grand Hall, navigating my way through the masses of antiques, my focus set firmly on getting to the library. I very nearly make it to the other side of the giant room, feeling my eyes tugging upward to the glass box that floats above the space, but I defiantly resist looking up, knowing it will only distract me again.

I'm nearly at the door.

Not far to go.

I lift my hand, armed with my card, ready to swipe the moment I make it there.

My eyes flip up involuntarily, seeing a familiar shadow beyond the glass.

Damn!

My stride slows, my lips part. The silhouette of the tall physique is perfect. I can make out every edge of the body, telling me it's naked. No clothes, just sharp, crisp, clear outlines.

My steps eventually come to a stop, my neck craned upward, and I fall into a trance. Not even the smugness he'll flaunt knocks away the desire to stare.

Then something happens, and it throws me off balance. Literally. My legs wobble as his hand touches the glass and he moves forward, bringing himself out of the shadows. My heart begins to race as I gaze up at him standing in his boxers, his face unadorned by his glasses. And his scorn. He looks sleepy. Like he just woke up.

'Morning,' he mouths.

My head tilts, my brow bunching, and he smiles a little at my surprise before looking over his shoulder and moving back into the shadows.

My eyes drop. *Morning?* Was he being nice? 'He's a fucking enigma,' I say to myself, hurrying for the door and swiping my card through the reader. Marching down the corridor towards the library, I try to wrestle the mental image of him virtually naked from my mind. '*Morning?*' I mutter, frowning. '*Morn—*' Something gets tangled between my legs, and I throw my coffee cup in the air so I can grab something to save myself. 'Shit,' I cry, grappling at the wall and knocking a René Magritte painting askew, coffee spraying the wall. I gasp my horror, quickly straighten it up, and snatch a tissue from my bag to wipe up the coffee. Jesus Christ.

My eyes fly to my feet when the sounds of whimpering registers, finding a big ball of fur cowering. 'Oh God, Winston.' I drop to the floor. 'I'm sorry, boy.' He whimpers and whines, backing away from me. 'C'mon,' I whisper, trying to earn his trust again. He likes me. Mrs Potts said so, and weeks of petting him has only brought us closer. Oh God, don't hate me.

I remain on my knees, my bum resting on my heels, and pat my lap, clucking and cooing. He eventually takes a cautious step towards me. The elation this tiny action brings overwhelms me. 'That's it. Come on.' He takes another step, and I shuffle forward a tiny bit, extending my hand to him. He sniffs warily, then takes one more step, so I reach up to his ear. But he doesn't let me rub behind it. Instead, he rolls on to his back and lets his tongue flop from his mouth, panting. I laugh loudly and make a real good job of apologising, scratching his belly until his back leg starts to twitch. 'You like that?' I ask, like he might reply. 'Oh, yes, you do.' I speed up my back-and-forth scratching, laughing harder when his whole body seems to go into spasm. 'C'mon,' I say, stopping when my fingers start to burn with the friction. 'I've got to get some work done.' I stand, delighted when Winston flips on to his paws and sits at my feet, looking at me all gooey-eyed. 'You wanna come with me?' He answers by trotting past me towards the library, and my eyes follow his path until he reaches the doors and drops to his arse again, looking at me. 'I'll take that as a yes.' He lets out a deep bark, and I smile, gathering up my coffee cup and joining him by the doors. 'Want to compare notes on Michelangelo and Raphael?'

His answer this time is a growl.

'Oh, okay. Not a fan?'

He growls again, deeper this time, and is up on all four paws in a heartbeat, his attention pointed down the corridor.

I follow his stare, frowning. 'What is it, boy?'

He starts backing away, his head dropped, his growl now bordering on a snarl. Every instinct tells me to back away with him, so I do, looking down the corridor at nothing. 'What's there, Winston?'

Then there's the sound of naked feet padding on the floor, and my back straightens when I realise where they're coming from. The curved staircase.

Becker.

I freeze, wondering why Winston is showing such aggressiveness at the impending arrival of his owner. His hackles are raised, and now his teeth are being flashed, too. Holy shit, the cute pup looks downright vicious. 'Shhhh.' I try to pacify him, crouching down, wondering what the hell has got into him.

I don't have to wonder for long. The clink of stilettos on the stone steps joins the naked padding of feet. *Oh, no.* I stand and weigh up my options, wanting to get away before I'm faced with another episode like yesterday evening, when they fell out of his office. I scramble to swipe my card in the reader, but my damn shaking hands aren't playing ball, and when I finally drag it through and push the doors, they don't budge. 'Come on,' I whisper, swiping again. The light on the card reader remains red. *Damn it!* Did the bastard only order me here for eight so I'd have to endure seeing him with that woman again? *What the hell, Hunt?* What can he personally get out of parading her in front of me again?

'Eleanor?'

'Yes?' I swing around and slap my back to the door. Becker's naked chest wallops me in the face like a wrecking ball, and I close my eyes tightly to escape it, while talking myself down from the burning rage his nasty tactic has spiked.

'All right?'

I keep my eyes firmly closed. 'Yep, just going to get the Spanish tapestry file you wanted.' I indicate blindly over my shoulder. 'I'll put it on your desk.' I turn back to the door before I open my eyes, then set about trying to get my card through the reader again. 'Damn you,' I mutter under my breath, adrenalin increasing my shakes.

I freeze when a firm hand clasps my wrist, no doubt soaking up my trembles. The heat that radiates through my entire body and travels down to between my thighs makes my jaw clench. His hold is solid, his body closing in behind mine. I beg every god above not to let that bare chest meet my back. Please, don't let another part of him touch me.

My breathing stutters when I feel the hot air of his breath tickle the hair around my ear, and my eyes close as I continue to pray. Then his hand squeezes mine gently. The further constriction feels like a silent message. And when he follows it up with some words – soft words – my trembles intensify.

'Stop shaking,' he whispers.

I'm completely befuddled by his actions and words. They were gentle. Reassuring. Very unlike Becker Hunt. I make to turn so I can see if I can read the intention in his eyes, but I only make it halfway before all hell breaks loose, and I'm snapped from my daze when Winston brings The Haven down with a relentless barking fit.

Becker releases his hold of me in an instant, and I turn the rest of the way to find my boss crouched on the floor, trying to calm a very rankled bulldog. 'Hey, pack it in,' Becker shouts, but he's flat-out ignored, and Winston just carries on yelling, the gruff barks piercing. I hold my hands over my ears as Becker looks up at me, a scowl on his face. I recoil. What did *I* do?

I disregard my boss's accusing look and focus on Winston, seeing him growling in the direction of the stairs, so I look . . . and I hate what I see. A woman dressed from top to toe in lace. Black lace. Sexy black lace. *Tiger bird.* I nearly vomit in my own mouth. I also nearly tell Winston to attack. She's looking at my doggy friend in disgust as she edges her way down the corridor.

'Becker, that dog is disturbed,' she whines.

'He's fine,' Becker grumbles, roughing up Winston's head with a swipe of his hand. 'He doesn't like you.'

'He doesn't like anyone.' The lace-clad woman looks across at me, her interest instant. 'Oh, you must be Becker's new skivvy.'

'Excuse me?' I cough.

'Shut up, Alexa,' Becker warns.

Alexa? Not Paula? This isn't the woman I spoke to on the phone? How many has he got on the go? Not that I care. *I don't damn well care.* Swinging towards Becker's crouched form, I glare at him. 'Skivvy?'

'I never said that,' he grates, just as Winston sets off on another round of barking and Alexa jumps back in shock, her perfectly manicured hand resting on her perfect boobs.

'You need to get that mutt chained up,' she spits, flicking her platinum-blond hair over her shoulder.

I fly to Winston's defence without thought or consideration of my position. 'The only mutt I see is on *two* feet,' I fire, my lip curling. She gasps in shock, and Becker disguises his laugh with a cough as I stomp over to him and virtually snatch his dog away, taking him by the collar. 'Come on, boy.' I throw a filthy look Alexa's way. 'She might give you fleas.' This time I manage to swipe my card just fine, and as soon as the light flashes green, I push into the wood, finding the heavy doors open easily, probably assisted by my fury.

I slam them behind me, bubbling with rage. Then I start to pace the library, back and forth, around and around, having a row out loud with no one in particular. It's a good job I'm alone because I think I'd take the head off anyone sharing breathing space with me right now … namely, Becker Hunt. Or that *thing* in black lace. 'What the hell does he see in women like that?' I ask thin air. 'Jumped-up cow.'

It takes a low whine from Winston to pull me from my hissy fit, and I look down at my feet, finding him looking up at me with droopy eyes, like he senses my annoyance. I sigh and crouch, giving his head a little scratch. 'I don't like her either, boy,' I say, letting out a little laugh when he barks his agreement. I like Winston more and more by the day. He's protective. Loyal. He's the type of man I need … when I venture down that road again. *If* I ever do.

I kiss his head and scratch his ears before I stand and head to the couch. 'Up,' I say, patting the seat. Winston immediately trots over and leaps on to the sofa with some effort, letting out a grunt as he does. 'Sit,' I command, and he drops to his arse in an instant. I cock my head on a smile as he looks up at me, panting. Add *obedient* to that list. 'Lie,' I order, trying to fill my tone with authority, but I only achieve a soft, almost begging demand. It makes no difference. Winston curls up into a big ball of fur and rests his chin on his front paws. 'You're just too bloody cute.' My aggravation is draining away. 'Right, Winston. I need to do some work.' I need to immerse myself in the history this library offers and forget what just happened. In fact, I need to forget about *every* encounter with Becker Hunt. Each and every one has been infuriating for one reason or another, and no good will come of analysing why the conceited twat gets such a rise out of me. What was last night about anyway? He had his bimbo in his tower and still found me on my date with Brent. He breaks the arsehole scale.

Work! I admonish myself.

I start to wander the length of a bookcase, my eyes drifting over the hundreds of spines, a smile beginning to tug at the corners of my mouth. That smell. It's like a tranquilliser. I feel my lingering frustration slip away as I drink it in.

I'm just about to select a random book – something to take a quick peek at before I locate the file for the sixteenth-century tapestry – when my attention is captured by . . . something. I'm not sure what. It's concealed behind a book, fixed to the back wall of the shelf. I would have completely missed it if I wasn't reading the spine of every book that my eyes passed over. I frown and slip my hand past the top of the book and beneath the shelf above, losing sight of whatever it is in an instant. Now, I only have my touch to guide me, so I fiddle around, trying to make out what it is.

Something clicks, and I retract my hand quickly, like I've been bitten. 'What the hell?' I bend to peek through the gap above the books. Whatever I'm looking at has released a little lever, and unable to control my curiosity, I reach in and pull it.

Then I stand back when I hear a flurry of mechanisms click and clunk and watch in wonder as a small section of the bookcase shifts and opens, revealing a dark compartment. A dark *secret* compartment. My mouth drops open a little as I tilt my head to get the best view. *Oh my.* I tentatively reach inside and feel around the space until I lay my hands on something. A book? On a furrowed brow, I pull it out, finding a leather-bound journal secured with a strip of cord that's tied neatly in a bow. The leather is dark brown, roughly the size of a standard sheet of paper, and embossed with elephants. And it's really, *really* heavy.

I carry it over to the couch and sit next to Winston. 'What's this, boy?' I ask him, but he's deep in sleep now, snoring happily. I pull the leather strip delicately until the bow unravels, and then pull the cover open.

The first page has a photograph of Picasso's *Harlequin Head* stuck to the paper and handwritten information is noted down the side. 'Wow.' I turn to the next page, finding a photograph of a Fabergé egg, again stuck to the page, and more paragraphs of handwritten information. The next page reveals another photograph, except this time the photo is of a violin. I pout, disappointed ... until I realise it's a Stradivarius. 'Jesus.' I gulp, turning another page. The pictures of priceless treasures go on and on, until I reach the back and find a folded piece of parchment paper. It's old, delicate, and I can see clearly there's a tear down one side. I gingerly push at the corner and frown, tilting my head. A map. A very old map of the world.

Curiosity gets the better of me and I open it up, seeing rips in the centre. A hole. It's not damaged from age or handling. A section has been ripped out, leaving a hole in the middle of the ancient map. I scan it, figuring out quickly that it's a part of Europe that's missing.

Wow. What is this?

My studying stops when I hear movements coming from outside the library doors. 'Shit.' I quickly fold it back up, carefully slot it in the leather book, and fly across the room like a bullet, trying to tie the cord as I go. I don't know how, but I manage to secure it before slipping it into the black hole and pushing the section of bookcase closed until it clicks. Then I bolt for the bookcase where the Spanish tapestry file is stored and pull it from the shelf, opening it up and beginning to walk casually up and down, my heart pounding.

I hear the library doors open, but I keep my nose in the file that I'm pretending to study, not prepared to give him the time of day. Or, perhaps, reveal my guilt for snooping. Then I hear the door gently close as I continue walking slowly up and down, my finger resting on some text and gliding from side to side as I read. I can see the words, but I'm not taking them in.

The only sound in the library is Winston's snoring and my light footsteps.

Until he speaks.

'I'd appreciate it if you didn't talk to my guests like that,' he says curtly.

I halt with my aimless wandering, my lips pucker, and my eyes close. Even if I wanted to fire off all sorts of thoughts on that one – which I don't because I promised myself I wouldn't let him get under my skin – I shouldn't because he's my boss. And like it or not, I can't be flashing my claws at his so-called *guests*.

'I'm sorry.' I release the words like they're acid on my tongue yet surprise myself that I actually sound genuine. Which begs the question whether I actually *am* being genuine. I don't know. I'm working on autopilot, and in a moment of pure lucidity, I realise why. I'm in self-preservation mode. This worries me. What am I protecting myself from? Him? Being fired? 'It won't happen again.' I brave peeking up a little, finding he now has a T-shirt on with some old worn sweatpants. And bare feet. I tense and throw my eyes to his face. Mistake. He has his glasses on, and for the first time I wonder how bad his eyesight is. His hair is all mussed up. Or sexed up from someone's fingers grabbing at it. I wince at my silent observation. The spikes of jealousy that stab at me repeatedly are baffling ... and, again, worrying.

I'm so busy weighing up all of these conflicting feelings, I almost miss the look of confusion on his stunning face. But I just catch it before he replaces it with indifference. 'Good.' He sniffs, wandering towards the couch. 'So, when I have female company, you won't insult them in future?'

'No. Like I said, I'm sorry.' I shut the file, proud of myself for not biting, and, again, catch a frown before he reins it in. I know he's wondering why I haven't questioned him on the whole skivvy business, or on his ploy to have me at work by eight, and I don't plan to. Questioning him will show him I'm bothered. I'm not.

'Good,' he says again. I can see his mind racing for his next words. This is getting easier the longer I'm faced with his perplexity, even if he's desperately trying to conceal it.

'Is that all?' I ask, my eyebrows rising in question.

His head definitely retracts a little. 'Um ... ye ... yes,' he splutters all over his words and seems to visibly try to pull himself together. 'Actually, no, that isn't all.' He strides over to me with purpose, almost aggressively, but I keep my feet rooted to the spot, interested by his agitation and attempts to spike a reaction from me.

He's towering over me quickly, but he doesn't speak. Oh no, he chooses now, when we're a whisper away from each other, to drink me in. Today I have on a simple little black dress and heeled pumps, and the slight shimmer in his hazel eyes tells me he likes it. So does the deep inhale he takes. And the flick of his eyes to my hair before they quickly return to my body.

He scowls and shakes himself back to reality. 'Winston shouldn't be on the couch,' he snaps.

I jump back, startled. Of all the things he's said in a childish attempt to get a reaction from me, it's his silly observation about his dog that finally gives him what he wants. And, bloody hell, I bite. 'You shouldn't subject him to *that*.' I swing my arm towards the door.

'What's *that*?' he asks, his chest suddenly heaving like a gorilla.

'Good fucking question,' I yell in his face.

'Oh.' He laughs. 'You mean Alexa?'

'Is that its name?'

'You know damn well what her name is.' There's victory in his tone. 'Just like you could tell me exactly what she was wearing, what colour she had on her lips, and what colour her nails were.' He stops and gives me a moment to absorb his words. True words. They bloody hurt like hell, but rather than confirming what he already knows, I hurry across the library and take a seat on the couch with Winston. 'Admit it, princess.' Becker walks over, his looming frame soon towering over me again. I peek up, seeing that rueful smile gracing his lovely face. I've given him what he wants, and, God, do I hate myself for it.

My gaze drops with him as he slowly lowers himself until he's crouching in front of me. He places his hands on either side on my knees and leans in. 'You. Are. Jealous.'

I breathe in some patience, so fucking annoyed with myself. But . . . 'Seriously, Mr Hunt. Are we going to talk about jealousy?'

'Yes, we are.'

'Fine. Then let's talk about you intruding on my date last night.'

'That was business.'

I snort. 'That was bullshit, actually.' What is his obsession with me feeling jealous? Why be so relentless about it? I'm his employee and nothing more.

He smiles. That damn fucking smile. 'Did you have fun?'

I should be telling him that's none of his business, but, of course, I don't. 'Amazing. Brent Wilson is a gentleman.' I smile, and his nose wrinkles a little. 'Now, can I get on with my job?'

'Suppose so.' He grins when I roll my eyes. 'I took a call in the night from the auction house in Tokyo where you sent the pearl brooch.'

I sit up straight, bringing us a bit closer together. He sees my interest, his eyes gleaming. 'And?' I question, adrenalin instantly racing through me.

'And it broke records.'

I feel excitement join the adrenalin, a squeal of delight threatening. 'Like broke records, or smashed records?'

'Smashed to smithereens, princess. A private collector bought it. Congrats.'

In a moment of pure ecstasy, I forget myself and dive forward, throwing my arms around his shoulders. 'That's so great.' I feel his palm meet the middle of my back, and the heat seems to snap me from my euphoria in a heartbeat. I shoot back, my lips straightening. 'I'm sorry.'

Becker stares at me for a while, still crouched in front of me. 'What?' I ask.

He's moves forward, coming closer. And closer. And closer. Oh, shit, what is he going to do? Kiss me? I slowly move back. He's my boss. This could get awkward. I quickly correct myself. This has *always* been awkward. 'I think you deserve a bonus,' he whispers.

Oh God. My eyes drop to his lips. He licks them. And I return the gesture.

Closer.

His eyes descend to my mouth. And mine to his. His breath stutters. My breath stutters, too. I need to pull away, but for reasons I may never know, I don't. Then our lips brush delicately, and I whimper. Oh, God, he tastes divine. Accept it. Accept *him.* But it's wrong. So wrong.

Stop it.

Don't stop it.

My mental debate stops there.

Woof!

Winston springs from his dreams and dives across the couch. He muscles between us, knocking the tapestry file to the floor and barking in Becker's face.

'Shit,' Becker yelps. My attempt to sit up straight is hampered by the giant bulldog standing on my lap, barking like he's just come across a burglar.

Woof, woof, woof!

'Winston!' Becker yells, but Winston doesn't let up, and his next round of barks cranks up a level, sending Becker falling back to his arse.

Woof, woof, woof!

'What the fucking hell has got into you?' he shouts, scrambling to his feet. The look he chucks me is filthy. 'What have you done to my dog?' He points at Winston but soon retracts his hand, a look of horror on his face when his beloved pet snaps at his fingers.

I say nothing, too mortified by what nearly happened. I seem to have a killing machine on my lap. Becker isn't impressed, standing before me while I look up at him in shock and Winston continues to make a racket. 'Shhhh,' I whisper in Winston's ear, nuzzling into his cheek. He shuts up immediately and nuzzles right back.

Becker looks down at his burly pet with pure condemnation. 'Traitor,' he mutters, grabbing the file from the floor before swinging moodily around and stomping out of the library. 'And get him off my couch.' The door slams.

My body starts convulsing the moment he's gone, and I realise it's yelling for some oxygen. I gasp, my lungs screaming when I finally give them some air.

Fucking hell.

That was way too close for comfort.

Chapter 12

Winston and I have been locked away in the library all morning together, him snoozing, me working non-stop to distract myself. As a result, it's been a productive few hours. After checking in with Mum, I worked my way through a whole case of books, sorting the reference books from the client files, and putting them back on the shelves in chronological order.

When Winston stirs a little on the couch – yes, I left him on the couch, fuck you very much, Mr Hunt – I look over and see him stretching out, his sleepy eyes blinking open. 'I need tea,' I declare. 'C'mon, big guy.' I slap my thigh as I make my way to the doors, hearing a thud as Winston lazily flops down from the couch.

He follows me down the corridor, but my steps falter when I hear a voice in the distance. Becker's voice. And then I hear Mr H's. I wouldn't have paid much attention, but a loud bang resonates from Becker's office, followed by a frustrated shout. I freeze, then look down to see Winston has made himself comfy at my feet.

'Calm down, Becker boy,' Mr H yells, and I purse my lips. It sounds like a very heated conversation and not for my ears, but just when I've convinced myself to move, Mr H goes on. And what he says has me standing stock-still again. 'I've seen the way you look at her.'

My hand reaches for the wall, my body suddenly needing the support, and my eyes tumble to the ground. They begin to dart, waiting for Becker's response. I'm not being presumptuous; I'm being shrewd. I need to know if what my intuition is telling me is the truth – I've seen the way he looks at me, too, and I've never been sure what to make of it. One minute, it feels like he's mentally undressing me, the next he's looking at me like he wants to strangle me.

'I don't look at her like anything.' Becker's voice is a raised whisper, his aggravation clear in his tone.

'Nonsense,' Mr H retorts. 'She's a no-go area, my boy. Keep it in your pants. Dorothy told me about your little performance outside your office last night, *and* that you demanded Eleanor to come in early this morning. It's self-serving, reprobate behaviour. Beneath you. And it's definitely beneath her. Stop playing games.'

I bite my lip, looking for the instructions I need to move, to send me to the kitchen where I was heading before their voices stopped me. I shouldn't be listening to this.

'I'm fucking trying,' Becker yells.

'Not hard enough.' Mr H's bellow is just as loud, but fiercer. 'Get your arse to a psychiatrist, Becker. Talk it out. Stop using women as your therapy. And leave Eleanor alone.'

The old man's demand shocks me. What is Becker, a sex addict? He's trying? What, to leave me alone? Well, clearly he's not trying hard enough.

'I don't need therapy. I'm done with it,' Becker snipes. 'I'm sick of someone trying to poke around in my mind. There's nothing wrong with me.'

Becker's grandad laughs sardonically. 'You need something. The way you carry on isn't healthy. Your mum and dad are gone, boy. Playing Russian roulette with our business and with your damn life won't bring them back.'

'Gramps, stop, please.' He sounds desperate, and my heart unexpectedly clenches from his plea. Because it really is a plea. But what on earth does Mr H mean? Russian roulette?

'What if she's different?' Becker asks out of the blue.

My eyes shoot down the corridor to his office door. Different?

'She isn't different, she's just forbidden,' Mr H snaps. 'You know she's off limits, and that is the *only* reason you want her so bloody much. I'm warning you, boy. Leave her be. She loves it here, and we love having her around. Don't you dare meddle with that. Do you hear me?'

'Yes, I fucking hear you.'

'Why did you employ her?' Mr H rants on. 'After all this time refusing to let anyone into The Haven to ease the strain on Dorothy, after turning your nose up every time we suggested we get some help, why now? Why did you agree to let her in?'

'She's clever. Smart. Knows her stuff.'

'And beautiful.'

Becker scoffs. 'That has nothing to do with it.'

'Don't lie to me, Becker boy.' He *is* lying. I know he is. 'You saw something you wanted and carved out a plan to get it. Bugger the feelings of whoever you hurt along the way. Women are a game to you.'

'What do you want from me?' Becker says, his voice anguished.

'To sort yourself out!' comes the angry reply.

'I'll call the fucking shrink,' he yells.

'Good.'

Becker's angry mumbles get louder, and I realise he's about to storm out of his office. So I bolt down the corridor, Winston tailing me, and let myself into the nearest door I come to.

Which happens to be a cleaning closet. I don't have time to fuck about. I reach down for Winston's collar and tug him in, slamming the door quickly, before crouching to fuss over him, hoping it keeps him quiet.

There are a few bangs, and then the clear sound of Becker's bare feet stomping up the stone steps. I hold my breath in the darkness, rubbing circles into Winston's ears, biding my time.

It's a few minutes, but eventually I hear Mr H hobble down the corridor.

Winston whimpers next to me, clearly wondering what the hell is going on. 'Okay, boy,' I whisper, hearing the door to the kitchen close. I exhale my relief and unfold from the floor, opening the door cautiously and peeking each way. 'Come on.' I usher Winston out and make fast work of straightening myself out, and when I think I've achieved the closest I'm going to get to composure, I head for the kitchen, my poor mind spinning.

I find Mr H sitting at the table, his silver hair neatly combed to the side and his face buried in a newspaper. 'Mr H,' I say, prompting him to look up. His glasses are resting on the end of his nose, and he dips his head to look over them at me.

'Eleanor.' He seems remarkably unflustered; there is no evidence that he's just had an argument with his grandson. Folding his newspaper neatly, he places it on the table before him. 'Come, join me.'

I indicate towards the stove. 'I was going to make tea.'

Mr H reaches into the centre of the table and taps the top of a pot. 'Freshly prepared by Dorothy.'

I smile and wander over, forcing casualness. It's hard. The conversation I listened to is playing on repeat. So many questions, but none of which I can ask without sounding like I'm prying. 'She really looks after you.'

'She does,' he agrees on a chuckle. 'Sugar?'

'No, just milk, please.'

'Sweet enough already?' He takes a clean cup and saucer and sets about pouring me a cup.

I laugh. 'Probably not.'

'Oh, you're being modest. How's your mother?'

'She's great, thank you.'

'Marvellous. I'm sure she's missing you.'

'A little,' I admit, though she would never tell me so. 'I'm going home in a couple of weeks.' I'm not looking forward to it at all and keep stalling to book my train tickets, but Edwin Smith has chased me yet again. There's only so long I can avoid clearing out Dad's store. And not only that, my ex is in Helston and apparently wants to make amends. Fat chance. I know as soon as I set foot off the train, news of my arrival will probably reach him before I arrive at my mum's house. I don't need to hear his apologies. They stand for shit and won't change a thing. Just waste my time.

Mr H adds milk to my tea. I try to ignore the chinking of porcelain as he hands it to me, but when his lips straighten and his face screws up in concentration, it becomes impossible.

'Are you okay?' I relieve him of the cup and saucer and place it down quickly, watching as he shakes his hands and head at the same time, clearly frustrated.

'Getting old has got to be one of the worst things to happen to a human being,' he says, forcing a smile as his old eyes find me. I try not to look sympathetic, knowing he probably won't appreciate it. His fingertip taps the side of his temple. 'Everything up here is sound as a pound. It's the rest of me that's the problem.'

'Do you mind me asking how old you are, Mr H?'

He lets out that sweet-sounding chuckle again, lifting his teacup to his lips. 'Ninety-three. Too old for you, lovely.'

'Well, damn.' I slap the table, screwing up my face in disappointment, making Mr H throw his head back on a laugh. I smile fondly across the table at him, my mind racing with a hundred questions I'd love to ask about the history of the Hunt Corporation and the magnificent treasures he must have seen in his lifetime. I bet millions of pounds must have passed through his fingers.

My beam remains fixed in place while the old man calms his laughter down, wiping under his glasses. But then his smile falls away, taking mine with it. He's gone from hysterical to super-serious in a nanosecond. 'And my adorable grandson might only be thirty-two, but he is too unruly for you.'

I purse my lips. 'That's a bit of a random statement,' I say, taking a sip of tea as I furiously fight away the blush creeping up on to my pale cheeks. Mr H's slight cock of his head and knowing smile tells me I've failed in my endeavour. I don't help my cause when I glance away to avoid his probing stare.

'You have fire in those brown eyes, Eleanor.'

I have no idea what he means. I sag a little and give up the ghost. 'Mr Hunt, forgive me, but your grandson is a little—' I snap my mouth shut when the only words that automatically come to me are insulting. I need to remember that this sweet old man is Becker's grandad, and Becker Hunt is, unfortunately, my boss. 'Testing,' I finish, pleased with myself for finding a replacement word for twat, bastard, arsehole, or knobhead. Or tempting, gorgeous, sinfully sexy and enticing.

His grin widens. 'You don't need to hold back with me, Eleanor. I love my grandson more than life itself, but I'm not deluded. The man is a maverick.' He leans across the table, and I find myself inching closer, intrigued. 'He's a modern-day Casanova.'

I snort impulsively, then, embarrassed, quickly apologise for it. 'Sorry.'

'Don't be. You don't agree?'

'Casanova? Wasn't he a smooth-talking charmer?' Becker's no smooth talker. He's a womaniser. His grandfather has said himself, not that I can raise that point since he's totally unaware I overheard that conversation.

'Yes. Famous for his love affairs.'

My brow furrows. 'Has he had many?'

'Casanova or Becker?' He's trying to conceal the twitch developing at the corner of his mouth, but I can see it as clearly as he can see my rosy cheeks. I'm asking too many questions for someone who couldn't care less.

'Becker,' I utter, and then hold my breath. Why didn't I say

Casanova? Because I sure don't want to know the ins and outs of Becker's love life. I can check Google again if I fancy torturing myself.

He sighs, giving me a compassionate smile. 'Oh, dear me, Eleanor.'

What? Something tells me that I don't want to know. I'm kidding myself, I do want to know. 'What?'

'Just . . .' He stands, and my gaze lifts with him, my eyes demanding an explanation. Using the table for support, he leans over towards me slightly. 'Oh dear, dear, me.'

I jump up and scoot around the table to assist him. 'What do you mean, Mr H?'

'Oh dear.' He shakes his head in genuine despair, and it hits me.

'Oh no,' I say. 'Oh no, no, no. Really, no "oh dear" whatsoever.'

'Oh dear,' he says once more. I want to scream my frustration. 'Casanova strikes again,' he quips. His attempt at humour isn't funny at all. There is genuine despair underneath it.

'But he hasn't.' I laugh nervously. 'Honestly, I'm immune.' I'm about to tell him exactly how immune to his grandson I am, but I'm interrupted by the kitchen door opening, halting another delusional lie from leaving my lips.

Mrs Potts stands in the doorway with her hands on her hips. I'm relieved, despite her looking rather cross. 'Eleanor, dear, would you mind peeling some carrots for me?'

'Of course,' I answer swiftly. Carrots I can do – anything to escape more *oh dears*.

'Donald, you're supposed to be having a nap.'

'Put a lid on it, woman,' he grumbles. 'We have a problem.'

'We do?' she says, ignoring his order.

'Yes, we do.' He takes my hand from his elbow and gently holds it, affectionately patting the back of it with his free hand. 'Eleanor here thinks she's immune to Becker boy.'

The overjoyed smile that jumps on to Mrs Potts face actually makes me feel better. 'That's wonderful.' She scurries over and takes my hand from Mr H's, repeating his move and rubbing furiously. 'I'm so pleased.'

'Me too,' I agree, soaking up the praise. Even if I don't deserve it. Because I'm a fraud.

'Oh, for the love of Hercules.' Mr H pulls my attention away from a pleased Mrs Potts. 'No, Dorothy.' He rolls his eyes. 'She *thinks* she's immune.'

My eyebrows meet in the middle. 'I *am* immune,' I say, keen to put their minds at rest. That I'm in denial is of no consequence. I realise the importance of repelling Becker, and not just because he's a player. It seems Becker didn't succeed in his attempts to settle his grandad's worry when it comes to me, so it's imperative that I do.

My eyes cast between the two old folks, as they slowly turn their attention towards me again. They're looking sorry for me. 'What?' I shift nervously on my heels. 'Why are you looking at me like that?'

'Oh, dear me,' Mrs Potts breathes.

'Oh my God,' I say in frustration. 'Really, no "oh, dear me".' I sound desperate. I *am* desperate. I will not go there.

'Yes, dear.' Mrs Potts places a pacifying hand on my bare arm and rubs soothingly. 'Anything you say, dear.'

'See?' Mr Hunt mumbles, starting to drag his heavy feet across the tiles to the kitchen door. 'Immune,' he scoffs.

If he wasn't so unstable and old, I'd drag him back and make him listen to my denial until he's convinced, but this little episode has exhausted me. My shoulders drop, and I give up, watching as Mrs Potts catches up with the old man and slips her hand through his arm. 'I feared the worst,' she says quietly, like she doesn't want me to hear. But I do hear. Perfectly.

'Oh, Dorothy,' Mr H replies, opening the door and gesturing for her to go first, a perfect gentleman, even though he still has to hold on to her as she takes the lead. 'The worst is yet to come.'

The door shuts.

And I'm alone.

'No "oh dear me",' I yell, looking around the kitchen for something to take my frustrations out on. I settle on the table and march over, giving it a firm slap, imagining it's Becker's face. What does this even mean? Will they sack me? Send me packing before the *worst* comes? And what did they mean when they said the worst is yet to come, anyway?

Woof!

I swing around to find Winston at my feet. If I wasn't totally sane, I'd suspect the happy pant he's got going on right now is him agreeing with the two old people. 'Don't you start,' I warn. Totally sane? I'm talking to a bloody dog.

Woof!

'What?' I ask, like he might answer. Funnily enough, he doesn't, but he does trot across the room and nuzzle at a leather dog lead hanging off the back of the door. 'You want to go for a walk?'

He barks and nuzzles the lead again, his tail wagging good and proper. I crouch and scratch his ear. 'Just let me peel some carrots for Mrs Potts,' I tell him. 'Then we'll go for a walk.' I could do with the fresh air, that's for sure. I need to clear my head and prepare my reassurance speech for Mrs Potts and Mr H.

Standing and brushing down my dress, I go on the hunt for some carrots. I open cupboard after cupboard, finding no carrots. 'The pantry,' I realise, heading to the tallest cupboard and pulling the door open. A wire racking system greets me, and I begin to scan the baskets, bending as my searching gets further south. 'Bingo.' I spot a sea of orange next to a sea of spuds and grab a few, raising and shutting the door.

'Oh dear.' The soft words come from nowhere, and my feet leave the floor from fright, the carrots tumbling from my hands.

I'm raging already, and I haven't even clapped eyes on him yet. 'You startled me.' I push the words through a tight jaw as I slowly pivot to confront him. He's leaning up against the work-top, looking all yummy, his glasses on. He's staring at me, his hazel eyes particularly green, as he munches his way through an apple. He seems to have composed himself after our little . . . moment in the library, and his little . . . *chat* with his grandad. The man I heard sounded like he was in emotional turmoil. This man looks far from it. Did he speak to his therapist? May-be he's had . . . his words suddenly register in my startled mind.

Oh dear.

Oh shit.

Did he listen in on that little episode between his grand-father, Mrs Potts and me?

'So, you're immune?' he says, like he's read my mind.

My cheeks burn up, but I ignore his question and fire one of my own. 'What do you want?'

He shrugs and inhales deeply, looking down at his feet, which are still bare, annoyingly. He starts to casually scuff them on the kitchen floor, like he knows I'm rapt by them. I rip my eyes away and return them to his pouting face. Stupid. It's always a lose–lose situation when I'm in Becker's company. There's nothing I can look at that lowers his sex appeal, so I have to rely on his 'charm' to deter me. And I'm willing it on right now. All of it. I'll take every bit. I know it's coming, so in an effort to move things along, I cock my head to prompt him to say more.

He grins. The fucking bastard. 'I love it when your cheeks go all red.'

I scowl.

His grin stretches. 'Imagine how red they'll be when I'm through with you.' He takes a tactical bite of his apple. And there we have it. Loud and clear. He should get a new therapist, pronto.

'Weren't you supposed to be somewhere this morning?' I ask,

referring to his supposed meeting about the Spanish tapestry, the one that required me to be at work an hour early. He's still in his sweats at midday. I dip and collect my scattered carrots.

'Rescheduled for this afternoon.'

I huff to myself. It's likely that the so-called meeting was never arranged for this morning in the first place. I reach for my final carrot and make to stand, but Becker crouches in front of me, his hand resting over mine on the carrot. The warmth paralyses every muscle in my body.

'I'd love to see how rosy I can make *all* of your cheeks.'

I flip my stunned eyes up. His face is deadpan. Beautiful. Mesmerising. All my cheeks? I can't do this any more. It's draining. I want no part of this game he's playing. It's beginning to frighten me, for no other reason than how it will end. Which, basically, will be me unemployed and bitter.

I force myself to hold his angel eyes in a show of strength. 'You're incorrigible.'

'Does that mean you like me?'

'No, it means you give me a headache. Stop it.'

'Stop what?'

'You know what.'

'Okay, then. You stop it, too.'

'Me?' I gawk at him.

'Yes, you.'

I give up. I snatch my hand from under his and stand, escaping to the other side of the kitchen. I yank drawers open until I find a vegetable peeler and a knife, then slap my carrots on to the worktop and start a carrot massacre. My hand viciously yanks the peeler down repeatedly until I have a pile of bald carrots. Then I start hacking at them with my knife, building up a mountain of questionably shaped pieces that Mrs Potts will no doubt disapprove of.

I know he's behind me, probably watching me cautiously. Or – given the knife I'm brandishing – he might have wisely dipped out before I can add him to my mound of carrots.

I hack and chop, feeling myself getting more worked up, and then . . . 'Ouch,' I hiss and drop the knife, glancing at my finger. *Blood*. 'Oh shit.' I grab a tea towel and press it to my finger. *Blood*. God, it makes me so queasy. I drop to my knees and blink repeatedly to clear my vision when it goes blurry, feeling hot, sweaty, cold, and sick. 'Fucking hell.' I squeeze the tea towel harder when my finger begins to throb. I won't cry. I also won't look at the damage I've caused. *Blood*. I feel my stomach turn and clench my eyes shut, trying to breathe my way through my light-headedness.

Then I feel his touch around my wrist, and my eyes open to find Becker kneeling in front of me. His lips are straight, his face serious. 'Are you okay?'

My bottom lip begins to tremble, stupid emotion sneaking up on me. I'm being a baby. It really doesn't hurt *that* much. Have our constant back-and-forth games worn me down? Exhausted me and made me all girlie? 'Ouch,' I mumble, dropping my head, feeling silly. Yes, they have. I'm drained of fight. Worn out by it all.

'Here, let me see.' He tries to pull my arm towards him, but I snatch it away.

'I'm fine,' I mutter, starting to unbend my body to stand. 'Stop being all nice and attentive.'

'Why?'

'It doesn't suit you.'

He rolls his eyes. 'Let me help.'

'I'd rather bleed to death.'

He laughs deeply, the sweet sound filling the kitchen. 'Yeah, well, I don't want the hassle of a dead employee's body to dispose of.' He swipes me from my feet in one swift move, making me squeal in shock, which he totally ignores, and strides over to the counter with me draped across his arms. I tense up in his hold, my lips clamping closed. 'As your boss, I'm ordering you to obey me.' He places me on the worktop and grins when he catches my look of disgust. 'Got it?'

I scowl, pulling at the hem of my dress which has inched its way up my thighs.

'Let me help.' Becker takes over the rearranging of my dress, his hand skimming my bare leg. I stiffen, and I know he's noticed, because he's smirking. Good God, the urge to slap him and snog him are causing havoc with my willpower. I imagine what it would be like to slap him *and* to snog him. I'm not sure which I'd enjoy most.

'Okay,' I say, pushing him away. 'The dress is fixed.'

Becker bats my hands down. 'Not quite.' He takes his time torturing me with strategic skims of his flesh over mine, nodding his approval and taking a deep breath once he's done. Then he braces his hands on the worktop either side of my thighs. I lean back as he stares at me. I'm caged in. Trapped. I'm a sitting bloody duck. 'Are you going to let me take a look?'

'At my finger?'

His chest concaves on an audible drag of breath, and his eyes scan my face, searching for . . . I don't know what. He looks a little confused, his eyes questioning. 'What else would I want to look at, princess?'

My lips purse, my eyes narrow, and I slowly lift my towel-wrapped hand up to him. 'Be gentle,' I warn.

'I like rough and dirty,' he murmurs quietly, almost questioningly, like he's reminding himself. Telling himself.

There's only one thing I should say to that, only one thing that comes naturally. 'Don't be a twat.' My insult breezes past my lips, and he gives me a strained smile.

Then, gingerly, he takes my hand, swallowing as he slowly unravels the material while I tense and hiss. 'Be a brave girl,' he teases, flicking his eyes up to me every few seconds. I couldn't possibly retaliate. I'm too busy holding my breath and sweating, and not because of my injured finger. He's so close.

Touching me. 'Close your eyes,' he murmurs. 'You won't feel a thing.'

I do as I'm told, happy to block out the sight of him. He's so gentle with me, each touch and movement carried out with the utmost care, making the whole process almost pain-free. But the heat of his skin on mine . . .

I gulp repeatedly, taking deep breaths and ignoring flash-backs of his naked chest. But it's hard to push something away when your eyes and mind take such delight in seeing and thinking about it. Damn me. He's fucking Alexa, and probably Paula too. He isn't adding me to his list. Becker Hunt is my boss, and above everything else, I need to remember that. I also need to remember everything Mrs Potts and Mr H have said. Falling for his relentless tactics would be monumentally stupid. It would be the beginning of the end for me at the Hunt Cor-poration. I must get over this silly crush.

It's all I *can* do. I love it here. I love all of the history, the . . . My thoughts are interrupted when my skin begins to tingle, and my sense of smell is bombarded by a familiar scent. *His* scent. Manly. Clean with a touch of citrus. It's strong. He's close. And then his hot breath clashes with my cheeks. My eyes flutter open, finding him as close as can be without touching, his perfect hazel eyes perfectly clear behind his glasses. He's leaning forward, arms braced on either side of me. Our eyes hold.

'It's superficial,' he whispers, taking my hand and holding it gently. 'You'll live.'

'I'm terrible with blood.' I can think of nothing else to say.

He nods in understanding, and for some unknown reason, it means something. He was gentle with me, when he could have been a prick and left me to suffer alone. But he didn't. He fixed me.

'Any particular reason?'

'When I was three, my dad sliced his finger on a blade when

he was repairing a clock. He went through eighty per cent of his thumb.'

He grimaces. 'That's gross.'

'Really gross. I thought he was going to die. The sight of blood makes me woozy.'

Becker chuckles a little. 'Then it's a good job I was here to save you.'

'Was it?' I'm not so sure. I don't like nice Becker. I don't know what to do with him.

'Yes, but this isn't the kind of red I wanted to see,' he says quietly, his face suddenly completely serious as he holds my hand in the air. My cheeks burn because of that statement, undoubtedly giving me away. I expect my red cheeks aren't the kind of red he wanted to see, either. At least, not the cheeks on my face.

He applies a light pressure to my hand, and I look down to see a small plaster covering the tip of my finger. That's it? I should feel stupid, but I don't. I can't feel anything beyond the conflicting thoughts running rampant in my mind. 'Thank you.'

'Welcome.' His reply is so soft. Comfortingly soft, and I cast my eyes back to his. I'm immediately hauled into their fiery depths. Passion, promise, and pleasure are all pouring from them. My body is singing. Alive. He inches his body forward a tiny bit, like he's testing me, trying to determine whether I'll retreat or accept him. I do neither. I remain a statue, keeping my eyes on his. He comes forward a little more, and I swallow hard when I feel his front meet my knees. His arm appears in my peripheral vision, his hand reaching towards my hair.

All the muscles in my body lock down. *Oh God.*

It takes everything in me not to move when I feel his finger slip delicately between the strands. He watches my hair as he plays with it. I can do no more than sit before him and accept his caress. This is wrong. This is so off limits. We both know it, and not only because he's my boss. He had another woman in his bed last night. I know what kind of man Becker Hunt is. I know he needs to be avoided. I know—

'We have a situation,' he murmurs, and my thoughts start chasing in circles. Yes, we do. But I can stop this. I *must* stop this.

I try to shake my head. Nothing happens. I try to speak, but no words form. The chemistry has been constant since the moment I clapped eyes on Becker Hunt. I've fought it. I've had to fight it. But the fighting has only added fire to that chemistry.

'I want you.' His nostrils flare, like it's taking everything to admit it. It probably is. 'Fuck, I really want you.' His palm drifts on to my cheek, and my eyes close, my mind spiralling into complete chaos. *Stop this, Eleanor, you fool. Why are you getting yourself into this situation?*

A slight squeeze of my cheek prompts me to open my eyes and face my situation. Becker is my situation.

'Do you want me?' His chest expands. Now he's holding *his* breath, bracing himself for what I might say. This isn't the behaviour of a confident man who always gets what he wants. He's unsure. Nervous.

'We can't. We shouldn't.' I splutter the words through my increasingly ragged breathing.

'We should,' he replies quickly and surely, and I withdraw a little on a swallow.

'Why?' He needs to give me one good reason. Or maybe he doesn't.

'Because I'm going to lose my fucking mind if we don't. I might lose it if we do, too. Who the fuck knows? But I've been slowly going mad since you crashed into my Haven, and I can't watch you getting lost in my treasure any more without knowing what it feels like to kiss you.' His eyes root to my lips as they part, my heart going wild. 'Tell me you're on the same page, princess.'

Oh fuck. 'You win.' The words are out before I can locate my willpower and dignity, and a carnal expression washes over his features, full of sex and power.

His hand moves to my nape and fists my hair tightly in his grasp. 'Of course I've won,' he growls, then moves forward fast, crushing his mouth to mine. He literally takes my breath away with the force of his lips on mine. His tongue plunges deep and demanding, swirling and stabbing as his hand in my hair holds me in place. My whole being comes to life and I accept it all, everything – the vigour, the power, the deep ache between my thighs. It's not long before I begin to voice my pleasure, moaning as I match his force, devouring him.

'Shut the fuck up, Eleanor,' he demands harshly, yanking at my hair. This should bother me. I should be pushing him off, telling him to fuck right off with his commands . . . except I like it. The build-up of frustration is draining away under his taking of me, because that's exactly what he's doing. He's taking me – unapologetically and however the hell he likes. Rough and dirty. Because I said yes. I gave in. I can no longer resist him.

I try to keep quiet as instructed, even as my hands find his shoulders and grab tightly, loving the feel of his bunched muscles beneath his T-shirt. I've seen these shoulders. Perfect shoulders.

'Becker,' I gasp into his mouth, earning myself a sharp yank of my hair again. I inhale sharply when he releases my lips, my eyes flying open. He's panting as he burns holes in me with the intensity of his stare, then roughly knocks my knees apart, making space for him to move into.

Which he does.

Slowly.

My heart bashes against my breastbone as he continues to fist my hair, moving his other hand to my lower back. I'm pulled into him with one easy tug until our torsos meet and every nerve ending explodes. 'Shit,' I whisper, searching his eyes, seeing raw hunger in them. I'm pretty sure the same hunger is in mine. I've never been so turned on.

Becker begins to nod slowly in agreement as his face moves closer, his attention dropping to my lips.

This is crazy. 'I can't do this.'

'You can.'

'No.'

'Stop it then.' His lips are a whisper away from mine. 'Go on, Eleanor. Stop it.'

'Oh God.'

'Exactly.' His voice is pure sex, and my body thrums. 'I'm going to violate you in the most delicious ways imaginable, princess.' Our lips brush a little, and I exhale in a sigh of surrender, falling into the soft motions of his kiss when he slips his tongue between my lips and swirls gently.

Then the sharp sound of barking makes us both jump.

No. Not now, Winston.

I'm released fast, Becker flying back, looking a little dazed and confused. The loss of support has me wobbling on the worktop, grabbing the edges to stabilise myself. The woofing continues, and I watch as Becker rakes a hand through his mussed hair, looking around the kitchen, disorientated.

I slip down from the counter and do my best to compose myself, but it's an epic fail. I feel like I could spontaneously combust. I'm so hot. Flustered. Lustful.

'What the fuck, Winston?' Becker asks when his eyes finally find his dog a few feet away. Winston answers by resting his arse on the floor, staring at his owner. This dog really does have doggy facial expressions, and right now he's giving his owner a miffed look. Becker stares right back, equally miffed. It's a glaring deadlock. 'What?' Becker throws his hands up in the air. 'You want her?' he asks seriously. Winston growls, making Becker take a wary step back, a stunned look on his face. It's hysterical, but I'm still too muddled to truly appreciate the comedy value. He's in a full-blown row with his dog . . . over me.

I take the situation into my own hands before they start wrestling. 'Here, boy,' I call, crouching, my voice shaky. Winston comes to me instantly, his backside swaying as he swaggers over and plonks himself at my feet, tail wagging in victory. I give him the fuss he's demanding and cautiously look up at Becker. His mouth is hanging open in disbelief and for the first time, I'm not so smug about Winston's blatant favouritism. In fact, I feel embarrassed. 'I'm sorry. I'm not sure what his problem is.'

Becker looks at me, all *what the hell?* before snapping to life and making a vain attempt at pulling himself together. Being hunkered down, I'm eye level with his thighs, and when his hand drifts to his crotch and he tries to discreetly rearrange himself, my stare wanders up a little and catches evidence of his . . . condition. He steps back, pulling his hand away when he realises where my eyes are focused. There's no concealing it, not beneath the loose, soft material of his sweatpants.

He's rigid.

My bottom lip slips between my teeth and bites down, my brain ignoring my stern demand to look away.

'Eleanor.' Becker's soft calling of my name pulls my attention up, and I find a pained expression on his face. Because of his current hard problem? Or because of what just happened? His eyes shut and he pulls in the longest breath. 'That shouldn't have happened.' His statement slices through me like a machete, yet I hear no conviction in his words. None. 'I can't . . . it's just not . . .' His fists clench into tight balls, his jaw pulses. 'You don't want me, trust me.'

I actually do trust him on that. He's warning me, just like Mrs Potts and Mr H. I should be grateful. So why am I aching everywhere with hurt and disappointment? And why his sudden change of heart? Has he remembered what his grandfather yelled at him? Has he kissed me and not enjoyed it? My confidence takes a bashing when I consider the latter. I've seen the women he's used to. God, he had one stuck to his lips right before me. I'm nothing like them. I have an arse, for a start. Oh my days, I've just willingly taken part in another round of his stupid game. *Idiot.*

I leave Winston and stand up straight, putting on a brave face. I have nothing else. 'I apologise, Mr Hunt.' I turn on the formalities automatically, falling straight back into protective mode, my focus now set firmly on keeping my job. 'It won't happen again.'

His jaw tightens, and a million expressions pass over his face, but it's the regret I catch most acutely, and I focus on that. I feel regret, too. I don't know where we would be by now had Winston not gone into psycho-dog mode. On the floor? Naked? Sweating?

'I was going to take him for a walk.' I blindly point to the space at my feet where I know Winston to be. 'Do you mind?'

'Course not,' Becker answers without hesitation. 'He probably needs to let off some steam. Might be why he's so' – he frowns at Winston – 'touchy.'

'Maybe.' I mirror Becker, looking down at his dog.

'I need to make a call.' Becker pulls his phone from his pocket and starts toying with it, almost reluctantly. Something tells me it's his therapist he needs to call. I bet he or she is on speed dial.

I waste no time leaving him to it. I grab the lead and I'm out of there fast, desperate to escape the awkward vibes. I don't need to call for Winston to come. He follows me out, all bouncy and chipper. I, on the other hand, want to curl into a ball of disgrace and hide. I've let myself down.

Winston didn't need to let off any steam at all. He doesn't bound across the park and run free. He just ambles alongside me, looking up at me now and then, like he is checking to see if I'm all right. I'm not all right. I'm ashamed. What on earth have I just done?

'Eleanor!'

I turn to see Lucy waving a frantic hand over her head, a bowl of salad in the other. She was more than intrigued when I texted to see if she was up for a lunchtime rendezvous in the park.

I stop and lean down to hook up Winston to his lead, letting out a sardonic burst of laughter when he grumbles in protest. 'You were hardly making the most of your freedom,' I say. 'Quit complaining.'

'Talking to a hound?' Lucy asks as she reaches us, looking down at Winston.

I straighten up and we start walking slowly down the pathway.

'Who does the dog belong to?'

I give her a tired look. 'My boss.'

'He makes you walk his dog?' Her disgust is obvious as she rearranges her bag on her shoulder. 'What are you, his skivvy?'

My hackles rise. 'I'm not his skivvy. I offered, and Winston seems to have taken a shine to me.'

'Okay,' Lucy says slowly, studying me with a forkful of salad halfway to her mouth. I look away, trying to conceal my irritation. 'How was your date with Brent Wilson?'

I shrug. 'All right.'

'All right? So why the emergency meeting?'

'Just because,' I snap a little too harshly.

'Jesus,' Lucy breathes. 'Who's pulled *your* chain?'

'No one,' I answer dismissively, at the same time wondering why I don't tell her when the reason I called her was to vent. To spill it all out. To find some reason from a sound mind, since mine constantly delves into dangerous places.

Lucy doesn't come back with any kind of retort, leaving a stretched quiet for her to fill with many silent assumptions. My curious mind begins to wonder if she's on the right track, and I peek out the corner of my eye to gauge her expression.

She's grinning. 'Is *no one* tall and lean with mousy hair?' she asks.

I look away.

'Is *no one* sinfully handsome, has a lovely straight nose, and a delicious body?'

'I never said he has a delicious body.'

'I bet he has, though, hasn't he?'

I sniff, tugging at Winston when he veers off the path a little. 'I wouldn't know.'

'Does *no one* have gorgeous take-me-to-bed eyes behind seriously hot glasses?'

I'm attacked by mental images of *no one*. 'He kissed me.'

Lucy laughs. 'I knew it.'

'It was incredible. Then Winston here interrupted, and it became uncomfortable. I feel stupid, it really shouldn't have happened, and now I'm worried I won't be able to work for him because of the awkwardness, or Mr H might fire me if he finds out.'

'Oh.' Lucy gives me a sympathetic look.

'He's in therapy,' I say, after a pause.

'For what?'

'I don't know. Being an arsehole, I expect.' I wince, thinking about his parents and how he tragically lost them both.

Lucy laughs lightly. 'Which do you want more?'

'Huh?'

'Which do you want more? Him or your job?'

I laugh. The question warrants it because the answer is very easy. 'The job.'

'Why?'

'Because I love it *and* it could be permanent or lead to other amazing opportunities,' I reply with no hesitation, sounding sure. I feel even better when Lucy nods her understanding. 'I can't risk a secure, long-term future for an uncertain, short-term fling with Becker Hunt.'

'Uncertain?' she asks. 'What makes it uncertain?'

'You've seen the pictures. He's a womaniser – a modern-day Casanova with eyes you want to melt in.'

'You could be different for him.'

Her innocent statement sucker-punches me in the stomach, reminding me of the same words Becker said to his grandad. *She might be different.* 'I don't think so.' I laugh nervously and reach up to my nape, feeling his hold there. He's dangerous. Rough and dirty. It doesn't escape my notice that I didn't give two shits about that when I was caught in the moment, being told to shut up when I so much as murmured. Hot sex. I was pretty sure it would be mind-blowing before our steamy kiss in the kitchen. He's a god. Woman fall to their knees for him. Now I know, beyond all doubt, that Becker's reputation precedes him. And though it physically pains me to admit it, I also know, worryingly, that I want him more than ever before. Hearing his vulnerable side when he argued with his grandfather shifted things. Outside the library, when he softly urged me to stop shaking, and then in the kitchen, where he was gentle and soft with me. Yes, he's harsh and unyielding, cocky and arrogant, but I discovered today that he's also tender. It's made him even more irresistible, and I never would have thought that possible. The way he looked at me. The torn expression on his face, like he was wrestling with an unconquerable opponent. I could be different?

I look at Lucy and she smiles as she drops her half-eaten salad into a bin. 'I'll be okay,' I say lamely. Lucy isn't daft, and even though we haven't known each other long, she gets that I need to put the earlier events at the very back of my mind.

'Good.' She rubs her hands together. 'Because tonight we're out.'

'What do you mean, out?'

'Like out, out. Proper out. I have VIP entry to a new club up west called Piper's. You game?'

'Yes.' I nod decisively, not needing to think twice. This is what London's about. Freedom, fun and liberation. 'I could do with a drink.'

'Fab.' She grabs my arm, pulling me to a stop, and I frown when her nose wrinkles in distaste. 'Um ...' She steps back. 'I think your new friend is about to take a dump.'

'What?' I look down to Winston, finding him squatting. 'Oh, no.'

'You know you're gonna have to pick that up, right?'

'What with?' I slap my hand over my mouth when Winston looks up at me, his whole body shaking with the strain.

'Don't tell me you came out to walk a dog without a poop bag?'

'I had other things on my mind.' I look around the park, desperately searching for another dog walker. There's no one. 'Fucking hell,' I curse, glancing down at Winston, who has now finished doing his business and is sitting at my feet with a pile of steaming hot poo next to him. 'Damn,' I mutter. He looks pleased with himself.

'I'd ask for a pay rise,' Lucy titters, and my shoulders drop, defeated, as I lower myself to unbearable levels, heading over to a rubbish bin.

Desperate times call for desperate measures. 'I cannot believe I'm doing this,' I whimper to myself. I'm in a lovely black dress with matching heels and a mac, and I'm about to rummage through a public bin – like a vagrant – to find something suitable to scoop up my sinful boss's dog's excrement. I really have reached an all-time low.

Once Winston is settled in his dog basket in the kitchen, I scrub my hands until they're sore and oversee the collection of the Rembrandt by the restorers, then I take a moment to evaluate my situation. I need to be a grown-up. I need to get a grip and stop with the dangerous games. I need to clear the air and be rid of the awkwardness before it goes too far. If it hasn't already. 'Yes,' I say to myself.

'Yes what, dear?'

I turn to see Mrs Potts scanning the kitchen for who I might be talking to.

'Oh, nothing. Just talking to myself.' I wave a hand flippantly in the air, brushing off her curiosity, but before I can stop it, the question that's plaguing my mind just spills right out. 'Why is Becker in therapy?'

Mrs Potts shoots me a worried look, and I find myself rushing to go on.

'I heard Mr H telling Becker to call his therapist.'

Her lips purse, her violet curls shifting as she shakes her head and goes to the pile of carrots I left for her, starting to scoop them into a large saucepan. 'He struggles.'

'With what?' I don't know why I'm asking. I heard plain and clear when Mr H yelled at him while I was hiding in the cupboard. I think I'm simply looking for validation. Trying to support the compassion I'm starting to feel for him.

She sighs. 'With his parents' deaths. First his mum in the car accident, and then his father. It's a lot for a young man to deal with.'

I fold a little on the inside with the confirmation. 'I'm sorry.'

'You mustn't speak of it,' she orders sternly, and I nod my understanding. 'He has an unhealthy way of dealing with things, and Donald hopes Dr Vass can help him work through that.'

'Women?' I broach tentatively.

'Among other things. He has a fear of affection. Doesn't like getting attached. He keeps things simple, hence the fast turnover of women.' She fires up the hob, effectively ending our conversation.

I accept the hint graciously, but wince as I turn and make my way from the room. Fast turnover of women. I've seen the photos myself. 'I'll be in the library.'

I can feel her eyes follow me all the way to the door until it closes behind me. She's worried, and she has every right to be. I shouldn't have pried, but I suspect she's fed me that little information as another warning not to go there. It might have worked. Or it might not have. I'm feeling empathy for my difficult boss. I can understand the level of his grief from my own. I lost my dad. Just one parent. Losing both would have sent me deeper into the black pit with little hope of clawing myself out.

I relax and lean my back against the corridor wall, looking towards his office. The thought of seeing him again frightens me. I'm already struggling to erase the memories – his taste, the feel of him, the rush of desire. Clapping eyes on him again is likely to make me struggle harder, but I need to face this head-on. Delaying it will make it harder. Nip it in the bud.

Swallowing hard, I brush my dress down and ruffle my hair, then start towards his office, speaking quiet words of encouragement to myself. The huge, intricately engraved double doors look threatening when I reach them, and my eyes fall to the handle as my brain gently encourages me to enter. I start breathing regulating exercises, brush my dress down again, fix my hair again, and repeat my encouraging words to myself.

Then I square my shoulders and ring the bell before taking the handle and pushing my way into his office. My eyes find him immediately, standing behind his desk. He's changed out of his sweatpants and T-shirt and is now looking impeccable in a grey three-piece suit. His hair is combed neatly to the side, and ... *oh fuck me*, his glasses. I sway on the spot and my eyes scan his tall physique, my heart kicking at the sight of him. Now that I have a good idea of what he's capable of, too, I feel conquered by him, without really being conquered at all. It was, after all, just a kiss.

A smouldering kiss. A kiss that made me dizzy. I'm certain there was affection there somewhere – somewhere amid the hair tugging and demands to shut the fuck up.

He's on the phone, but he gives me a subtle smile as he stares at me, listening intently. 'I've been busy. Apologies,' he says, keeping his eyes on me. I shut the door, and he points to a chair opposite his desk, inviting me to sit with an encouraging nod. 'I have it here waiting. We'll discuss money at the viewing.' He puts his palm over the receiver and lifts his chin up. 'You okay?' he whispers, regarding me carefully. He's worried.

My head begins to bob a bit too much, my instincts telling me to assure him that I'm fine. 'I can go.' I point over my shoulder.

He holds his finger up and scowls down the line. 'There will be no negotiation. Sotheby's are keen to hold the sale, and I'm not averse to giving it to them. Let's not waste each other's time. It's a Louis the fourteenth table. It's solid walnut with marquetry, and the legs are gilded as you would expect. It's a rare and beautiful example of its era, Burgess. Let's not fuck about with insulting offers.'

I smile internally. Damn, talking business just makes him even bloody sexier.

He scoops his mobile from the desk when it starts bleeping, holding his conversation on the landline. Glancing at the screen, his eyes narrow a little as he looks up at me, thoughtful, before connecting the call and handing it across the desk.

I take his phone tentatively and do as I'm bid. 'Becker Hunt's phone. Eleanor speaking.'

'Oh, hi. Paula here. Where's Becker?'

Oh, he did not. No matter how hard I battle, I can't stop the sizzle of annoyance from rooting deep in my belly. He knew who this was when he handed me the phone. Why would he be such a dickhead? 'Busy,' I say tightly, watching Becker wander a short distance away from his desk, leaving me to deal with another current fuck. She'd better not ask me to schedule a date in his diary.

Paula chuckles. She's sensed my frosty reception. 'Eleanor, I feel I should make it clear,' she begins, clear and confident. 'There's never been, nor will there ever be, any physical relationship between Becker and me. I can only imagine the women you have to endure.'

Oh? My unwarranted dislike for Paula fast converts into respect. He's not fucking her? A quick check tells me Becker is still deep in conversation. 'I'm sorry, it's just . . .' I have no idea what else to say. Bottom line, I'm jealous of Alexa, and I would have been jealous of Paula too, had she turned out to be one of Becker's screws.

'Really, there's no need. I've encountered a few of them myself.'

'Lucky you,' I quip, wondering why I'm extending a conversation, fuelling it, when we shouldn't even be having it. I don't know who this woman is.

'Not that it matters to me, of course,' I rush to explain, cringing as I do. *Who is she?*

She laughs. 'How are you settling in?'

'Great,' I answer swiftly, grateful she's taken the initiative to turn the conversation around. 'Keeping my head down.'

'Best way. And keeping that adorable maverick in check?'

Her question gives me pause. 'Trying to,' I murmur, staring at the adorable maverick's back.

'Get him to call me. I need to pick his brain about something,' Paula says, and then she hangs up, and I place Becker's phone back on his desk.

'Good,' he says as I allow my eyes to climb his back. 'I'll be in touch.' He slowly turns and places the receiver into the cradle. And then he stares at me. And I forget why the hell I came in here.

'Eleanor?' He nudges me from my trance, and I quickly fix a strong, sure look on my face.

'Paula wants to pick your brain.'

He laughs lightly. 'Oh, I bet she does. I'll call her.'

Silence falls again, but before it becomes too awkward, I go on, keen to clear the air. 'I just wanted to come and clear—' I snap my mouth shut when the bell rings and the door swings open behind me. Glancing over my shoulder, I find Mrs Potts gesturing for someone to enter. And my eyes quickly widen. 'Brent.' His name passes my lips on a gush of stunned air.

'Eleanor.' He smiles brightly, walking into the office as Mrs Potts quickly scans the situation before shutting the door on a look that can only be described as despair. Understandable, since I told her I would be in the library and I'm not.

I'm on my feet quickly, but they feel like lead, preventing me from leaving. I want to leave, I *need* to leave, because I know what's coming. But my muscles refuse to play ball.

'So lovely to see you.' Brent reaches me and takes my shoulders, leaning in, kissing one cheek first, then the other. My eyes automatically flick to Becker, seeing him stiff as a board behind his desk, the muscles of his jaw ticking wildly.

I manage to step away from Brent, but the discomfort filling the room remains. 'I . . . I . . . didn't realise you had a meeting with Bec . . . Mr Hunt,' I stammer.

'Your boss is going to fix me up with an endorsement, aren't you, Hunt?'

We both look to my boss, who has a death stare aimed at Brent. The atmosphere is cutting. I need to go.

'I was just leaving.'

'I was hoping I'd see you while I'm here.' Brent's looking at me thoughtfully, maybe wondering why I'm not as receptive as the last time he was here. I could be, if I wanted the stupid battle of the biggest ego between these two men to continue. But I don't, not just because of what happened in the kitchen a couple of hours ago. But because I know Brent only took me on a date to rankle Becker.

My stare bounces between them, uneasiness crippling me. One man looks pleased to see me, smiling as I stand before him all awkward and fidgety, and the other is looking at me like he wants to rip off my head.

God, get me out of here. 'Is there anything I can get you?' I ask Becker, reclaiming some composure and relying on my professional demeanour. I focus my attention on him with a straight expression. I haven't any desire to rile my boss. Not now.

He eventually drops his eyes from mine. 'No,' he murmurs, faffing randomly with some papers to the side of his desk.

I nod and take the few steps that will get me to the door, giving Brent a small smile when he looks at me questioningly. I can't even muster the strength to say goodbye.

'Eleanor?' he calls as I leave the room, clenching my eyes shut, hoping he doesn't follow me. 'Eleanor,' he repeats, this time more urgently.

I increase my pace, but only make it halfway to the library before I hear footsteps coming after me. Taking a deep, confidence-boosting breath, I stop and turn, plastering a fake smile on my face.

Brent skids to a stop, frowning. 'Are you okay?'

I look over his shoulder when Becker emerges slowly from his office and stares down the corridor at me. His hands are in his trouser pockets, his stance wide as he regards me with prob-ing eyes. I break our eye contact before Brent notices that I'm distracted. 'Yes, I'm fine,' I chirp, straightening my shoulders. 'Just busy.' I don't give him a chance to extend the conversation, turning on my heels and hurrying towards the library.

'Tonight,' Brent calls. 'Dinner again?'

What the actual fuck? No, my head's already twisting be-cause of my sinful boss's games. I'm not up for another round of Brent's game, thank you very much. 'Thanks, but no thanks,' I say. 'Out with a friend.' I swipe my card quickly and throw my weight into the door before closing it just as fast and collapsing against the back of it.

Shit.

So much for clearing the air.

Chapter 13

I'm ambushed by a very excitable Lucy as I climb the stairs to my flat, my feet aching, along with my brain for overthinking about … certain things. She has giant rollers in her hair and half a face of make-up on. 'It's six thirty,' she screeches at me, hurrying over and taking my arm. 'What's taken you so long?'

'Um, London rush hour,' I answer, as I'm practically hauled down the corridor to my front door. 'What's the rush?' Admitting to her that I could quite easily curl up on my couch in my jammies would be stupid. I know I won't be allowed to do that tonight. She's ready to paint the town red.

Taking my bag from my shoulder, she starts rummaging through it while I look on. 'You have an hour,' she tells me, dragging out my keys and opening the door for me. I accept my bag when she hands it back, then she pushes me through the door. 'For your reference, I'm going with tits tonight.'

My brow furrows. 'What?'

'Tits.' She rolls her eyes. 'Not legs.'

'Should this mean something?'

She sags on the spot, shaking her head. 'Tits or legs, Eleanor. Never both.' She grabs the handle and pulls the door shut. 'An hour,' she repeats before the wood comes between us and I'm alone.

I head for the shower but just before I get there, I hear my phone ping. I pick it up to find a message.

From my ex.

157

I damn my stomach for churning, and damn myself further for opening it.

Your mum is still refusing to tell me where you are, and you won't answer my calls or messages. Just talk to me, please.

What part of *we're finished* and *I never want to see you again* doesn't he understand? I huff my disgust and make a quick call to Mum. Her voice is chirpy when she answers, and it doesn't falter when I apologise for David's persistence.

'Don't you worry about that,' she says cheerfully. 'It's not hard to say no to him.'

I smile and settle on the couch. Although I was pretty much emotionless when I told Mum about David and Amy, she saw through that but knew I didn't want sympathy. Anger, possibly. Sympathy, nope. 'Everything okay?'

'Never better.' She wouldn't say if it wasn't, yet I know she's doing well. The attentive close community of our village helps her, whereas it suffocated me. We chat for a while, her telling me about the gossip of home, which isn't a lot, and me bringing her up to date on my new life in London. Well, most of it.

Apparently, David isn't the only one who's been sniffing around. 'Amy stopped by,' Mum says tentatively. 'Asked how you are.'

'That's nice,' I mutter, brushing off my mother's reference to my ex-best friend. 'Did you ask *her* how David is?'

Mum lets out a light laugh. 'They both insist it was a stupid mistake. David wants you back.'

'David can go swivel. Tell him *that* if he comes sniffing around again.'

'Okay, darling,' she replies, and I know she will.

'Anyway, I'm out tonight with Lucy,' I say, moving things along as I unfold my body from the sofa.

'You must bring her home to meet me. She sounds like a doll.'

I don't think Lucy will appreciate a trip to the countryside after she's only just escaped it. 'Soon, perhaps. Maybe I'll bring her when I come home to clear the shop.' Lord knows I could do with the help.

'Darling, I've told you I can deal with that,' Mum says, sounding less than enthusiastic. I know she'd rather poke nails in her eyes. I wouldn't land that burden on her. She's sounded good these past few months. I'm worried that sending her into Dad's shop to clear it out would only put her back a few hundred paces. The reminders of him, the stock he loved, even the familiar smell of the old store that was always embedded into his clothes when he got home. Or would she be fine? Is she okay, and it's simply my guilty conscience dictating my decisions? Because, after all, once that store is sold, everything Dad built up, albeit junk, will be gone. What would he think of that? I swallow and try to push back those thoughts before they take hold and have me nosediving into melancholy.

'It's fine, Mum. I have it in hand.' This is my responsibility. I need to pull my finger out, book my train ticket home, and face what's waiting for me there. Plus, Mum needs to be relieved of the financial strain that shop has on her while it's sitting collecting dust. Literally. 'I'll call you next week.'

'Okay, darling. Have fun tonight.'

'I will.' I hang up and head for the shower.

'Oooh, you went for legs.' Lucy struts over as I lock my front door. She's in a pair of fitted black trousers and a seriously racy plunge-neck blouse, eyeing up my slinky black off-the-shoulder number. 'Sexy.' She halts in front of me, smiling as she reaches up to my hair. 'I have serious hair envy.'

'Don't,' I say as I pat my mane down.

'Why?' she asks. 'Shiny, vibrant, thick, falls perfectly. I need to freeze mine into place once I've burnt it to death with heated rollers.' We start to head down the stairs together.

'Yes, but the colour seriously limits my wardrobe.' My fire-red hair clashes with most pretty colours, leaving me with a wardrobe full of black, navy, and natural tones. On the odd occasion I can get away with pink and pastels, depending on the shade. 'Well, I have arse envy,' I tell her.

She peeks over her shoulder, looking down at her butt. 'I don't have an arse.'

'No, because God gave your quota to me.'

She laughs. 'You have an amazing arse. Curvy. Womanly. Mine looks like it's been dragged down a cheese grater.'

I chuckle, opening the door and gesturing for Lucy to lead on, which she does after curtseying on a giggle. 'Have you been drinking already?' I ask, catching a whiff of wine.

'Just a glass while I was getting ready.'

'Hey, don't peak too early.' I'm looking forward to a night out to drown my sorrows. Or drain out my thoughts. Either will suffice. I've seen Lucy smashed. She's a handful.

'Oh, be quiet.' She pulls me to a stop, her amusement falling away, and she holds me in place with serious eyes.

'What?' I ask, nervous.

'Whatever happens tonight,' she begins, and I frown, wondering what's coming next. 'Don't let me go home with a man.'

'Should that be a concern?'

She sniffs and reaches into her bag, taking out her blood-red lipstick and reapplying. 'Well, you know. We're both looking pretty hot tonight. And my willpower sucks when I'm pissed.'

I raise my eyebrows at her, waiting for her straight expression to crack. It takes roughly two-point-five seconds. We *both* crack up, giggling uncontrollably as I link my arm through hers as we start to sashay towards the main road. 'Okay,' I agree. 'But the same goes for me, not that it's likely to happen.'

'Famous last words.' Lucy chuckles.

We enter the club via an old factory-style lift, the original mechanism visible through the bars as it creeps up a couple of floors. A doorman on the other side pulls the sliding door open. 'You're good to go,' he rumbles, swooping his arm out.

'Wow.' I gulp, my mouth gaping as the club floor comes into view. Everything is white, with pink lighting illuminating the stark space. An enormous circular bar holds court in the centre of the room, the dance floor surrounding it edged in tubular lighting that's flashing from pink to white constantly.

'Pretty cool, huh?' Lucy directs us over to one of four bridges that crosses the dance floor to the bar.

'Yeah,' I agree, taking in the atmosphere. Eurythmics 'Sweet Dreams' is pumping, the dance floor is packed, and the bar is ten deep. Not that my final observation registers with Lucy. She pushes her way through, dragging me behind her, and I follow her indication when she points up, seeing a sign stating 'VIP GUESTS' glowing above our heads.

'What makes us VIPs?'

'These.' She flashes two pink cards. 'Mark gave them to me.' She grins. 'Even though I told him I was busy tonight.'

'Found out if the rumours about him and the girl from floor eighteen in the printing room are true?'

'Sadly, yes.'

'Oh. How?'

She shrugs. 'I asked the girl from floor eighteen.'

'That was rather bold of you.'

She snorts, just as a barman arrives. 'What are we having?'

'Grey Goose and tonic. Make it a double,' I say, turning my back on the bar and glancing up, seeing podiums scattered around the club with half-naked women adorning them, dancing suggestively. 'Wow.'

'The Bubblegum Girls?' Lucy passes me a highball, and my lips find the straw without taking my eyes off one of the girls atop a podium.

'Bubblegum Girls?'

'Yes, he told me about them. He's probably had a few.'

'He?' I look at Lucy, noting she's nearly worked her way through her drink already.

'Printer-room guy.' She gives me a look. '*Mark.*'

'And what does *Mark* look like?'

She shrugs nonchalantly. 'Blond, beard, cute mole on his cheek. Come on.' She starts pulling me away from the bar before I can press her on Mark, but I make a mental note to do so once we've found a base in the club.

'Are you on a mission tonight?' I ask.

'Yes.' We arrive at a cornered-off section, with booths lining the curved wall. Lucy flashes her pink card to the doorman keeping guard, looking over her shoulder and winking at me when he grants us immediate access.

'Pick a table, girls,' he grunts, indicating a few empty ones in the centre. 'It's yours for the rest of the evening.'

I give Lucy wide eyes, and she giggles before hotfooting it over to one right in the middle with a perfect view over the dance floor. We get comfy and I glance up to see one of the Bubblegum Girls approaching.

She sets a bottle of champagne in the middle of the table with two glasses. 'I'm Evette. I'll be serving you this evening.' She smiles, resting her weight on her hip. 'Champagne is courtesy of management.'

'Then keep it flowing,' Lucy says, grabbing the bottle and pouring. 'We'll take another in about ten minutes.'

Bubblegum Girl sashays away as Lucy pops the cork and pours. 'Hey, calm down,' I warn when she downs her full glass in one swoop. 'What's the rush?'

'No rush,' she says, topping it back up. I eye her warily across the table, suspicious, her words from the bar still at the forefront of my mind. Her eyes are flicking back and forth to a table of blokes not too far away, and after observing her for a few moments, seeing her jaw tightening by the second, I turn to see what's got her attention. A guy. Quite a hot guy, with blond hair and a well-trimmed beard. I can't see the cute mole, but I'd put my life on the fact that it's there.

'Mark,' I blurt, swinging my eyes to Lucy. 'That's Mark, isn't it? Printer-room guy.'

'That's him.' She rips her eyes away.

'Not gonna say hello?'

'Nope.' She slumps back in her seat, swirling the champagne in her glass. 'Anyway, how was the rest of your day?'

My glass pauses on its way back to the table as I cautiously glance up, finding an expectant look on her face. 'I intended on clearing the air, but when I went to his office to do so, Brent Wilson turned up.'

'Oh, no.'

'I know,' I say. 'I've never been in such an awkward situation. He asked me out again.' I neglect to mention the fact that the veins on Becker's neck looked set to burst at that point. She'll only surmise what that might mean, and I'm worried about what that could be.

'And you said—?'

'No.'

'Why?'

I sit back, evading her gaze. 'I didn't want to,' I murmur lamely.

'Why?' She's not giving in.

'Just . . . because.'

'Because of *no one*?'

My lips purse, and she smiles at me, her tongue pushing into her cheek mischievously.

'I know it's a bad idea,' I admit. 'And I have a feeling I'm just a game to both of them. I'm not interested in that at all.'

'A game?'

'I don't think they like each other.' I shrug.

Lucy's face screws up a little in disgust. 'Urgh, testosterone at play. Men. They think with their fucking dicks.' She lifts her glass to mine. 'Here's to not being one of the many, but maybe being *the one* someday.'

'I'll drink to that.'

'Good. We need more alcohol.' Lucy waves the bottle above her head, and a fresh one is soon delivered. I cast my eyes past her, relaxing a little, thinking tonight is shaping up to be a good one – a great club, great music, free champagne, and my best fr—

What the fucking hell? I stiffen all over as I spot someone. Or *no one.* My neck cranes, my eyes squinting a little as my mind tries to decide whether I'm seeing right. I don't know who I'm trying to kid. I'd know him a mile off. Plus, my heart is doing what it usually does when he's nearby. Going wild. 'Oh fuck,' I breathe, tipping another whole glass of champagne down my throat.

'What?' Lucy asks, turning in her seat to see where I'm staring. 'What's up?'

'Nothing,' I squeak, ducking a little in my chair before he spots me. 'Can we go?' I can't believe it!

'No way.' She swings back to face me, disgusted by my suggestion. 'Free champagne all night? The only place I'm moving to is the dance floor.' She downs her drink in demonstration, then tops it right back up, this time knocking the bottle on the side of the glass. She's well on her way and I'm not far behind. A bad condition to be in when Becker Hunt is around, *and* we're not on work time.

Shit, he's mere feet away, looking spectacular. He's ditched the jacket of his suit, leaving him in grey trousers and a white shirt. His collar is open, his sleeves rolled up, revealing lickable forearms, and he's wearing his glasses. Those fucking glasses.

My eyes close as I gather breath. Lots of it. He was smiling, a bottle of beer in his hand, lapping up the attention being rained on him by the women flocking around him.

Oh God.

When I finally find the strength to open my eyes, I'm confronted by Lucy's frowning face. 'Seriously, Eleanor, what's up?'

'My boss,' I whisper. She can't possibly have heard me over the music, but she must have read my lips because she swings around, wide-eyed and mouth agape.

'Where?' she gasps, her head swaying from side to side. 'Which one?'

'Trousers, white shirt, glasses.' I hope Lucy will take note quickly, spot him quickly, and turn away quickly.

'Motherfucker,' she says, throwing her arm out in Becker's direction. 'His photos do him *no* justice.'

'I know,' I grate. 'Stop pointing.' I grab her arm and yank it back.

She flashes me excited eyes. 'You missed *magnificent* on that list of yours.'

I pout to myself. I do have *magnificent* on my list. I just didn't share it with Lucy, just like I didn't tell her that he intruded on my date with Brent, or about that tremendous tattoo on his back.

'Go and say hi.'

'Are you insane?' I hiss. 'I'd rather put on some pink fluffy knickers and join a Bubblegum Girl on one of those podiums.' My gaze flicks in Becker's direction, my face screwing up when my eyes are assaulted by a ton of women all vying for his attention. My repulsion only multiplies when I notice that one of the clingers-on is the woman from The Haven. Tiger bird. Alexa. I snort my revulsion and throw another glass of champagne down my throat. Is he for real? He had Alexa in his bed last night. Kissed me this afternoon. And now he's out with her again? Oh my days, someone hold me back before I go on a rampage. The wanker. The dirty, philandering, low-life wanker.

'Someone's touchy,' Lucy says, watching me closely as I shift and fidget in my seat. She's getting a kick out of this. I'm just about to tell her exactly why I'm touchy when my attention is captured by another man walking towards us.

Oh? Interesting.

I slowly cast my eyes back to Lucy.

Then I smirk. 'There's someone on their way over.' I cock my head and widen my eyes for effect, now taking a leisurely sip of my champagne. 'Blond. Beard.'

She sits up straight and grabs her glass with both hands. 'No,' she murmurs, shaking her head slightly.

'Oh, yes,' I counter, looking over her shoulder when Mark comes to a stop behind her. There's that mole. It really is cute. 'Hi.' My voice is so completely over the top. 'I'm Eleanor.'

Mark gives me a sideways smile, obviously amused by my enthusiasm. Or maybe just confused. 'Hi,' he says as he rounds the table until he's between us, looking at Lucy. 'Lucy?'

I purse my lips, only just managing to rein in my grin. My friend mouths something that I don't catch, which doesn't bother me because I'm guessing it wasn't pleasant. Then she slaps an exaggerated smile on her face. 'Oh, hi, Mark.'

'You made it, then?' he says. 'I thought you had a date tonight?'

I cough over my champagne, earning a filthy look from Lucy. 'Sorry.' I thump the side of my fist lightly on my chest. 'Bubbles.'

'Change of plan.' Lucy relaxes back in her seat, bringing her glass to her lips and holding it there, slowly gliding it from side to side as she gives Mark sultry eyes. I want to laugh at her tactics, but she's doing too good a job of it. 'Eleanor has man trouble,' she tells him. 'She needed a friend.'

I shoot Lucy a shocked look. 'Have I?'

'Yes.' She looks out the corner of her eye at me. 'She's fallen for her boss.'

I nearly choke on my tongue when I inhale sharply. 'I have not fallen for my boss.'

'And she's in denial.'

'I am not.'

'See?' Lucy points her glass at me. 'Denial, right there.'

Mark gives me a sympathetic look, and I throw Lucy an indignant one. I'm rendered speechless. In the space of sixty seconds, she's made me out to be a sad, hopeless fool, when she's the one who's tactically dragged me to this club so she can see her work crush.

Outraged, I stand and swipe up my glass. 'I'm going to the ladies'.' My hair swooshes through the air as I swivel, whipping my hot face. 'She wanted to be the girl in the printer room with you, Marky boy,' I call over my shoulder, catching Mark's eyes widening and Lucy's jaw falling into her glass. I smile to myself, my hips gaining some sway as I saunter off, smug as can be. I take a detour – so I don't bump into a certain *no one* who's likely to make my eyes bleed – and then the bouncer frees me from the VIP area.

I bump and shimmy through the crowds to Kygo's 'Here for You', spotting a sign above pointing to the ladies'. I'm relieved when I fall through the door, not only to be free from the sea of people, but because I need to check my face. Because I'm hot. And a bit of dabbing with some powder might be required to soak up the sweat. I peek in the mirror and note there is no sweat. But I still drag my powder out and have a quick brush, followed by a touch-up of lipstick. And some mascara, just for good measure. Then some blusher, because it's feeling left out.

Five minutes later, I've reapplied everything, including a squirt of Issey Miyake behind my ears. My hair has been ruffled and my dress smoothed down. 'I have not fallen for my boss,' I say to my reflection. 'Because he's a first-class twat.'

'Sounds like a catch.'

I look to my left, finding a perfect stranger washing her bag. 'Sorry. Thought I was alone.'

She smiles into the mirror. 'Messy business, getting involved with your boss.'

I laugh, shaking my head and packing my lipstick into my purse. 'I'm not getting involved with my boss.'

'Of course,' she says on a laugh, shaking her hands and looking me up and down.

'You sound like you're talking from experience,' I say tentatively, wondering why I'm getting into such a conversation with a woman I don't know.

'I am.'

'And how did that work out?' I ask, fearing I know exactly how.

She cocks her head and raises her eyebrows at me. 'I'm unemployed,' she states matter-of-factly with clear bitterness, making me deflate on the spot. She throws me a little wave before exiting, leaving me alone again in the Ladies.

I gaze at myself in the mirror with pity, my freshly applied make-up perfect, but all I see is a total clown. That will be me if I'm not careful. Bitter, twisted, and jobless if I continue partaking in his silly game. For the love of all things dignified, I'm better than this. He can have the Alexas or whichever beautiful model-like women he wants. He's just a man – yes, a sexy, gorgeous man – but a man to be avoided for many reasons, all of which I should list to remind myself. One: he's with someone else. Two: he's troubled, and even his grandfather warned him away from me. Three: he regretted kissing me, and I deserve better than Becker Hunt's swaying mood. I'm not in London for this. I'm in control of my future.

Yes, I am. I pivot and make my way back to the club. I'm not at all surprised when I arrive in the VIP area to find Lucy on Mark's lap. Both are laughing. Both have roaming hands. And both look at me with excited eyes when I arrive at the table, yet I know the excitement has nothing to do with my return and everything to do with those wandering hands.

'What took you so long?' Lucy asks, shuffling off Mark's lap and stumbling towards me. 'We have more champagne.'

I glance past her, seeing Mark waving the fresh bottle with a smile. I'm squiffy, but I'm perfectly lucid, whereas Lucy is too drunk to make wise decisions. 'Hey.' I move in and get close to her so Mark can't hear or lip-read me. 'Why don't we move on?' I ask, injecting some enthusiasm into my tone, like I'm trying to convince a child that an utterly boring plan is actually a super-exciting plan. It's easy, especially since leaving this club is probably the best idea I've had. Becker Hunt is self-absorbed and clearly enjoying being surrounded by his harem. I don't give a flying fuck who he spends his personal time with. But it doesn't mean I want to hang around and watch him revel in the swooning attention.

'Never,' Lucy screeches, clearly disgusted by my suggestion. I shake my head. I know when I'm fighting a losing battle. She isn't going anywhere, and I'm not about to leave her alone with Mark. The least I can do is make sure she finds her way home and not into Mark's bed. So relenting to my fate – which is to stay longer in this club than I really want to – I slide on to my seat and claim my fresh glass of champagne.

By the time I've taken my first sip, Lucy is back on Mark's lap and hands are wandering again. Fabulous. They're giggling, whispering, and I have a front-row seat to the whole shebang. I could look away, take in the club and my surroundings, but then I risk getting an eyeful of the vultures stroking Becker. I mustn't let my eyes stray. I need to keep my dignity, not to mention my temper.

With little else to do, I'm quickly working my way through another bottle of champagne.

Don't do it. Don't. Fucking. Look.

I blame the champagne, because I'm almost desperate to catch a glimpse of him. My brain, on the other hand, is telling me that no good will come of taking a peek. *Remember who you are, Eleanor.* Remember who *he* is. *She* was in his bed last night. *He* regretted your kiss today.

'Bollocks,' I breathe, my eyes winning and casting over to my left, spotting him lapping up the attention. Jealousy rears its ugly and unwanted head, and my blood begins to simmer dangerously. Here's me, analysing every detail of what's happened between us, chasing in circles, obsessing about that kiss, beating myself up. And there's him. Clearly fine. I'm not costing him a thought while he laps up attention from other women.

I can't take it. Shooting up from the table, I grab my purse as I down the rest of my drink. I won't subject myself to this any more. 'I'm going,' I declare loudly over the pounding music, getting no acknowledgement from my friend. I lean in and knock Lucy's arm, interrupting her sloppy snog. She looks at me all gone out, completely dazed, her lipstick smudged, and when I quickly peek at Mark, he's sporting a nice red smear up his cheek. She's going to regret this in the morning. 'Why don't you come with me?' I suggest, trying to be as diplomatic as I can. Her face takes on a serious edge and she shakes her head slowly, making my shoulders droop in defeat. I bend and get eye level with her, smiling fondly when her lips purse. I don't care if Mark hears me this time. 'I don't want you to regret this in the morning.'

She smiles and falls towards me clumsily, prompting Mark to snake his arm around her waist so she doesn't slide off his lap.

She thinks hard for a few moments. 'I really like him.'

'But you're worth more than a one-night stand.'

'Who said it would be a one-night stand?' she asks, looking injured.

'When it's alcohol-fuelled, it usually is, Lucy. Take his number. Go out on a proper date.'

'I'll do that, too,' she says, delighted that she seems to have found the solution to my problem. 'I'll be fine, honestly.'

I eye her suspiciously, nibbling on the inside of my mouth. Then I glance past her to Mark. He catches my look and speaks up before I have a chance to warn him. 'I'll make sure she gets home safely.'

'Via your place?' I ask sardonically, eyebrow raised.

'Maybe.' He smiles and tugs Lucy back a little. 'She'll be fine, I promise.'

I give Lucy a quick peck on the cheek and unbend my body, tucking my purse under my arm. 'Make sure she is,' I warn. 'I know where you work.'

He laughs. 'Hey, speak to the blond guy on the door. He'll call you a cab.'

'Yes.' Lucy nods enthusiastically. 'And text me the moment you're home.'

'I will.' I leave Mark and Lucy laughing, keen to break free of the club, and when I've made it to the edge of the dance floor, I'm certain I've evaded a certain ... *no one*. But just as I think that, I glimpse to my left ... and fall straight into panic.

Oh God, it gets worse.

Brent's head is craning around a few people who are blocking his path. He's here too? And he's spotted me. *Fucking hell.* I dip and weave through the crowds, my feet moving urgently to get me out of here. I can't promise I won't slap his face if he asks me out again. I can't promise I won't—

My wrist is seized, and I swing around violently, coming face to face with ...

Becker?

A funny sensation comes over me, and I roll my shoulders back to shake off the prickles that have just jumped on to my skin.

He's breathing heavily, his angel eyes hard. 'Don't go home with him,' he says urgently, and then he's gone, disappearing among a sea of people, just as Brent breaks free of the crowds on the other side of me. I release the air in my lungs, my breastbone rolling in waves of shock, confusion and fear. He delayed me. I could have got out of here before Brent made it to me, so why didn't he just let me? I look past Brent's smiling face, searching for Becker.

And my ability to breathe is stolen from me the moment I find him.

His eyes are not on me any more, because they're directed at the woman in his arms. What is he doing? And *why* is he doing it to me? What fucked-up game is he playing?

'Eleanor?'

I shoot my dry eyes to Brent. He's frowning at me. My head is spinning, but as I stare blankly at him, clarity seems to descend.

Don't go home with him.

Becker could have escorted me out. He could have taken me away from Brent, and both of us know I wouldn't have stopped him. But he didn't, and the reason why is suddenly so obvious. He wants *me* to reject Brent. He wants me to reject him *after* he told me to. Why? I should slap myself for asking such a stupid question. Because then I've bowed to him. I've done as I'm told, and though everything unreasonable within me is yelling at me not to, I still do. 'I'm leaving.' I back away, ignoring Brent's perplexed expression.

'Stay. Have a drink.' He motions to the bar.

'No.' I give my simple refusal with no further explanation. It's just a no. What more would I say? That I want to slap him for taking me for a fool? That I want to slap Becker harder, and I might do exactly that if I remain in this club? That I'll spend all my time glaring at Becker, working myself up until I talk myself into doing something stupid? Like taking whatever Brent's obviously willing to give. Not because I want it, but because Becker doesn't want me to have it. Because my arsehole boss told me not to go home with him, which means I might do exactly that in a fit of revenge.

No. It's just a no.

I turn and make my way to the exit, and Brent doesn't stop me. My frame of mind must be obvious. I don't try to cover up my despondency; I don't have the energy.

The doors to the lift open and I step inside, turning slowly to face the club. Brent is watching me, still looking a little baffled by my behaviour. I look past him. There are a million people between me and the VIP area, but my eyes zoom straight in on one spot. A surge of energy bolts through me when our eyes lock. My surroundings fall silent. The path to Becker is clear, and it's calling, almost lit up, like it's encouraging me to follow it.

Go to him. Slap his face. Give him a piece of your mind.

He simply stares, and something tells me he's waiting for me to do exactly that. Like he wants me to. Like he feels he deserves it. Then his eyes slowly look to the side, and I follow Becker's line of sight until I find Brent. He's looking at Becker, and Becker is looking at him. Two wolves in a staring deadlock. Brent's head starts to shake mildly as he comes to realise why I'm leaving.

Go on, boys. Carry on playing your game with each other. This girl is out.

'Cab, love?' The distant question has my eyes casting slowly over to the doorman as he takes the door handle. I just nod and then allow my gaze to fall to Becker again. He smiles mildly and gives me a subtle nod. He's encouraging me, praising me.

He's still telling me to go. Then I lose sight of him when the door slides across.

My lungs drink in a sharp blast of cool air when the lift abruptly starts to descend, my eyes darting around at my feet. Becker doesn't want me. So no one else can have me, either? Is that what this is? The notion shocks me back to life. And I suddenly realise: I'm not in control at all. He is.

Anger sizzles dangerously in my belly, and my hand shoots out and grabs the rail when the lift shudders to a halt on the ground floor. The doorman quickly yanks the door open, but I remain tucked neatly in the corner of the lift, my mind screaming at me not to go there. I need to leave this club. Going back up there will serve no purpose. Using Brent will serve no purpose, other than proving a point to Becker. He can't dictate who I see. He can't tell me what to do. He can't entice me in, tempt me, then push me away and expect my compliance.

'Miss?'

I look up to the doorman, who's staring at me with concern. His expression worries me, because it tells me that I look as unbalanced as I feel. I'm about to do something incredibly stupid. My mouth opens, intending on instructing him to shut the door and send me back up to the club, but only a wisp of air breezes past my lips. The fact that my mouth refuses to allow the demand to escape should be a sign. But I ignore the sign and force the words to materialise. 'Could you shut the—'

I don't get the opportunity to complete my request. Becker appears from nowhere and prises my hand from the rail, pulling me from the lift. I yelp, stumbling along behind him, my skin burning from the heat of his touch soaking into my flesh. His fingers are entwined with mine, locked tightly, eliminating any potential of breaking free. He was upstairs one moment and downstairs the next. How? He's showing no signs of exertion from running down here, just signs of . . .

What?

A firm yank of my hand hauls me out of the nightclub, and a further string of aggressive but precise movements has me flying around until my back is against a wall. He pins me to the cold bricks with his front, not that the cold registers. The heat of his torso pressed to mine is too consuming. And so are those hazel eyes that are burning with such intensity, they threaten to melt his glasses. He releases my hand and rests his palms on the bricks on either side of my head, heaving long, deep breaths in my face. He's all coiled up.

And I realise.

He's pissed off. With me?

'You were going to go back into the club. You were going to go back to him,' he growls in my face, bringing me down to earth in the harshest possible way. He's livid, and I should be, too. But I'm too stunned to locate my spunk and rip him to shreds. So I remain where I am, nailed to the wall by his body as the sizzling of our combined heat begins to spark. 'Damn you, Eleanor,' Becker hisses. 'Just fucking leave.'

He's not just pissed off. He's fuming.

And with just a second to talk some sense into my tattered mind, I'm right there with him. Long gone are the sparks of pleasure. Acid is coursing through my veins.

How dare he?

My hands come up, my palms slap into his chest, and I throw my weight into shoving him back. 'You came down to check that I was going?' I yell, my anger unleashed. 'It's not pathetic enough that you told me to and I fucking did? You had to check?' The blood is rushing to my head, making me dizzy. Pathetic. That's what I am. Fucking pathetic.

'Yes, I fucking did,' Becker bellows, making me physically recoil. 'And you *were* on your way back up to the club. To him.'

Fucking hell. I'm vibrating with fury. 'You had no right to tell me to leave.'

'I know!'

'Then why?' I scream.

He swings away from me and pulls at his hair, roughing it up and looking up to the night sky. Then he shouts at the blackness, a long roar of frustration. 'For fuck's sake.' He's quickly facing me again, breathing heavily, his chest pulsing with each laboured inhale. I'm suddenly wary of his volatile reaction, and I have no clue what to do with it. This isn't simply anger. This is Becker out of control.

'I'll tell you why.' He sounds hostile, his eyes wild. 'Because there's only one reason you went for dinner with Brent Wilson.' He comes closer, and I push myself back into the wall some more. 'To piss me off. You don't want him. You want me.'

When I should be denying it, I say nothing, strengthening his claim. But he feels it, too. The conflict. *What if she's different?*

He wants me, and it's driving him mad. Making him angry. Frustrated. Why? Because he struggles with affection? Because I'm putting up a fight? Because all he knows is seducing women and having them lick his feet, beg him for it? Because I'm not falling all over myself to please him?

But I don't voice my questions, which leaves a long, difficult time with no words, just loud breathing.

When I can't watch Becker Hunt shaking with rage before me any longer, and my brain is tired out from trying to evaluate this situation, I push him away, peel my back from the wall, and start to walk away from him on shaky legs.

'Yes, go home,' he shouts after me, his words laced with fake conviction. I can hear his voice trembling. He's not fooling me, but I ignore his apparent uncertainty and keep up my pace. 'And don't be late for work.'

I clench my eyes closed, determined not to cave and retaliate. I need to stock up on self-control, locate the willpower I need to keep strong, whether his goading is weirdly playful, or deadly serious. Right now, he's deadly serious. I don't like either, but I'm missing the roguish, arsehole Becker, and I never dreamed I'd think that. The guy behind me seems unhinged. It's like he's winding me in, tempting me, and then pushing me away when I get too close. I can't fathom him at all. He's mercurial, not a maverick.

Never in my life has my mobile ringtone been such a delight to hear. I don't care who it is, but their timing is impeccable. I grab it and connect the call. 'Hello.' My greeting is clearly strained as I continue marching on my way.

'Eleanor?'

The familiar voice brings my dogged marching to a halt. 'Brent?' I only manage a surprised wheeze of his name.

'Are you okay?' He sounds genuinely concerned, but then I remember the game. 'Where are you?'

'On my way home.'

'On your own?'

'Yes, on my own.' And it's going to stay that way. 'Just grabbing a cab.'

'You'll do no such thing. Stay where you are. I'll come and get you.'

'No, Brent,' I argue quickly. The last thing I need is Brent adding another dimension to this spiky mix. 'I can get myself—' I don't get to finish. Because my hand is suddenly missing my phone. 'What the hell?' I shout, turning fast and coming face to face with Becker. He doesn't look any less pissed off, which only serves to heighten my own anger. 'What are you doing?' I make a grab for my phone, missing by a mile when he dodges my swiping hand. 'Give me my fucking phone, Becker.'

'Dream on, princess,' he snipes, cutting the call with the filthiest look on his face.

'Don't call me princess.'

He scoffs and lifts his arm high, a threatening look on his face. His intentions are clear.

'Don't you dare.'

Oh, he dares. His lip curls and his arm comes down fast, releasing my phone and slamming it into the ground. It smashes to smithereens, and pieces of my dead mobile dance around at my feet. *What the fuck?* But as if he isn't happy enough that he's destroyed my phone, he starts kicking the pieces all over the place, shouting and grunting as he does.

I watch with wide eyes and my mouth sealed firmly closed while Becker has a physical punch-up with my helpless mobile phone. *Fuck.* How am I meant to survive without my phone? In bloody London. Is it Becker Hunt's ambition to completely ruin my life?

I'm not sure how long I stand staring at the scattered pieces – maybe a minute, maybe ten – but when he seems to be done and is puffing and panting from his exertion, I bring my eyes up to confront him. His handsome face is contorted with rage, though I detect a slight wrinkle of his brow, indicating confusion. He's shocked by his actions, too.

'Why did you even give me the job?' I ask.

'I was enjoying the foreplay,' he growls without hesitation.

I'm speechless.

Almost.

'I quit,' I scream, kicking away a chunk of plastic near my feet before pivoting on my heels and storming off.

'Good,' Becker yells, the word punching into my back like a boulder. My poor mind is rampant with anger, too many emotions stirring, and before I can stop myself, I swing around to attack him with some home truths and hateful words. I've got nothing to lose now. As far as I'm concerned, he isn't my employer any more. I just quit.

Yet when I open my mouth, no scathing words materialise, the insults getting caught behind the lump in my throat. His dishevelled magnificence hits me in the forehead like a bullet, leaving me standing like a useless lump of body parts before him. I'm . . . empty.

I came to London to escape the constant feeling of weakness that dogged me. I wanted to take charge, start fresh, discover a stronger me. I wanted desperately to chase my dreams, to live the life I choose, not the one dictated by my shitty circumstances. I've battled my conscience too long to get to this point in my life. This man currently staring me down, looking at me with a mixture of loathing and wariness, was a sure-fire way to fuck it all up. And he has. And worse still, I let him.

Closing my eyes and taking a deep breath, I shake my head a little, backing away, so disappointed in myself. I willingly let him drag me into his stupid mind games. I willingly let this happen.

'Where are you going?' he snaps, but I ignore him, turning and walking away with no urgency. 'Eleanor.'

'Home,' I call over my shoulder, cool and collected.

I hear the even pound of his shoes beating the pavement behind me. 'How?'

'Cab.' Just as I utter the word, a black Bentley pulls up to the kerb and the window slowly rolls down.

Brent.

'You shouldn't be wandering the streets this late at night, Eleanor,' he says, leaning over to the passenger door and pushing it open. 'Get in.'

I stall for a moment and look over my shoulder. Becker has come to a stop a few paces behind me, his face twisting, his nostrils flaring dangerously. I don't want to aggravate him further, but right now my options are limited. I can get in the car with Brent Wilson and risk pissing Becker off even more – if that's possible – or I can decline Brent's offer, hang around for a cab with no phone, and risk getting caught up in another stupid row with my boss. I correct myself. *Ex*-boss.

It's an easy decision.

I get in the car.

He doesn't try to stop me, and I hate myself for feeling hurt by Becker's lack of intervention. My head is fucked.

I pull on my belt and centre my attention forward as Brent pulls away. The wing mirror catches my eye and I see the reflection of a man walking on heavy feet in the middle of the road behind us. His stance is wide and he's getting smaller in the distance, until we round a corner and I lose sight of Becker watching me leave him.

Chapter 14

The atmosphere is thick with awkward vibes on the drive home. At least, it is for me. Brent seems oblivious as he rambles on about . . . I don't know what. All I seem to be able to focus on is the image of Becker as we drove away.

'At the risk of it sounding cheesy, can I come up for coffee?'

Brent's question makes every muscle in my body tense. I should have anticipated this when I accepted his ride. Of course there's an ulterior motive. And why the hell is he being so indifferent to the fact that he just whisked me away like a knight in shining armour from a man who he knows, a rival? They didn't even acknowledge each other. Nothing. I believe Brent is up one point to Becker.

I smile as I unclip my belt and open the door. I have no intention of seeing him again, just like I have no intention of seeing Becker. It shouldn't be difficult. I'm not contactable now, after Becker had fisticuffs with my phone. Plus, I was crafty – or wise – and asked Brent to drop me off around the corner from my flat, therefore eliminating the chances of him turning up when he can't contact me on my number.

Both of them, gone.

'No coffee,' I say assertively. *But I'll happily give you a slap.* 'Thanks for the lift.'

He smiles and starts to inch forward. Oh shit. He's moving in for a kiss? How thick is this man's skin?

I dive out of the car urgently and clumsily. 'Goodnight,' I squeak, slamming the door with a bit too much force.

The window comes down instantly, Brent leaning across the car, almost laughing. *Yes, this whole situation is rather hilarious, I agree.* 'I have a meeting with Hunt tomorrow. Pop by and say hello?'

He does? They just totally ignored each other. Whatever. I won't be there, and I no longer care. Brent doesn't need to know that I don't work for Becker Hunt any more. He'll find out soon enough. 'Maybe.' I strain a smile as I back away, and he pulls off promptly. I sag in exhaustion, wondering how I got myself into this diabolical situation.

I laugh to myself as I make my way down the street. Because I'm stupid, that's how. I thought I could take on Becker Hunt and all he threw at me. But I can't. I have no idea how to handle him.

I walk slowly down the road with the weight of the world on my shoulders, and when I take the corner into my street, the sight of the door to my building fills me with comfort. I'm already picturing stripping down and tucking myself up in bed with a cup of tea. The thought makes me smile, but it's soon wiped from my face when the roar of a car engine has me jumping out of my skin, and then almost diving into a hedge to hide when I clock where the loud sound is coming from.

A car.

Brent's car. He came back?

'Oh shit,' I whisper, keeping myself concealed in the shadows. 'Shit, shit, shit.' I remain deathly still while I watch his car cruise past.

'He's gone, princess.' Becker's even tone snaps my spine into shape, but I don't swing around startled. I'm too busy trying to figure out why the hell he's here.

There are a few moments' silence; him waiting for me to react, and me slowly getting more and more worked up. It's like a natural reaction to him, and in this moment, I realise it's my fault. Not Becker's. Most of the blame lies with me, because

I can't control myself when I'm around him. My temper, my irritation . . . my desire. And that's why I'm in this mess.

It's like an epiphany. My body is buzzing in response to his closeness, and no amount of willpower and sensibility seems to be able to dull it. And that makes me angry.

My feet kick into action, and I start striding away from him. No looking back. No engaging. No show of emotion – anger or anything else. *Walk away. Don't even think about why he's here.* Why is he here? To continue with our row? To see if I invited Brent in?

My fists clench tightly, and I find myself flexing life back into them when I reach for my keys. I don't even have to check to see if he's following me. I can feel him close behind, my back tingling in response to his stare nailed to me. Or did he come here to violate me in the most delicious way imaginable? My previous questions are suddenly forgotten when my final question sits heavily at the front of my mind, demanding an answer.

'Why did you get in the car with him?' he asks curtly. 'To piss me off? Because it worked.'

My fumbling hands falter slightly but soon fly into action again, locating my key and putting it into the lock. I'm not answering him, not only because I don't owe him an explanation or have nothing to say – I have plenty to say, like asking why the fuck he destroyed my phone and paraded that woman in front of me – but also because I need to remove myself from this situation. My time is worth more than this ridiculous game. *I* am worth more.

'Eleanor, answer me.' Becker's voice has taken on an edge of impatience and sternness, which stirs unsettling feelings within. The key turns, and I stumble into the lobby of my building. 'Answer my fucking question, woman,' he growls as I push the door closed, getting a glimpse of his face. There's aggravation written all over it. *Woman?* Oh, he's going the right way about tipping me over the edge. He always does, whether it's the edge of lust or insanity. I'm struggling to fathom which is most rampant within me now. What I do know, though, is that neither is safe.

The space between the door and frame shrinks and his face vanishes, but just when I begin to feel safe and relieved to be away from him, a weight presses against the other side of the door. Instinct has me pushing too, fighting the force coming from the other side. He doesn't speak. I don't speak. There are no sounds, not even heavy breathing, as we wrestle against each other to win – me to keep him out, Becker to get in. But while my efforts are great, I realise his aren't, and it's only a few moments before I comprehend something: he's holding back. There's no way my strength could equal his. He could push this door open with a flick of his finger, so why the bloody hell isn't he? Is it because he fears what might happen if he does?

'Fuck off, Becker,' I yell, panting as we continue with our ridiculous wrestling match.

'No.' His answer is short and sharp as he continues to fight me, but there's still no exertion from his side.

He's not trying to get in.

What's his game?

I don't know, but I continue to push against him, now using my shoulder instead of my palms. 'Let me close the door.'

'No.'

'What game are you playing, Becker?' I shout. 'We both know you could get in.'

'I don't want to.' He's hissing the words past clenched teeth, and I frown.

'Then what the hell are you doing fighting with me?'

He shoves hard, forcing me to throw some more effort into keeping him out. 'I don't want to force my way in,' he says in a snarl. 'I want you to surrender.'

'Not a chance.' I snort, disgusted. Hell will freeze over before I let him past this door. Surrender? Never. Not this time. The torrent of emotions I've undergone since I caved into my want has been unbearable. I'm not fuelling it.

Another jar of the wood has my heels digging in further. Literally.

'Please, Eleanor.'

I pull up but hold position, the begging in his tone settling deep. It's a total turnabout from the hissing and spitting of a moment ago. 'What?'

'Surrender.'

'Why?' The one-word question is simple and falls past my lips without thought. I want to know, however dangerous the answer might be.

The door is thrust again in temper. 'Because I fucking want you,' he shouts. 'And the moment you release this door, I'm having you, Eleanor. Every fucking bit of you. I'm not forcing my way in. You'll let me in, because you want me just as badly.'

I gulp, my muscles seizing and holding the door. *I'm not forcing my way in. Fuck . . .*

'Let me in,' he breathes.

Let me in. My body comes to life, my blood singing in my veins. He wants me to *let* him in. Clarity has me releasing the door and stepping back, inviting him in, *letting* him in, but he doesn't fall over the threshold like I expect. The door remains closed, me standing on one side, Becker on the other. My breathing is all over the place now, my skin damp with sweat, my cheeks flushed as I stare at the wood. Then he pushes the door and it slowly opens, and there he is. Mr Mercurial.

Dishevelled but gorgeous.

Angry but gorgeous.

Dangerous but gorgeous.

Our eyes lock, and my heart wedges itself in my throat as Becker reaches up and removes his glasses, tucking them into his pocket. 'Invite me in,' he murmurs, blinking slowly, his eyes lazy and angelic.

My lips part, and I step back a few paces.

'I want to hear it, Eleanor. I want to hear you tell me you want this.'

Oh my God, what am I doing? 'I want it.'

He's fast, slamming the door behind him and stalking towards me, purpose seeping from every delicious piece of him. I don't move, but let him tackle me and push me against the wall. He's pressed into me everywhere, looking down at me, his hand on my nape to hold me in place.

He thrusts his knee between my thighs, encouraging me to spread. Which I do – no thought, no hesitation. He brings his lips close to mine, and my gaze flicks between them and his burning hazel eyes. 'Say it again,' he demands.

I take a deep inhale of air and lift my eyes from his mouth, up his perfect nose to his stunning eyes. 'I want it,' I repeat on a wisp of lusty air.

The grin that slowly creeps on to his face is wicked and victorious. 'Say please.'

I've lost my mind. 'Please,' I whisper.

He attacks me full force, his mouth crashing to mine and instantly consuming me. My hair is tangled roughly in his grasp, his tongue plunging deeply. He's frantic in his approach, rough and wild, his free hand finding my thigh and squeezing hard. There's no room in my desire-drenched mind for hesitancy or second thoughts. Right now, under his demanding attention, I'm his to do with as he pleases. I'm lost. My mind has abandoned me. His lips meld with mine, his tongue exploring my mouth, it's all reminding me of the kiss we shared in the kitchen at The Haven earlier today, except this time I know beyond doubt nothing will stop him. The all-consuming, built-up frustration is going to be sated in the best possible way. My internal muscles are already clenching in anticipation. I'm about to be violated in the most delicious way imaginable, and I have no willpower or strength remaining to fight it.

A small whimper of pleasure slips past my lips when his touch slides higher up my thigh and cups me over my knickers. 'Shut the fuck up, Eleanor,' he growls into my mouth, again reminding me of our kitchen encounter. The potential of him expecting me to keep quiet through what is about to happen hits me hard, though I don't voice my concern. I'm unable to anyway, because his palm has replaced his lips over my mouth and serious eyes are boring into me. 'I only want to hear your pleasure when I say so. Got it?'

I'm reluctant to agree, but I find myself nodding anyway. What on earth have I just let myself in for? We're not even naked and I'm already set to scream in ecstasy. Good God, this could be torturous. Then his finger slips past the seam of my knickers and that *could be* turns into a *definitely*. My jaw tightens, and I swallow hard, closing my eyes and praying silently to God. His hot touch teases my flesh for an eternity, like he's testing me, seeing if I can fulfil my agreement to keep quiet. It's looking doubtful, but I'm determined to try.

'Good girl,' he whispers, his breath tickling my ear as he moves in closer, his fingertip lightly rounding my clitoris painfully slowly. My hands are aching from the harsh grip I have of his shoulders, the feel of lean muscle beneath spiking flashbacks of his chest. 'You feel good, princess. So fucking good.' He slips his finger out of my knickers, his words and action prompting my eyes to open. There's still evidence of that salacious smirk as he brings his finger up and removes his palm from my mouth. 'Open.'

My lips part and he slips his finger into my mouth, raising his eyebrows in a silent instruction that I catch immediately. But he voices his wish anyway.

'Suck.'

I close my mouth and do as I'm bid, relishing the carnal want in his eyes as he concentrates on my tongue lapping slowly at his finger. His head tilts thoughtfully, then he slowly brings his eyes back to mine, withdrawing his finger lazily. 'On a scale of one to ten,' he murmurs, low and husky, dipping and nibbling at my bottom lip delicately, 'how turned on are you right now, princess?'

The back of my head meets the wall, surprised by his question, even if it's dead easy to answer. 'Ten.' I'm not stroking his ego. I'm pulsing everywhere, ready to sacrifice anything to maintain this feeling of ecstasy. I'm not stunned by my admission. I know Becker Hunt is bad news, but right now he's making me feel too good to question what I'm getting myself into.

A devilish grin appears, making his boyish good looks more boyish, and his hand comes up to cup my cheek, his head shaking mildly. 'Trust me, princess.' He plants a chaste kiss on my lips, then rests his forehead on mine. 'You're not even at a one on the pleasure scale yet.'

Now, I'm stunned, and my wide eyes show it. 'What?' A one? The pleasure scale? No, I'm at a ten. He needs to trust me on that.

'I'm about to pleasure you like you've never been pleasured before.' He pulls me from the wall and hoists me up his body, my legs automatically spreading and wrapping around his waist. He's looking up at me, his hazel eyes darkening as he starts to carry me up the stairs.

'Cocky.' I have to stop myself from laughing at his arrogance. I can't prevent my thighs from clenching, though. His conceitedness shouldn't be attractive, but as I expect his declaration to be 100 per cent correct, it's hard not to be totally bewitched by him.

'But true,' he adds, coming to a stop at my front door. 'Down.' He pushes my legs from his body and takes my purse from me, helping himself to the keys in my hands. I give them up willingly, freezing when he moves in, pushing his front into mine. He opens the door over my shoulder, putting his mouth to my ear and blowing softly. 'Get inside.' Every nerve ending explodes, and I wobble on my heels.

I can't move. My situation has just hit me hard, and I can't figure out why I'm not stopping this. He's a modern-day Casanova – I've seen the proof and had it confirmed by his dear old grandad and Mrs Potts. He drives me wild, and not always in the best way. He's in therapy, for crying out loud, and could possibly put me in therapy too. He destroyed my fucking phone in a tantrum. He has unhealthy relationships with women, unhealthy ways of dealing with his parents' deaths. He's going to fuck me. Nothing more. No feelings. No affection. I'm going to be another conquest, another woman who's about to be charmed into bed by him. I've lost all self-respect. I must have. So why my feet are moving, stepping back into my tiny apartment, is beyond me. I've lost my fucking mind.

The door closes, and Becker relaxes against the wood, looking me up and down, taking his time about it too. My condition is plain to see. I'm shifting from one heel to the other, my hands twitching by my sides, and my mouth is open slightly to grab valuable oxygen. Oh my days, he looks poised, ready to pounce. 'Take off your dress, Eleanor.' He drops my things to the floor.

I have no idea where my next words come from. Maybe my own ego is trying to retain a little control. Or maybe I'm just plain stupid. 'Say please.'

The moment his eyes find mine, I realise I'm the latter. They're laced with a threat I wholeheartedly comprehend. 'Now.' He supports that threatening look with an equally threatening tone.

I'm not just stupid. I'm *very* stupid. 'Say. Please.' I spell it out boldly, and quite bravely, too. If I'm going to do this, I'm going to have *some* control. It'll make me feel better about being so completely and utterly foolish.

Becker steps forward, shaking his head, watching me closely. 'You want me to say please?'

I nod.

He chuckles quietly, glancing away as he pinches the bridge of his nose, squeezing his eyes closed. He seems amused, but that doesn't stop me from being on my guard. I recognise power when I see it, despite having an unreasonable desire to test it.

He growls, reaching forward quickly, and rips my dress from my body in one fast yank. It splits straight down the middle, and I suck in a shocked shot of air, jumping back from Becker, who's currently screwing up the two pieces of my dress. 'Abra-fucking-cadabra.' He smiles at me.

'Oh my God,' I gasp, my naked skin warming under his scrutiny.

'I don't say please, princess.'

'Yes, you do,' I laugh. 'You pleaded with me to let you in. You pretty much *begged* me to let you have me.'

His smile falls away fast, being replaced with confusion. I can see him mentally rewinding back a few minutes, trying to recall my claim. He can't possibly deny it, and if he does then I'll gladly jog his memory with a complete run-through of how he ended up in my apartment. He wants me. And he basically begged. He's not taking that away from me. This isn't only what *I* desperately want.

His brow wrinkling actually fills me with relief. He remembers. 'You'll pay for that.'

'Excuse me?' I laugh, my hands coming up to cover my chest. 'For making you beg?'

'Yes. Drop the hands.'

'Say please,' I retort through a tight jaw, narrowing my eyes.

'Abra-fucking-cadabra,' he bellows, and for reasons unbeknown to me, my hands drop, and he charges at me. I inhale and brace myself, yelping when his body collides with mine and he throws me up on to his shoulder. This is just another part of our cat and mouse game, both our frustration and impatience making for a very fiery encounter – an encounter I know I'm going to enjoy more than I should.

Becker paces determinedly across the room and chucks me on to the bed, and my knickers are being tugged down my legs before I've gained my bearings, my body flipped over soon after so he can access the clasp of my bra. It's whipped from me as I gasp and squirm, anticipation ruining me, before he flips me on to my back again.

I blink my eyes open and brush my hair away. He's standing at the end of my bed, stance wide, hands by his sides, looking at me through his long lashes. He looks like something to be worshipped. God-like. Holy. A saint.

Without a word, he slowly reaches up and starts to unfasten the buttons of his shirt, one by one, slowly, never taking his eyes from mine. I watch, completely rapt, buzzing from the tips of my toes to the very top of my head. Then the heaviness in my tummy drops straight into my clitoris and begins to pulse slowly. The delicious sensation makes me fidget on the bed, yet my eyes remain on his hands working his shirt buttons until they're all undone and the white material is hanging open. My teeth bite harshly on my lip as I cast my gaze up to his face, finding him holding back a smile. I know what he's thinking. He's thinking I'm going to voice my impatience at any moment, but he's wrong. I can only see a sliver of his flesh right now, but I have a good memory. That chest has been imprinted on my brain since the moment I clapped eyes on it at The Haven when he and that woman fell out of his office, and *that* is what I'm seeing now . . . minus the woman.

'You're rather quiet, princess,' he says on a husky murmur, holding each side of his open shirt with steady hands.

I make sure I remain that way as I lie before him, naked as the day I was born and completely unbothered by it. His appreciative eyes, as they make sporadic trips up and down my body, leave no need for shyness. He likes what he sees, and while my thighs and arse might be a little on the curvy side, now isn't the time to admit to my body hang-ups.

It takes everything in me not to sigh when he finally shrugs his shirt off, every lean piece of his torso rolling methodically, making my greedy hands twitch, desperate to touch.

'Want to touch?' he asks, like he's read my mind.

'I'm happy with the view.' I smile when he laughs, moving my hands behind my head, all casual and settling in for the show. I want him to turn around and give me a glimpse of that gorgeous back and magnificent tattoo.

'I didn't say you could speak.' He takes his hands to his belt and yanks it open.

'Stop me,' I breathe, raising cocky eyebrows at him. I realise, given all the signs of Becker's sexual nature, I might regret my obstinacies, but my natural instinct is all I have, and I'm depending on it. And anyway, he's ignited this spirit. He can damn well deal with it.

He pulls his belt from the loopholes of his trousers and drops it to the floor. 'Was that a challenge?'

My lips press together. I should quit while I'm ahead. Impossible. 'Yes.'

'Oh, princess.' He kicks off his shoes and pushes his trousers down his thighs, leaving him in grey marl boxers with a thick white waistband. My sass is shot down in flames, and I blink, attempting to restrain my awe. I know I fail. 'I can sense your regret already.' He slips his hands into the waistband of his boxers and pushes them down just a little, set on making a meal of this, too. I stare at the hair peeking over the top of the waistband, mentally licking my lips. Regretful? Nope, can't say I am.

'Take them off, Becker,' I demand, looking up at him. 'Now.' I feel like I've waited an eternity for this.

He can't hide his surprise. 'Say—'

I jump up to my knees and yank them down his legs, leaving them falling to his ankles. 'Abra-fucking-cadabra.' I grab his neck and pull him to me, and our lips collide harshly. I fall to my back, taking Becker with me, and he doesn't try to stop me. Like me, he's instantly drunk on the raw chemistry exploding as a result of our bare flesh touching.

'Oh shit, you feel fucking amazing,' he rasps slowly, pushing me up the bed with the force of his kiss. My tongue is aching already, but I'm not stopping. Not for love nor money, not even for sanity – which is currently misplaced amid a torrent of indescribable lust and want. 'I'm in control,' he grunts, grappling to seize my hands, maintaining the frantic duelling of our tongues. 'Give me your fucking hands, Eleanor.'

'No,' I snap, dodging his grasp and plunging my fingers into his hair, relishing in the feel of his naked skin against mine.

'Fucking hell, give them to me.' He brings his knee up between my thighs, spreading me and resting his naked body between them. The feel of him, solid and ready, only heightens my desire to fight him. I writhe, ensuring our mouths remain locked tightly together, my tongue dancing madly as our kiss becomes more and more feverish, but my tactical wriggling only causes more friction. It makes me crazy, almost breaks me in two, and I cry out.

My hands are claimed and roughly shoved above my head. He has me where he wants me. I'm captured – at his mercy, puffing and panting – my hair a tangled mess in my face. My lips are released and his face falls into my neck, his breathing laboured and erratic against my hot skin, matching mine. We've not even reached penetrative sex and we're both already exhausted, our naked wrestling match taking too much out of us, and for what purpose? I've drained myself, hindered my energy levels in a pointless attempt to gain the upper hand.

'Well, princess,' he pants, sucking on my neck, drawing my flesh into his mouth and circling his tongue. My head drops to the side, pushing into his face, trying to halt the wonderful sensations before I scream my pleasure-induced agony. 'That's foreplay out of the way.' He bites my neck, and my spine bows violently when he pushes his groin firmly into me. 'Time to violate you.'

I don't have time to reply or fight him. Or the willpower, for that matter. He flips me over on to my tummy, shifting to keep his hold of my hands above my head, then spreads himself over me. My cheek is squashed into the pillow, my eyes trying to find something to focus on now I don't have Becker's mouth's attention to relish in. The feel of his solid chest compressed against my back warms me through. Then his hot breath at my ear has me drinking in air and attempting to calm my breathing.

'Every time you've pissed me off,' he whispers seductively, pushing one of my legs out a little, exposing my throbbing core, 'I've wanted to punish you so fucking hard.'

'How have I pissed you off?' I pant.

'By making me want you so fucking much.' My hands are suddenly held in one of his, giving him one spare. I clench my eyes shut when I comprehend exactly what he plans on doing with it.

Imagine how red your cheeks will be when I'm through with you.

But nothing prepares me for the force he puts behind it. His palm comes down and delivers a stinger of a slap to my arse, stealing my breath. 'Fucking hell, Becker.'

'Oh, yeah, princess.' His touch is soft now, massaging the burning pain on my bottom, stroking delicately, lovingly. 'I've lost count of the amount of times you've pissed me off.' His hand leaves my right cheek, and though I can't see, I painfully accept that it's getting ready to connect harshly with my backside again. Yet something unreasonably stubborn prevents me from pleading with him to stop. I take a deep breath and turn my face into the pillow, just in time for his belter of a thwack. My body jolts, my teeth clamp down on the material of my pillow as my muffled scream rings in my ears. I only vaguely register my immense gratitude that he chose my left side this time. But now both cheeks are burning, probably glowing bright red, and I'm sweating, concentrating on stabilising my breathing while Becker rubs some life back into my arse. We're both heaving, our bodies sweating, except where my breathlessness is a mixture of exhaustion *and* craving, I know Becker's is simply raw desire. He has plenty of energy, and it's beginning to scare the crap out of me. What have I got myself into? 'Are you sore, princess?'

'Yes,' I wheeze, seeing no point in denying it, and knowing he gets a sick thrill from having it confirmed. The bastard.

He keeps his hold on me and inches down my back, dragging his lips across my skin as he goes, sending me delirious, my eyes rolling in my head as I moan and groan and twitch and whimper. 'You really aren't getting the hang of this silence business, are you?'

I moan again in reply and hear him chuckle. I don't take his amusement as acceptance of my defiance, or my inability to shut the hell up. He'll find a way to put me in my place, but he's stark raving mad if he expects a woman to keep quiet when he's inflicting this kind of pleasure and pain on them. And if there is any woman in existence who has, then I'd like to meet her and shake her hand. Or rip her head off.

His lips reach my bum, and he hums in approval, rubbing his palm gently across the two peaks. 'Perfect,' he says, dropping a light kiss on each before crawling back up my body and dropping his mouth to my ear again. 'Now that's the kind of red I wanted to see. Your arse carries rouge as well as your hair. Fucking beautiful.'

'Make the most of it.' I just can't help myself.

He bites my ear, and I feel him smile against it. 'Still stinging?'

I close my eyes and nod, praying he's through with the spanking session. 'Probably for another week.' Could possibly be a year. It's on fire.

I hear the rip of a packet, and I see him in my mind's eye pulling a condom from the foil with his teeth. His sharp inhale makes me want to spin over and watch him sheathe himself, but his hold on me is solid. I'm going nowhere until Becker lets me.

'Do you know how long I've wanted this?' His fingertip travels the crease of my bum, down to the apex of my thighs. I hold my breath as his touch slips easily across my opening. And it's no wonder. I'm dripping wet. He's just slapped me stupid. I should be 100 per cent fucked off, but I'm ashamed to admit I'm only mildly miffed. The majority of me is begging for all he has to give.

'What's taken you so long?' I push the question past my fitful breaths.

'A fucking conscience I never knew I had.' He surprises me with his answer as he slowly pushes two fingers into me, purposely breathing deeply in my ear. 'I need to make you sore here, too.'

My body bucks beneath him and every internal muscle I possess grabs on tightly, never wanting to let go.

'Every time you talk about work, about my treasure, my cock turns to stone.' He thrusts deeper with his fingers, and I whimper. 'Every time I see you lost in what you love, my fucking dead heart kicks a little.' Another hard thrust, one that blanks my mind from reading too much into that statement.

'Becker.'

'You want me, Eleanor? Do you want me buried inside of you, fucking you hard until you beg me to stop?'

'I'll never tell you to stop.'

'I hope you fucking don't.' He moves fast, pulling his fingers free and rolling his hips, slamming home on a guttural yell. 'Holy shit!'

A choked scream bursts past my lips, filling the room, the force he's adopting almost too much to handle so suddenly. There's no gently breaking me in. Oh no, he's done with foreplay.

With my hands now free, I can hold something for support, and I do. My sheets get a punishing grip and a few angry yanks. He grabs my hair and fists it, drawing his groin slowly back until he's hovering over my entrance, his hips raised. 'I'd ask if you're ready, but I'm not in an accommodating mood.'

'Fuck you,' I yell, raising my backside, egging the fucker on.

'Oh, fighting talk.' He slams forward, hitting me deeply and grinding super-slowly, ensuring I get to feel every inch of his cock stroking my passage. 'You're a bad girl, Eleanor.'

Bang!

'Arhhhhhhh.'

'A bad, bad girl. You made me want you. You made me want you until it drove me fucking mad.' He pulls at my hips. 'Up.'

My movements are sluggish as I literally drag myself on to my hands and knees, moaning in despair when his cock slides free, stimulating every nerve ending I have, making me buzz and tense and twitch and shake. I'm experiencing too many sensations. I can't deal with it.

'Congratulations.' He's mocking me. 'You managed to fulfil a request without too much fuss.'

'Don't get used to it.' I feel his fingers dig into my hips, getting a good grip, and then he levels up and launches into action, taking me by surprise, thundering forward on a deafening roar. Every breath I have is punched from my lungs under his force. And I'm not given the opportunity to get it back. He finds his pace quickly and powers on, over and over, hitting me to depths beyond my comprehension, and though the twinges of pain are there, there is also a ton of unspeakable pleasure backing it up, clouding it. My arms stiffen and brace into the mattress, my arse flying back continuously and smashing against his groin, each hit delivered with as much determination and passion as the last, if not more. And with each thrust comes a shout from Becker or a scream from me. We're loud. Our voices. Our bodies. Sweat pours from my forehead, drips plummeting to the bed, my hair whipping from side to side, my vision becoming hazy.

I can feel the blood rushing to the tip of my clitoris, an orgasm looming, teasing me as it shows signs of bursting free, before it stubbornly retreats, denying me the opportunity to grab hold of it. My mind is making the most of this. It's telling my hasty body to slow down, to relish the moment.

'I'm going to come,' Becker declares, panting each word behind me.

I panic. 'No.'

'Fuck, Eleanor, I can't hold off.'

'Just wait.'

He yells, flexing his fingers, driving on. 'Tell me when.'

I concentrate hard, feeling the heaviness descending again, and this time I won't allow it to retreat. No way. I'm not ending this until I have the satisfaction of a mind-bending orgasm. I can feel it. It's coming. I've waited too long for this.

'Eleanor, when?'

'Soon,' I breathe, ramming my backside on to him.

'Oh Jesus, woman, you're fucking killing me. Why the fuck am I listening to you?'

'When,' I scream, grabbing hold of my climax and letting it hijack every piece of me. I zone out, start to vibrate, and I can dimly hear Becker behind me moaning his release, his pace slowing, his groin rolling firmly into me, milking us both dry of pleasure.

'Oh my fucking God.' He collapses behind me, forcing me to fall to my front on the bed, caging me in with his solid, sweaty body. Our gasps for breath fill my flat as he throbs inside of me, my internal wall instinctively constricting and releasing around him. 'Fuck, that feels good,' he wheezes into my hair, and I lamely nod my head in agreement, allowing my heavy lids to close. I'm sated and content. Too content, even more so when he bites into my shoulder before tracing his lips across the top of my back to the middle, his hands dragging up my arms until they find mine. He laces his fingers through mine and squeezes gently, then gives me one last deep swivel of his hips before lazily rolling off me, falling to his back on a deep sigh. Now I know his lovely face is within my sights, my eyes open willingly and with little effort. They're delighted by what they see – a naked Becker, panting up at the ceiling, hair damp, palm resting on his stomach, skin glistening. I push myself over on to my back and match his pose, my front thankful for the blast of cool air.

His head drops heavily to the side to look at me. And we stare. And then he smiles. And I smile right back. 'It was inevitable,' he sighs, returning his focus to the ceiling.

'Becker . . .'

'Shhhh.' His index finger comes up to his mouth and shushes me. It's sexy as hell, even as a warning, but I still ignore it.

'A conscience you thought you never had?' I murmur.

His head falls to the side again. 'Dorothy and Gramps love having you around,' he says quietly. 'I've been told not to fuck it up. You know that.' He laughs sardonically under his breath as he removes the condom and leans over to drop it in the bin beside my bed. 'I fucking tried.'

'You didn't try very—'

'Shhhh.' That finger rests sexily on his lips again, interrupting me. 'Trust me, I did.' His eyes fall to mine, soft but doubtful, as he reaches for me and encourages me on to my side, facing away from him. I go with ease until he's curled around me. 'Good fucking night, princess.' He kisses my neck and constricts his arms, tugging me in closer.

Spooning. Isn't this a little too far?

I don't know the answer to that, but I do know it's nice. Becker Hunt is good at spooning, and my eyes quickly become heavy. 'Good night, beast.'

I drift off with every inch of his front spread across my back.

Chapter 15

I bolt upright in my bed, sweating and disorientated, my heart thundering. My eyes are darting around my flat. 'Becker.' His name leaves my lips on a rush of air before my brain has engaged, and my eyes fall to the mass of sheets tangled around my naked body. On closer inspection, I see certain sections are folded neatly under here and there. Like someone has tucked me in.

Casting my gaze to my right, I find an empty space beside me and, ridiculously, my heart sinks. He's gone. Of course he's gone. What did I expect? To wake with him lovingly wrapped around me? I shake my head, angry with my stray, unreasonable thoughts.

My head falls into my hands in despair and shame. We just fucked. Nothing more. That was raw, carnal screwing, rough and dirty, and that's a good thing. We both had an itch to scratch. Done. I'm no different from the other women at all. I need to see it as a leaving present from my boss, because, essentially, that's exactly what it was. I'm no longer an employee, therefore fair game. There's only a little piece of me that's sorry at this particular moment in time, where I'm deliciously sore between my thighs. Tomorrow is another day, though. Tomorrow, I am jobless, and any remote possibility or hope I had of walking back into The Haven to resume my duties have been colossally ruined in the haze of a mind-blowing orgasm . . . delivered by a hunk of a man who proved just too irresistible. I made my choice. And I'm living with it.

My muscles are just about to loosen and send me plummeting back to the mattress when a collection of loud bangs and clatters freezes them into position again. My spine uncurls, my brain now fully awake and listening carefully for the source of the noise.

'Eleanor.' My name is shrieked, and then what I can only describe as something that sounds like a battering ram hits my door. 'Eleanor!'

I'm up in a flash and grabbing my dressing gown from the couch as I hotfoot it to the door. The wood visibly vibrates before my eyes with all the banging, and when I swing it open, Lucy falls into my arms. 'Oh thank God,' she cries, throwing her arms around me. 'I thought you were dead.'

'What?' I hold her up, trying to wrestle her into a steady standing position.

'I've been calling you since you left the club. You were supposed to text me to let me know you were bloody home.' She pulls back, and I finally get a good look at her. She looks surprisingly sober in comparison to the last time I saw her.

'What time is it?' I ask.

'Two in the morning. Where's your phone?' She marches past me in a huff, leaving me to follow her path, as guilt creeps up on me.

'I think I must have left it in the taxi.' I wince as the night's events storm into my mind in vivid detail, all of it – the row with Becker, the massacre of my phone, the ride home with Brent ... the filthy sex. 'I'm sorry.' There's just enough room amid my remorse to feel bad for Lucy's worry.

She swings around, all dramatic, and throws her hands into the air. 'I was so worr—' Her mouth snaps shut, her attention cemented to the floor, and wondering what's caught her sharp interest, my eyes drop to the floor, too. My face begins to burn as her accusing finger points to the offending object and her stunned eyes land on my flaming face. 'What's that?' she asks, her head tilting.

'Nothing.' I shoot over and swipe my dress from the floor, except my dress isn't safely in my grasp. At least, not all of it. Half of it is still puddled loud and proud by my feet, laughing at me.

Lucy moves fast, crouching down to pick up the ragged material, then flaps it out as she stands again, holding it up in front of her, hiding what I know will be an interested face. Too many awkward seconds pass before she slowly lowers my tattered dress and hits me with reproachful blue eyes.

'You mean to say that while I've been repeatedly calling you and racing across town to get home and make sure you're safe, you've been getting some action?'

'No, I—' My feet start moving back, away from Lucy's threatening stance. Many lame excuses start to jump into my fraught mind. 'I caught my dress on the railings outside.' And I choose the lamest.

'Eleanor,' she yells, making me flinch. 'I've just cast aside a hot bloke to come looking for you.'

'I'm sorry.' I throw the half of my dress I'm still holding to the ground in a temper. 'I didn't plan it. He followed me home.'

'Who did?' She looks at me with narrowed eyes, making me inwardly squirm.

'My boss,' I mumble moodily under my breath.

Any hope I had of forgetting about everything that's happened has just been blown away with the shocked breath currently gushing from Lucy's mouth. 'Him?'

'Or ex-boss,' I correct myself quickly. 'I quit.'

'Oh, this is fucking perfect.' She mimics my actions and throws her half of my dress to the ground, too, although hers lands with much more force. She's really pissed off. 'I can't talk to you right now.' She storms past me, and I sigh, thinking she's being ridiculously melodramatic, but telling her so probably won't help my cause. So, I remain with my mouth zipped safely shut and watch her walk across the corridor to her own flat. The key is slipped into the lock, the door pushed viciously open, but before it gets slammed, she turns and raises her chin in the air, looking me up and down. I brace myself for a scornful attack. 'Did he really rip off your dress?'

My lips press together, and I nod, that regret creeping back up on me. 'It's one of my favourites as well.'

'And you quit?'

I nod again.

'I want to hear all about it tomorrow,' she sniffs, and then slams the door, leaving me alone again. But now, I'm wide awake and dreading tomorrow more than ever. Silent torture would be bad enough. Having to give Lucy a blow-by-blow account of my reckless encounter with Becker Hunt makes me want to leave London immediately.

Chapter 16

I avoid my inbox like the plague when I start my laptop the following morning, concentrating on ordering a new phone to be delivered tomorrow before trawling the job sites for anything remotely appealing as I spoon cornflakes into my mouth. It's nine, I'm still in my PJs, and Lucy has made a brief appearance to tell me I'm meeting her for lunch to provide *every* detail. She looked especially lovely today, and it doesn't require a genius to figure out why. I'm keen to hear what goes down at Lucy's place of work this morning with Mark, but I'm not so eager to share the events that resulted in me spending all morning searching for another job.

My eyes flit across my unmade bed, and then to my door where he stood, poised and ready to jump me – which he did like an animal. I relax back on the couch, my spoon held limply in my hand as my mind wanders. I can still feel him between my thighs, that soreness he promised, making it impossible to forget about my mistake. Then I shift on the couch and wince, the tenderness of my bottom adding to my memories. With all these physical reminders, I anticipate it to be a good week before I can make any serious effort to move on, and an irrational part on me wonders whether that was his intention. I wouldn't put it past him. Becker Hunt likes to leave a lasting impression.

Before I can fall too deeply into the whys and wherefores, I sit up straight and return my attention to my laptop, clicking through page after page of jobs, seeing nothing that even remotely fits the bill, and after I've lapped the same pages for the third time, I finally give in to my fate and click on an advert for a waitress position. 'It's just for the time being,' I tell myself, scanning the ad for a telephone number. I find it and go to stand, set on calling before I talk myself out of it, but then I remember . . . I have no phone. Because that bastard destroyed it. 'Shit.' I then spot an email address on the ad. This should be a simple task, an easy alternative to calling, but the thought of loading my email account stalls me. There could be all kinds of monsters from my past lingering there. Could be. There might not be.

I open my inbox. I shouldn't have. Three emails are staring at me, two from David, and one from Amy Petitt. My ex-boyfriend and my ex-best friend. *Fuckers.* I hover over the open icon, my mind whizzing with what these emails could possibly say. It'll be nothing I haven't already heard or read. They'll be full of apologies and excuses. But what do either of them hope to gain? Peace? Forgiveness? And does David seriously think I'd take him back?

I grab the screen of my laptop and slam it shut. Whatever. I'm not interested. I don't need their apologies, and I'm certainly not interested in easing their guilt for them, or getting back with David.

Any person who can call themselves a friend or boyfriend and cheat is not someone I want in my life. *I deserve more.* I'm no longer desperate for morsels of love. What's done is done.

My mental annihilation of David and Amy is cut short when a light knock at my door distracts me, and I jump up, not giving too much thought to who it could be.

Until I swing it open, and I'm confronted with Becker Hunt.

My blank mind gives me no heads-up on what I should say, so I wind up just staring at him like an idiot. And he stares right back, his eyes vacant behind his glasses, obviously no right words coming to him either. An invisible protective shield flies up around me, and after a long period of silence – our eyes the only connection – his potency wins, penetrating my defences, and the shield shatters. My eyes plummet to my bare feet as a result, and I fold in on myself, searching for words.

Becker finds some first. 'You're late for work.'

I give myself whiplash when my head shoots up in shock. 'Pardon?'

He slowly pulls up the sleeve of his jacket a little, looking down at his watch, a gorgeous antique Rolex. His leisurely move gives me a fleeting moment to skate my annoyingly greedy eyes down the length of him. He has jeans on, lovely fitted jeans that hug his thighs in all the right places, and a navy suit jacket over a pale blue shirt. 'It's nine forty.' He speaks with an even, business like tone, releasing his sleeve as he looks up at me, catching me in the act of admiring him. But when I would expect him to give me a cocky, knowing look, all I get is a straight face instead. It's silly for me to feel injured by his indifference, I realise that, yet I can't deny the hurt is there. If I didn't still have the evidence of our encounter stinging my arse, I'd think I dreamed it. 'You're late,' he repeats. 'Mrs Potts is worried.'

'I quit,' I remind him, raising my chin in an act of equal in-difference. It doesn't matter that it's fake.

His jaw tightens. 'I didn't accept your resignation.'

'I didn't resign.' My body begins to heat up, and it isn't with desire. 'And I believe you yelled "good" a second after I quit, Mr Hunt.'

His face twists in annoyance, his head dropping back in ex-asperation. I wish he wouldn't do that. His stubble is the perfect length on his taut throat, begging for me stroke it. My own face twists too, and I struggle to grab control of my traitorous mind and stop it from wandering to forbidden places. I can't. Now he's flesh and blood and standing right in front of me, the memories are like a tidal wave, crashing over me relentlessly. His chest, his mouth, his power. *Oh, flipping heck.* In a panic, I grab the door and violently throw my weight behind it, waiting for the loud bang to ricochet around my apartment, except that loud bang doesn't come. Well, it does, but it's delayed. Becker pushes his way past the door and puts my forceful attempts to shame. I jump back when the wood hits the frame, but quickly gather myself, ready to blast him with my viper tongue. I just about manage to load my lungs with air, ready to fire, when he tackles me around the waist, flipping me up on to his shoulder.

'What the fuck, Becker?' I yell, brushing my hair from my face. 'Get your filthy hands off me.'

'Shut up, princess,' he snaps, striding into my bathroom and reaching to turn on the shower.

'Don't call me princess.' I thump his back in my temper, ignoring my brain when it reminds me I didn't complain last night when he used the irritating pet name.

'I said, shut up.' He dumps me on my feet and grabs my hair on either side of my temples, getting way too close for comfort. If he didn't look so aggravated, I would think he was moving in for a kiss.

My hands come up fast and smack him away. 'Get out,' I demand.

He rolls his eyes. He actually rolls his eyes at me. What's he on? 'Get in the shower.'

'I will not.' I pivot on my heel ... and go nowhere.

'Where do you think you're going?' he asks, calm as can be, seizing me and opening the shower door.

I wriggle like a demented worm to no avail, and then the fact that no steam is emanating from the shower cubicle grabs my attention. I stop fighting him, but only long enough to spot the shower dial and note that the twat turned it the wrong way. Then my squirming hits new heights as I come closer to the spray. 'Becker,' I yelp, kicking back into his shin, getting some mild satisfaction from the curse that bursts from him. 'You've turned it to cold.' He completely ignores me and shoves me into the cubicle. 'No!' The water hits me like a million ice spears, stabbing my skin, and my body goes into shock. Every muscle shuts down as I'm attacked by the icy water. 'Oh my God.' My words come out broken and my teeth begin to chatter, the material of my shorts and vest clinging to me and my hair soaking up every freezing drop raining down over my defenceless body.

'There,' I hear him say as I slowly shuffle around, finding him on the other side of the glass – the dry, warm side – brushing off his hands, a smug smile stretched from ear to ear. 'Wasn't so hard, was it?'

I'm so fucking cold, I could cry. 'I hate you,' I choke, making a grab for the door handle, my only purpose now to escape. But he pushes against the frame, keeping me prisoner in the ice box. 'Let me out.'

His head cocks and he brings his face close, pushing his lips to the glass and giving it a smacker of a kiss. 'You looked like you needed to cool off, princess.'

I mentally scream and finally find the sense to swing around and locate the temperature gauge, flipping it to the maximum heat and pinning myself to the tiles while it warms up. Taking the sponge, I hold it under the spray and squirt some shower gel on it. 'When I get out of this shower, you'd better be gone.'

'Or else?' He raises an interested eyebrow that I only just catch before steam engulfs the glass and his infuriatingly handsome face is no longer visible.

I have no *or else*. 'Get out.' I toss the drenched sponge over the top of the door and hope he's close enough to cop the soppy bomb. Then I begin to strip out of my sodden pyjamas, my skin burning from the mix of cold and hot, as I mutter under my breath every name for Becker I can think of. He expects me to return to work like nothing's happened? Is he insane?

The shower door swings open and the sponge sails through the steam, slapping me right in the face before dropping heavily to the shower floor. 'You'll need that.' The door closes, and I stand with my eyes closed, taking deep, calming breaths. 'You still smell of me.'

I don't rise to his taunt, but I do bite down on my lip and slowly sink down to collect the sponge. Then I start to wash the smell of Becker Hunt from my skin.

I've been standing looking at the bathroom door for an age, wrapped in a towel, psyching myself up to face him again. I know he's still here. I might not be able to smell him on my body any longer, but I can smell his scent lingering in the air. And I can *feel* him close by. He's gone full-force into wind-up-merchant mode. Irritating mode. Joker mode. It's like nothing ever happened.

Just get dressed and go out. Pretend he isn't even there. Sounds simple in theory. In practice, though, I'm aiming for the impossible. But I'm willing to give it a go.

On entering the small space of my apartment, I catch him sprawled on the couch, looking comfy and at home. I resist the overwhelming urge to go over and batter him with a pillow, instead heading straight for my wardrobe. Grabbing the first thing I lay my hands on – some jeans and an oversized blush-coloured shirt – along with some underwear, I pelt back to the bathroom, chickening out on my brash intention of dressing in front of him. After last night, I'm zapped dry of brazenness, and I hate him for it.

I ignore the feel of his eyes on me as I make my hasty escape and shut the door, throwing my clothes on a nearby rail. My urgency to be out of here won't allow time to moisturise, so I throw on my clothes, haphazardly slap on some make-up, then blast my hair with the dryer. It's the fastest I've ever got ready.

Before I venture out of the bathroom again, I plot my escape, mentally locating my cute suede ankle boots, my leather jacket, and my bag. I'm a little early to meet Lucy, but I'll find a park, where I can sit on a bench and clear my head.

Straightening my back and raising my chin, I casually exit the bathroom and calmly find my boots, slipping them on while feeding my arms through the sleeves of my jacket. I can feel him watching me, probably with a frown on his face, but I succeed in disregarding it. My bag and keys are my last claims before I'm out the door and walking purposefully down the stairs to the main entrance hall. I can smell freedom as the street comes into view, my feet picking up pace.

Just as I feared, soon I hear heavy footsteps in pursuit of me. 'Eleanor, wait.'

I ignore his call as I fasten the zip of my jacket and take the pathway to the street. My shoulder jars a little as Becker overtakes me, skidding to a halt and blocking my way. 'Excuse me,' I say politely, stepping to the side to pass. He moves with me, so I take another step to the other side, all in vain. Becker shifts, too. I refuse to look at him when I speak. 'I'm not playing your games any more,' I tell him, maintaining my calm. I'm surprised that I actually mean it. I've lost a little self-respect. I've lost a job I truly loved. He got his way, I didn't. I'm done. *Again.*

'My game?' he asks, stunned. The nerve of him. 'You can't be serious.'

'Deadly serious. Just fuck off, Becker.' I start to pass him, but he grabs my arm to stop me. *Keep your cool, Eleanor.*

'But Mrs Potts is wondering where you are. She's worried about you.' He steps forwards, prompting me to move back, away from his closeness.

'Then you can tell her she needn't be.'

'I can't go back to The Haven without you.'

I pluck up the courage to look at him. Is that . . . embarrassment coating his features? It takes two seconds flat to figure out why. 'Oh.' I laugh sarcastically. 'Too ashamed to admit to her why I quit?' I ask, getting a sick thrill when he drops his head in shame. It's all very clear why he can't go back without me, and it fucking hurts like hell. I bet Mrs Potts will go, well, potty. 'You left me no choice but to quit, then fucked me with a clear conscience, making it impossible for me to work with you again.'

He snarls, getting his face up close and personal. 'I'd say it was pretty fucking impossible to work with you before we fucked, wouldn't you?'

'Because you behaved inappropriately.'

He recoils, offended.

'Don't look so horrified.' I wail, pointing an accusing finger in his face. 'You knew what you wanted, and now you've had it.'

'Don't pretend you didn't want it, too.'

'You made it impossible to resist.' The fact that I'm now drowning in despair as a result of my weakness and where it has got me is beside the point.

'So did you,' he shouts, and I withdraw, aghast.

I don't need this. I never tempted him. He's not pinning any of this on me, just to ease his conscience. He can go back and explain to Mrs Potts why I'm not at work today. I hope she attacks him with her watering can.

I pick up my feet and make a dash for the road.

'Oh no you don't.' He seizes me around my waist and lifts me from my feet, yet this time I don't scrap with him, and I don't know why. I have plenty of spunk locked and loaded and ready to unleash. Is it because I secretly want him to take me back to The Haven? The knowledge that I'm being missed by some-one warms me through. Or is it because his chest is currently pressed into my back and is *actually* warming me through?

Stopping the side of my head from pushing into his cheek when he brings his face close to mine is a killer. 'Please,' he begs, surprising me. Becker doesn't say please. 'Please, Eleanor.' He keeps me secure against him as he takes a deep breath. 'Last night shouldn't have happened. You know it, and I . . .' Another deep breath. 'I shouldn't . . . I can't.'

Ouch.

I try to nod my head into him, knowing he's 100 per cent correct, but the damn thing won't move, like it's stubbornly refusing to accept that he's right.

'Please come back.' He drops me to my feet and turns me in his arms. Then he steps back, giving me space I haven't asked for, or, infuriatingly, that I want. His next words are spoken in a mechanical tone. 'I promise to stay out of your way. I won't behave inappropriately or push your buttons.' There's no emotion or conviction, nothing to make me believe him, yet I do. Begrudgingly, I do.

Because he's had me. Itch scratched. *Next woman, please.* I'm falling to pieces on the inside. Crumbling.

'Since you've been around, Dorothy is much less stressed,' he says. 'She can focus on my grandad now. And Gramps loves you,' he finishes, cruelly yanking at my heartstrings. I adore Mrs Potts. I don't want to leave her in the lurch. And his gramps? I love him, too. Goddamn him. Becker's reached an all-time low, using emotional blackmail. 'What happened last night will never be spoken of again.'

And there it is. I'm determined to not let this break me, because I knew going in that this would be the result. I knew it. But it doesn't matter how sorry I am that I allowed myself to venture there, because Becker's regret has just shredded my own. It's like a kick in the teeth. *He* made a mistake. *He* went against Mrs Potts and his grandad's wishes, and now he's trying to fix things. *He* will carry on as normal, wielding his charisma and potency around other willing women, and before a week passes, our night will be forgotten. And me? Well, at least I have my beloved job, and hopefully he'll be a man of his word and stay away from me. *Surely I deserve that.* I can't let my obstinacy and disdain for Becker get in the way of the only thing that's brought me joy since my father died. That would be cutting off my nose to spite my face. And I can't abandon Mrs Potts. My conscience simply won't allow it, not for the sake of punishing Becker. Or myself, for that matter. Because walking away from my job would be a punishment.

So, plucking my professionalism from nowhere, and disregarding the fact that I'm doing Becker a favour, I square my shoulders and knock every reason to decline out of my mind. 'You owe me a new phone.' My statement is an agreement without actually agreeing, and the hopeful look that springs on to his face tells me he gets that.

'Done,' he says, his eyes shining with happiness. It makes me appreciate just how much he wants me back to help Mrs Potts, and that realisation makes me see Becker in a mildly different light. Maybe he isn't such a selfish knob. It also makes me pull up and think carefully, because judging by his quick agreement just now, I could probably demand anything and get it.

Maybe it's time to test my boundaries. 'And I want a pay rise.'

'Done.'

I purse my lips and think harder still. Will he really agree to anything? The potential has my mind racing, conjuring up demands while I've got him where I want him. 'No poking me or winding me up.'

'Agreed.' He nods.

I push some more. 'No pieces of arse at The Haven during my working day.'

'Whatever you want.'

'Really?' I blurt, shocked. I have no right to demand such a thing, and in all honesty, I have no clue where it came from.

'Yes, really.'

'Oh.' I'm stumped. Nearly. 'I want Fridays off.'

His eyes narrow, and I realise I've reached my limit. 'Don't push it, princess.'

'Oh,' I squeal, when the most obvious demand comes to me – the one I should have demanded first. I poke him in the shoulder. 'You don't get to call me *princess* any more.'

He sniffs his thoughts on that. 'Well, we won't have to worry about that if we stay out of each other's way, will we?'

'Fine,' I snap, knowing he's suggesting the impossible. I work for him. Avoiding each other is a luxury we can't have. He knows that. I know that. That's where resistance and control needs to come into play, though it sounds like Becker's not going to struggle in that department.

'Good,' he snaps right back, pointing behind me. 'Get in the car. I'll take you to work.'

I pivot haughtily and come face to face with a red Ferrari. A super-shiny one. It's the epitome of showy. My nose wrinkles in distaste. 'This is yours?' I don't know why I'm asking. Who else could it belong to?

'Yes.' He circles round to the driver's side and leans on the roof. 'Maybe you should get the Tube.'

I frown. 'Why?'

'Because, you know, your hair clashes with my pretty motor.'

I cough all over his shiny red car, outraged. 'What happened to not goading me?'

'I can't fucking help it.' He's halfway between hysterics and exasperation as he shouts over the roof at me. 'Just looking at you makes me want to poke you . . . or fuck you.'

'Then don't look at me.' I'm offended, I'm disgusted, and, for my fucking sins, I'm instantly turned on. 'And for the record, looking at *you* makes me want to slap you. You're like an irritating gnat that won't fuck off.'

'A gnat?'

'Yes, a gnat.'

'Nice.' He gives me doubtful look as he jumps into his car. 'Come on, princess. You're over an hour late. You can work late to make up the time.'

I roll my eyes and begin to search for anything resembling a door handle on his pretty motor. There's nothing. 'Becker, where's—' I'm interrupted when the engine roars to life, but not content with making me physically jump out of my damn skin once, he begins revving it, over and over, the noise each time making me jolt with fright. 'Where's the—' The horn begins to sound, accompanying the unbearable booms of the high-powered engine, making my ears ring and my hands cover my face to muffle my incensed scream. He just can't fucking help himself. He must either play with me or flirt outrageously with me. There's no in between.

In a temper, I draw my foot back and launch it into the side of his Ferrari. Silence falls. Until Becker scrambles out of his car and begins to rant like a sailor, firing fucks all over the place. 'What the fuck are you fucking doing?' he cries, running around to my side and closely inspecting the paintwork of his baby. 'Jesus, Eleanor, have you any fucking idea how much this machine cost?'

I shrug insolently when he looks at me in disbelief, casually inspecting my nails. I couldn't be any more disrespectful if I tried. 'I couldn't find the door handle.'

He makes an overdramatic job of pointing at it, the muscles of his jaw ticking madly. He looks ready to clout me one. 'Get in,' he orders, releasing the door.

It glides up smoothly, revealing what can only be described as a spaceship inside. 'Ooh.' I give him a fake astonished look. 'Fancy.'

'Get. In.'

I fall apart on the inside but manage to keep it together on the outside, as I slide in and pull my belt on. I have a feeling if I show my amusement, Becker might wring my neck. The door comes down gently and he's next to me in a moment, probably fearing what I might do to the inside of his precious car.

'I don't want to hear a murmur out of you,' he orders through gritted teeth. 'Not a peep.'

'Fine by me,' I retort, watching as he fiddles with some buttons on the steering wheel. After the shock my hearing has had from him revving the engine, the booming music that blares from the millions of speakers surrounding me has little impact. I still, however, throw him a filthy look. Not that he acknowledges it. No, he just relaxes back in his posh leather seat and skids off down the road.

I lose the urge to go crazy all over his arse when the track registers. Freemasons *Uninvited*.

Me? Am I uninvited?

Then why is he so passionate about me staying?

Chapter 17

I try not to show my confusion when Becker misses the road to The Haven, but my head slowly turning as we pass gives me away.

'Now you can never quit again,' Becker says. He looks at me out the corner of his eye, before returning his attention to the road and turning down a dusty alleyway.

'Why?' I sit back in my seat, not liking the serious look on his face.

'Because you're about to see the secret entrance.' He swings the car to the left, and I spot huge, battered iron doors covered in graffiti sliding open ahead.

'The secret entrance?' What is he on about? We slip between the moving doors and they immediately begin to close behind us. The car comes to a stop and darkness descends, the sound of the engine reaching a whole new decibel level with us enclosed in what can only be described as a factory unit. It's derelict, old, and grubby. It's a shithole.

'Yes, princess.' He looks at me, that serious face still present. 'You're now in Becker's Circle of Trust.'

I laugh nervously, not grasping where he's going with this. 'You show me a manky old factory and that puts me in your circle of trust?'

'Precisely.' He flips the sun visor down and presses a white button, keeping his eyes on me.

'What's that?' I blurt, grabbing the side of the car when it starts to move without Becker controlling it. 'Oh my God.' The floor starts to rise around us, closing us in, making me come over all claustrophobic. 'Becker, what the hell is happening?' I move away from the window when I see concrete creeping up the side.

'Calm down.' Becker's hand lands on my knee and squeezes gently, and I find my hand shooting down and claiming it, holding it tightly. 'It's an automatic ramp into my garage, that's all.'

The sensation of being at an angle suddenly registers in my panicked mind, and I peek over my shoulder, noting the rear of the car is lowering and I'm pinned to the back of my seat. 'Why can't you have a proper garage like normal people?'

He laughs and uses his free hand to put the car into reverse. 'I'm not normal people, Eleanor. Haven't you figured that out yet?' The car rolls off the ramp into a vast white room, and Becker turns off the ignition. I watch the ramp rise back to the ceiling with the assistance of a few hydraulic arms. I'm rendered stupid. Becker isn't normal people, I knew that, but last night and this morning has taken my conclusion to a whole new level of *not normal people*. Normal people don't fuck like Becker. Normal people don't wind me up like Becker. Normal people don't make my pulse race like Becker. And normal people definitely do not have secret underground garages that are accessible through the concrete floors of manky factory units.

Now I'm wondering what I've got myself into, but for a whole different reason. I've been working here for weeks. Why didn't I know about this monstrous underground space?

When Becker's hand flexes in mine, I quickly snatch it back, embarrassed, before blindly reaching for the door handle and grappling for a few mindless moments. Becker takes it upon himself to reach over and help me out. 'Thank you,' I say quietly, keeping my attention on the section of ceiling slotting back into place as I slowly get out of the car. A hiss of air sounds, and I find my eyes journeying the expanse of white above me, seeing five more sections in the ceiling, all with metal machinery attached. Then my gaze drops to floor level, seeing cars set back from each area. Posh cars. I clock a silver Porsche 911, a black Maserati, a flashy black 5-series BMW, a grey Audi RS7, and I can't see the final car because it's hidden beneath a cover. My mind is blown.

My hand waves around senselessly. 'You like cars?' I state the obvious like an idiot.

Becker laughs lightly, pressing the button of his key fob. The Ferrari makes a few threatening noises, and it speaks. Actual words come from the car. 'Alarm engaged,' Becker mimics, strolling over to a metal cabinet mounted on the wall. When he peeks into a little black dial, the thing just springs right open.

'Did you bring me to MI5?' I ask, laughing in disbelief. 'Hey, you're not a secret agent, are you?'

He laughs loudly and pushes the cabinet shut once he hangs the keys inside. 'No, princess, I'm not a secret agent, and this isn't MI5.' Slipping his hands into his pockets, he slowly turns towards me, regarding me carefully.

'What?' I ask, feeling uncomfortable under his close scrutiny. 'Why are you looking at me like that?'

'You've seen what I deal in.'

My mind mentally places me in the Grand Hall, where a mass of historical treasures live. 'Antiques,' I squeak, feeling a little silly for stating the obvious again.

'And art, and let's just say there are many people out there who would go to great lengths to get their hands on some of those pieces.'

'Can't they just buy them from you?'

He's laughing again as he wanders across the garage to me. 'Yes, because everyone I know has a spare million here and there to buy pretty shit.' His arm rests lightly around my shoulders and encourages me onward.

'They try to steal from you?'

'If anyone ever breached the security at The Haven, I'd happily eat my arm. I have the most valuable collection of antiques and art in the world stored here, Eleanor. Each and every piece is like my baby until I find a new owner for it. I don't sell to any Tom, Dick or Harry, either.'

'Like Brent Wilson?'

He peeks down at me, smiling. 'Like Brent Wilson.'

'You have something Brent wants,' I say. It's not a question, just a statement I know to be true, since Brent told me on our date that Becker Hunt has a habit of obtaining things that he wants.

Becker looks at me out the corner of his eye. 'I think I have a few things Brent wants.'

I let that one slide. He's being cheeky. I can live with that. 'Why won't you sell to him?' I ask, resisting the urge to snuggle into his side.

'You're not for sale.'

'Becker.' I shove into him roughly, making him chuckle. He's relentless, but I'd be lying if I said this affability isn't charming. 'Tell me.'

He pulls me back into his side and he kisses the top of my head. He actually pulls me into him and drops his lips to the top of my bloody head. What the fuck was that? 'I'd rather burn every treasure I have to ashes than sell them to him.' There's violence in his tone. Pure, scathing violence.

'Why?' I ask quietly.

He looks off into the distance, thoughtful and suddenly uptight. 'Let's just say I don't appreciate his appreciation for antiques.'

'Then why is he always here?'

'I like letting him think he might get his smarmy hands on something special.'

I'm even more confused. Hasn't he got better things to do? 'Why?'

'Keep your enemies close, princess,' he whispers, traces of resentment heavy in his quiet tone. I've figured out that Becker and Brent don't like each other, but enemies? 'Make a call to Bonhams,' Becker orders, changing the subject swiftly. 'Arrange a private viewing for me of their classic car exhibit sometime next week.'

'Sure,' I reply as he opens a door for me and gestures me to go through with a gentlemanly sweep of his arm.

I pass him on a small smile and find myself in the corridor of The Haven, just past the sweeping stone staircase that leads to his apartment. When Becker shuts the door behind us, it blends right into the wall. There's no sign of it being a door. My mouth hangs open. 'A secret door?'

He smirks. 'You're in Becker's Circle of Trust now, princess.'

An odd thrill dances through me. 'Then I'm honoured.'

'Trust me, you should be.'

I smile and continue down the corridor, Becker following. It's quiet now, neither of us speaking, and the easy comfort I've thrived on in the past half-hour transforms into electric energy again.

He's studying me. I can feel his eyes on my back, and I roll my shoulders and flex my neck.

Professional. Keep it businesslike. This is going to be so fucking hard.

Chapter 18

'Thank you for your help.' I hang up to Bonhams and make a note of Becker's private viewing as I wander to the kitchen. I smile when Winston clocks me and scurries over to say hello. 'Hey, boy.' I drop to my knees and make a thorough job of scratching his ears, laughing when he falls to his back and his leg starts twitching as he groans, his tongue hanging limply out the side of his gaping mouth. 'Did you miss me?' I coo, moving my scratching to his tummy.

'Morning.'

I look up and find Becker's grandad sitting at the table in his dressing gown. 'Morning, Mr H.' I unfold myself from the floor and grab the kettle.

'You look particularly chirpy today, Eleanor,' he remarks, raising a cool grey eyebrow. 'Did you have a good night?'

I clam up as I turn the tap on, feeling like he knows something he shouldn't. 'So-so.' I brush aside my worry. He couldn't possibly. 'Tea?'

'No, thank you,' he answers. I hear the squeak of a chair and turn to see him struggling to his feet, so I dash over to lend a hand, ignoring his grimace. 'I should have dedicated my life to discovering the fountain of eternal youth instead of dealing in ancient treasures.' He accepts his cane with a shaky hand when I hold it up, rolling his eyes as he straightens up on a wince, before stepping back to demonstrate his stability. My hands are still poised, though, ready to dart out and steady him if required. 'Like the priceless objects I've devoted my life to collecting and preserving,' he says wistfully, 'the human body gets more and more delicate the older it gets. It too needs to be treated with care and respect.' He sighs. 'But sadly, the human body doesn't become more desired and beautiful when it's been around the block a few times. It just becomes a burden.'

Sympathy grabs me. 'You're not a burden, Mr H.' I link my arm with his.

He laughs and taps the top on my hand. 'You're sweet, Eleanor.' I raise a doubtful eyebrow as we wander to the kitchen door. 'Spirited and full of zest for life.' I look up at him as he comes to a stop and turns into me, letting the handle of his walking cane slide on to his wrist and hang so he can hold the tops of my arms, keeping me in place. I expect it's probably keeping *him* in place, too. His old eyes, a match of Becker's lovely hazels, but slightly paler, no doubt from age, hold me still. 'I remember being your age. What would that be? Mid-twenties?'

'Twenty-eight.'

'Twenty-eight,' he muses, smiling fondly. 'Feels like yesterday. You know, I was in India when I was twenty-eight. Discovered my first solid-gold Buddha.'

I mirror his smile, seeing a gleam in Becker's grandad's eyes as he talks about his passion. 'Your first?'

'Yes, I found another in the sixties, except it was a whopper.' He releases me and measures a space between his hands, indicating its size. 'Weighed a bleeding ton, it did.'

'Not the *Phra Phuttha Maha Suwan Patimakon*?' I smile. To think I almost walked away from this place. This man.

He laughs loudly. 'Could you imagine? Five bleedin' tons of solid gold.'

'No human is lifting that sucker,' I say seriously, increasing his amusement.

He shakes his head wistfully, falling into thought again. 'How did we get on to that?' he asks, genuinely confused, and

I cast my mind back, too, wondering the same thing. 'Oh, yes.' He raises an old finger that's bent terribly, probably riddled with arthritis. 'Twenty-eight.'

It all comes back to me, and old Mr H is holding me in place again with a firm grip, his grave eyes back. 'Sometimes I wish I could go back to twenty-eight. I'd do a few things differently.'

'Like what?'

'Oh, bits and bobs, this and that.'

I narrow questioning eyes on Becker's grandad. Something tells me there's more to this than he's letting on, and when he coughs and stands back, I know I'm on to something. 'Like?' I ask again, studying him closely.

Mr H seems to think long and hard before answering. The silence feels like it's stretching for ever, giving me too much time to drive myself mad with wondering. 'Everything,' he finally says quietly and with a slight shake in his tone.

'I'm not sure I follow.'

He laughs lightly and reaches forward, tenderly giving my cheek a little rub. 'Not now, Eleanor. But I have a feeling you'll be around long enough to hear the Hunt family legacy.'

'Oh, no, Mr H, we're not going over this again, are we? I told you, I'm immune.' How can I lie to a dear old man?

He smacks the bottom of his cane on the floor, chuckling. 'Yes, yes, so you say. I meant to work, Eleanor. You'll be around a while to *work*.'

I blush profusely. 'Of course,' I mutter, because if I was around for the reason I mistakenly thought he was referring to, I wouldn't actually be around for long at all.

'Just remember what I told you.'

'What did you tell me?' The old man has spoken a whole lot of nothing.

'My Becker is spirited.'

I frown. What relevance does that have in all this, for crying out loud?

'You're a very spirited young woman, too, Eleanor. That spirit has only flourished since I first clapped eyes on you, and I'm wondering why.' He seems to take immense pleasure in watching me disintegrate under the heat of my own cheeks, his old eyes sparkling like I haven't seen in the short time I've known him. 'Something tells me it's not just the beauty of our Haven and its treasure.' I keep my mouth firmly closed as his hand comes up to my face and he strokes my cheek gently again. 'Don't let anyone take that fire away from you. I like you. I don't want to see you hurt. We love having you around, Eleanor. Women who get caught up with Becker don't stay around for long. Call me selfish, but I want to keep you.' He winks. It's so endearing. And then he ambles out, meeting Mrs Potts in the doorway. She's wrapped up warm and loaded with two very heavy-looking shopping bags. It's a perfect distraction. Mr H's words make perfect sense, and I hate that he's right. My spirit has definitely grown, and has been ... nurtured since I've been at The Haven. What Becker said last night is true. They love having me around and know Becker could fuck that all up. My conscience is being attacked by guilt. I feel rotten. That was a subtle reminder. Or not so subtle. He knows his grandson will hurt me. Annoyingly, he already has, but I'm all for damage control. This wonderful place can still be *my* haven, too.

I dash over and claim the bags from Mrs Potts, and she takes old Mr H's arm. He shrugs her off. 'Dorothy, please, I'm walking thirty feet to the courtyard to get some fresh air.'

'Aren't you going to get dressed?' she asks, dropping her hold begrudgingly.

'Might do. Might not.' He pushes Mrs Potts back into the kitchen and takes the handle. 'I'm not going to die if I don't take a shower for another hour, am I?'

'Don't get smart with me, Donald.'

He flips me another wink before shutting the door so Mrs Potts and I are alone. Now I have another cringeworthy confrontation to face. This morning is full of them. Bracing myself for her imminent inquisition on my lateness, I start emptying the bags, a ploy to avoid having to look at her when she hits me with the questions I know are coming. Except they don't. Mrs Potts takes the items I'm removing from the bags and puts them away in silence. This worries me more, because now I'm worried she's annoyed with me. Becker's grandad's little speech about spirit and his subtle warning, and now Mrs Potts's silent treatment. The last time we were all together, I was having *oh dears* thrown at me left, right and centre. They can't know about last night, and I plan on keeping it that way. Call me pitiful, but I don't want to disappoint them.

The silence drags and drags, until I have no more things to empty from the bag. It's painful. At least, it is for me, and when I've slowly folded the carrier bags into neat little squares, I cave, unable to take the discomfort any more.

'I'm sorry about this morning, Mrs Potts.' I turn and rest my bum on the counter, wincing at the flash of pain. 'I broke my phone last night and had to order a new one.'

She's across the room on her tiptoes, trying to get something down from the top shelf of a wall cupboard. 'What, dear?' she says, shifting a bag of sugar back further with her reaching fingers. 'Bugger.'

I scoot over and grab the packet for her. 'I said I'm sorry about this morning.'

'What about this morning?'

I slowly retract my hand when she's taken the sugar, confused. 'For being late.'

She bursts into laughter and trots across the room, leaving me bemused as I watch her potter around happily. 'You silly girl,' she says. 'I've been in town all morning fetching some shopping. If you hadn't mentioned it, I would never have known.' She laughs some more, and my confusion begins to subside, something else taking over. 'Although your honesty is appreciated.'

She hasn't been here all morning? She hasn't been worrying about me? The fact that Mrs Potts isn't suspicious should be a relief. But it isn't. I'm too mad to appreciate it. He lied. The dirty scoundrel lied through his teeth.

Mrs Potts turns and smiles at me. I might look completely composed on the outside, but on the inside I'm ripping everything in sight to shreds, and a few things out of sight, too. Namely, Becker Hunt.

'Are you okay, dear?' she asks. Okay, maybe I'm not so composed.

'Yes,' I squeak, pointing to the kitchen door. 'I'd ... um ... better get on.' My legs are itching to break into a run, but I manage to hold them off until the kitchen door is shut behind me, and Mrs Potts is out of view. Then there's nothing holding them back. I'm sprinting down the corridor towards Becker's office like a madwoman, knowing I need to rein myself in, but unable to find the self-control to do so. He lied to me, the conniving bastard. Played with my conscience.

I don't bother ringing the bell when I get to his office door, I just steam right in, my temper getting the better of me. 'You lying arsehole,' I blurt through my laboured breathing, slamming the door behind me.

Becker looks up, and it takes a few moments to register something that I should have checked first: he isn't alone. 'Mr H,' I breathe, my eyes widening. Becker's leaning over the desk, his palm is resting lightly on his grandad's shoulder, where he's seated in Becker's chair. Both men are staring at me, one shocked, one annoyed.

'You just can't find the staff these days,' Becker says quietly, removing his glasses and rubbing his eyes. A derogatory statement like that from him would usually have me preparing to attack, but I've just noticed someone else in the room, too.

Brent slowly turns in his chair, a stunned look on his face.

'Good morning, Eleanor.'

Oh fuck. What the hell is he doing here?

'Morning,' I reply, taking the handle of the door, desperate to escape the three sets of eyes all focused on me.

'I think that's my cue to leave,' Mr H says as he rises from the chair, giving me a knowing look and Becker a pat on the shoulder. A pat that's a bit too firm to be mistaken as fond.

'No, really, I'll go.' I open the door. 'I thought you were in the courtyard.'

'I was heading that way until I found Becker and Brent in the corridor.' Mr H makes his way around the desk and holds out his hand to Brent, who takes it quickly and gives it a firm shake. 'Good to see you, son.'

Brent stands in a gesture of respect. 'And you, Mr H.'

I definitely don't miss the look of condemnation on Becker's face at their exchange as he rounds his desk, and it makes me wonder whether his grandad is aware of the animosity between these two and the game they're playing. 'You don't need to leave, Gramps.' Becker shoots me a filthy look that I accept willingly. I deserve it.

'Oh, yes' – Mr H points his walking stick at me – 'I think I do.'

I cringe all over the office and mentally smack myself around the head with the cane currently pointed at me. Yes, perfectly immune.

'I don't think it's safe to be alone with her,' Becker mumbles under his breath. I accept that too. In fact, if he sacked me on the spot, I wouldn't blame him. He looks to Brent. 'We're done. I'll see you out.'

I turn and exit sharply, but I only make it a few metres down the corridor when my arm is gripped harshly. 'Ouch,' I hiss.

'Wait in the library.' Becker is speaking through a clenched jaw, trying to disguise the threat.

'Mrs Potts didn't even know I was gone,' I whisper-hiss,

allowing him to guide me away for fear of creating more of a scene in front of his grandad and Brent, who are trailing some way behind, chatting.

'She would have, had I not got you back here before she arrived.'

'That's not the point.'

'Shut up and get in there.' He swipes a card, then roughly pushes me inside, and I turn to find Becker trying to close the door and Brent holding it so he can't.

'A moment of her time, if you don't mind,' Brent says confidently, going to pass Becker. I cringe as Becker blocks him.

'She's busy,' he retorts sharply, yanking at the door again, but Brent isn't giving in. His expression is determined, and so is his hold on the door.

'I won't take much of her time.' Brent speaks coolly, but there's no escaping the gritty edge to his tone. Not that I expect it to make an ounce of difference to Becker's subtle refusal. I've just caught a glimpse of my boss's profile. He looks indomitable. This could turn messy.

I'm still furious with Becker, but *this* I'm staying out of.

'You won't take *any* of her time,' Becker says, the hollows of his jaw pulsing steady and slow. He's trying to keep his cool. I don't know how long he can do that. Especially since Brent Wilson seems to get a sick thrill out of pushing Becker's buttons where I'm concerned.

Brent goes to retaliate but gets no further than drawing breath before Becker steps into the library.

'Gramps, see Wilson out, please.' He shuts the door in Brent's face with brute force, locking us in.

I'm so pissed off, for reasons that are unwarranted and so fucking childish. Brent's brashness, Becker's behaviour, his lies. I need to take deep breaths. Quickly. 'I might have wanted to speak with him.' I simply cannot help myself.

Becker swings around, his face awash with disbelief. 'You

had him drop you off at a fake address. And anyway, private client and employee relations are against the rules. Check your contract.'

I'm about to ask about employee and *employer* private relations, but the final piece of his little speech has just registered. 'What contract?'

'Your employee contract.'

'There's nothing about private relations in my employee contract,' I splutter. He knows damn well.

'The other contract. The separate NDA.'

'What NDA?' I ask, running over the paperwork in my mind that I signed on my first day at The Haven. There definitely wasn't a separate NDA, only a section dedicated to non-disclosure in my employee contract, and, like I said, there was no mention of client and employee relations.

'It's a document that might do you and me some favours, princess. An addition to your standard terms of employment.'

'Good,' I yell. 'Make sure you include something regarding sexual harassment while you're at it.'

Becker's mouth drops open, stunned by my outburst. Then his face screws up in contempt. He doesn't know what to say to that. 'Wait here,' he barks, turning and swinging the door open, slamming it, and leaving me alone in the library with nothing to do except as I'm told. That thought alone makes me want to bash the door down, but as I take a long, calming breath, I remind myself I'm at work. I'm on Becker's time. This isn't personal.

I hesitate a moment, fighting for clarity. But it *is* personal. This all started because it got bloody personal, and now the areas between work and my private life are becoming grey. When is it okay to retaliate, and when is it inappropriate? My head falls into my hands. I can't cope. There have been grey areas since day one.

On a long exhale of a tired breath, I turn, coming face to

face with the bookshelf nearest the door. The one with the secret compartment. Secret compartments, secret garages, secret doors. Suddenly, my despair is drowned out by an odd sense of excitement, and a wicked thrill steamrolls through my bloodstream. I scoot down gingerly, flicking a cautious look over my shoulder before tilting my head to peek through the dark gap.

'Don't ever storm into my office again!' The door slams and I fly up, swinging around. 'I'm your fucking boss. You work for me.'

A million words hang off the tip of my tongue, many justified, but they remain exactly where they are, unprepared to back me up, and probably wisely too. I've way overstepped the mark, and although Becker is responsible for destroying boundaries too, I'm certain now wouldn't be a good time to remind him so. He's currently fighting his way out of his blazer, shouting while he's at it. He's fuming.

'Where's your fucking respect?' His jacket gets lobbed on to the couch, then he begins yanking at his tie. 'Barging into my fucking office. Shouting and fucking swearing.' The fucks just keep coming and coming, and I accept them all, standing deathly still while he stomps around the library, getting himself into a worked-up, sweaty mess. 'And in front of my grandad.' His rant goes on for a good few minutes, Becker jabbering on, me pretending to listen, when what I'm actually doing is silently drawing my own conclusion: his tantrum has nothing to do with my behaviour in front of his lovely gramps, and everything to do with him struggling with grey areas, too. This side of him – the unsure, vulnerable side – is like a redeeming quality. It makes him more human. Shows he has feelings. I'm not sure if that's a good thing or a bad thing.

It's bad. Definitely bad.

My eyes follow him marching around the library until he finally comes to a stop and yanks his phone from his pocket. He punches in some digits aggressively. 'Vass,' he barks.

I frown as he begins his dogged march around the library again. Vass? Dr Vass? His therapist? He's going to have a quick phone session while I'm here?

'Becker Hunt,' he snaps. 'Have her call me back. It's an emergency.' He hangs up on a grunt and looks at me with guarded eyes for a few moments. 'How come you're so quiet?' His question is quite endearing.

An emergency? Am I the emergency? Honestly, right now, I want to hug him. My head could also fucking explode. I should ask him to put me in touch with his doctor, too, because I sure as shit need to see a shrink. 'I didn't want to interrupt you,' I say, joining my hands in front of me.

'Oh.' Becker's brows meet in the middle. 'Well, I'm done now.' He makes a futile attempt at composure.

'Okay.'

'Okay?'

'Yes, okay,' I reply, super-calmly.

'That's all you have to say?'

I stop myself from asking why he needs to speak to Dr Vass. That's *his* business. Besides, he doesn't know I know he has a therapist. 'Do you want me to tell you how disappointed I am with you?' I quietly praise myself for my self-control.

'You're disappointed with me?' He laughs, but it's a nervous laugh, one filled with apprehension.

'Yes, I am. You lied to me. There should be trust if our relationship is going to work.'

One of his eyebrows hitches up a little, worry plaguing his face. 'Relationship?'

'Working relationship,' I clarify, getting a thrill from seeing the discomfort that silly word causes him. 'If you were so desperate to have me back, you should have just said so instead of resorting to using Mrs Potts and tugging on my emotions.'

'Hey, hey, wait a moment. Desperate?' He laughs, stepping forward gingerly, like he's too scared to come close. 'I don't do desperate, princess. You're getting a bit ahead of yourself now.'

'Am I?' My question is nonchalant but cocky as hell.

'Oh my God.' He looks to the ceiling. 'Is there any part of you that doesn't wind me the fuck up?'

'Clearly not,' I answer quickly, turning to exit. 'Maybe it's best if I leave.' I have him all figured out.

'No, Eleanor, wait.'

A smile tugs at the corners of my mouth. Oh, I really do have him worked out. This business between us isn't done. The chemistry hasn't been snuffed out by last night's encounter. If anything, it's worse, so why on earth am I feeling so happy about that? I should be fearing the worst. I guess I'm finding comfort in the fact that he's as frustrated and confused by the whole mess as I am. But I still have more to lose, even if it feels like I have the upper hand right now. In reality, I don't.

Pulling to a slow stop, I turn, not allowing my smile to break free. It's hard. I'm all over Becker Hunt and his supposed re-spect in the workplace. 'Calm your britches, Mr Hunt,' I say cheekily. 'I was only going to make some tea.'

His eyes nearly pop out of his head, his mouth twisting, no doubt to hold back the filthy look he wants to fire at me. But through the horror of being nailed, I see amusement begin to surface. He's fighting a smile. 'You drive me fucking crackers.'

Putting on my best warning stare, I point a finger at him. 'Don't lie to me again.'

'I won't.'

'Good.'

His smile breaks free, soft and beautiful. 'Get to work.'

'Straight away.' I back towards the door, watching as Becker watches me, his smile stretching. It's a sight to behold, a true happy smile. Then he robs me of it when he turns and wanders over to a nearby bookshelf, putting extra effort into his sexy saunter. It's intentional. He's testing me. This man is seriously an arrogant arsehole, and I wish I actually hated him. But I don't. For my sins, I like him.

I come to a stop when my back meets the door, my eyes drifting down to that special place, seeing it tense and swell with his long strides. I can't help it. I relax against the door and fall into a trance. He's playing.

'Stop looking at my arse,' he says over his shoulder.

'No.' My refusal comes without thought, and I'm suddenly not looking at his arse any more, because he's spun around, giving me something else to feast on. Something I'm now on first-name terms with, so to speak. Something I've been acquainted with, and my filthy mind is off on a tangent, wondering if I might have the pleasure again anytime soon.

'What did you say?'

'Pardon?' I land on planet Earth again with a mighty thud when the shock on his face registers.

'Just then,' he says, walking forward a few steps. 'What did you say?'

My hand blindly feels for the handle behind me as I search for the right answer. 'Straight away,' I stutter lamely, avoiding his questioning eyes. 'I'll get back to work straight away.'

'No,' he says slowly. 'After that. When I told you to stop looking at my arse.'

I clam up, not knowing how to respond. He heard. I know damn well he heard, so the fact that he wants me to repeat myself tells me he simply wants to hear it again. Surely if he wanted to forget about last night, or pretend he hadn't heard what I just said, he wouldn't push me to repeat myself. My conclusions are only strengthening by the minute, which means I'm currently holding the cards. I'm the one who dictates what happens next, but I've just realised something. A *significant* something.

I want it to happen again.

He makes me feel alive.

Whether I'm raging at him or struggling to keep my hands off him, he makes me feel alive. My heart pounds every time

I'm with him. He makes everything colourful. I keep coming back for more of the predictable, intoxicating clashes because deep down, I'm addicted to the rush of blood to my head each time he pokes me. I like the way I feel around him. I like *him*. Unconventional, daring, cocky but smart. Unapologetic for who he is. Passionate about his passion. A total maverick, just like his gramps said. Truly spirited. And he's unearthed a spirit in me, too. Everything had been sucked out of me – my soul, my heart, my essence – leaving a void, which rapidly filled with sadness and bitterness that was slowly drowning me. There was no spirit. There was no passion. I had become an empty shell who existed, who went through the daily motions of life without . . . life. Or hope. Any smile I cracked was followed quickly with gut-wrenching guilt. Any attempt to distract myself, to move on, was followed rapidly by a mental beating by my conscience.

'Eleanor?' Becker breaks into my reflections with his soft tone, and I realise I'm looking straight through him, seeing things from my past that need to stay where they are. Miles away. But now I'm here. In my present. I should be sensible, given that Becker seems to have momentarily lost his reason. 'What did you say?' he repeats, starting to breathe heavily, bracing himself.

I'm going to be sensible. I have to be sensible. 'I said . . . no.' Rational thought has abandoned me, as it always does when I'm with Becker Hunt. It's been ambushed by recklessness, and in this enlightening moment, I seem to have lost the inclination to reason with my idiocy. 'And you really don't want me to stop looking at your arse,' I add.

He gives me a lopsided grin. 'It's a good arse.'

'You have no idea,' I breathe, feeling something between us shift. It's acceptance.

But then his smile falls away and his gaze falls with it, before he breathes in deeply and slowly lets his eyes climb up my body again, pausing now and then. When we're staring at each other, for what feels like minutes, he asks, 'What's happening here, princess?'

'I don't know,' I admit quietly, willing him to give his thoughts on our confusing clashes – both the mental ones and the physical.

'Me neither.' His whole forehead creases as he slips his hands into his pockets. 'You piss me off on an hourly basis.'

'Likewise.'

He smiles. 'You also turn me on as often.'

'Likewise,' I say again, no holding back.

'Trying to be angry when my cock is throbbing isn't easy. It's like the anger enhances how much I want you.'

I lose my breath, my hand beginning to shake on the gold doorknob. I'm not sure whether it's safe to release it. My legs feel like jelly. He's *really* not holding back. 'Becker, I love this job.' I need him to know that.

He begins to nod slowly in understanding. 'And I love you being here.'

'To annoy you?'

'To look at you.' He starts to approach me, and my back instinctively melds to the door. 'I could look at you all day, princess.'

'You don't get to call me princess,' I murmur. I'm being arrested by a desire so potent, I'm struggling to remember what he *should* be calling me. What's my name?

He reaches me in a few lazy strides and presses the whole of his front into mine, pinning me to the door. I gulp, scared to look into his eyes. Becker doesn't have the same fear. He rests the tip of his finger lightly under my chin and applies the lightest of pressure, not forcing me at all, so when I lift my face to confront him, he knows it's with nothing but willingness. Our mouths brush. If I let my tongue venture past my lips, I could taste him again. This close, it's all I can think of. But then he speaks, and my hunger reaches unbearable levels. 'What I choose to call you won't feature in that pretty little head of yours, princess, when—'

'You're violating me in the most delicious ways imaginable.' I let the words out on a wisp of lustful air and release the doorknob.

'Precisely.' He grabs me with conviction, sinking his fingers into my hair and gripping hard. 'Any final words, Miss Cole?'

'Yes.' I link my hands around his shoulders and push my forehead to his. 'This doesn't count as my bonus.'

His eyes gleam in wonder. 'And what I'm about to do doesn't count as sexual harassment.'

'Fine.'

'Fine.'

Our mouths smash together violently, Becker pushing me into the door roughly. My mind is bombarded with a million memories from last night. Amazing memories. Memories I want to keep for ever. And memories I'm about to build on.

My hands take on a mind of their own, pulling at his shirt, wrenching it from his trousers so I can slide my hands over his chest. I moan my happiness when my palms find his stomach, my fingers tracing and discovering the perfect ripples all over again. He rolls us suddenly and his back slams against the door harshly, creating a deafening thud.

'Fucking hell.' He grabs my spare hand and directs it to the bulge beneath his trousers. I squeeze as I pant, and he clenches his eyes shut, sliding his hands on to my bum and massaging gently. The light pressure on my tender cheeks reminds me of the last time he was there. 'Me and your arse are going to become very friendly, Eleanor.'

I moan and shamelessly push into his hands, nibbling on his chin, then I'm rolling, my back against the door again. His hands move to the waist of my jeans and slowly drift to the front, skimming my skin lightly on their way. Every inch of me is tingling, my mind spacing out as he tackles my mouth again.

Bang.

My body jolts forward, pushing into Becker's, but I don't give up his mouth.

Bang.

I fly forward again, this time with more force, and Becker abruptly drops my lips *and* me.

He looks past me to the closed door that I'm currently propped against, then to me with worried eyes.

'Damn door.' Mrs Potts's irate tone drifts into the room, blanketing the heavy breathing that was saturating the erotic space a moment ago.

My eyes bulge with panic and my hand slaps over my mouth.

'Shit,' Becker says, backing away, his hands urgently tucking in his shirt. I fly forwards once again, except this time I don't have Becker to bounce off, but he reaches for me, just catching me before I stumble to my knees. 'She's a burly old bird,' he grumbles, steadying me quickly before moving away and leaving me to fend for myself.

I spin around, not knowing what to do, certain my face is red and my clothes all out of place. It's a dead giveaway, but before I have time to contemplate my best move, the door swings open with brute force, revealing a rankled Mrs Potts. 'The door's sticking again,' she barks, grabbing it and swinging it back and forth a few times.

I take her momentary focus on the door as an opportunity to dash to the nearest bookshelf, grabbing the first book I can lay my hands on.

'I'll have someone look at it,' Becker says, and I look up to see him fighting a smile as he watches me flick through the pages aimlessly.

I give him a pained look and a roll of my eyes. He looks perfectly composed, while I'm battling to rein in my overwhelming panic. I'm fidgeting, and that only becomes worse when I feel

Mrs Potts looking at me. 'What happened to you?' she asks.

I want to die on the spot. Immune? 'Nothing,' I squeak, placing the book back and taking hold of the shelf, leaning against it casually. It's not casual at all. I must look as guilty as I feel. I let go and ruffle my hair. Becker looks like he could fall about laughing at any moment, but he soon puts a lid on it when Mrs Potts flicks her suspicious eyes his way.

'What?' he asks, cocky as ever. He's loving this. The daring maverick.

'You tell me.'

'What would you like me to tell you?'

'Don't give me your lip, Becker boy.' She waves a threatening finger in his face, taking a peek at me again, no doubt seeking further evidence. I shy away, unwittingly giving her that evidence.

'Nothing to tell,' Becker says, unconvincingly.

She scoffs and wanders over to him, all casual, looking him up and down. Under any other circumstances, Becker cautiously backing away from the little old lady would be comical. I'm too worried to laugh, though. Mrs Potts has warned me, and I know she's warned Becker, too. She doesn't approve. She knows the consequences, as do I.

Becker only stops when the backs of his legs meet a couch, and Mrs Potts eyes come to rest on the collar of his shirt. She slowly reaches up and takes the corner lightly between her fingers, musing thoughtfully. I frown, but then get all kinds of worried when she turns and slowly makes her way to me. Like Becker, I back up until I'm cornered against the bookcase. She purses her lips and narrows her eyes. 'Nice shade of lipstick you have on today, dear.'

My fingers reach for my mouth, and my eyes cast over her shoulder to see Becker quickly look at his collar before he brushes at something. A smear. From my lipstick. Then he looks to me, his mouth dropped open. His coolness has been superseded by Mrs Potts's *super*-coolness. Now he looks guilty, too.

Caught.

She hums, and I force an innocent, sweet smile, for what reason I don't know. I'm kidding no one. My appearance, my behaviour, the evidence, it's all labelled me guilty as charged. No interrogation required. 'You have the Countryscape auction this afternoon.' Mrs Potts is speaking to Becker but looking at me. 'You mustn't be late or you'll miss the lot.'

My discomfort is suddenly transformed into excitement. Countryscape? I've heard of it. Or read about it. A private auction house in a sprawling mansion. It has showcased some of history's most famous pieces. To say it's super-exclusive is an understatement. Only the richest and most credible pass those doors. *By endorsement.* Fucking hell.

'I'm expecting a call from Doc—' Becker stops mid-sentence and flicks me a dirty look. Dr Vass. *His therapist.* I'm insanely curious. Has he discussed me with his therapist? 'I have a conference call,' he says. 'Then I'm leaving at two. I'm taking Eleanor.'

'You are?'

'You are?' Our stunned replies collide, and we both gawp at Becker like he might have lost his mind.

'Yes,' he says, picking up a book from a nearby table and pointlessly inspecting it, casually brushing off dust that isn't there.

'That's not wise, Becker boy.' Mrs Potts's tone is dripping with warning.

He slides the book on to the table and raises his chin confidently. It's laughable, but I'm unsure how to interpret his misplaced valour. 'Buying is part of this business, Mrs Potts. It will be good for Eleanor to experience it.'

'But ... we ... she ...' Mrs Potts stammers, her coolness disappearing. 'You never take company to auctions,' she snaps, worry lacing her tone. 'You need to concentrate.'

I keep my mouth firmly shut. I'm intrigued. Part of me desperately wants to go, but I'm too afraid to speak up for fear of being sliced by Mrs Potts's angry tongue. My decision to zip it is only reinforced when she turns and studies me carefully. I have no idea what's going through her mind. Maybe she's wondering who instigated the events she just walked in on. That should be an easy conclusion to reach. Except it's not. We're both guilty, and I can tell she senses it. I feel like she's delving into my mind and reading it.

'I'll be in my office,' Becker announces.

What? My eyes shoot to him as he edges towards the door, and I shake my head, forbidding him to leave the library for me to face the wrath of Mrs Potts alone. The friendly old lady looks truly formidable right now. She isn't happy. We might both be guilty of fooling around like a pair of sex-starved desperadoes, but the latest bombshell – him taking me to Countryscape – is Becker's idea and Becker's alone. I'm shirking all responsibility.

Shrugging apologetically at me, he continues to move towards the door, ignoring the angry eyes I'm sending him, something I'm trying desperately to hide from Mrs Potts.

'Bye.' He whips the heavy doors open and zooms out.

The bastard.

I remain in place, awkward as hell, waiting for it. Time seems to slow to a stop, dragging out my torture as Mrs Potts takes her duster to a bookshelf nearby and flicks it across a few shelves. I should run, but just as I'm about to make a dash for it, she sighs heavily. Then she turns and wobbles across the library, heading for the doors. That's it? Just a sigh? I thank my lucky stars, deflating on the spot.

But I'm holding my breath again when she pauses, her hand resting on the gold doorknob. 'Eleanor,' she says quietly, but not quietly enough for me to pretend I didn't hear. I wouldn't be so disrespectful, anyway.

'Yes, Mrs Potts?' I maintain my respect and face her when

she turns, hoping I've cleared my expression of all guilt and apprehension. At least, I try my very best. I have no clue if I've succeeded, and her straight face isn't giving me any hints.

'There is no happy ending here, dear.' Her voice is soft, almost pitiful. Maybe it's the distressed undertones telling me she's speaking sense, or maybe it's my gut instinct. 'Unless, of course, I'm mistaken in my assumptions.'

I almost manage to disguise my frown. I know exactly what her assumptions are and there is nothing I can do to prevent her from assuming what she's assumed. My mind is running away with me as I stand like a statue under Mrs Potts's glare, and my reply is delivered with conviction I'm faking to within an inch of my life. And I feel so guilty for lying to the dear old lady. 'Nothing has happened between Mr Hunt and me.'

'That's good. I already told you, Eleanor, he has an unhealthy way of dealing with his parents' deaths. Don't be one of those ways. Leave that to the Alexas of this world.' She nods and leaves the library. My relief should be evident in the deflation of my lungs, but I'm not relieved at all. Her words have stung like a monster wasp. I'm instantly transported to the nightclub last night and the women draped all over him. And to outside his office when he put on a special show for me. And just like it was then, my ability to breathe is stolen from me. My heart constricts painfully in my chest and worrying fury burns my mind, like acid has been poured over my brain. *Leave that to the Alexas of this world.* The temporary women. The *many* temporary women.

My craving for Becker has made way for uncertainty following Mrs Potts's subtle nudge and blunt words. It's ridiculous. Anyone with semi-functioning vision could see plain as day what was going on in here. I'm not naïve enough to believe Mrs Potts bought my lame lie. She knows damn well. This is a backward, mutual understanding, that's what it is. A twisted way of acknowledging it, but jointly pretending it never happened.

The knife twists. I'm in mental fucking agony. Problem is, I'm not sure who to blame for my hurt. Really, it's my fault. All me. For being weak in the moment. I quickly remind myself I have a job I love, and I should focus on keeping it.

I laugh to myself and my stupidity, as I find a chesterfield and drop into it. The warnings, the disapproval. I'm not about to fall in love with the arrogant twat. My thought process, in particular my last thought, hits me like a brick. Categorically, that isn't going to happen, which leads me to my next sobering thought, assisted conveniently by a flashback of my encounter with the bitter woman in the ladies' at the nightclub last night. What's the point of encouraging anything between us? It has a sell-by date, and what happens then? Namely, with my job? My palm comes to rest on my throat when I begin to feel suffocated. I wouldn't be able to work here. We'll have our fun, one of us will get bored and end the affair – probably Becker – and then it will be impossible to work together. The whole friends thing never works, and the whole employer–employee relationship definitely won't. Oh God, what have I been thinking? Mrs Potts is trying to do me a favour. She said herself that she needs me here. She knows as well as I do that a reckless affair with Becker will be the end of my time at The Haven. One night alone nearly destroyed it. She wants to keep me. It's no wonder she's trying to prevent it. *She's* seeing sense. This is good, since my sense has abandoned me all too often lately. I came to London to pursue my dream career. Not to get caught up in a fling with a notorious womaniser. What am I thinking?

I don't get a chance to analyse the situation any further, not that I need to. The door opens and Becker's head pops around. 'Is it safe?'

'Thanks for that,' I say sarcastically. Why's he looking all smiley?

His shoulders jump up on a tiny shrug and he slips in, closing the door quietly behind him. He wanders over to me casually and when he makes it to me, he crouches and cages me in on the couch. I lean back, wary, and he frowns, confused by my withdrawal. It's the cutest expression, if a little annoying. I'm certain Mrs Potts would have found him and given him a reality check, too. Or a warning. Whichever. Doesn't he care any more? Well, I do. Mrs Potts's looks of disdain and sobering words are currently stomping all over my mind. I won't be forgetting any of *that* in a hurry.

'What's the matter?' he asks, straightening up. He looks worried, and so he should be.

'Didn't she just give you a subtle warning?'

'I've been on a call.'

He's been on a call. To his therapist? What's this therapist saying? What are they talking about? Is this thing between us being encouraged? Or discouraged? Whatever, his behaviour now doesn't seem like he's had the same dose of reality shoved down his throat that I had. Does he actually want to carry on where we left off?

It looks like it's up to me to put a stop to this crazy shit once and for all. I stand, forcing him to stand, too. 'I'll be getting on.' My voice is shaking, and I'm staring at his chest. I can't look at him. I mustn't look at him.

'Right,' he says quietly, stretching the word out for ever. He doesn't move, so I shift to the side, seeing his brogues move with me.

'Is there anything else?' I ask, forcing my vocal cords to remain steady.

'Yes, there is.' He moves in, taking my chin in his fingers and lifting my face, surprising me. I know what's coming, but I don't put up a fight. He dips and claims my lips, but his brutal tactics are long gone. He's gentle and slow, tender. It sends my confused mind into a further tailspin.

'Mr Hunt, please.' My hands meet his chest and push lightly. Unconvincingly.

'Quit with the Mr Hunt bollocks, princess,' he mumbles into my mouth, coiling a well-formed arm around my waist. 'Your attempt at formal isn't gonna wash.' I'm compressed against him, my palms on his chest now trapped. It's a bad place for them to be. He's almost reverent, his tongue lazily roaming my mouth.

'Please.' This kiss is making me dizzy. Dizzy with delight, dizzy with doubt. He's swallowing me up, immobilising me with the sensation of his soft lips and delicate tongue. It's so, *so* good. 'Please,' I whisper again, begging feebly. 'Please stop.'

Our kiss slows. A tiny nibble of my lip followed by a delicate peck nearly floors me, nearly has me fighting my trapped hands free and throwing my arms around his neck. But I don't. I allow him to break away and desert my unstable body.

'Okay.' He reaches under his glasses and rubs his eyes wearily. 'It's done. We're done.'

Again, I think to myself. It's done *again*, but this time there will be no next time. Perspective is a glorious thing. It also hurts like fucking hell. My hand goes to my blouse and I cough, clearing my throat. 'Thank you.'

He nods, his lips forcing into a straight line as he watches me. He's trying to figure me out, and knowing I'm displaying all kinds of uncertainty, my eyes flick away from his for a split second. He sighs and gestures to the clock. 'It's noon. I'd still like you to come to Countryscape with me, given that you seem to be taking this job quite seriously.'

He's trying to be funny, trying to lighten the mood. I'm grateful, but I'm not sure spending any more time with him would be a good idea right now, no matter how much I'd love to experience Countryscape. 'I don't think that'll go down well with Mrs Potts,' I say, indicating towards the door. 'Your private viewing at Bonhams has been arranged for Friday next week. Nine o'clock. The Rembrandt has been returned and the hair-line crack on the frame repaired.' *Keep it business,* I tell myself.

Keep it safe. 'I should get on before Mrs Potts hunts me down.'

He laughs, but there's annoyance lacing it. 'I'll deal with Dorothy. I want you to come.'

I recoil, unsure. 'It won't look good. You and me going off—'

'Would you like to come with me, Eleanor?' Becker asks quietly, something lingering in his eyes that I've seen before. Desperation? He *wants* me to go?

I nod and swallow hard, thinking I might be my own worst enemy. 'Yes, I'd love to.'

'Good, we leave in an hour.' He makes for the door, his long strides eating up the distance in the blink of an eye, limiting my viewing time of his arse. I try not to be disappointed. I'm waiting for his usual quip when he knows I'm staring at it. Except it doesn't come.

Taking the handle, he pulls the door open, but then pauses. He doesn't turn around. 'Wear something pretty,' he orders softly. 'It's the countryside. All manor-ish and posh.' The door closes, and he's gone, leaving me in a sudden state of panic.

Something pretty? I look down at my jeans and shirt combo, then to the clock. I have an hour to pull something together.

Shit, I'm supposed to be meeting Lucy for lunch. I mentally track my phone down . . . to the pavement outside the club. I dive towards the phone on the coffee table and call directory enquiries to get Lucy's work number. Then I make a quick call to cancel lunch, feeding her small scraps of information that drive her wild. She only lets me hang up once I promise to fill her in later.

Chapter 19

I can't believe I did it. Like a madwoman, I ran down Regent Street, searching for a store, any store, to find something suitable to wear. I would never have got home, changed, *and* made it back to The Haven in time, so I'm not going to beat myself up for being a little frivolous in my hour of need. My credit card is for emergencies, and this is an emergency. That's my excuse, and I'm sticking to it. I'm even okay with the fact that I not only bought a new dress – a lovely blush-coloured button-through swishy piece that hugs my breasts and hips before tons of material tumbles to my knees – I also grabbed a lovely nude traditional mac that complements it. The assistant said it was 'wow' and my leather jacket just wasn't doing it. Neither were my ankle boots, and that's why my feet are now graced in some gorgeous nude heels. And my neck was cold, so I finished the look off with a massive cream silk scarf. And the cream leather gloves to match.

I disregard the obscene amount of money I've just blown, and the reason I've blown it, and sashay down the familiar alleyway. I'm smiling ... until I emerge into the peaceful tranquillity of The Haven's courtyard and see Mrs Potts waiting for me. My feet stutter to a halt, and I stand quietly while she takes in me and my new attire. Heck, I've made too much effort, and it's not escaping her notice. Has Becker spoken to her about Country-scape? And if he did, is she pissed off?

'You look lovely, dear,' she says, stunning me. 'You'll fit right in.'

Oh? I brush down my new mac. 'Thank you.'

She smiles sympathetically. She thinks I'm trying to impress him. When she's out of sight, I drop my head back and look to the skies in exasperation. No, I'm not. I just want to . . . fit in.

'The grumpy face kind of ruins the elegance.'

My head snaps down, and I find Becker in the distance, regarding me closely. I come over all restless and start faffing with anything I can lay my hands on, starting with my scarf. Oh, good God, he looks magnificent in a brown tweed suit, with navy brogues and matching tie and hanky poking neatly out of his top pocket. His hair has been manipulated to the side. His glasses are gracing his perfect face. His jaw is peppered with stubble.

I'm fucking doomed.

'Will you just stand still for a moment?' he calls, halting my fidgeting.

'Excuse me?'

'You look perfect. Stop fiddling.'

I force myself to obey and push my shoulders back, my breasts jutting out as a result. I didn't mean to do that. I was trying to stand tall and elegantly.

'Better,' he says on a smirk, wandering over, his eyes sparkling in pleasure. 'You didn't need to go to all this effort, princess.' There's humour in his tone, and I leap to my defence.

'You said it's posh. I didn't want to feel uncomfortable.'

'And do you feel comfortable?'

I wriggle my shoulders on a little grimace. 'Kind of.'

He laughs as he reaches forward and affectionately pushes a stray lock of my red hair over my shoulder. The gesture is soft, sweet, and *way* too inappropriate, and it has me freezing, looking out the corner of my eye to his hand that's hovering close to my cheek. Becker's frozen too, and silence falls as I watch his eyes shimmer, the green shining through. I don't know what to do. Shy away?

He bites his bottom lip. I swallow as a result.

Oh God.

A loud clatter from across the courtyard makes us both jump back, widening the space between us. We both look to the same place at the same time, finding Becker's grandad poking at an old beam outside the Grand Hall with his walking stick.

Becker curses and shoots over. 'Gramps, what are you doing?'

Old Mr H totters around at the sound of his grandson's worried tone and smiles the brightest smile I've ever seen. It warms me to the bone. 'Becker boy.' He accepts Becker's offer of support, linking arms with him and giving his cheek an affectionate pat with his old, deformed hand. 'Just checking for woodworm.'

Becker rolls his eyes. 'There's no woodworm, Gramps.'

'I know that because I just checked. Can't be too careful, Becker boy. If those little buggers find their way into the Grand Hall, we'll have a catastrophe on our hands.'

I chuckle to myself as I wander over to join them, watching their exchange fondly. 'Good afternoon, Mr H.'

'Afternoon, Eleanor,' he says, flicking his eyes to me and doing a double take. 'Oh, I say.'

I sag and wait for it.

'Do you have another date?'

I turn tomato red. 'No, I'm going to Countryscape with Mr Hunt.'

Now Becker rolls his eyes at me, and I shrug, giving him a *what?* look. If we don't tell Mr H, Mrs Potts will. 'Thought she would learn a lot,' Becker sighs, flicking his grandad a wary look, like he's waiting for the backlash.

Mr H is looking at his grandson like he's lost his mind. 'You're taking Eleanor to Countryscape?'

Becker nods decisively.

'But ... what ...' He does a damn fine rendition of Mrs

Potts, who was equally as stunned by Becker's proclamation. What's the big deal? The old man gathers himself and flicks me a cautious look before returning his attention to his grandson. 'You work alone, Becker boy. No distractions.'

Oh, I get it. When you're spending God knows how much on precious things, you need your wits about you. But I suspect that's not the only thing concerning Becker's grandad. He's worried about us being alone.

'Trust me, Gramps,' Becker says. 'My focus can't be hampered. Not by *anything*.' He tosses me a deliberate dirty look, highlighting that *anything* means *me*. I have no intention of distracting him. I'll be still and quiet and take in this new experience. He won't hear a peep from me. I take my pinched thumb and forefinger to my lips and pull an imaginary zip across, making Becker's filthy look disintegrate fast. He shakes his head on a small smile. 'Come on, you old fool.' He redirects his attention to his grandad. 'Let's get you to your suite.'

Mr H looks at his grandson, startled. '*I'm* the fool?'

Becker avoids his grandad's question, making Mr H sigh with a subtle shake of his head. 'I hope you know what you're doing.'

'I do,' Becker answers adamantly, looking at me. I shrug, unsure how to take their exchange. The old man doesn't think I should go, just like Mrs Potts. Don't they trust me enough? The thought injures me.

'I'm actually very interested to see this process, Mr H. Maybe it's too early in my learning curve, but eventually, I'd love to know how this part of The Haven's business works.'

He looks at me with a benevolent expression. 'Yes, of course, Eleanor. And it will definitely be a learning curve for you.' His face sobers, and I frown as he flicks Becker the death stare. 'Get me back inside before the crows swoop in.' The old man's quip, which is intended to be light-hearted, in fact comes across more solemnly, and I wonder if Becker comprehends his grandad's feeling of hopelessness. He must. He can't be *that* wrapped up in himself. I've known the old man for a matter of weeks, and it breaks my heart to know he feels like a burden. He travelled the world and ran this renowned business. Now he potters around The Haven feeling like a loose part. He feels redundant.

Right here and now, I decide that tomorrow I'm taking Mr H out for lunch. And I don't care what Becker says. Or Mrs Potts. I'll sneak him out if I have to.

As Becker hits the lights in the underground garage, I'm nearly blinded, the surge of energy powering them creating a glare in the sterile space. There's plenty to hold my attention – an array of luxury cars, for a start – but it's that god-loving arse currently meandering over to the key cabinet that my eyes are held rapt by.

'Stop looking—' Becker halts mid-sentence, his steps faltering, and his shoulders visibly tense. A long, lingering silence falls. An uncomfortable silence – one that needs to be broken quickly before I finish that sentence for him. Strangely, his uncanny, blind observation each time my eyes are rooted on that special place is becoming endearing. 'Never mind,' he says to himself, going through the steps required to open the cabinet. I wince on his behalf, telling myself I need to fight my natural instinct to admire him, if only to help Becker fight his instinct to tease me about it.

After selecting a set of keys, he turns and shows me the trace of an embarrassed smile, but he quickly turns it into a cheeky one. 'Today, princess, you get to meet the only woman in my life.' He wanders across the garage, leaving me processing that declaration. 'Only woman besides Dorothy, anyway.'

I have to physically stop myself from blurting *who*. My mind might have just started sprinting, but I'm not about to show it.

So instead of acknowledging my unreasonable spinning mind, I follow him to the other side of the garage. I don't want to know. *Who is she?*

'Why the need for so many cars?' I ask, not that I'm interested in what his answer might be. It's just a ploy to stop myself asking another question.

Damn it.

Who?

He reaches the only car in the garage that's draped in a protective cloth. 'Not *need*,' he muses, heading around the front. 'More *want*.' He takes the sheeting at the edge and whips it off, revealing a very shiny silver car. It's gleaming, sparkling with flickers of twinkling lights as the bright lighting from the garage ceiling competes with the paintwork. 'Wow,' I say, looking to Becker, who's smiling at it fondly.

'Meet Gloria,' he says proudly, discarding the sheet and running a palm carefully down the side.

'Gloria?' I say on a small laugh.

He looks at me, offended. 'Yes, the only woman in my life.'

The penny drops. 'Gloria,' I say slowly, shaking my head, ignoring the elation that washes over me because of Becker's announcement.

'She's the perfect woman,' he begins, and my eyes roll. 'She's beautiful, she doesn't answer back, and she does exactly what I tell her to.'

He never ceases to amaze me. 'She's also old,' I point out unreasonably. I only know this because Becker is currently taking the soft top down manually. Everything else looks brand-spanking new.

'She's a 1966 Aston Martin DB5, the queen of the classic cars, and I'm in love with her.' He huffs and puffs as he fights with the mechanical roof. 'Don't be jealous, princess. Just be happy for me.'

I scoff at the absurdity of his comment, an over-the-top,

totally dramatic scoff. 'She also has no feelings, so it makes sense you get along.'

Making his way around to my side, he gives me that adorable lopsided grin as he opens the door and swoops his arm out in a gesture for me to get in. 'My lady.'

Slipping in and pulling on my belt, I watch him walk around to the driver's side, wondering how the rest of the day might pan out.

'Just remember,' he says, sliding into the black leather seat and inserting the key into the ignition, 'you're at work today.'

That answers my question. I'm at work, therefore I should be professional. There's a problem, though. I can be professional, but I struggle to maintain that professionalism when Becker pushes at the boundary lines. We're always either in the grey or hovering very close to the edge of it. 'And so are you,' I politely remind him. He needs to remember that detail too.

'Have no fear, princess,' he teases, pressing a button that starts to lower a platform from the ceiling. 'When I'm focused on something precious and priceless, there's nothing else on my mind.' The hissing of hydraulics almost drowns him out. Almost. I wish it had, because now I'm furious with myself for silently wishing he was incapable of thinking of anything else but me. I'm pathetic. If I wasn't on my way to Countryscape, I might bail and decide this is a terrible idea. I'm not sure I appreciate friendly, playful Becker. It makes controlling my urges more tricky.

Once the ramp has lowered, Becker pulls slowly forward, and then presses another button that has us rising steadily. The cold air of the derelict factory unit hits me, and it's only now that it occurs to me that we're in an open-top car. In November. The low winter sun has been present in recent days, but with clear skies comes lower temperatures. It's bloody freezing. Is he mad? I shiver and pull in my coat, gazing around as we rise to the factory floor. It's going to get colder when we roll out of here, and colder still when we're sailing down an open road. The pretentious Ferrari is suddenly very appealing. 'It's a bit chilly,' I mumble to myself, pulling on my new gloves.

The car jolts, indicating the end of the climb from the garage, and Becker turns to me. 'Come here,' he says, reaching over and taking my scarf. My head recoils instinctively in response to his move, not that he notices. Or if he does, he ignores it. He calmly folds and smooths the material of my scarf under my close observation until he has a large triangle. Then he drapes it over my head, sheltering my hair and my ears, before tying a bow under my chin with the loose ends. I smile as he concentrates on tucking some misbehaving locks of my red hair into the edges, a frown jumping on to his forehead when they refuse to remain where he's put them. 'Even your hair's irritating,' he mutters, his eyes meeting mine and holding them for longer than is acceptable for an employer–employee relationship. 'Perfect,' he says quietly, nodding decisively. We both seem to find reality at the same time, each of us snapping out of the moment and looking away.

'My duties for today?' I ask, aiming to get us back on track quickly.

'Don't piss me off,' Becker fires shortly, revving the engine and flipping a switch that has the factory doors sliding open. 'Do you think you can manage that?'

'No problem, sir,' I answer cockily. I can't promise that. Pissing Becker off comes naturally.

'Don't call me sir,' he says quietly, and I look across to see him shudder, remembering him barking those same words at me in the library one time.

'Why?'

He glances out the corner of his eye. 'It doesn't help me when I'm having to resist you, Eleanor.'

I breathe in and quickly return my focus forward. 'Okay.'

'Good.' He hits the pedal, and we're zooming out of the garage like lightning. 'Get ready for the ride of your life, princess.'

I'm inhaling again. I try not to, but it's impossible when he's chucking innuendoes all over the place. Actually, the first wasn't an innuendo at all. It was a statement. An honest statement?

'I mean in Gloria,' he clarifies, returning his attention to the road. 'It's thrilling.'

Forcing myself to disregard Becker's inappropriate comments, I breathe in the fresh air currently whizzing past my face at high speed, and when music is introduced to the mix, I'm more than thankful. It seems neither of us can say the right thing, so filling the empty space with INXS's 'Need you Tonight' is welcome. And a bit . . . suggestive.

It takes a solid hour to get out of London. We hit the country roads, and Becker opens up Gloria, putting his foot down and relaxing back in his seat. It's nippy, but he has the heater blasting and the scarf he so thoughtfully secured over my head is keeping my ears warm. I'm relieved I took the initiative to transfer my shades from my other bag. Becker has replaced his normal glasses for sunglasses, too, and despite the music having stopped about ten miles ago, I'm no longer uncomfortable. Becker is right. Gloria is one hell of a ride.

'Mr H and Mrs Potts really didn't think it was a good idea for me to accompany you today,' I muse, waiting to see what reaction that statement draws.

'You still have a lot to learn about the Hunt Corporation, Eleanor.'

'Like?'

'Many things.' He looks across the car and smiles. 'You'll learn along the way.'

I return his smile, looking forward to learning everything there is to know. 'Your grandad seems sad.' Becker appears unaware of his grandfather's feelings. Or is he just ignoring them?

He laughs it off. 'Is that a statement or a question?'

'It's an observation.'

'He's an old man.' He flicks his eyes briefly to mine. 'He hasn't been the same since he lost Mags.'

'Your grandmother?' I ask, shifting to face him. Am I about to learn a little more about the Hunt family history?

'Yes, my grandmother.' He's talking with complete detachment. 'Died twenty-five years ago.'

'I'm so sorry.' Human nature has me reaching for his left hand, which is currently holding the gearstick, and squeezing gently in a sign of compassion.

'Don't be.' He glances down and flexes his fingers. I snatch my hand back, injured that he didn't accept my offer of comfort.

'And your father?' I ask tentatively, wondering if he'll open up about him.

Becker laughs, not the reaction I was expecting. 'Jesus, princess. What's with the twenty questions?' He's trying to evade my enquiry, but I'm now more intrigued than ever.

'If it's too painful, I understand.'

'It's not painful,' he mutters. 'I'm over it.'

I flinch at his brutality, his harsh assertion cutting deeply. I hate to think what his grandad would make of that. So he's in therapy for fun, is he? I detect hot resentment, and despite Mrs Potts's warning words to never speak of it, I go for the jugular. 'Do you want to talk about it? I'm a good ear.'

Becker looks at me out the corner of his eye. 'Can I call a friend?'

My lips straighten, unamused.

'What about fifty-fifty?' he asks.

'Not funny.'

'Okay, I'll ask the audience,' he relents on a sigh, taking a corner fast.

'You have no audience.' I gasp, grabbing the door handle for dear life. He seems to be getting faster and faster, and I wonder if it's because I'm getting personal. It's making him edgy.

His attention is being divided equally between the road and me, back and forth. 'Why not ask about my mother?' That resentment has just doubled.

I swallow hard, now unsure of how to handle this. 'She died in a car accident.'

'Well done,' he says coldly. 'Now ask about my father's death.' The playful, cheeky Becker has been lost amid my questioning, and I seriously dislike myself for it. 'C'mon, Eleanor.' He laughs callously. 'Don't wimp out on me now.' Another corner is taken fast, this one sharp, and then he's swinging into the right-hand lane to overtake a tractor.

I clutch my seat, fear beginning to grip me. He's being reckless. I've sparked anger in him – deep-rooted, damaging anger. 'Becker.' An oncoming car sounds its horn and flashes its lights as it coasts towards us. 'Becker, stop.' My hand flies out and grabs his arm. The car is getting closer and closer, the horn louder and louder, and then, as smoothly and calmly as can be, Becker zips back on to the correct side of the road. He makes it just in time. The car sails past, the horn a continuous blare until it fades into the distance.

My palm slaps on my chest to stop my thundering heart from breaking free.

'They're both dead, Eleanor,' he says calmly, like he hasn't just given me the fright of my life. Was that a warning? Don't pry again, or I'll scare the god-loving shit out of you? 'I'm sure you wouldn't appreciate me asking about *your* dead father.'

My mouth falls open. 'How . . .' My question fades to nothing. Of course. His grandfather must have told him.

He flicks me a sideways glance. 'I'm sorry for your loss.'

'Don't be,' I snap. 'I've come to terms with it.' His acknowledgement of my loss was hardly sincere. It was lip service. He couldn't give a flying fuck about my loss. I should adopt the same detachment where his heartbreaks are concerned. Problem is, he doesn't seem heartbroken. He seems more . . . angry.

He breathes out deeply, and I look down at his hand when it lands on mine, squeezing. The move is unexpected and definitely in the grey area of our working relationship. 'I'm sorry. I shouldn't have been so short with you.' He gives me a faint smile, one that I find easy to return. I should have listened to Mrs Potts and kept my mouth shut.

'I shouldn't have pried.'

He shrugs. 'Tell me about your father.'

I laugh a little. 'He'll probably be looking down on me now shaking his head.'

'Why?'

'Because he never really appreciated the high-end world of this business.'

Becker smiles, shaking his head in disbelief. 'He didn't leave you any priceless treasures then?'

'The only thing Dad left behind was a dilapidated workshop full of junk.'

Becker gives me a sympathetic sideways look. I brush it all off with a flippant wave of my hand. 'Why are we going to Countryscape, anyway?' I ask. There will be no junk there.

His smile broadens in a heartbeat, and he returns his attention to the road and his hand to the gearstick. 'Michelangelo.'

'The ninja turtle?'

He turns disbelieving eyes on to me, his face an expression of pure horror, until he sees my grin. 'Hilarious, princess. Fucking hilarious.'

'You mean a real Michelangelo?' I ask, fascinated.

He laughs, a sweet-sounding laugh – soft and low. 'Why, is there a fake Michelangelo?'

I give him a tired look. 'You know as well as I do that there are forgers far and wide.'

He hums on a nod of agreement. 'The piece has been authenticated by the world's top expert.'

'Holy shit.' My mind is blown, but Becker seems to be taking it all in his stride. 'What piece?'

'*Head of a Faun*. Presumed lost by some—'

'Or Michelangelo destroyed it himself,' I cut in, my excitement uncontainable. 'Oh my God.' I slump back in my seat. 'He created more sculptures than he did paintings. All have been accounted for, except *Head of a Faun*. It's been missing for centuries, and now it's turned up out of the blue?'

He nods his head, smiling at my astonishment.

'Where was it found?'

'In the attic of the Saunders country mansion when it was repossessed.'

'Wow. Bet it's not getting repossessed now.'

He chuckles. 'No, I expect now the Saunders are moving to Monaco.'

'Hey.' I turn in my seat to face him, something quite unbelievable coming to me. 'Is that why we're here? To buy it?' Fucking hell, I'm no expert, but it must be worth millions.

Becker nods, and my mind blows further. Then he says something that worries me. 'Brent Wilson wants it, too.'

I look at him, my mouth agape. 'He does?'

He glances at me, catching my stunned expression. 'It's a private auction. He's been after my endorsement to get him in.'

'Oh . . .' Becker has something Brent wants. An endorsement to Countryscape. So *that's* why he's sniffing around, and I bet Becker has loved every moment of flatly refusing his request. I had wondered why a multimillion-dollar hotel mogul had the time to visit The Haven so often of late. 'And you won't endorse him?' I ask. It's a stupid question.

'No.'

'Because you want it and if he's there, he might get it.' That's the crux of it.

'Precisely.' Becker smirks, and I roll my eyes. 'And—'

'Yeah, yeah, I know.' I return forward and centre my attention on the road. 'You'd rather burn it than let him get his hands on it.'

He nods his head in acknowledgement. 'Problem is, someone else endorsed him.'

'No.' I shoot Becker a disbelieving look, knowing what this means. A bidding war. 'You can't let him win.' I don't know what's come over me, but I really don't want Brent to get the long-lost treasure. I've seen The Haven and everything it represents to the antiques and art world. *Head of a Faun* deserves to be within its walls.

'I knew I liked you for a reason.'

I flash him a surprised look. Did he just say that? 'Pardon?'

He begins to shuffle in his seat, flustered, refusing to look at me. 'Didn't say a word.'

'Yes, you did.' I take off my sunglasses and start to chew one of the arms as I study him. 'In fact, you said eight words. Would you like me to remind you what they were?'

He brings his forefinger to his lips and holds it there lightly. The move spikes a memory of last night, and I fidget unnecessarily. I know what's coming. 'Shhhh,' he whispers. The simple whoosh of noise sounds erotic, adding to my fluster, and immediately has me crossing my legs subtly. Becker Hunt doesn't miss a trick, and he didn't miss that. He turns a cocky grin on to me. 'Okay there?'

'Super.' I delve into my bag for something to do, other than look as desperate as I am. 'How long until we arrive?' I pull my lipstick out and the sun visor down.

'We're here.' He gestures towards acres of empty fields.

'Wow,' I blurt out, seeing a magnificent country estate set on a hill in the distance.

He takes his phone from his inside pocket and taps a few buttons before putting it back. Then he flicks the stereo on, and Coldplay's 'Clocks' kicks in before he puts his foot down and we zoom down the country road. I grab my scarf and hold it to my head, laughing.

'Welcome to Countryscape, princess,' Becker shouts over the wind and music, turning a disarming smile my way. 'Let's buy ourselves some lost treasure.'

Chapter 20

Classic cars. Everywhere. It's the first thing I notice when we drive up the gravel driveway. I could have been transported back in time. The impressive building, constructed with a deep orange stone, rises from the ground proudly, the brickwork intricate around the stained-glass windows. It's majestic, the stone cherubs edging the roofline only adding to the magnificence. There are dozens of them, one different from the next, all facing the driveway, welcoming visitors.

From a distance, sitting high on a hilltop, this place looked breathtaking. Close up, it's beyond spectacular. But there's a strange sense of foreboding lingering around the ancient brickwork. It's welcoming but intimidating. I'm in awe but feel vulnerable. I can't figure out whether I like it or not.

Becker slows down to a crawl, stretching out our approach to the house. It gives me more time to absorb my surroundings, to try and decide if I'm comfortable or not. It's time I don't need. I feel edgy. I feel like we're creeping up slowly so as not to disturb the angels keeping guard. 'Why so slow?' I ask, a little irritably.

'The gravel. Too fast and it'll kick up and chip Gloria.' He rumbles to a stop, pulling up behind a Bentley. I'm not sure if he's scowling at my question or at the car. 'Piece of shit.' He may as well be growling.

I look at the Bentley, thinking it looks far from a piece of shit, but I know he isn't referring to the prestigious car. Does this mean that Brent's here already?

Becker cuts the engine and swaps his shades for his Ray-Bans.

'I want to set some ground rules before we go in.'

'I won't talk to him,' I murmur, letting myself out of Gloria. I wouldn't want to, anyway. I straighten and turn to close the door, finding Becker is still sitting in his seat, looking up at me. 'That was what you were going to say, wasn't it?'

'Yes, he'll be picking your brain on things that don't concern him.' He jumps out and begins to pull the roof across.

'I wouldn't disclose anything work-related to anyone,' I clarify, though I expect he wasn't only referring to work.

'I should hope not,' Becker says, throwing me a warning look. 'Since you're in Becker's Circle of Trust, and it's in the NDA.'

'You mean the NDA that doesn't exist?'

'It will do soon,' he replies flippantly, rounding the car and taking my elbow. 'A few other ground rules we need to be clear on, princess.'

'Like what?' I look up at him, my mind sprinting through what he'll possibly say.

'Like don't speak unless spoken to.'

What am I, a child? I gawp at him, trying not to feel slighted. I fail on every level. 'You mean like a good little girl?'

'Just like that.' He doesn't give my affronted state the attention it warrants. 'And when you do speak, don't mention anything about your work at The Haven, The Haven itself, or me.'

'So basically, I'm best saying nothing at all.'

'Ideally, yes.'

We reach the oversized stone steps leading up to the entrance and start the mammoth climb. Each side is flanked by imposing stone columns with topiary trees nestled between each towering pillar, concealing the entrance to the mansion. 'What if I'm asked a question I shouldn't answer?' My slight has made way for panic. I'm going to spend the afternoon hiding behind a plant pot in the hope that no one sees or speaks to me.

'You have a quick mouth, Eleanor.' He flashes me an ironic look, not that it makes me feel any better. My so-called quick mouth works best when dealing with my aggravating boss. With Becker, it comes naturally. I can't guarantee it will function within the walls of this place.

'Why did you bring me here?' I ask, rattled by the pressure he's placing on my shoulders. I should wait for him in the car. Or go for a walk in the countryside. My earlier excitement about an afternoon out with Becker at Countryscape has dissipated. Gone completely. My uncertain feelings towards this building sliced my enthusiasm slightly, but Becker's demands have just severed them beyond repair. I want to leave.

'Now you're in my circle of trust, it's time for you to see what it's all about,' he says quietly.

I shoot him a look. 'What *what's* all about?'

'Me.'

'You?' I already know what Becker's all about. Have done since I clapped eyes on him. Or maybe I'm kidding myself and there's more to him than meets the eye.

'Me,' he confirms, giving me a sideways grin. 'Hope you're ready.'

'I am,' I answer confidently. What a joke. I've never been ready for Becker Hunt.

When we cross the threshold of the entrance, my desire to probe further dies the moment the activity inside hits me. It's bustling, well-turned-out people everywhere, some laughing, some in serious conversation. Becker leads me through the centre of the vast entrance hall, not acknowledging a single person on our way. But his arrival is noticed by everyone we pass, every person noting the presence of the famed Becker Hunt. People pause conversations, some men look at him with awe, some with disdain, and then there are the women. Too many of them, all dressed in high-end designer labels, and all dripping in diamonds, pearls, rubies, emeralds . . .

Every precious gem you could possibly think of is present in this space, dangling from ears, draped around necks, adorning well-manicured fingers. Blimey, there must be millions of pounds' worth of sparklers in here.

When I finally rip my eyes away from the beauty of these women's jewellery, I find sparkling eyes too. Lots of them. Those sparkling eyes soon turn to curious eyes when they clock me shuffling behind the man who's clearly known by every single person in the room. It's like the parting of waters, everyone standing aside to let us pass. I couldn't feel any more uncomfortable. I remember Mrs Potts's proud declaration. *He's the best dealer out there.* The Hunts are famed in this industry, but Mrs Potts specifically said Becker was the most talented in the long line of Hunt men. What makes him better than the rest? Why's Becker so special? I wonder if most of his clients are women, because that would explain it perfectly.

I'm about to ask what the deal is with the grand entrance, when I remember the ground rules. Don't speak unless spoken to. Does that include speaking to him? He didn't say, so I go right ahead and ask my question. 'Bit over the top, isn't it?' I say quietly, looking right ahead to the white double doors we seem to be heading towards.

'What's that, princess?'

'The grand entrance.'

'I walked into a building.'

'And everyone fell silent.'

'I have a presence.'

'You have a big head.'

He nudges me in the side gently. 'One more ground rule.' Looking down at me, he keeps a straight face, though I can see the playful twinkle in his eyes. 'You can't insult me in public. A few eyebrows might be raised if I spank that peachy arse of yours in front of everyone.'

I press my lips together to stop from laughing out loud,

as Becker's pace slows a little when we reach the doors. But just when I'm about to follow suit, something meets my lower back, encouraging me on. Becker's hand. I'm wrapped up warm in my coat, but I can still feel his heat through my layers of clothes. I swallow and allow him to guide me into the room. The ridiculously flamboyant décor of the space doesn't grab my attention like it should. None of the incredible paintings, all originals – a Monet, a Dalí, to name just a few – have my mouth hanging open in astonishment. The ceiling mural, a depiction of the Last Supper, doesn't have me staggering to a stop in admiration. No. I can't concentrate on anything except the sizzling heat plaguing every inch of my skin beneath my clothes. It's crippling me to the point of being unable to walk steadily, so I speed up a little, breaking the contact. I need to keep my wits about me. This place is daunting enough, without the added handicap of Becker's attentive touch. It's alien to me. I can cope with his arsehole/playful behaviour, bounce off it. This isn't as easy to deal with, especially when he's already loaded the pressure on me with his *ground rules*. Besides, it's definitely a grey area. I can think of a few ground rules myself.

'Where to?' I ask, noting the rows of chairs facing the rostrum. He doesn't answer me, but when I'm about to turn and face him, I feel a familiar heat closing in again, this time near my ear. I jump out of the way like a skittish kitten, unable to control my reaction to his proximity. If he whispers anything in my ear, even a simple direction, I'm likely to melt into a pathetic pool of uselessness.

Turning confidently, as if I haven't just practically banged my head on the lovely ceiling from the height of my startled jump, I plaster a smile on my face, but it wavers when I find Becker still bent, his lush lips poised at the spot where I expect my ear was a second ago.

I start to draw breath, ready to ask again where we sit, but my question gets no further than the end of my tongue. Then I virtually bite it off to avoid shrieking an expletive.

What is *she* doing here?

Tiger bird. Weighed down by a huge fur coat, which, quite frankly, looks utterly ridiculous. Her glossy blond hair is cascading down one side of it, her pink lips pursing as she approaches. Oh, no. I can't guarantee my silence. She's not even made it to us and I already want to launch her into outer space. She has one of those faces. One with a constant sneer. One that you instantly want to slap. Add to the equation that I know Becker has screwed it, I'm in souped-up, ultra-bitchy mode. I don't want her to be one of the ways Becker deals with his demons. I don't want just *any* woman to be his outlet. My revelation doesn't cause me the worry it should, because I'm too focused on keeping my cool. I clamp my teeth down harshly, my jaw instantly aching under the pressure. We're in a posh, renowned private auction house. I can't be flashing my claws or cursing.

I can't be flashing my claws or cursing.
I can't be flashing my claws or cursing.
I can't be flashing my claws or cursing.

'What's that mutt doing here?' I spit quietly, not feeling too bad for failing in my endeavour. At least I whispered.

Becker frowns and glances over his shoulder, right as Alexa makes it to us. The air around me is electric with nutty female hormones. Alexa is giving me daggers. 'Becker,' she purrs, presenting him with her cheek for him to kiss, while keeping her eyes on me.

'Alexa.' He feeds her open need to rile me, placing his lips delicately on her cheek. I immediately want to bleach his mouth. I huff and look away, knowing I've failed in my delayed attempt to appear untouched by her tactics. She thinks she's superior to me. She probably is – all precious gems, fur coats, and designer make-up. The fact that everything under it all is fake lessens my resentment a smidgen. What is she doing here

– a place that requires endorsements to even be considered for admittance?

'Are we still on for tonight?' I know Alexa's looking at me, and though I have no right to silently demand it, I'm begging every god that's ever existed that Becker bums her off.

I can feel her eyes boring into me. I despise the thought of Becker with her. It makes me feel sick to my stomach.

I don't wait around to hear Becker reply. Instead, I wander further into the room before I lose control of my mouth, making myself focus on the paintings gracing the walls. I home in on a Dalí, smiling at the oil painting of a woman's back. It's one of the artist's less controversial creations, and also one of my favourites. *Woman at the Window in Figueres*. It still fascinates me how he got away with such erotic edges to his paintings at a time when talking about sex in public was pretty much taboo. And even though this picture is a little tamer than his other works, there's still evidence of Dalí's sexy imagination. Her bottom, for starters. Protruding and curvaceous, it's what most people see first when they study the image. And her skirt. It's see-through.

'So you brought the skivvy along,' Alexa says, loud enough for me to hear.

My attempt to distract myself from them talking nearby is dashed right there. I could have the *Mona*-fucking-*Lisa* in my grasp, and I still couldn't ignore her. I swing around, incensed. I couldn't give a toss where I am. How the fuck dare she? She's concealing a conniving grin, and Becker is watching me with caution. He should be. I'm about to rip that fur coat from her body and stuff it down her throat. Holy shit, where has this rage come from? I start marching forwards, but I only make it two steps before Becker intercepts me and steers me away,

I know it's for the best, but that doesn't curb my rage. He gives me a look to suggest I should zip it. But I can't. 'If I ever see her face at The Haven again, I'm quitting.'

'Okay.' He shrugs my scathing promise off with ease. 'We already agreed no pieces of arse at The Haven during working hours.'

I recoil. 'Oh.' Pieces of arse? Why do I feel so comforted by his referral? Does he see me as a piece of arse? Lord knows, I have enough of an arse, and Becker seems to like it.

'Is that all?'

I narrow my eyes on him. 'Are you hooking up with her tonight?' I have no right to that information, and that I've asked makes me look as jealous as I feel.

'Tonight isn't during working hours,' he says quietly, watching me closely for my reaction. I don't disappoint. My breath stutters, his reply stinging so much I'm probably wincing. 'But that's okay, right?' he goes on, his eyes laser beams on me. 'Because we're done.'

'Where to?' I ask, forcing an even tone while swallowing down my unreasonable hurt. Yes, we're done.

He regards me with probing eyes as he gestures towards a row of chairs. I ignore that look, following his outstretched arm and scooting down the aisle. Sitting down on the final seat, I look up to find Becker standing at the end of the aisle watching me. Eventually, he takes a chair three rows behind, in the very back row.

He gets comfy and pulls a brochure from the back pocket of the seat in front, then starts flicking casually through the pages. I return my attention to the rostrum, wondering if I should join him. He directed me to this row. Then took a different one. I can't sit with him?

I mull over the things I recall Mrs Potts and Mr H saying earlier today – the working alone, the concentrating, the never having company. My decision to remain where I am comes quickly, assisted by our moment back then. We're done . . . right?

I take the brochure in front of me and start browsing, looking up when I hear people starting to filter into the room. I try my hardest not to appear dumbfounded by the mass of wealth coming at me from every direction and closing me in as they all take their seats, but it's hard. Very hard. I feel inferior. I'm so far removed from my father's store, I could be on the moon. Peeking over my shoulder discreetly, I spy Becker looking down and assume he's engrossed in the pages of the glossy catalogue, but a subtle movement reveals his mobile phone in his hand. He smiles and slips it back into his pocket before returning to flicking the pages, bringing his ankle up to rest on his knee. My wayward mind wonders what he's smiling at. Alexa? Did she text him?

'Afternoon, miss.' The greeting from my left tugs my attention away from Becker to a stout, grey-haired man who's grinning down at me. 'I'm Peter. Peter Ramsbottom.'

I politely smile my hello, thinking it's best to limit my interaction with anyone. No interaction means no concern about what to say. Then I return to my mindless viewing of the antiques adorning the pages in my lap. I fear the worst when he lowers to the chair next to me.

'Haven't seen you here before.'

I smile down at the pages like an idiot, avoiding eye contact. He's going to try and make conversation. This doesn't bode well. 'First time,' I say, not offering anything more in the hope it'll deter him. He looks like a chatty type, but I'm in no mood to chat. And I'm not *allowed* to, anyway.

'Then welcome to Countryscape.'

'Thank you.' Maybe I could excuse myself and hide in the ladies' until Becker's done.

'Are you buying?' he asks, leaning in to see what page of the catalogue I'm viewing. It's only now that I notice the title of the piece on the page before me. *Head of a Faun*.

'Ah.' His pudgy finger lands on one of the photographs of the sculpture. 'Causing quite a stir, this one. Who do you work for?'

My tongue thickens in my mouth as I take in the lost piece of treasure currently looking up at me with narrow, somewhat evil eyes. Many people have anticipated what it looks like. For years, a cast was held in the Bargello Museum and was attributed as Michelangelo's *Head of a Faun*. That thing looked pretty creepy, but it hasn't a snitch on what I'm looking at now. It looks like pure evil, could possibly even be mistaken as a depiction of the devil.

'Who do I work for?' I repeat his question mindlessly, buying some time. If I answer, I could spike a whole other barrage of questions that I don't know how to answer. 'Um—' I race through my options, and just as I'm about to take the easiest, most obvious escape and declare my need for the loo, a laugh captures my attention.

I deflate and sink into the chair in despair.

'Good afternoon, Peter.' Brent takes a seat on my other side, cornering me, and reaches across my tense body, offering Peter his hand.

Peter takes it and shakes mildly, but he's reluctant. 'You got in, Wilson,' he says with as much enthusiasm as his handshake. I can only assume that Brent clearly tried Peter for an endorsement for Countryscape, too. It doesn't sound like Brent Wilson is very highly thought of. Or maybe everyone is playing the same game, trying to limit competition.

'I certainly did.' Brent's clearly chuffed with himself. 'So, you've met the lovely Eleanor.'

'Yes, but she's a bit taciturn.'

I cringe, wishing they'd hurry up with their frosty greeting so my path is clear to escape. If I was a suspicious type, which I am, I'd think their joined hands in front of me is an ploy to keep me where I am.

I can feel Brent staring at me, but I refuse to indulge him. 'I wonder why that is,' he muses, releasing Peter's hand, much to my relief. I engage my muscles, ready to stand, but Brent's hand falls straight to my lap and scoops up the catalogue. 'You've been reading up on this incredible piece.' He turns into me, making it impossible to pass him if I try to leave, which I suspect is another ploy.

I narrow my eyes, thinking now would be a great time to deliver that slap I've been mentally promising him. 'There's not much I don't know about Michelangelo.'

'This is quite exciting for you, yes?'

I pluck my catalogue from his hand and return forward, going back to browsing it. 'Yes.'

'Did I mention, Peter,' Brent muses casually, 'that Eleanor here works for Hunt.'

'Oh, she does?' Now Peter turns into me too, and I resign myself to sitting still and shutting up, not because Becker told me to, but because these two are clearly out for information. What information that might be is beyond me, but their interest in me now has my alarm bells ringing.

'Nice to see you and Becker seem to have sorted your differences out,' Brent says softly, and with zero sincerity.

I look out the corner of my eye, finding him watching me too closely. He's fishing, trying to wring me for information. That's been his game since day one, as well as riling my boss. The Hunt Corporation is notoriously cloak-and-dagger. The whole antiquing world respects the famous family run business. And I bet they're all curious about the private dealings.

'Silly misunderstanding,' I tell him with a sickly smile.

'I bet,' Brent muses.

I pull my shoulders in. My personal space is being invaded, and it's beginning to piss me off. What information do they think they can extract from me? How much Becker is prepared to pay for the sculpture? I don't know, and I wouldn't tell if they tortured me for the information.

'So, what's it like working for the Hunts?' Peter asks.

'Interesting,' I answer quickly and dismissively. Brent laughs, and I turn a disdainful look on to him. 'Is something funny?' I ask.

He shrugs. 'Not at all.'

'Boy, would I love a peek in the famous Grand Hall,' Peter says. 'Is it as magnificent as they say?'

'No comment.' I work myself up further and further, sidestepping a few more seemingly harmless questions and answering some with short, one-word answers, until I've had enough. I will not sit here accepting their obvious attempts to wring me for information. If neither man moves, I'll climb over the seats. I'm not being held hostage. I stand abruptly. Maybe I'm being too cagey, giving them something to be curious about. 'Excus— oh.'

My feet leave the ground, and I'm hauled up over the chairs, landing on my feet with less style and grace than I'd like. Blowing my hair from my face, I find Becker throwing daggers at Brent and Peter.

'Excuse us,' he says, perfectly civilly, but there's threat lacing his tone. He takes my hand and pulls me to the back row. 'Sit,' he orders firmly, tugging me down to the seat as he lowers to his own. He doesn't release my hand and though it's a monumentally stupid thing to do, I don't wriggle free of his firm hold. 'You did good.'

'What?' I ask on a hushed whisper, seeing the room is now filled to capacity in the time I've been interrogated. Then it hits me. 'You planted me there?' I ask, horrified. 'To test me?'

He keeps his attention ahead. 'Let's not be all dramatic. You passed. Congratulations.'

His disregard for the difficulty of my situation astounds me. 'You're a wanker,' I mutter, yanking my hand from his. The boundary line just got buried.

'Ground rules,' he says quietly and calmly, ignoring my spiteful insult.

'You can shove your ground rules where the sun doesn't shine.'

'Shhhh . . .'

I scoff and go to stand, now needing the ladies' to splash my cheeks and cool down my growing rage, but I'm pulled firmly down to my chair. I make a rubbish job of wrestling out of his hold inconspicuously.

'Stay where you are,' he warns, cool as a cucumber. 'You'll want to see this.'

My curiosity is piqued immediately, and I hate myself for it. 'What?'

'Just behave and pay attention.'

I obey, looking around for what might be the subject of my supposed interest. I see nothing, except a sea of people and a suited man upfront, taking position behind the rostrum and tapping the mic. 'Good afternoon, ladies and gentlemen,' he says. 'Welcome to Countryscape.'

A flurry of low mumbles emanates from the crowd and a few people applaud the speaker's arrival. Not Becker. His face remains straight, revealing no indication of his mood. I can't believe he set me up like that. A test. That I passed the test is irrelevant, and I'm going to ignore the pang of pride I feel because of that. He's immoral, and as soon as we're out of here, I'm going to give him a piece of my mind.

The auctioneer launches into a detailed speech. It goes on and on, with no one seemingly paying attention as he rambles about the history of Countryscape. I expect they've heard it all before, as have I, but I still settle in for the introduction and listen attentively while he talks through the history of the building – about how it became such a prolific, worldwide-famous auction house, a meeting point for some of the best-known art historians in the world. Built in 1752 by the Masons – a family held in high esteem in the aristocratic world, and famous collectors of antiques – Countryscape is famous for housing and exhibiting some of the most famous historical finds in recent history.

Situated in the countryside with no neighbours for a ten-mile radius, it boasts a church, a gatehouse, a lake, and a woodland. The current Masons live in a smaller dwelling on the grounds and kindly opened up Countryscape in 1945 to the elite art and antiquing world. It's still very fascinating, however old the story is to me.

'Here we go,' Becker says, nudging me and nodding to a door behind the auctioneer. It opens, and a suited man appears, wearing white gloves. He has a small tin in his hand. It's non-descript, a plain silver case, from what I can see. I'm buggered if I know what it is.

'A cigarette case,' Becker whispers, obviously sensing my perplexity. 'Belonged to Marilyn Monroe . . . supposedly.'

'Supposedly?'

He hums, glancing around the room. 'I'm sceptical.'

'You think it's a fake?' I ask, keeping my voice to a whisper.

His finger comes up to his lips, quietening me before he has a chance to add the inevitable sexy shush. But he does anyway. 'Shhhh . . .'

I shudder, fighting off the flurry of tingles his gesture spikes.

'Starting the bids on the phone at ten thousand pounds,' the auctioneer declares, pointing his wooden gavel towards a balcony, prompting me to look up. A row of suited men line the space, all with mobile phones poised at their ears. 'And we have eleven thousand in the room.' My attention flies down, seeing a round paddle held in the air a few rows in front. I can't see who it is, but the red nails and fur-cuffed wrist tells me it's a woman. 'Twelve.' He's pointing back at the balcony, but I don't get a chance to follow his gavel again because the lady up front shouts, 'Thirteen,' before I can look away from her.

'Thirteen in the room.'

No matter how much I try to disguise my amazement, I fail. My mouth is agape and my head turns back and forth from the room to the balcony continuously as the bidding gets higher and higher. A cigarette case? I bet if the asking price of every piece that passed through my father's shop over a year was added together, it wouldn't come close to the sum this piece is poised to achieve.

'Twenty-five thousand once,' the auctioneer yells, his gavel hovering in the air. He looks over his glasses, scanning the room. 'Twice.' I'm tense, waiting. 'Sold to the lovely Miss Depont.' I jump in my seat when he smashes the gavel down on the rostrum, and everyone in the room starts clapping as the lady who paid a crazy amount of cash for a silver cigarette case stands and takes a bow. My astonishment only increases tenfold when I get a glimpse of her face. She's a dead ringer for Marilyn Monroe.

'Did she really just pay twenty-five grand for a cigarette case?' I look to Becker, who's bashing out a text on his phone. He isn't the least bit fazed. My desire to crane my neck to see who he's texting nearly gets the better of me. What I shamelessly do instead, though, is glance around for Alexa to see if she's engaged in any mobile activity. God, I'm pitiful. I force my attention back to the front.

'She's probably the most renowned Monroe impersonator in the world.' Becker looks past me and reaches for something. 'Espresso?'

I turn and find a tray being presented to me. I accept the small glass of black coffee and smile my thanks.

'If she's bought it, it's the real deal.' Becker takes a shot of caffeine and downs it in one swallow before placing his empty on the waiting tray. I keep hold of mine.

'But still . . .' These people must have more money than sense. 'Twenty-five grand?'

'You've seen nothing yet, princess.' Becker slips his phone back into his pocket and nods towards the front again.

Over the next hour, I sit through a dozen lots. I watch as a dozen people part with insane amounts of cash for pieces of art and historical antiques. The most insane being a music box from the twelfth century sold for £400,000. It was stunning, made of pink crystal and edged in a silver trim, with white diamonds embellishing the lid, but I was still staggered by the winning bid. My knowledge of antiques and art is vast, but I've neglected to appreciate the worth of the treasures I've indulged in over the years. The history. That's all that mattered to me.

I'm the perfect spectator. I don't speak, just absorb it all, flicking through my catalogue to the right page each time a piece is presented on stage. Becker hasn't breathed a word. He's sat next to me, hardly paying attention, busy on his phone. I've left him to it.

My attention is stolen momentarily by the coffee man again, and this time I take a tall latte, replacing my empty espresso glass at the same time.

'This is what we're here for.' Becker nudges me in the side, and my head snaps around, knowing what I'm going to find. The gasps of shock filling the room only confirm it. It's not being handled by delicate white-gloved fingers like everything else presented today. Instead, it's in a glass case that's being wheeled on to the stage by two rather smart-looking, albeit massive, guys. The room is quickly a hive of chatter, people leaning in to each other and whispering. The excitement is palpable, but again Becker remains expressionless in his seat, not giving anything away. I watch him closely as he gazes around the room for a few moments before letting his eyes settle on the lost piece of treasure. His face remains impassive, which is probably a good thing, since Brent keeps flicking glances our way. I wrap my fingers around my latte glass, sinking deeper into my chair, like I have something to hide. I'm nervous. Becker wants that sculpture desperately. Does everyone here know that? No idea, but I do know Brent does.

The auctioneer waits for the chatter to die down, looking around the room with a smile on his face. Once it's quiet, he remains silent for a long, extended length of time before he begins to talk. It's a tension builder, if ever there was one, and it works. Everyone in the room is holding their breath, except Becker. His eyes are still rooted firmly on the glass cabinet.

'*Head of a Faun*,' the auctioneer begins, low and dramatic, slowly gliding his gavel through the air until it's pointing at the glass cabinet. 'The lost sculpture of the Italian Renaissance master Michelangelo himself.' A few whispers start again, but only briefly before silence falls and the auctioneer continues. 'It's been authenticated by world-class Michelangelo experts. We all know that many of the master's pieces have been found hidden in obscurity. This is a perfect example. I won't bore you with what you already know.' He chuckles to himself, and for the first time I hear life from Becker in the form of a tired sigh. He might look impassive, but he's bored out of his mind. I smile and bring my coffee to my lips, feeling relaxed for the first time since they brought out the sculpture. 'A true discovery,' the auctioneer continues. 'I'll say no more and start with a commission bid of ten million pounds.'

Ten million pounds? I inhale sharply, sucking back the coffee I just tipped into my mouth. It hits the back of my throat and I proceed to cough all over the place, spraying milky liquid in every direction. *Ten million.* I splutter uncontrollably, my hands now vibrating, the remaining coffee in my cup swishing around precariously. Ten million? I couldn't have heard him right.

I'm so busy trying to compose myself and wipe the dribbles of coffee from my chin, I don't notice that everyone in the room has craned their necks to see who's causing the drama.

'Smooth,' Becker mutters, whipping a hanky from his jacket pocket and dangling it in front of me without looking at my frightful state. 'You're dribbling.'

I peek up through my lashes and spy a million eyes, all narrowed, looking my way. I wince, shrink into my chair until I'm practically lying on the floor, and blush harder than I ever have before. And that's an achievement, given my susceptible colouring. Everyone is staring at me. I feel like a total tit.

'Thank you,' I murmur, reaching for his handkerchief before dabbing at my face gently, all ladylike, pretending I didn't silence a whole room of aristocratic hoity-toity old farts in one of the most famous auction houses in the world. Good God, I'm an absolute disgrace.

When I'm done with my clean-up operation, I muster some bravery and confront my spectators, devastated to see that I'm still the centre of attention. There's nothing I can do to redeem myself, so I sniff and raise my chin as I straighten my shoulders. I'm squirming on the inside. Positively dying. Humiliated. I bet Becker's all kinds of regretful for bringing me along. If the auctioneer doesn't pick up where he left off soon, I'm making a run for it. There's only so long I can sit here with everyone staring at me.

'Eleven million.'

The announcement from a couple rows in front of us does the trick. Everyone in the room swings their attention away from me, and I follow their lead. Brent catches my eye and smiles, shaking his head at me. 'Eleven million,' he repeats, turning away from me to face the front, raising his paddle.

I gawp then swing my eyes to Becker, looking for his reaction. His attention hasn't wavered from the sculpture.

'Eleven in the room. Do I hear twelve?'

'Twelve.'

A sea of heads swing up to the balcony, then back into the room quickly when Brent shouts, 'Thirteen.'

The gasps grow louder with each bid.

'Thirteen in the room from Mr Wilson.' The auctioneer points his gavel at Brent. 'Do I have fourteen?'

'Here.' Back our heads go again to the balcony, where the guy on the phone is waving his paddle in the air. It's clear from all the way down here that he's sweating, his head shimmering under the lighting above. I would be, too, if I were bidding this kind of money on someone's behalf.

The chatter in the room accelerates, people hushing each other, some holding the arm of the person sitting next to them, bracing themselves. I'm thoroughly caught up in the hype, getting a rush of adrenalin from the tension and excitement. Brent catches my eye again, his profile clear as he looks up at the balcony, scowling at his competitor.

'Fifteen million.' He pushes the words through clenched teeth, slowly turning back to the front of the room and lifting his paddle. His bid takes the hype up to another level. Someone at the front stands and looks back at Brent, and someone else whips out their phone and starts frantically hammering at the screen. It's a frenzy of stunned activity. You can almost hear the heart of every single person in the room beating.

I turn my eyes on to Becker, desperate to see what he's making of this. Why hasn't he bid? He's still simply staring at the glass cabinet showcasing the sculpture. I nudge his knee discreetly with mine to get his attention. He doesn't look at me, choosing to keep his focus on the lost treasure.

'Fifteen,' I breathe, taking a cautious peek around me to ensure no attention is on me. I have nothing to worry about. All eyes are on the two men in the bidding war.

'The people on the phone are a museum in Florence,' Becker says quietly, not breaking his focus from the sculpture. 'They can't go any higher than sixteen.'

I swing my eyes up to the balcony, just as the man on the phone yells, 'Sixteen.'

But Brent yells, 'Seventeen,' in quick succession, putting the museum in Florence out of the game. I look up to the sweaty guy on the balcony and see him shaking his head, confirming what Becker's told me.

'Seventeen in the room.' The gavel points to Brent.

'Becker.' I turn into him, my sensible side kicking in. 'You can't spend this kind of money.' Especially if this is a war of the egos between him and Brent. It's crazy. I don't care if it's a Michelangelo. 'Let—' My mouth snaps shut when I catch his finger rising slowly to his mouth.

'Shhhh.' He hushes me, the low, seductive whoosh silencing me in an instant. 'Calm your britches, princess. I'm not that crazy.'

Everything in me relaxes. 'Good, let the idiot blow his fortune.'

'Precisely.' Becker looks at me and lets a small smile crack the corners of his mouth, then I watch in confusion as he slowly raises his paddle into the air. 'Twenty million,' he bids.

My mouth drops open. *What the fucking hell?* He stares at me, that boyish, cheeky smile gracing his beautiful face, while I gape at him, feeling the attention in the room divert to us. People cry out in delight, in shock, in awe.

'Twenty million in the room.'

'Becker, what are you doing?' I ask, unbothered by the sound level of my voice. There's not a chance anyone could possibly hear me through the hustle and bustle.

He brings his paddle down and leans into me, putting his lips at my ear. My eyes close and everything around me fades to nothing. 'I hate him, Eleanor.'

I frown into my darkness, totally confused, but when I open my eyes, Becker is smiling, getting comfortable in his seat again. He winks at me and returns his focus to the glass cabinet.

'Your hate must be of epic levels if you're prepared to part with so much cash, just to stop Brent from getting hold of the sculpture.'

'Epic doesn't cover it,' Becker says.

Swallowing hard, I settle in my chair and work hard to ignore the excited faces glaring at us. All excited, except Brent. He's scowling.

The auctioneer looks over his glasses to Brent. 'Do I have twenty-one?'

Brent's shoulders are tense, nearly touching his earlobes. He wasn't happy at fifteen million. I can only imagine he's absolutely insane with frustration at twenty-one. Being outbid by such a huge amount *and* by his arch-enemy, no less? Fucking hell, I wouldn't be surprised if he launched himself over the chairs and attacked.

'Twenty-one,' Brent spits, reaching up to his face with his paddle-free hand. I expect he's wiping the sweat from his brow.

'Thirty,' Becker says coolly.

I don't move. I don't say a word. I mimic Becker's poise and stare at the priceless sculpture. Why does Becker hate Brent so much? His explanation in the garage this morning seems feeble now. Keep your enemies close? He'd rather burn a priceless object than see Brent Wilson get his hands on it? What, even if it costs him millions? There's more to it, there has to be, but now really isn't the time to ask.

'Thirty-one,' Brent bellows in response. The room is silent. Not even the auctioneer can recite the bids before the counter bids are declared.

'Forty million.' Becker spells it out clearly and concisely without a hint of his mental state, which I'd say is fucking crackpot right now.

There are screams this time. The whole damn place plummets into complete chaos. It's hardly surprising. Nothing would stop me from reacting to that one, either. Forty million? Who has that kind of money? I should laugh at my silent, *stupid* question. The Hunts. That's who. Becker isn't messing around. Brent is creeping up in pathetic one million-pound increments, while Becker is slamming down fucking colossal bids. He really doesn't want Brent to have *Head of a Faun*.

Amid the madness of people surrounding us, Brent flies up from his seat. He's furious. 'Fifty million,' he yells. His hair is in disarray from his jerky movements. He looks a state, whereas Becker looks perfectly composed and together.

Things are getting out of hand, and I start to wonder where this ends. Becker wants that piece, and so does Brent. I don't expect either man to relent and lose face, so I settle in, looking ahead to the treasure that's sent this auction room into pandemonium.

The auctioneer points at Brent. 'Fifty million from Mr Wilson.'

I wait for it. It's coming.

Any.

Moment.

Now.

Except it doesn't. Becker is silent beside me, and while I know the money being bid here is astronomically stupid, even for a long-lost Michelangelo, I'm suddenly overcome by an unreasonable wish for him not to let Brent win. Maybe it's the wicked glint in Brent's eyes as he looks over. Or maybe it's because that piece belongs somewhere special, like a museum or at The Haven. Or maybe it's simply because I want Becker to win and *really* want Brent to lose. For me, that would be the best slap in the face, even if I'm not technically delivering it.

'Going once.'

I look across and find Becker staring blankly at the cabinet, oblivious to all eyes on him, waiting for his counter bid. He looks like he's in a trance. Or is he thinking? I can't be sure, so I nudge his knee. He turns his face slowly to mine. 'It's on you,' I prompt, nodding my head towards the auctioneer.

'Going twice.' The auctioneer is looking at Becker like everyone else, his gavel hanging limply in his hand.

I have no idea what to make of the expression Becker is giving me. It's vacant, but there's fondness in there somewhere, too. 'Are you okay?' I ask.

He takes a deep breath and reaches for my hand, taking it

gently and weaving his fingers with mine. I look down, confused by his move, but not so confused by the growing heat of the blood in my veins. Everything around me is silent again. Gone.

'Just in case I forget to tell you when we get out of here,' he says quietly, and I look back up at him, finding a calm, expressionless face. But those eyes. They're alive and dancing, and gazing affectionately at me. 'I've loved every second I've spent with you today.' He smiles.

Of all the crazy shit that's happened in this room, it's this moment that takes my breath away and refuses to give it back. He squeezes my hand gently and turns to the auctioneer. 'I'm out.' He snaps to life, stands and pulls me up by my hand. Becker nods courteously to Brent like a true gentleman, gracious in defeat. 'Congratulations, Wilson.'

'Sold to Mr Wilson for fifty million.'

Bang!

Brent's chest is puffing with pride. 'Thanks.' He gives our joined hands a scornful look, before quickly restoring his superiority when everyone in the room loses interest in Becker and rushes to offer Brent their congratulations. He laps it up. It's sickening, and while Becker seems to accept defeat with perfect grace, I can't help feeling bitter.

'Come on, princess.' Becker tugs my hand, and I look up to find him studying me with a hint of amusement on his face.

'What?' I ask, failing to erase my sulky expression.

'Nothing.' He pulls me through the crowds of people, politely asking to be excused when people block our path.

'He shouldn't have won it,' I grumble, dodging bodies as I trail Becker.

'He didn't win it, Eleanor. He paid for it.'

We break free of the packed room and hit the marble floor of the entrance hall. 'I didn't mean win in that sense. I meant it only in the sense that Brent Wilson feels like he has one up on you. *Head of a Faun* belongs somewhere special. It belongs at The Haven.'

Becker peeks down to my moody face as he strides onward. 'Are you becoming a bit protective of your boss, princess?' he asks seriously, raising his eyebrows as he removes his glasses. 'Because that might be seen to be inappropriate.'

'Or just loyal,' I retort, forcing our joined hands up so he can see them. '*This* is inappropriate.'

Becker smiles and drops my hand as we continue walking. It makes me wish I'd kept my stupid mouth shut. 'I'm glad I brought you here today.'

'You are?' I thought he would regret it after my coffee-spitting performance.

'Yes, your reaction to Brent winning the sculpture confirms something.'

I look up at him, keeping up with his strides. 'Confirms what?'

'That I can trust you.'

'Trust me to sulk when you lose, you mean?'

He chuckles. 'You've nothing to be worried about. I never lose.'

My steps falter, causing me to fall behind him until I come to a stop. 'But you just did.'

Becker looks back when he notices I'm no longer at his side, and his soles skid to a stop. He places his hands in his pockets and walks back to me, closing the distance between us. I watch him closely as he slowly dips his head until his eyes are level with mine. He looks way too cheerful for someone who lost out to their arch-enemy. His smile is bright. Happy. I'm confused.

But then he speaks and transforms my confusion into horror. 'I didn't lose, Eleanor. Brent's just paid fifty million for a lump of marble that *I* could have sculptured.'

What?

My hand flies to my mouth to stop my shriek of shock. 'It's fake?' I hiss.

Becker looks up to the ceiling, thinking. 'Yes, I'd say so.'

This doesn't make any sense. Why would Becker bid on a piece if he knows it's fake? The answer comes swift and fast and without the need to ask. 'You tricked him.' Becker pushed the bids up, forced Brent to pay well over the odds. Oh my days.

'How do you know for certain it's a fake?' He could be wrong. It might be genuine.

He straightens up, looking at me with a hint of mischief in his eyes. It worries me. It tells me I'm not going to like what he says next. 'Because,' he murmurs quietly, leaning into me a little, 'I know where the real one is.' He slips his shades on, swivels on his heel, and strolls right out of Countryscape, leaving me with my jaw on the posh mosaic floor.

Chapter 21

I'm still standing in the exact same place, who knows how long later. Becker knows where the real one is? He just bid obscene money on a fake? Good Lord.

'Becker,' I yell, willing life back into my dead legs and sprinting after him. I hit the top of the steps outside Countryscape and skid to a stop before I fall down the damn things in my rush. I spot him at the bottom. 'Becker.' I'm off again, unable to calm my urgency to get to him and demand an explanation. Perhaps there's a bit of panic in that urgency, too. I feel like a crook fleeing a crime scene.

I charge down the steps like a madwoman, disregarding the potential of falling and breaking my neck, which is a definite possibility in these shoes. Landing at the bottom in a flustered mess, I find my boss has removed his sunglasses and is looking up to the clear blue sky, inhaling the fresh countryside air with a look of pure exhilaration on his perfect face. He's just divulged something wildly unbelievable and strolled off like it's all so very normal. And now he looks the happiest I've probably seen him. I'm stumped for words. I frown to myself while Becker gazes up to the sky, waiting for him to finish up with his ... moment.

It's a nerve-racking few minutes. I'm constantly checking behind me for anyone who might run out of the mansion shouting allegations of corruption.

'Do you smell that?' He finally speaks, taking one last deep inhale through his nose before he lets it stream out of his mouth.

I smell. I actually sniff the air around me. I'm such a twat. Whatever smell Becker is currently taking great pleasure from, no one else can smell it. This is personal. 'What?' I ask, confident of the answer I will get.

'That, princess, is the smell of retribution.' He drops his head on a broad smile. His eyes are twinkling madly. 'You okay?'

'Actually, no,' I cry, wincing at the sound level of my own voice and quickly looking over my shoulder. It's all clear, but this isn't a conversation for here. In fact, this isn't a conversation to have within a ten-mile radius of here.

I grab his arm and roughly drag him over to Gloria. He doesn't bother trying to stop me, nor does he complain about my rough handling of him. Good job for him. My desire to flee Countryscape, coupled with my desire for an explanation, has made for one determined princess.

'Open the car,' I snap, my eyes darting around us. I'm jumpy. I can't help it. Becker, on the other hand, is unruffled and highly amused by my edginess.

He makes no attempt to obey my demand, and rolls his eyes, making a mockery of my concern. 'Calm your britches, princess.' He moves in fast, scooping me from my feet.

'Oh,' I cry, grabbing his shoulders when my feet disappear from beneath me. He walks straight past Gloria, and my head cranes, seeing her getting further away. Aren't we leaving?

'Let's talk.' He places me neatly on something, and for a second I wonder what, until I notice the sparkling silver Bentley winged motif next to my thigh.

'Why have you sat me on Brent's car bonnet?' I ask incredulously, scrambling to get off. I don't get very far.

Becker pushes me right back on. 'Stay where you are.' His palms land on each side of my legs, closing me in. Then I hear a high-pitched noise that cuts right through me. Metal on metal. My palms go straight to my ears to protect them from the cutting sound, and Becker gives me a feigned surprised look.

I glimpse down to see the metal strap of his watch resting on the Bentley. 'Oops,' he says, lifting his wrist to reveal a monster scratch.

I look at his smugly satisfied face in horror. 'Why did you do that?' I ask, licking the tip of my finger and frantically rubbing at the mark. I'm being stupid. I heard the damage and now I can see it. That's one deep scratch. Oh my days, I'm going to be arrested for all kinds of crimes. An accessory. Aiding and abetting. Criminal damage. I've never got my nose dirty before. Now I'm a criminal. 'I don't like you very much today,' I grumble mindlessly. 'Isn't it enough that you've just conned Brent for fifty million without vandalising his posh car?'

Becker halts my fruitless attempts to make the scratch magically disappear and takes my hands, holding them in front of me. 'Look at me.'

'No, you might steal my eyeballs.'

He bursts into a fit of laughter at my sulky quip, head tossed back, the lot. 'Eleanor, I'm no criminal. Look at me.'

I begrudgingly peek up through my lashes, nearly being knocked unconscious by the smile on his face. 'You had no right to put me in the centre of your pathetic game with Brent.'

His smile fades a little, and I know why. He's read between the lines of that statement and interpreted what I haven't said but want to. It isn't just today. I've been a constant pawn for both men, and there's no question in my mind that Becker not only brought me along to test my trust, but also as a little dig at his nemesis. I'm his, except I'm not. He has no claim on me in that respect, and I have no claim on him. I know it. He knows it. Mrs Potts knows it. Gramps knows it. Alexa knows it. Even Winston fucking knows it. Becker loved every second he spent with me today? Yeah, I bet he did, because I played his game unwittingly. This isn't about impossible attraction. This isn't because he can't help but *fucking want me*.

This is about him showing me who he is. Letting me see.

I hope you're ready.

Never, Becker. Never ready for you.

I want answers. 'How do you know where the real one is? And how do you know *that* one's not real?' I point to the mansion. 'Who are you, the world-renowned expert?'

'No, I'm the man who paid the world-renowned expert to authenticate that one in there.' He points to the mansion, too.

Oh my God. My palm reaches up to my throat and rests on my skin. I can feel the noose there. The one that's going to hang me when the authorities find out about this. 'That's despicable.'

'No, that's clever, princess,' he corrects me quickly, seizing my hand when I lift it to point an outraged finger in his face.

'It's despicable,' I argue. 'How did you even manage that, anyway? No expert held in high esteem would be mad enough to risk their reputation.'

'Greed is a terrible thing.' Becker shakes his head in dismay. There's no sarcasm. He truly believes his claim, and I can't possibly argue with that because he's right. The antiquing world is as corrupt as they come. I never imagined in my wildest dreams that an outfit as reputable and notorious as the Hunt Corporation would be involved in such a scandal. No wonder Mr H and Mrs Potts were so opposed to me coming. That dear old man and sweet old lady? They're in on this? My mind has just exploded.

'But you didn't want Brent here,' I remind him, now speaking for the sake of it. All those times Brent was vying to be hooked up at Countryscape and Becker took delight in refusing, it was all an act. 'You asked someone else to endorse him, didn't you?'

'I wouldn't be very clever if I gained him entry knowing he wanted what I wanted, would I?'

'But you didn't want it.'

'Yes, but I didn't want Wilson to know that.'

He's too clever. That's the problem. Smart beyond what I gave him credit for, and I thought he was pretty smart, anyway.

'How do you know where the real one is?' I ask.

'Because I have a map.'

I can't contain my gasp. He's searching for *Head of a Faun*? Flashbacks of the library, the secret compartment that I found *and* the map inside, explode in my mind, yet I can't say anything. He doesn't know I've found that book or what's in it. He'll think I'm a snoop. So I take a different angle. 'Where's the map?'

'Somewhere safe.'

Damn. I can tell by the sour expression on his face that he isn't going to give me any more on that. 'Why somewhere safe?'

'Because Brent—'

'Was looking for the sculpture, too,' I finish for him, clarity biting me on the arse and sinking its vicious teeth in. 'And now he thinks he's found it.' My eyes dart across my lap as my mind tries to wrap around the astonishing realisation.

'Well,' he sniffs. 'Someone else found it. Brent bought it.'

I exhale my disbelief. 'Holy shit, this is unbelievable.'

'This is win–win, Eleanor,' Becker says quietly, chucking my cheek like I'm a child he's trying to pacify. I peek up at him. He's still smiling. 'My family gets the sculpture, the Saunders don't lose their estate thanks to me, Brent Wilson is confirmed a dickhead, and I get a thrill from it all.' He gives me that lopsided, cheeky grin. 'Wait . . .' He glances off into the distance for a moment, thoughtful. 'That's a win–win–win–win.'

My disgust at his disregard gushes out on an exasperated sigh. 'And if Brent decides to sell it and it's authenticated again' – I swing my arm towards the mansion behind me – 'everyone will know that one is fake.'

'And?'

And? Why isn't that a problem for him? With no other instruction coming to me, no thoughts, no words, I slap his arm for his insolence. It spikes the most gorgeous-sounding chuckle. It makes me want to hit him continuously so my ears are drowned in the dizzying sound for ever.

Becker gazes at me as the sound fades, until there's only silence left between us again. We simply stare at each other. He wanted me to know all this. He wanted to share this with me. He's brave, trusting me for a start, but more than that, he's opened up to me, whether he realises or not.

He smiles. 'The rivalry between my family and Brent's goes back nearly a century, Eleanor. I'm continuing the family legacy. That's all.'

'Your dad was looking for the sculpture?'

He nods. 'And my grandfather, and Brent's grandfather, and Brent's father. But I'm going to find it. Please don't let morals cloud your judgement. Brent's father ripped my dad off for a lot more than fifty million.'

I pout, unable to comprehend such a sum. More than fifty million? But I still ask. 'How much more?'

'A fucking lot.' His smile is quickly gone, and I'm not sure what to make of the misery slinking on to his face, drowning out the elation of a few moments ago.

He's feeding me scraps. I want a three-course meal. 'How much is a fucking lot?'

He pushes himself off the bonnet of Brent's car, swallowing. 'Don't make me go down that road again, Eleanor. I just needed you to know there's a method to my madness.' He plasters a false and rather inappropriate smile on his face. 'Brent Wilson thinks he has his smarmy hands on *Head of a Faun*, so now I can focus on finding the real one without an Indiana Jones wannabe tailing me all over the world.'

Every scrap of my irritation slides away. I have my very own treasure hunter. It's crazy for me to find his simple explanation acceptable. Really crazy. Maybe Becker Hunt is making me crazy.

'This has become more about pride and winning.' Becker taps the end on my nose. 'It's not about passion for treasure.

Brent's just proven that in there.' He points to the mansion. 'He isn't selling that sculpture anytime soon. He'll keep it for his own sad, private satisfaction. He thinks he's won, princess.'

'You said you can focus on finding the real one. I thought you knew where it is.'

'I do. Like I said, I have a map.'

I shake my head, stunned by it all, but I don't see this as foolproof. Becker must have thought about the consequences. 'If it's discovered that Brent Wilson bought a forgery, the authenticator will be hung, drawn, and quartered.'

'He's long gone with a few million in his off-shore account. Retired. This is a testing business, you know.' He smirks.

I have nothing to say to that, but then I think of something else. 'Brent will want his money back. Surely the Saunders can't keep all his money.'

'The Saunders family are financially ruined. They'll use the money to pay off their debts.'

'He'll sue them,' I fire. Jesus, fifty million quid gone? Just like that? Brent Wilson will have a hernia. And that hernia will burst if he knows Becker is responsible.

'*They* didn't authenticate it,' Becker points out quite rightly. 'And anyway, you can't sue someone for something they haven't got. This is all ifs and buts, princess. Wilson will never share the fact he's been conned, *if* he finds out. His ego is too big.'

His ego is too big? Hilarious. But I'm done. I've presented every hole in his plan and he's filled them in swiftly. 'You're immoral.' It's all I have left.

He grins and slides his hands on to my waist, lifting me from the car and holding me against him. We're in that grey area again. It doesn't stop my hands from sliding around his neck, though. Or my eyes from feasting on his obscenely handsome face. Or my body from becoming hypersensitive to every part of him that's touching me.

His soft hazel eyes shimmer with happiness. I can't fathom

why it blankets my worry right now. All I know is that I feel I know Becker Hunt so much more than I did an hour ago, and he made that happen.

'I'm not immoral, princess.' He chastely kisses my cheek, making an over-the-top noise about it, too. 'I'm a fucking saint.'

I smile, and it is beyond my ability to hold back. It's also beyond my ability to break free of his arms as he carries me to Gloria. 'Saint Becker?' I ask, letting him lower me to my feet and open the door. 'I'm not so sure about that.' I slip in and pull my belt across, then jump when Becker virtually throws himself across the bonnet of the car like a stuntman, his shoulder meeting the metal first and the rest of his body following fluidly in an expert roll. He lands lightly on his feet on the driver's side of the car and brings two fingers up to his lips. I shake my head in dismay when he blows across the tops of them before holstering his imaginary gun and strutting to the door, opening it swiftly and falling into his seat.

He starts the engine and makes Gloria roar in delight. 'Did I tell you about the time I skydived off the Burj Khalifa?'

'Really?' I gasp sarcastically, and he grins. I shouldn't humour him when he's being so reckless. Becker Hunt is pretty damn hard to dislike when he's being a total twat. When he's all playful, daring, and roguish, it's impossible. He's a maverick for sure. Today has proven that. The risks he's taken are reckless, but I've no doubt his plot has been deeply thought through. He's spirited too, just like his grandad said. Wild and audacious. Passionate and loving. Sex appeal exudes from every pore of his gorgeous body, and his face is so handsome it should be classified as dangerous. Which it is. I can attest to that.

But setting all those silent summaries aside, I really should be asking myself something. Something important.

What does his grand gesture mean?

Chapter 22

I'm surprised when Becker pulls off the country road into a pub car park and declares we need to eat. I don't argue. Apparently, being an accomplice to a con artist builds up quite an appetite.

We chat non-stop over dinner about Rome, the couple of years Becker spent there studying Italian Renaissance art, and I listen in awe and envy. We touch briefly on me, and I find myself shutting down, wondering what my straight-laced father and all his junk would make of what I've been involved in today. I should be back at his shop trying to keep his memory alive, not getting myself caught up in con jobs. Because that's exactly what it is. Illegal.

It seems that Becker detects my mental torment at that point, because he coolly diverts the conversation, sending my nagging conscience sailing into the distance with his animated stories from his days in Paris, Madrid, Buenos Aires, Moscow . . .

The list goes on and on. He's been everywhere, and he talks with passion about each and every place. I could listen to him for ever. There's been only playful banter, no pokes or . . . I stop my direction of thought immediately. There have been pokes. Lots of them, but both of us have bounced them right back on a grin or a laugh. It's different today. I don't know what is different, or why, but there's been a huge shift in our relationship, and I can't help but think it's for the best. I've come to love the Hunt Corporation, my sense of belonging, my job, Mrs Potts and Mr H, and not even the events of today has made that waver, and that really is crazy.

I feel revitalised, and I can't take that away from myself. Becker Hunt is thrilling and daring, and it feels so good to be thrilling and daring with him. I just need to get past those moments of rhapsody whenever Becker touches me or gets too close. I can do that. To maintain this exhilarating, belonging, and purposeful feeling within me, I can do that.

I *should* do that.

Can I do that?

The ride home from the pub goes too fast, assisted by Becker actually driving too fast. The evening air is bitter and at eight o'clock, it's already dark. When we pull up outside my building, I choose not to look at him, concentrating on pulling my coat in and my scarf up my neck. My actions say more than I'm cold. They say I'm distracting myself, maybe even trying to use my clothing as a protective shield from . . .

I don't know what. Him? My uncontrollable and unreasonable attraction to everything he represents? I'm instinctively protecting my heart from being broken. Because the tiny vulnerable part of me is worried he'll infiltrate my defences again.

'I'll see you tomorrow,' I say, keeping it short and sweet and, most importantly, professional. It's taking *so* much energy. 'Thank you for taking me. And for dinner.'

'Was it everything you hoped it would be?' he asks, turning off Gloria's engine.

I brave looking at him, sensing genuine curiosity. I could laugh. 'And a whole lot more, but you know that, don't you?'

He seems to drift into thought, his eyes falling to my lap. Something tells me he's seeking my approval. Or acceptance. Can I give him that? 'Coffee?' he blurts out of the blue.

Coffee? Is that code for sex? *Be wise, Eleanor. Be professional.* 'I think I'll pass,' I say, giving him a small smile when he starts nibbling his lip, his mind clearly whirling. Is he wondering how he can convince me? He can't. I'm not making that mistake again. He'll have to wait for Alexa. He can pick her up on his way home. 'You should go,' I add, worried he might find a way to sway me. I'm not at my strongest when Becker unleashes his charm on me. I take the handle of the door. 'Thanks again.'

His hand is on my arm fast, and I'm inhaling quickly, searching for my grit. 'Please,' he murmurs quietly. My eyes lift, my shock obvious. Becker Hunt doesn't say please. And I don't do casual fucks. Especially with my boss.

Taking his hand from my arm, I drop it in his lap. 'Mr Hunt, I believe you have a date tonight.'

His frown is quite cute, and then his phone rings, pulling our eyes to the centre console. I smile to myself, seeing Alexa lighting up the screen. 'She means nothing to me,' he says when it rings off.

'Oh, I know,' I assure him, taking the handle of the door again. 'And I'm not interested in meaning nothing.'

His stunned eyes dart to mine. 'I've no intention of making you feel like nothing.'

'Your lack of intention doesn't mean you won't, Becker.' I open the door and get out, leaning down to look him straight in the face. The poor man seems a little lost. 'I know you well enough by now. Let's keep it professional.' I have to be the sensible one, since it's obvious Becker can't control his urges. A tiny part of me is quite satisfied. But a bigger part of me knows there's nothing in it other than an urge. Tomorrow, Becker will have had his itch scratched, and I will be back in that place called shame and weakness. No. 'It's been a lovely day. Let's make sure tomorrow is lovely, too.'

His phone starts ringing again – Alexa *again* – and I smile as I push the door closed, pulling my bag on to my shoulder, so proud of myself and my strength. But no sooner have I taken a step, Becker is in front of me, his phone held up. I blink at the illuminated screen as he accepts the call and takes his mobile to his ear, looking me straight in the eye. What is he doing?

'Yeah, hi,' he says, and is quiet for a few moments, no doubt listening to Alexa detail exactly what she has planned for him. I force myself not to wonder what that is. 'Afraid not.' Becker's stare remains nailed to mine. 'No, I can't see you any more.'

I move back again, uncomfortable, not just by Becker's closeness, but by what he's doing. What *is* he doing? I don't know, but I don't like the feel of my heart's increasing speed. I step to the side to pass him and get blocked. 'Becker, go home,' I say, getting worked up.

'Yes, I'm with Eleanor,' he says down the line, reaching for my arm to hold me in place. 'Bye.' He hangs up, and then silence falls. So what does he expect to happen now? That I'll dive on him? Drag him upstairs? Thank him?

I look at him to be sure he can see my resolve, as well as hear it. 'That was a waste of a gesture.'

Is that hurt I see in his eyes? Yes, it's definitely hurt. Oh my days, he really did expect me to shower him in appreciation. What does he take me for? Just because he fancies a different woman tonight, and I'm the lucky girl, he expects me to melt and swoon all over him? I feel my anger simmering. It'll boil over soon.

'It wasn't a gesture,' he says. 'I meant it. Honestly, I never want to see her again.'

I laugh out loud, staggered. '*Honestly?*' I mimic. 'With all due respect, Becker, I just spent the day watching you lie to hundreds of people. I watched that poker face of yours fool everyone. So please don't talk to me about honesty.' I pull my arm from his grip. 'And at the same time, you used me as a pawn.' I storm past him. 'I have more respect for myself than to be at your beck and call.'

'You're not a pawn, Eleanor,' he shouts after me, but I keep walking on a huff of disbelief. Sure I wasn't. 'Goddamn it!' He lands in front of me, blocking the way to my door. 'You're not a pawn, and I *really* need you to know that.'

'Then what the hell am I, Becker? Please tell me. An employee? An accomplice? A lay?'

His jaw pulses under the fierce bite of his teeth. I'm even more furious that my question angers him. I've never met such an obtuse man in my life. 'You are not a fucking lay,' he says. 'You're the fucking queen of the chess board, Eleanor. Superior to all. Got it?'

I withdraw, blinking.

'I didn't take you to Countryscape to use you,' he yells. 'You want honesty, I'll give you honesty.' He cups my cheeks and brings his face close to mine. 'I took you because I have an annoying fucking urge to let you in.'

'What?' I step away, and this time he doesn't close in on me.

Becker sighs, closing his eyes briefly. 'I took you to Countryscape because I want you to see what no one else sees.'

'Why?' I murmur mindlessly, and he smiles mildly.

'Because you like me in a way no one has liked me before.'

Oh God. There he is. The young man who is craving acceptance. The man who doesn't want to end up alone. But . . . 'I don't like you.' *Lies.*

'You really do need to work on that poker face, princess,' he says on an ironic laugh, glancing away as he pinches the bridge of his nose. He sighs. 'You love my passion, and I can't even begin to tell you how much I love yours.'

I also need to work on my willpower, because I can feel my walls beginning to crumble. I can feel my heart shouting louder than my head. I need to get out of here. 'I'll see you at work tomorrow,' I say, skirting past him quickly.

'That's it?' he asks, bewildered.

'That's it,' I say. 'You said yourself it should never have happened. You need to remember why.'

'I can't remember a damn thing when you're around, Eleanor.'

'Then try,' I shout, glancing up to my apartment window, thinking about the quiet, lonely space beyond it. Quiet is good. Lonely is good. I need some space to kick my mind back into line before Becker captures my foolish side again. But my thoughts are cut short, as well as my steps, as I wonder if I'm seeing right.

'What is it?' Becker says, picking up on my unease. I look back blankly at him, seeing a face awash with concern. 'Eleanor, what?'

He joins me, and I look up again. 'My window,' I go to point, but my arm refuses to unwrap from around my midriff. 'It's . . .' I trail off when I register my window is closed. 'Oh.' Now I'm frowning. It was open.

'What about your window?' Becker prompts, pulling my puzzled face away from the building. He's frowning too.

I shake my head, dismissing my mistake. 'It looked open. I must have been seeing things.'

'You don't sound sure.' He glances up to the building and runs his eyes from left to right a few times, checking for himself.

'It's dark. I wouldn't see my hand if I held it up in front of me.' And I'm certainly not thinking straight right now. I turn and make my way up the path, keen to escape the cold. As well as Becker and his revelations.

My freezing hands take for ever to locate my door keys, and once I've finally picked out the right key, I spend precious seconds in the cold trying to insert it into the lock. 'Damn,' I curse as I drop the bunch to the floor.

I kneel to retrieve them, but Becker beats me to it, swiping them up. 'I'll see you up,' he declares, opening my door and stepping in first.

'There's no need.' I want him to go now so I can fall into my bed and ponder every thought currently tangling my mind.

'That wasn't a question.' He looks at me expectantly, showing me an expression that definitely isn't going to relent. 'Are you going to stand in the cold all night?'

I sigh a long, tired, exasperated sigh, then I do as I'm told. Becker shuts the cold out and stops me from proceeding any further, moving in front of me and taking the stairs. 'I was mistaken,' I say to his back, following him up. 'You really don't need to do this.'

I'm flat-out ignored, so I save myself the effort and shut the hell up. Let him see me in. Let him leave. Simple.

He strides towards my apartment, his shoulders tense, and makes fast work of opening my door, pushing it wide open and scanning the space.

Waiting patiently behind him, I look over his shoulder and see nothing out of the ordinary. He's being overly suspicious.

'There you are!' I swing around to find Lucy breaching the top of the stairs, dragging a laptop case behind her. It's not the only thing trailing her. Mark appears, suited and booted, looking a lot fresher than he did the last time I saw him. I backtrack through the week in my head. The last time I saw him was last night. Shit, has it really only been a day?

'Hey.' I smile my hello to Mark, who nods, choosing to remain quiet, before I return my attention to Lucy. 'Sorry about earlier.'

Lucy's grin gives me the reassurance I need. 'It's fine. Mark and I had lunch.' Her eyes widen, telling me everything I need to know. Last night might have been a washout for Lucy, thanks to me, but tonight looks set to get her right back where she wants to be. I give Mark a wicked grin and get a smack on my arm from Lucy for my trouble.

'Look at you, fancy pants.' She says, giving my outfit the once-over. 'Good day?' She wiggles her eyebrows suggestively. I wouldn't know where to begin on today, so I don't entertain her, returning the favour and slapping her arm. She snickers, but her amusement vanishes the moment her eyes flit past me and catch sight of who's currently stalking around my apartment with a scowl on his face.

'Oh?' Lucy cranes her neck to get a better look, trying to muscle past me. I move to stop her. Something tells me Becker won't tolerate girlie banter right now.

'He's just checking things out.' I push her back into the corridor and pull the door closed behind me.

I get a slighted look tossed at me. 'How bouncy the bed is?'

'Security,' I blurt, keeping hold of the door handle.

'Security?' Lucy repeats, flat and bored. 'He's checking security? How exciting. How about checking *your* security?' She nods to my crotch area. My lips purse at her cheek and Mark lets out a sharp shot of laughter. Oh, her scream is going to reach the valleys of Wales when I fill her in on the last twenty-four hours. Or what I *can* tell her, anyway. 'Take it you have your job back?' She eyes me suspiciously.

'Coffee in the morning?' I ask, nodding my head, telling her the answer to that question should be a resounding *yes*.

Her eyes light up like fireworks and she nods with me, backing away. 'Eight?'

I'm still nodding. 'I'll—' The door is wrenched open, my body following it on a clumsy stagger back. 'Whoa,' I cry, colliding with Becker's tall, too solid frame. Quickly gathering myself, I toss him an indignant look. 'Watch it.'

My scathing threat has zero impact. He gives Lucy and Mark the once-over while they both stand silently and accept the inspection they're under, before he takes my hand and pulls me into the apartment, swinging the door shut behind him. I catch Lucy's bemused face and put my hand up, mouthing, '*Morning.*' She won't forget, especially now she's spotted Becker.

'Did you leave the pillows scattered like that?' He marches forward and assesses the cushions that are strewn haphazardly all over my couch.

'Yes.' I avoid rolling my eyes for fear of being caught and

reprimanded. He's on a mission, yet what that mission could be is yet to be established. He should know the pillows were all over the place. He was sprawled on them this morning.

'Did you leave the lemonade on the worktop?'

I glance over to my kitchen area and see many things littering the work surface. Is he going to ask about each and every item? 'Yes.'

'Was your bed made this morning?'

I purse my lips and note my messy bedcovers. He was in that bed last night. Does he even remember? 'No.'

'Was the bathroom door open?'

'Yes.' I sigh my answer this time, wandering further into my apartment and throwing my bag on to the couch.

He's standing in the centre of my space, looking around, pointing out random things. 'Was the rug all bitty?'

My patience evaporates. He was here this morning. He's seen it all. 'So I need to vacuum.'

He huffs his agreement and strolls over to my window. 'Was this picture on the floor?' I watch him pick up a framed photograph of me and my mum and put it in its rightful place. On the windowsill.

'No.' I frown to myself, searching my mind for any clue that will lead me to the reason why it would be on my apartment floor.

Becker pulls the blind up abruptly and looks outside into the darkness. 'Didn't think so,' he murmurs quietly.

I look back to my front door. 'Did you close the door?' I ask, but I know I heard it slam as he stalked after me this morning.

'Yes, I closed the door.' His hand reaches for something on the windowsill, and he turns around, playing with it as he stares down. I have to step forward to fathom what it is. My eyes widen when I realise. 'The window lock?'

'Correct,' he mutters as he strides across my flat to the

bathroom. I don't move. I've been frightened into silence and immobility. Someone has been in here?

'Is anything missing?' he calls, and I immediately scan the space, looking. Not that I have much to take, apart from my laptop.

Which is currently on my bed. 'No,' I say quietly, frowning.

'We probably disturbed them.' Becker marches out of my bathroom with arms full of various bottles and cosmetics. 'You're staying with me.' He dumps them on the bed. 'Get a bag.'

His order and follow-up demand soon yanks me from my stomach-knotting worry, catapulting me into panic. 'I can't stay with you.' That's a bad idea. Stupid.

'It wasn't a question, princess.' He's back to that irritating, inconsiderate arsehole-like behaviour. I want to object further, but as I gaze around my tiny apartment, I realise something very quickly. I don't want to stay here. I feel vulnerable and exposed. 'I'll go to Lucy's,' I suggest. 'She won't mind.'

'You're staying with me.' He gives me an expression that dares me to argue further. 'Bag.'

I shake my head in silent refusal, making him fall deeply into thought. After everything that was said downstairs, that's a bad, *bad* plan. 'Not a good idea, Becker.' I didn't need to follow up my head shake with that statement. He knows.

'Why?'

'I'm not rehashing everything. You know why.' I turn and drag my bag from under my bed. 'I'll stay with Lucy.'

'Well, maybe I *do* want to rehash everything.'

I look at the ceiling. I really don't have the energy to go over it again. Or even the willpower to maintain my resistance. Maybe he suspects that. Or senses it. My lungs are shrinking by the second, the air slowly draining until I'm holding my breath. There's something tugging at my whole body, an invisible connection from him to me, making me quiver as I prevent it from drawing me closer to him. 'I'm staying with, Lucy,' I repeat, facing him.

He steps forwards. 'I want you to stay with me.'

Our eyes hold like magnets, never faltering. 'Give me one good reason, Becker. Just one.'

He moves closer. 'Because if I don't win this battle, Eleanor, I'll feel like I've thrown away the chance of something fucking incredible.' Another step. My heart quickens. 'Is that a good enough reason for you?' I swallow. He's within touching distance now. Smelling distance. Every sense I possess goes into overdrive. 'Please, Eleanor,' he whispers, reaching up slowly and sliding his palm on to the side of my neck. He trails his thumb lightly up and down my throat, and my eyes close, soaking up the tenderness of his touch. 'I want to make the last seconds I spend with you today unforgettable,' he murmurs. My cool bloodstream ignites and sizzles, but my head still starts to slowly shake fractionally in his hold. My body is begging for him, but my mind is vehemently refusing to let it happen again. 'Yes.' His one word is barely a breath, as he moves his hold to my nape and applies a light pressure that manipulates my neck back, exposing my lips to him. 'Good God, aren't you tired of fighting this?' His soft whisper tickles my cheek, and my relaxed lids squeeze shut tighter, hiding from him.

Then his lips brush mine and demolish every scrap of doubt, because that's the moment my mind decides to remind me of his earlier words.

I took you to Countryscape because I wanted you to see what no one else sees. Because you like me in a way no one has liked me before.

Oh God. I can feel the doubt and caution being replaced with belief and willingness. His groin expertly rolls up into my lower tummy as he kisses me and lightly laps his tongue through my mouth, holding my head securely to keep me in place. My lack of fight in this moment gives him his answer. Distraction has been my friend since I arrived in London. My new purpose at The Haven has given me life and enthusiasm. My guilt has faded, and my heart has been repaired. Becker has the potential to annihilate it all. My hard exterior, my closed-book approach, my impenetrable heart. It's all at risk. He could strip me bare and expose my fragile centre – send me back to places in my past I'm scared of revisiting.

His kiss is worshipful. It's soft, slow and powerful. I expect it's also a strategy to get what he wants. So I break it. And it hurts like hell. 'And what about tomorrow?' I lightly push away, cowardly lowering my head to avoid his eyes. They'll be dark. Full of heat. Soaked in promise. All of which I won't be able to resist. He dicks around, I join in the fun. He tosses an insult, I lob one right back. I play the game, he invents the rules. He casts a spell, I fall under it.

Trying to figure out in my conflicted mind if what's developing here could be a good thing or bad thing is continuously hurting my head. The conflicting emotions are confusing. The potent sensations and feelings he creates within me are addictive.

This could be heaven.

It could also be hell.

I promised myself this wouldn't happen. How could it when he winds me up every second of my working day? This is his fault. I'm blaming him. I both love him and hate him. I hate him for failing to be professional. I hate him for pushing the boundaries. Or destroying them. However, I also love what he stands for. I love him for being so bold and daring, so confident and determined, and I love his passion and grit to get what he wants. I've seen many sides of him, and I admire each one. But I suspect there are more. He's a multifaceted man, and I can't help wanting to solve the puzzle that is Becker Hunt. For my sins, I'm captivated by him.

He eventually pulls in a deep inhale of air and takes my cheeks in his hands, forcing my face to his. Those eyes. Angel eyes. I begin to wobble on the spot. 'Tomorrow is tomorrow, princess.' He runs his fingers through my red hair. 'Today is now. Don't dwell on the past and don't fear the future.' His words strike a chord within me – something deep and lost. Dwelling on the past is natural and unstoppable. But Becker is right. I can't fear the unknown. Some things you can't control. Some things you can't prepare for.

It seems I can't control my feelings for Becker, and I definitely wasn't prepared for him.

He scans my face for the longest time. 'You make me smile,' he says simply. 'I look at you, and I just can't help but smile. I want to talk to you, watch you, share my love for my treasure with you.'

A lump jumps into my throat, surprising me, and I fight to swallow it down before it escalates into something more.

'I can see your determination to keep your distance,' he goes on softly. 'And I hope you see my determination to prove to you that I'm a better man than you think. So, please. Let me do that, princess.'

Oh wow.

I draw breath and hold it until my stressed lungs are screaming for oxygen. God, never have I wanted anything like I want Becker Hunt. It's uncontrollable, unexplainable. Maybe even crazy. But I want him. All of him – his secrets, his passion, his words.

Yet, amidst the realisation are errant wisps of wisdom. Mr H's certainty that *I am not different.* Mrs Potts's unwavering assertions that Becker will always remain aloof to true and deep affection. *There is no happy ending here.* He says he's brought me into his circle of trust, but I'm not really sure he's opened that door. And, if I give him my heart, there is no guarantee he'll put it back in one piece when he's done with it.

He could ruin me. But he could also fix me. To a certain extent, he's already repaired my broken spirit. Every minute I've spent with him so far has been memorable. A new drive consumes me; a new, unquenchable thirst for life impels me. Saint Becker Boy Hunt and his enthralling charisma is slowly taking over my heart. He's stealing it, no matter what I do and what I tell myself to try and stop it. Today has been amazing, wonderful, crazy good. The guilt I feel I'm constantly battling seems like a tiny smudge on the horizon of my existence whenever I'm with Becker. Whether that time with him is driving me around the bend or driving me to unimaginable depths of desire. It's all explosive. Every moment is consuming. I'm taken by him. Completely taken. It's like a fog has evaporated. He's right. I can't live on *what ifs*. I can't live my whole life so cautiously. It'll defeat the whole point of me breaking away from the constraints of my old life in Helston. What if this could be something fucking incredible? What if this is where my life's journey was meant to take me? To him?

I look Becker in the eye, and something happens. The level of understanding that slowly creeps on to his face makes me believe he's read my mind. Absorbed my thoughts. Comprehended them all. I hope he has. His eyes roam my face in wonder. 'You're not and never will be *nothing* to me, Eleanor Cole. *You*, I need to keep close. *You*, I want to see every day. I'm hungry for your smiles. I'm desperate for your smart mouth. I feel amazement and deep respect for your knowledge, talent, and love of all things at The Haven. And all who *live* there. I'm in awe of your talent for winding me up. You keep me on my toes, and I love it. Every minute is a surprise with you, I never know what to expect, and for a thrill-seeker like me, that's really saying something.' He reaches for me and wraps his arm around my shoulders. He holds me tightly, like he's found something he never wants to let go of. 'I'm fucking addicted to you. I need to understand what this is.'

'That makes two of us,' I murmur, staring ahead to the window where I can see the picture of Mum and me. *I'm fucking addicted to you, too, Becker.* And all those words just now have floored me.

I absolutely need to understand what this is too.

Chapter 23

I pack a few sets of clothes to take to Becker's, unsure of how long I'll be staying at The Haven, at the same time wondering how long it might take him to understand what's happening. And what happens when he does? Do I even understand myself? Of course I do. I'm exposing myself to the potential of falling for someone I shouldn't be falling for.

I leave Becker on the couch, engrossed in his phone, and spend five minutes in my bathroom sitting on the toilet looking at the photograph of Dad and me. Words run riot in my mind. So many words, but the strongest one is *sorry*. I'm apologising to him, but for what I don't know. Abandoning his shop? Abandoning Mum? For loving my new, thrilling life in London? Or for getting caught up in Becker's web of corruption?

Who knows. But I'm sorry.

Once I gather the strength to leave the bathroom, I grab the picture of Mum and me, checking for cracks on the glass before putting it safely in my bag with my photo of Dad and me. After sheepishly cancelling tomorrow morning's coffee with Lucy and telling her I'm staying at Becker's, I make my way down to the street where he's loading my bag into Gloria. He holds my hand in his lap the whole journey back, releasing it only when there is the need to change Gloria's gears. His thumb strokes lightly over the top of my hand until the friction begins to warm my skin. He is pensive. I am pensive. The atmosphere has an air of awkwardness that we are both well aware of.

As the mechanical car lift lowers us into the bowels of The

Haven, my mind is still swimming with what the remaining hours of the day might bring. And what it might mean. Despite my better judgement, I've opened up my mind to my heart. I've unwittingly allowed Becker to dismantle my defences. One part of me, the sensible part, is demanding I rebuild them this instant. The other part of me, the spirited, curious, hopeful part, is throwing away the bricks.

'You okay?' It's a question that could be referring to one of two things: am I okay because I'm here with him? Or am I okay because my apartment has been broken into. With no obvious answer coming to me, for either possibility, I murmur a feeble, 'Yeah.'

I'm not okay. Someone broke into my apartment, yet it isn't that that's frightening me the most. Crazily, it's the revelation of what's happening between Becker and me. Hating him was easier. Or pretending to hate him was easier. Accepting that I love what he represents is twisting my gut with agony and pleasure too fast for me to get a hold of myself. He's a free spirit, something I've longed to be all my life and only recently come to taste. He's strong-minded and wilful, he's intelligent and passionate. He's courageous and assertive. He's unleashed a spirit in me, a zest for life, and, cruelly, I feel like he's the only person who can keep it alive.

'You sure?' He sounds worried, and a quick glance out the corner of my eye confirms it. 'You look . . . worried.'

'So do you,' I reply, and he shakes his head in what I know is frustration, getting out of Gloria.

I follow his lead, pulling my bag from the back seat while he puts the keys away. 'You must be thirsty.' He takes my bag, slipping his arm around my shoulders, frowning at me when I tense. I'm all edgy, and I can't bloody help it. He might have detected my reaction, but he doesn't remove his arm and he doesn't make any mention of it. 'You sure you're okay?' He looks down at me, concerned.

Fucking hell, I tense up again. What's the matter with me? Where's my reasoning of half an hour ago gone? 'Fine.'

'Am I going to have to slap that arse of yours?'

I'd usually have some smart-arse comment to lob back at him but my mind's a blank. 'Don't mind.'

This time, he brings us to a stop. Damn. 'What's going on?' He pins me in place with expectant eyes, and I find mine darting away from his gaze. 'Hey.' He grabs my cheeks with a firm grip, forcing my face back to his, demonstrating his frustration and commanding my attention. Again, when I would usually have slapped him off, I'm blank. A mass of stupid uselessness. 'Answer me.'

'My flat has just been broken into,' I remind him, shamelessly copping out on sharing the truth of my lacking bite. I should get away with it. It's a perfectly feasible explanation for my unease, even if it's a big fat lie. But, now I'm thinking about it, should I be worried? Were they still there when I looked up at my window? Did we disturb them? And most importantly, who was it and what did they want? My head begins to pound. 'I should call the police.'

'Of course,' he mumbles, almost in shame, stepping back. 'Um ... yeah ... we should do that.'

I close my eyes and wish above all things that our normal routine of banter and rubbing each other up the wrong way resumes soon. I'm used to it. I can deal with it, handle it. This? I don't know how the hell to deal with this, this, this ...

What the fuck is this?

My head is suddenly swimming again, my resolve wavering. I need to know what happens now. I find the courage to face Becker to ask him what is happening between us, only he's no longer standing in front of me. He's already disappearing through the door that leads to The Haven. Great. So what now? I've hurt his feelings. I should be pleased he's even got any to hurt.

I go after him, determined set things straight with him, but that fortitude is quickly shot down in flames when I enter the kitchen and find Mrs Potts and Mr H sharing a pot of tea, both looking at Becker's back. He's currently roughly pulling open cupboard door after cupboard door and slamming them on moody grunts.

'Where are the apples?' he barks, throwing his arms into the air in a strop.

'Fridge,' Mrs Potts answers, her teacup poised at her lips. 'Where they always are, Becker boy.'

He ignores her sarcasm and stomps over to the fridge, yanking it open and grabbing what he's looking for. He's sunk his teeth in before he has shut the door and is ripping the flesh of the fruit away when he swings around and takes in his spectators. He can't talk. His mouth is full, so he throws a *what?* look at them.

Mrs Potts and his grandad slowly drag their stares to me, looking for enlightenment. I'm not going to give it to them. Not intentionally. I can't, however, help the involuntary blush that springs over my cheeks.

Guilty. As. Charged.

A wash of worry falls over Mr H's old face, and he rises to his feet with too much effort. But he doesn't question what's going on between Becker and me like I suspected he would. 'The sculpture, did you intercept the sale?'

'Yes.' Becker nods on a scowl, agitated by the question.

I frown across the kitchen at him, bemused by both his grandad's question and Becker's answer. Intercepted the sale? Like stopped it? Becker looks to me guiltily, wrapping his lips around his apple again.

'Oh, thank Aphrodite.' Mr H collapses to his chair, relieved. 'I bet it caused quite a stir.'

'It did,' Becker says, now refusing to look at me. Yes, it caused quite a stir, but something tells me that they aren't on the same page.

'And have we any idea who crafted the fake?'

'No,' Becker grunts through his chews, still refusing to look at his grandfather.

'Well, I for one am raging with curiosity.' He laughs. 'I don't know what planet that authenticator was on. I mean, it was a damn good forgery, but even I could see it was a fake. Now the museum has the map, we can move on and put this poisonous rivalry with the Wilsons to bed. We've done our part. We've done what's right.' He nods, satisfied, a huge smile on his old face.

I just about manage to conceal my gasp, but I don't refrain from shooting Becker an alarmed look. He catches it. I know he does, even though he's pretending he didn't. I've just grasped what's amiss here. Everything just slotted into perfect place.

Oh my God.

Mr H has no idea that his grandson bribed the expert. He thinks Becker has declared the fake and handed over the map – the map I found. The map everyone thinks I don't know about. That map I *know* is still in the secret compartment I found in the library. I'd put my life on it. The rivalry with the Wilsons, the one Mr H seems to think is over, isn't done in Becker's eyes. Mr H and Mrs Potts don't know about the stunt Becker's pulled. He's deceived them, too. And pulled me into the middle. Why? He was supposed to prevent the museum from buying the fake sculpture, but he wasn't supposed to trick Brent into buying it. But this is a rivalry that goes back generations. And what happened today was payback for his father being ripped off. Retribution.

Oh Jesus.

I start laughing. I actually laugh. It comes from nowhere, surprising me as much as everyone else in the room, who all shoot me frowns. I shut up and clear my throat, smiling awkwardly. I'm going to give Becker away soon. I've started toying with my gloves, and I'm a nanosecond away from starting to whistle while looking around the kitchen casually, Becker's words that he said outside Countryscape bombarding my mind.

Mrs Potts looks doubtful. 'And the fake?' she asks.

'What about it?' He flips a quick look across to me. My eyes widen pleadingly, and I silently scream at him for putting me in this situation. Does he want backup or something?

'Where is it?' she asks.

'I don't know.' Becker shrugs. He's doing a terrible job of lying. Shockingly bad, and I somehow find comfort in that. It worried me that he could so easily fool hundreds of people at that auction house. His ability to deceive is alarming. That he's struggling to maintain his mask with his grandad and Mrs Potts is actually soothing me.

But I'm still standing here, cringing. Becker must know they'll find out sooner or later. The news of Brent Wilson getting his smarmy hands on *Head of a Faun* would be top gossip in the antiquing world.

Mrs Potts steps forward, her head lowering, her eyes narrowing. 'Where is it?'

'Wilson bought it.' Becker confesses before chomping on another bit of apple.

'For the love of Achilles.' Mr H is up from the table again, this time like a lightning bolt, his anger taking years off him. He's mad. Very mad. Seething, in fact. His face has gone bright red. 'Becker, I told you it's done. Ancient history. Let it go.'

'I can't,' Becker splutters, pieces of apple firing from his mouth. 'It's harmless. Just a joke.'

Becker's grandad wobbles on the spot, but it has nothing to do with his unstable legs. 'And how much did that harmless joke cost Wilson?'

Becker's mouth snaps shut, and he glances at me. I gulp, thinking his grandad might have a heart attack if he knows that bit. But again, surely he's going to find out one way or another. Why's Becker looking at me, anyway? This has nothing to do with me. 'Less than they took from us,' he whispers.

My eyes dart between the men. *Less than they took from us?* What's going on here?

'How much?' Mr H roars, but Becker doesn't even flinch. He stares at me, and when I glimpse across the kitchen, I find Mr H and Mrs Potts watching me closely, too. I shake my head, unsure whether I'm trying to convince them I don't know, or I simply don't want to tell them.

'Well?' Mr H asks, planting his palms on the table and leaning in towards me.

I laugh now, nervous as shit, looking to Becker for help. He just stares at me.

'You were with him all day, Eleanor. Don't play ignorant. How much?'

'I . . . it's—'

'Tell me, or I swear on Odysseus, I'll get really mad.'

He's not already? 'Fifty million,' I blurt out, shooting Becker an apologetic look, noting the disbelieving drop of his head on his shoulders. Holy Greek god. Becker's grandad's already seething. I'm not stoking his anger by refusing the information he's demanding. He'll find out soon enough anyway.

'Fifty million,' he bellows, actually sounding like a Greek god shouting from the heavens. 'Fifty bleedin' million!'

I've tipped him over the edge. I recoil and back away, fearing for Becker's life.

'Calm down, Donald,' Mrs Potts says, trying to push him down into his seat. 'You'll have a funny turn.'

He shakes her off, finding strength in his anger, and marches over to his grandson, using his stick to wave threateningly at Becker. 'You promised me. You promised to let bygones be bygones. No more games.'

'He's a fucking prick,' Becker retorts, but his grandad doesn't back off. No, he gives his grandson a whack with his stick in temper. Becker jumps back in shock. 'Fuck, Gramps.'

'We agreed,' he yells. 'Declare the fake, give the museum the map, and wash our hands of it.'

'I'm not giving up that map. I'm going to find the sculpture, Gramps.'

'At what cost? Your great-grandfather, your father, we all searched for years. It can't be found. Your damn father didn't listen to me. And look what happened to him. Looking for that stupid sculpture. I will not lose you, too.'

'He's dead because of the Wilsons,' Becker growls, shaking with rage. 'Dad was pushed to make stupid decisions. I won't make that same mistake. Wilson thinks he has the sculpture. Now I can find it without him following me around the fucking world.'

I step back, shocked, Becker's words coming back to me.

Less than they took from us.

The Wilsons took a fucking lot. Like his father's life? It's clicking together like a slow-forming puzzle, and I'm beginning to grasp the enormity of what I'm witnessing. A wannabe Indiana Jones tailing Becker around the world. Brent's dad also tailed Becker's father while he searched for the sculpture. They think the Wilsons had something to do with Becker's father's death? How?

'Enough,' Grandad roars. 'No more. You. Will. Forget.'

'I fucking can't,' Becker yells back. 'How can you ask me to do that? How can *you* do that?'

'Because it will eat me alive from the inside out for the rest of my godforsaken life, that's why. And it will you.'

'It already has.' Becker throws his apple maliciously across the kitchen and stalks out.

I feel like an intruder. I shouldn't be here. I shouldn't have heard that. But Becker put me here. He wanted me to know all of this. He wanted me here when the shit hit the fan with his gramps. Good God, does he simply want one person in this world to understand his plight and support his quest? Do I? I thought I did, but now? Now I've heard how serious this rivalry is, I'm not sure.

'Now, now, Donald.' Mrs Potts moves across the room to Mr H with an agility of a much younger woman. 'Let it be.'

'It consumes him, Dorothy.' His breathing is laboured from his overexertion. 'He has to stop. Dear God, please make him stop.'

'He's wilful, Donald. A trait you can surely relate to.'

He huffs. 'He's a fool, just like I was. And his father. A daring son of a bitch with no regard for anyone but himself. He'll waste his life, like we did. And there will be nothing left for him at the end of it, except regret. No sculpture. No satisfaction. Just regret.' His head falls into his hands, his old body deflating.

Seeing the old man in such a state of helplessness and desperation does more than tug on my heartstrings. It cuts straight through them. I want to offer my comfort, yet I don't feel it's appropriate. This rivalry isn't a battle of the biggest ego. It might have been once upon a time, but now it's escalated into something more. Something fucking huge. Mr H once told me he'd do things differently if he had his time again. He means this. The family rivalry. Of course, my mind is rampant with unrelenting curiosity, but it would be silly and selfish of me to dream of prying into such a delicate, painful matter.

I slip silently out of the kitchen, leaving Mrs Potts to console Becker's grandad. I'll stay with Lucy. Mark will just have to put up with me. I'd rather be the cause of another night of no action for Lucy than be here where everyone's emotions are so volatile. I should have kept my mouth shut, but in the same breath, Becker expected that showdown. He's put me in the middle, knowing what I would face, what I would see, what I would find out.

I blow out air, my brain burning further as I head for the courtyard, making a conscious effort not to be distracted by the stone staircase when I pass it. I do well, keeping my focus forward.

Until I hear him.

'Where are you going?'

I slow to a halt and glance up the stairs into the blackness. I can't see him; he's hiding in the shadows. 'I didn't mean to cause such a row,' I say quietly. 'You should have told me.'

'He'll get over it. Always does.'

His detachment rattles me. How can he be so selfish? 'Well, he's not in good shape. You should tend to him.' I continue on my way, but come to a stop when a question pops into my mind that I'm surprised I haven't thought to ask before. 'If you have the map, how come you haven't found the sculpture? You said you know where it is.'

I hear movement on the stone steps behind me, followed by a deep breath. 'I'm missing a piece.'

I swallow hard. The rips. The hole in the old map. He needs that missing piece. He's looking for that, too? God, it goes on. He doesn't know where the sculpture is at all. He needs to find the missing piece of map before he can find the sculpture. My mind spirals.

'Eleanor?'

I don't turn around. What would be the point? I can't see him, and speaking to darkness is something I'm sick of. I feel like I've been doing it from the moment I met him. 'What, Becker?'

'Don't go.' The quiet demand is whispered in my ear, and I flinch, turning around to find he's silently crept up on me. He's expressionless. But the sadness and frustration behind his hazel eyes is obvious. 'Please.'

That follow-up plea slices me in two, his vulnerability weakening me. 'I don't know what I'm doing here,' I admit, dropping my eyes.

'You're here to help me understand.'

My head whips up, annoyed. If there's anyone who needs to understand shit around here, it's me. I've had a tidal wave of revelations poured all over me. 'Understand what? Us?'

'Yes.' He steps into me and nuzzles my cheek, the bristle coating his jaw comforting. I could cry for him. I could cry for me, too. My morals and conscience are demanding I run. Yet my heart is refusing to let me give up on him. This crazy revelation hasn't made a scrap of difference to how I feel about Becker. If anything, it's made me realise how passionate and lost he really is. How determined. And how fragile. This has given a whole different perspective on his therapy. Women are a side effect. Something to distract him when he allows them to. Because in every other facet of his life, he's on a hunt. An unrelenting, solitary quest. For that sculpture, but also for retribution. For peace. To find what his father and his grandfather couldn't.

A small part of me wants to leave because I know it's the right thing to do. To ease my conscience. But I can't win. By easing my conscience, I'll be breaking my heart. I need to figure out which one I can live with.

My answer comes out of nowhere.

I relax into his body, accepting how right it feels, my hand coming up of its own accord and cupping his cheek, holding him to me, soothing him . . . tumbling deeper into his corrupt, conflicting world.

I'm choosing to stay.

Chapter 24

I wait patiently in Becker's office while he goes to find some snacks. I didn't offer my assistance. I don't know where his grandad and Mrs Potts are, and I didn't want to risk bumping into them. Smart? Yes. Gutless? Definitely.

Becker returns with a tray and slides it on to his desk, revealing a selection of picky bits – breads, cheeses, pâté, and olives. 'Bon appetite,' he says, brushing his hands off. He's taken his jacket off and pulled his shirt out of his trousers. The first few buttons are unfastened, his tie loose and hanging low, and he's rolled his sleeves up. He looks casually relaxed and delicious. 'Don't ever tell me I don't know how to treat a lady.'

I frown at what Becker's chosen as our sustenance. 'Really?' He's hardly gone to much trouble.

He drops down into his chair, unravelling his tie with lithe fingers. Slowly. Watching me. A heavy, distinctive pulse drops into my nether regions with an almighty bang. He smiles. That damn smile disarms me in a flash. And the bastard knows it.

'Let me reword that.' He tosses his tie aside and reaches for an olive, popping it in his mouth and chewing purposely slowly. My eyes are glued to his lips. Double bastard. 'Don't tell me I don't know how to treat the devil woman.'

'Hey.' I grab a pen and throw it at his head, but he ducks and it sails past his ear. He stops chewing and his surprised face follows its path until it comes to land on the floor, bouncing a few times by the clock. His sharp inhale is loud. And fake. I devilishly wish he'd choke on the olive he's storing in his mouth. 'Why, princess . . .' His hazel eyes, full of light and humour, slowly reveal themselves as he swallows deliberately. It's a calculated move designed to drive me nuts, but not in a mad way. In a seductive, teasing, torturous way. 'That feisty side coming out to play?'

'It's ab—'

'Ah, ah, ah.' That finger appears. 'Shhhh.'

My mouth closes speedily. I didn't tell it to. The cocky fucker sitting opposite me did. Triple bastard. He's pulling out all the stops, the smile, the teasing, the humour, the sexy shush. And I want to kiss him for it. This is better. Normal. This is us.

Trying to fool him into believing his gallant attempts to bring me back around aren't working would be . . . well, foolish. But I do, anyway. I shrug nonchalantly and take an olive for myself, slipping it past my lips. I'm buying myself some time to think carefully about what my next words should be. I've learned a lot today, almost too much to process. It's been a tidal wave of revelations.

'I have a whole lot of shit on you, Hunt,' I say quietly.

'Maybe that's the point.' He regards me closely. 'You're in Becker's Circle of Trust now, and once you're in, you never get out.' He picks up an apple. Damn. My body stiffens. If I had the strength and inclination I'd look away, but I don't. Instead I find my gaze tracking the slow delivery of the green fruit to his mouth. Once you're in, you never get out. I'm stumped as to why this thrills me more than it frightens me.

'How many people have there been in Becker's Circle of Trust?' I ask, reading between the lines of his statement.

'Including you?'

'Including me.'

'One,' he answers assertively, taking a big, clean bite of his apple. His answer delights me as much as the sound of him crunching his way through his favourite fruit. So why me? Why now? 'Don't look at me like that, princess.'

Like what? Awed? Mesmerised? Excited? Or am I now watching him in wonder? Eating apples shouldn't be erotic, it just shouldn't, but every time I witness him sinking his teeth into one, it's all I can do not to dive on him and lick the juice from his lips.

'Look at you like what?' I ask cockily, tossing that errant thought away. I regret my comment the moment his lips curve into one of those disarming, lopsided smiles. They send my knees bandy. Even when I'm sitting down.

'Like you want to share this apple with me.' He holds it up and spins it expertly in his hand.

I do, tickles my lips as I watch the fruit, held rapt by its shiny skin and the manly hand holding it. Forbidden fruit. It's a sign. I'm Eve being enticed by the devil in disguise. Is Becker in disguise? Do I know who I'm dealing with? The mystery and intrigue attached to him holds a certain element of addictive danger. I could fall spectacularly from the beauty of The Haven into a hellish place of sin and temptation. Or am I Snow White, being tricked into accepting an appealing offer that could destroy me completely?

'About that NDA.' Becker breaks into my thoughts.

I regain my focus. 'You mean the one that's a figment of your imagination?'

And it happens again. A big bite from the apple accompanied by a smirk. I'm forced to endure a painful stretch of time while he munches through it and swallows. 'Not any more,' he announces, producing an envelope. He places it neatly in front of him, then uses two fingers to leisurely push it across the desk to me, achieving maximum, dramatic effect. My eyes are rooted to it. Something tells me it's going to be unconventional. Something tells me not to read it. Something even more powerful demands I definitely shouldn't sign it. My teeth nibble the inside of my lip thoughtfully while I stare at the harmless envelope. At the same time, all I can hear are the sounds of crunching, reminding me of who put the NDA there. And, more significantly, who wrote it.

'Open it.'

I look up to find Becker's burning gaze on me. His eyes are dark. I'm wary of them. Then I look at the envelope again. My hesitance is clear. I'm cautious, but I'm also curious. But as seems to be the way of things for me recently, my curiosity breaks through my defences. I've discovered some utterly unbelievable shit today, and I'm still here, for Christ's sake.

I reach forward and take the envelope, slipping the paper out. Becker remains quiet, allowing me to read and absorb the non-existent NDA that isn't so non-existent now. It has been penned by Becker, and I expect Becker will demand full committal. We'll see. I can read it. There's no contract that says I have to sign it.

I unfold the heavily embossed ivory paper, finding the Hunt Corporation's logo and company details emblazoned across the top, all displayed in a pretty gold font.

I dive in and my eyebrows get higher with each term I read.

NON-DISCLOSURE AGREEMENT (NDA)

This Non-disclosure Agreement (the 'Agreement') is entered into by and between Becker Hunt ('Disclosing Party') and Eleanor Cole ('Receiving Party') for the purpose of preventing the unauthorised disclosure of Confidential Information as defined below. Furthermore, it shall outline basic requirements of the Receiving Party, as stated by the Disclosing Party. The parties agree to enter into a confidential *relationship* with respect to the disclosure of certain proprietary and confidential information and with a clear understanding of what is expected from each party.

1. *Definition of Confidential Information.* For the purposes of this Agreement, 'Confidential Information' shall include all information or material that has or could have commercial value or other utility in the business in which Disclosing Party is engaged, whether in written or oral form.

2. *Exclusions from Confidential Information.* The Receiving Party's obligations under this Agreement do not extend to information that (a) is publicly known at the time of disclosure or subsequently becomes publicly known through no fault of the Receiving Party; (b) is disclosed by the Receiving Party with the Disclosing Party's prior written approval.

3. *Obligations of the Receiving Party.* The Receiving Party shall hold and maintain the Confidential Information in strictest confidence for the sole and exclusive benefit of the Disclosing Party. The Receiving Party shall carefully restrict access to Confidential Information to anyone as is reasonably required. The Receiving Party shall not, without prior approval of the Disclosing Party, use for the Receiving Party's own benefit, publish, copy, or otherwise disclose to others, or permit the use by others for their benefit or to the detriment of the Disclosing Party, any Confidential Information. The Receiving Party shall return to the Disclosing Party any and all records, notes, and other written, printed, or tangible materials in its possession pertaining to Confidential Information immediately if the Disclosing Party requests it. In addition, the Receiving Party agrees to the following terms of this agreement, which are included for the benefit of both parties, and to define and clarify their relationship.

The Receiving Party will:

3.1 Sign this contract with no fuss.

3.2 Stay at The Haven for as long as the Disclosing Party deems appropriate.

3.3 Sleep in the Disclosing Party's bed.

3.4 Keep the Disclosing Party's fruit bowl full of apples. Green Granny Smith's with juice spots.

3.5 Allow the Disclosing Party to violate the Receiving Party in the most delicious ways imaginable.

3.6 Answer the Disclosing Party's calls within the first five rings.

3.7 Answer the Disclosing Party's text messages within five minutes.

3.8 Accept that the Disclosing Party will call the Receiving Party 'princess'.

3.9 Never ask the Disclosing Party to say 'please'.

3.10 Never stop looking at the Disclosing Party's arse, even when he tells the Receiving Party to.

3.11 Be considerate of the Disclosing Party's feelings. He does have them.

3.12 Accompany the Disclosing Party to the Annual Andelesea Gala and wear what he picks out for the Receiving Party.

3.13 Never engage on a personal level with clients of the Disclosing Party. This includes but is not limited to accepting dates, calls, and flowers.

3.14 Never share any information about the Disclosing Party or his family to anyone at any time.

4. *Time Periods.* The non-disclosure provisions of this Agreement shall survive the termination of this Agreement and the Receiving Party's duty to hold Confidential Information in confidence shall remain in effect until the Confidential Information no longer qualifies as a trade secret or until the Disclosing Party sends the Receiving Party written notice releasing the Receiving Party from this Agreement, whichever occurs first.

5. *Relationships.* Nothing contained in this Agreement shall be deemed to affect the private relationship of the Receiving Party and the Disclosing Party.

6. *Severability.* If a court finds any provision of this Agreement invalid or unenforceable, the remainder of this Agreement shall be interpreted so as best to effect the intent of the parties.

7. *Integration.* This Agreement expresses the complete understanding of the parties with respect to the subject matter. This

Agreement may not be amended except in writing and signed by the Disclosing Party.

8. *Waiver.* The failure to exercise any right provided in this Agreement shall not be a waiver of prior or subsequent rights. This Agreement and each party's obligations shall be binding on signature.

(Signature)_____

Becker Hunt_____ (Printed Name)

Date: 30 November 2019

(Signature)_____

Eleanor Cole_____ (Printed Name)

Date: 30 November 2019

I stare at the paper for a good five minutes after I've read it three times. It couldn't be any clearer. 'When did you write this?' I ask. It was only agreed that I come here an hour ago.

'While you sat in your bathroom battling with your conscience.' He raises his eyebrows, and I purse my lips guiltily.

'And what if I want to add something to your little NDA?'

'If it's within reason, go right ahead.' He passes a pen over, and it's all I can do not to laugh. Within reason? Yes, because everything on here is perfectly reasonable.

I take the pen tentatively. 'Not seeing other women, is that reasonable?'

'You or me?'

Now, I do laugh. 'You.' Then I hold my breath. The anticipation of his answer has fear swirling in my tummy.

'I'd say that's perfectly reasonable,' he says quietly. 'And it also goes without saying.'

Air enters my lungs and burns them. 'Okay,' is all I manage to say as I look down and add my own little addition to his NDA. Then the pen hovers over the signature strip.

'Sign it,' Becker says quietly, obviously seeing my hesitance. 'What—'

'I refer you to item three point one.'

'But—'

He shoots up from his chair and slaps his palm on his desk, using it as leverage to launch himself across to my side. I fly back in my seat in shock, my eyes landing on my knees where his hands are resting, his body bent, his face close to mine. 'You're signing that paper, princess. You know it and I know it.'

'What—'

His finger meets my lips and my eyes fall to his mouth. 'Shh-hh.' He hushes me and waits a few moments until he's sure I'll comply. Then he removes his finger and crouches in front of me, turning the contract around and scribbling his name across the bottom. 'Your turn.' He holds up the pen for me.

I suddenly realise something key. 'I won't tell anyone about today,' I murmur quietly, because I expect that detail is an issue here. Now I have something against him. Something that could stir an enormous shitstorm, a scandal of epic proportions. Everything tells me there is so much more than what I already know, and I astonish myself when I realise, out of the blue, that I want all of Becker's secrets. Every single one.

'I know.' He strokes my thighs, stirring up my unrelenting desire for him, crumbling my morals more. His jaw pulses, and my eyes drift from the indentations on his cheeks, to the perfection of his nose, where his glasses sit as perfect as always. 'But it's actually item three point two and three point three that I'm particularly passionate about.'

I don't need to look at item 3.2 and 3.3. They're stuck to the front of my brain. 'You should have asked me to sign this before you exposed some of your secrets.'

'Maybe.' He shrugs a little, not perturbed by the suggestion that I might not sign it. 'But it's a moot point, because we both know that you are signing that contract.'

'What makes you so sure?'

'Because you love working here,' he says, pausing briefly, like he's waiting for me to reply. It's silly. He knows how I feel about my job. 'Because it excites you, and because life is too short and you're too curious.'

I take a long, deep breath. He's right. I can't deny it, and I won't.

'This is a Non-Disclosure Agreement, princess. That's all. It's standard business practice.'

I laugh. 'With a few added extras.'

'Would you like me to remove them?'

'No,' I answer before my brain engages, but it's too late to retract it.

He smiles and nods down at the papers in my hand. 'You're already in Becker's Circle of Trust, princess. This simply makes it official.'

I reason with myself for just a moment, because that's how long it takes to talk myself around. I'm overthinking. This NDA is simply a measure to ensure my silence. I wouldn't dream of breathing a word to anyone about what I've learned today. Discretion is part of the job, I knew that. So it really is a moot point. The rest? The added extras? Well, my stomach somersaulting is scaring me. I don't think Becker realises how significant his moves have been – the secret entrance, the Countryscape trip, the con, the family feud. He's inviting me in. Or dragging me. Either way, I'm not putting up much fight.

Throwing caution to the wind, I take the pen and scribble my name across the bottom of the paper messily. Done. I'm being discreet about more than I ever imagined, but it's irrelevant. I can't even be bothered to find the concern I should be looking for, let alone analyse it.

The pen is whipped from my hand before I can print my name below. Becker tosses it on his desk and scoops me up from the chair, cradling me in his arms. 'Super,' he whispers, taking my lips like they belong to him. Right now, they do. And so does every other piece of me. 'Now I get to violate you.' He paces out of his office with conviction, placing me on my feet sooner than I'd like. I blink repeatedly and glance around, grasping my bearings. 'Turn around,' he orders gently, taking my hips and encouraging me. I come face to face with the opening of the stone staircase that has been a fascination to me since the very first time I encountered it. My pulse thrums in my ears, and my trembling hands come up to rest over Becker's on my hips as I stare into the darkness. I squeeze them, indicating where I'm at. I'm looking for reassurance, and when he closes in behind me, returning my squeeze, pushing his chest into my back, I know he's comprehended that. 'Don't be scared.' His breath tickles my ear, increasing my pulse rate.

Yes, I am a little scared. But nowhere near enough to hold me back. My muscles engage, and my right foot gingerly comes up to rest on the first step. He doesn't push me on or express any impatience. He just manipulates our hands so they're entwined, still held at my hips, and waits patiently for me to find whatever strength I need to negotiate the steps.

One by one, I tackle them, willingly venturing into the darkness. My legs are stable and unfaltering now, my mind accepting, yet I still feel like I'm stumbling into the unknown.

We round the circular staircase, our feet hitting the treads the only sound, until a dim light comes into view, seeping from under a wooden door.

Becker gives me one final super-squeeze of my hands and releases them, stepping to the side and swiping his card. The door creeps open, bathing us in hazy light and revealing the mystery of the glass wall that keeps guard over the Grand Hall.

Becker's apartment.

Chapter 25

I take it all in on a quiet hitch of breath. It's sparse, a massive contradiction to the rest of The Haven. The floor is black, with flecks of sparkling glass broken and engrained within the smooth marble, and the walls are covered in a graphite-grey wallpaper behind silver frames of various sizes. In every frame is a black-and-white map of a country, the smaller ones displaying islands and slighter countries, the bigger frames showcasing countries such as Russia, China and America.

'I'd show you around, but I'm feeling a little impatient.' He whirls me around and yanks me into him. My body crashes with his, and I look into his eyes, my breathing shallow. A light fingertip ghosts across my brow and down my cheek, Becker's eyes trailing it, until he reaches my lips. Then he secures my nape with a firm palm and moves in, lowering his mouth to mine.

My groan of pleasure echoes in the space around us, welcoming him to do what he has full intention of doing. Possess me. I have no influence over that now. I'm vulnerable and weak. Yet somehow calm and strong.

My hands find his hair and I take the greatest of delight when he moans his pleasure, weaving through the strands and gripping harder when he ups the ante of our kiss. 'Skin,' he mumbles, desperately pulling at my dress. My hands free his hair and my arms rise, permitting and willing him to hurry. My dress is gone, almost as quickly as abra-fucking-cadabra, except this time it's still in one piece. Not that I care. It's tossed aside blindly, and then he's up close again, burrowing into my neck while his hands locate my bra strap.

Closing my eyes, I inhale and drink in his scent, feeling drunk on pleasure and anticipation. I feel the clasp of my bra give. I feel his hands dragging across my skin as he pulls it around my back. I feel his teeth biting lightly into the flesh of my shoulder. I feel his cock pressing into my stomach. I feel his heart hammering against my chest. I feel mine, too. 'Becker.' His name is more a plea, released on a shaky breath of air.

'Shhhh,' he soothes, taking my bra straps lightly and stepping away, breaking all contact between us. I hate it. I want him close again, touching me. But Becker has other ideas. He releases my straps and watches as my bra slides down my arms and tumbles to the floor, exposing my nipples to dark, appreciative eyes. I stand before him in just my satin knickers and heels. 'The heels stay,' he whispers hoarsely, his lip slipping between his teeth as he runs his eyes up and down my body. I have no desire to conceal myself. I don't feel shy or hesitant. Not even when he drops to his knees and slips his thumbs into each side of my knickers. Looking up at me, he lazily drags them down my thighs and I step out of them as soon as they reach my ankles. Then he rests back on his heels and gazes up at my body, his eyes heavy and hooded. His pose could be mistaken as submissive, but I'm under no illusion that he will be. I'll get no control here. And I don't want any. Whatever he does to me this time, *he* will instigate. I won't protest or hamper his natural instinct. And his instinct right now is to rise and bury his nose into the apex of my thighs.

I cry out and grab his head, knowing I'll get reprimanded for it.

'Hands, princess.' He reaches behind him and pulls my fingers from his hair, squeezing hard in warning when I make it as tricky as possible for him. It doesn't hinder him much. 'Here.' My hands are settled by my side. He's asking the impossible.

I'm wrong. Very wrong, in fact. It's actually quite easy until he lays his palms strategically on my upper thighs and uses his thumbs to reach between them and separate my soaked folds. My head falls back, my mouth mumbling mindless prayers to the ceiling. And then he takes the torture to another level and flicks his tongue over my hypersensitive clit. I nearly double over, screaming in beautiful agony. This is just the beginning. Oh God, I'll never remain upright for this.

'Legs apart.' He knocks the inside of each ankle in turn and, hungry for more torture, I comply, stepping out, widening my stance, opening myself up to him – no objection. I'm willing, I may as well be begging. In mindless desperation, my hands find my own hair and yank, bracing myself for what will come next.

It's his fingers. They circle provocatively, spreading my wetness, slicking back and forth, each time scarcely breaching my entrance. It's too much. I could step away, try to compose myself, or grab his hand and push him into me. Yet I don't. I remain a statue before him, my feet rooted, accepting anything he gives me.

'That good, princess?' The roughness of his tone enhances the feeling of his fingers between my thighs, pushing me to flex my hips in answer. 'Tell me.'

'Yes,' I whisper, my head rolling, my moans saturating the air.

'In the eye, Eleanor. Look me in the eye and tell me.'

My head drops limply. No second thought. No hesitation. My mind isn't my own. It's like it's wired to fulfil whatever he demands. He's looking up at me, still fully clothed, but the absence of his bare skin doesn't feel like a loss. I can't get past his eyes. They're brimming with carnal need, overflowing with satisfaction of the best kind. Kneeling at my feet like this, he shouldn't be exuding so much power. 'Never stop,' I tell him. My voice is shaky but certain. 'Ever.'

Growling, he puts some weight behind his caressing and pushes into me with two fingers, circling skilfully when he hits me deeply and pushes the tip on his thumb on to my clitoris. My knees buckle and my hands fly out to grab his shoulders for support. Stomach muscles I never knew I had constrict, forcing me to bend at the hips, my hair tumbling forwards. He doesn't give me any respite, drawing out and plunging forward again, nibbling on my thigh, licking and swirling his tongue expertly.

'You smell fucking amazing, princess.' His lips vibrate against my skin, sending tingles racing down to my toes. I shudder, clawing my fingers into his shoulders, clenching my eyes shut. 'Taste even better.' Strong fingers pull out and stroke up my front, leaving my core bare and begging for him to return his attention there. 'You're going to climax,' he says confidently. 'Then you're going to suck my cock and watch as I come all over your pretty tits.'

I use what strength I have to lift my head and open my eyes, leaving me without any remaining energy to answer him. I nod, looking him straight in the eye as I gasp for breath. Every nerve ending I possess is screaming excitedly, the ones at my centre the loudest when his mouth starts to drift forwards, his eyes never leaving mine.

'You'll watch,' he whispers, flicking his tongue out to catch the zinging tip of my clit.

'Oh shit.' I blink, keeping my eyes closed a moment too long.

'Open,' he barks, slapping my arse with an accurate palm.

My eyes open wide in shock, the hard whack not only putting me in my place, but reminding me I've already been here once before. The sting is instant. So is the thrill.

'Do as you're told,' he warns, gliding his palm over the tender spot. 'Or don't do as you're told. Choice is yours.'

The choice is mine. Whether I get another pound to my arse is my choice. That's what he means. He gets as much pleasure out of spanking my arse as he does out of having me obediently comply with his commands. And much to my surprise, so do I. He talks dirty. He fucks dirty. He does business dirty.

And I love it. I shouldn't, but I do. It's as though until now, my life has suffocated me. Stifled me. But somehow, this dirty, controlling, sexy man is breathing much-needed air into me.

I nod my understanding and watch with rapt attention as he comes closer again, except this time he takes longer, driving me wild with impatience. 'Hurry,' I let the word slip past my lips and immediately regret it. Because now he'll do the exact opposite. He pulls away, smiling cunningly.

My eyes close, devastated, angry and insane with desperation. *Thwack!*

'Fuck,' I yell, my hips shooting forward, my arse feeling like it has burst into flames.

'Open your goddamn eyes, Eleanor.'

'Becker, please.'

Slap!

'Open.'

'Ah,' I scream, clawing my nails into his shoulders, throwing my head back in despair. My vicious act has little effect.

Thwack!

'I told you, princess. Choice is yours.'

My screams are not filled with pain. Yes, it stings like a fucking bitch each and every time he tans my arse, but the frustration . . . it's making me lose my mind. I'm buzzing between my thighs, dripping with need, fraught with desperation to find that explosion. I realise I'm my own worst enemy, but insanity is preventing me from finding the reason I need to fix that. I could cry.

'What's it to be?' He grabs my nipple and twists, multiplying that frustration by a million. 'I'll slap this gorgeous arse all fucking week long, princess. And I'll love every minute of watching it heat and cool between my strikes.' He rubs at my burning bottom, and I finally convince my lids to peel open and reacquaint myself with who's before me.

Becker.

Smug Becker.

On his knees, ready to give me the orgasm of my life. All I need to do is watch him give me that orgasm. Sounds easy as pie. In theory. It's a shame theory isn't reality.

I pull it together, reaching up to wipe the sheen of sweat from my forehead. My hair's wet, sticking to my damp skin. I'm a sexed-up mess. 'I'm ready,' I declare, stabilising my legs and breathing in. I've never been reduced to this before. I've never had to psyche myself up for an orgasm. Shit, this infuriating man has me constantly dancing on the edge of madness.

'You sure about that?' He cocks a self-assured brow at me, stroking my heated arse cheeks simultaneously before giving each a cheeky squeeze. 'No more spanking?'

'No more spanking.' I speak through gritted teeth, my flushed cheeks receiving a new dimension of red. I'm guessing they're crimson now, the craving and anger mixed together creating a vivid hue. 'Make me come, Becker.'

'With the greatest of pleasure,' he says on a calculated smirk, licking straight up the centre of my core while watching me, waiting for me to give him the green light to indulge in my arse again. It takes everything out of me, but I manage to keep my eyes from closing. Another long lick starts the shakes in my legs, and another carries the shakes up my torso. I'm trembling, feeling the agonising slow build-up of pressure swirling in my lower tummy. I need to grab it. I need to concentrate. My hips start to sway with Becker's motions, rolling on to his mouth in perfect time with his firm, long licks.

Closing my eyes is the natural thing to do, but the threat of him stopping helps me through the struggle. As do his hazel eyes, which are still looking at me, watching me falling apart before him. The build, the anticipation.

My climax strikes me with a force I'm unable to compre-hend. 'Oh my God.' I come undone when he latches on to my clitoris and sucks softly, yet I keep my gaze on Becker, the appreciation and pure satisfaction staring back at me making it easy. My body convulses, every muscle solidifying. Clenching my bum cheeks, he pushes me on to his mouth to finish me, sucking my release from the deepest parts of my body. It flows and flows, the pleasure, the scream, the tension. I'm mesmerised by his tongue slowly swirling, being as gentle as can be as I pulse against him. 'Perfect,' I breathe, sliding my hands up his neck and on to his head, giving his mousy, messed-up hair a tug. Good God, the man has serious mouth talent.

Our eye contact remains firmly intact while he patters gentle kisses across my thighs, working his way up my tummy as he climbs to his feet, his hands keeping a firm hold of my arse. 'I'm staking a claim on this.' He pinches my bum, and something inside me pleads for him to stake a claim on every other part of me, too. 'It's all mine, princess. To spank, to caress, to admire. All mine.' Dropping his hold after a final crush of my flesh, he takes one step back, forcing me to relinquish my grip of him. 'Go stand by the wall.' He nods over my shoulder and reaches up to his shirt buttons. He's going to get naked. He's going to reinstate the need he's curbed by undressing in front of me, and worst of all, he's insisting on me standing too far away from him to touch should my impatient hands want to hurry him along. 'Now.'

I'm stepping back before I know what's happened, my wired mind not failing him. I hate the distance between us, but the glimpse of his chest when his shirt falls open eases the blow. Solid flesh. Cut and smooth. Tanned and rippling in soft waves as he shrugs the white material from his body and lets it drift down to the floor. My back meets the wall with a forceful smack. My palms follow. I'm pinned to the paint by an invisible force. He's debilitating. Everything about him. The unstoppable power of those sleepy, angel eyes backed up by a mouth that looks ready to break into a cocky smile at any moment. It strips me of any cognitive thought, and, worst of all, the desire to get it back.

'Play with your nipples.'

I'm on autopilot. Like a button has been pressed, my hands leave the wall. The sensitivity of my solid nubs doesn't hold me back. The first gentle brush makes me hiss a little, but I fight my way through and grip them hard, rolling them through my pinched fingers and thumbs.

Having his bare chest out of reach is beautiful cruelty, which leaves me wondering with building panic how I'll deal with him fully naked. His hands slowly find their way to his belt and yank it open aggressively. The grip of my nipples increases as a result. Then he whips it out of the belt loops and tosses it aside with force. I grip harder. Then he unbuttons his fly and pulls his trousers open, revealing the thick red waistband of his boxer shorts. I whimper, clamping down harder, like I'm punishing myself for being so weak and desperate. 'Red boxers?' I wheeze, dropping my nipples and banging my head against the wall, hearing my pulse begin to pound in my ears, the dull whoosh of blood making me dizzy and disorientated.

'Power red.' He smiles seductively and pings the waistband, keeping his full composure. Power red. Fuck, I bet he felt awfully powerful today, and I bet he's feeling pretty powerful now.

How can he do this to me? My head collides with the wall again. I don't know why I'm putting myself through this. I could go to him, tempt him, make him cave under the pressure of his equal want for me. I have no idea how he's controlling it. He's calm and measured, getting a sick kick out of playing with me. He's a fucking control freak, that's what he is. A sick, power-tripping womaniser. Yet here I stand, pinned to the wall with no intention of moving until he says so. 'Fucking hell,' I curse out loud, punishing my skull with another sharp smack against the wall.

'Struggling there, princess?' He pushes his trousers down and kicks them off. And I nearly faint. His neck, his chest, his flat stomach. The material of his boxers hug the tops of his thick thighs in the most sinful way, but they only get a moment of my appreciation. The outline of his cock may as well be glowing. It's pulsing, speaking to me. It's telling me that hours of pleasure can be found there. I lick my lips as Becker prowls towards me, stopping far enough away so I can still admire the bulge he's packing. I want to touch it. I want to feel, kiss, and caress it. Now, tomorrow, the next day, and the next. 'Kneel,' he breathes into my face, placing his palms on my shoulders and pushing me down. He doesn't need to try very hard. I slide down the wall willingly until I'm face to face with Becker's groin. 'At your leisure,' he says, pulling my face up to see him, placing a hand on the wall behind me. 'Like, now.'

My fingers slip past the red waistband of his boxers faster than my eyes drop back to his crotch, and they're dragging the material down his muscled thighs in quick succession. The wonder that is Becker's manhood springs free, the tip nearly skimming my nose.

'Aren't you hearing me, princess?' He takes hold of himself and draws back, then slips the head that's slick with cum across my lips. 'I said now. Suck.' The pressure of his hardness forces against my lips a split second before my mouth drops open, and I virtually swallow him whole, grabbing his arse and wrenching him forward. 'Son of a bitch.' His shocked bark only spurs me on. I dig my nails into his flesh and pull back, giving a wide swirl of my tongue around the tip before taking him all the way again. I've never loved giving a blowjob. The taste, the feeling of choking, but this . . . Becker's cock? I can't get enough. Won't get enough.

'Sweet mother of fucking God.' His spare hand finds my hair and pulls painfully, wrestling with my locks. 'Steady.'

I'm not steady. Don't plan on being, either. I lap and suck like a starved lion, determined to inflict torture to rival his own.

I'm confident of a victory. His sharp gasps for breath tell me I may have already won. Releasing one clawed hand from his arse, that fucking delectable arse, I tickle my way between his legs and find his balls, relishing in the whimpers and groans before I revel in the more satisfying sound of a high-pitched yelp. I grab on. Probably too hard, but the constant firm strokes of my mouth over his taut flesh are achieving the perfect mix of pleasure and pain. His body is quaking with pleasure and stiffening with delicious pain in between. He's unravelling before me. I've quickly sensitised myself to the sounds and feel of him, adjusting my touch from soft and giving to raw brutality. I stroke and tickle his heavy sack and follow it up with a tight squeeze. I run smooth lips up and down his cock and round it off with a firm bite – not too hard, just enough to have him tensing in uncertainty.

'Shit, Eleanor. How the hell do you do this to me?'

I look up to see his eyes clenched shut. *Back at you, Hunt.*

'You . . . fuck. Fucking, fuck, fuck, fuck.' His head drops, followed by a few beads of sweat, dripping from his wet brow. He shakes his head at me, torn, gritting his teeth and letting out a gruff bawl. Then he starts to convulse, his stomach concaving to control the sensations hijacking him. He's coming. My hold of his balls slackens and my tongue relaxes, my hand beginning to work in unison with my mouth. 'Oh, Jesus.' He smashes the wall above me with his fist, then drops his head back and yells at the ceiling, screaming for help from the gods. He's losing his mind. He's crumbling. 'I can't fucking see.' His head drops limply and rolls uncontrolled, his hips now taking on a mind of their own and meeting my advancing mouth. 'I'm coming,' he pants. 'I'm fucking coming.' He roughly pushes me off him, and takes over, his hand flying over his shaft urgently. My back meets the wall, my lungs screaming for breath as I heave, sweating and breathless. And then he comes, in long, hot, surging spurts, moaning and directing his release to my breasts. I accept it all, closing my eyes and melting into the hard wall behind me, feeling his heat slide between my boobs, down to my tummy.

'A-fucking-men,' Becker pants, dropping to his knees in front of me and slapping his palm on to my breast. Then he makes sure every inch of my front is coated in his essence.

Dropping my chin to my chest, I watch his hand glide across my skin with ease, and feeling him looking at me, I peek up through my lashes. He half-smiles, revealing a glimmer of that boyish charm. And I smile right back. 'You're a fucking she-devil, Eleanor Cole.'

'And you,' I puff, 'are a fucking saint.'

'A saint who's now going to fuck you like the filthy princess you are.' He takes my hands and lifts me as he rises. 'How's your arse?'

I pout. 'Sore.'

'Good.' He flips me around and shoves me forward so my front splats against the wall. 'I quite like it this colour.' He gives my right cheek a light smack, not painful as such, but reminding me of the delicate condition of my poor abused flesh. He pushes his body into every curve of my back, moulding us together. I swear he must be charged, because my flesh is sizzling like a metal prong powered with a thousand volts is being held against my skin. Then he takes my hands and braces my palms on the wall. 'I'll work hard to keep it this colour.'

I wince at the very thought. I'm going to be flinching every time I sit down for a good few days. Taking my waist lightly, he steps back, bringing my hips with him, bending me into position. Then I hear the rip of a condom packet, followed by a tiny hiss as he rolls it on.

'I'm constantly fucking solid for you,' he pants, taking hold of my hip, guiding himself to me. 'How dirty are you, princess?' He rubs the tip of his cock up and down between my swollen lips, sinking his teeth into my shoulder.

Fuck me, I'm on the brink of self-combusting. 'Dirty,' I

whisper – like I'm ashamed to admit it. Average sex. Just the kind that sees the job done. That's all I've had.

This? This and last night are as far removed from my previous sexual encounters. This is all kinds of illicit and dirty and so fucking good.

He slips in on a guttural groan, the sound rumbling up from his belly. 'How fucking dirty, Eleanor?' He holds himself deep, and my mind spirals into submission once again.

'Filthy,' I shout. 'I'm a filthy fucking whore.' I don't know what I'm saying. Jesus, I'm slipping further into debasement by the second. His carnality, his kink, his secrets. I'm falling for it all. And I couldn't give a flying fuck. 'Fuck me,' I plead, ramming back, impaling myself on him and hoping it locks us together for ever. Everything is forgotten – everything – my name, my history, everything that has made me *me*. It all disappears, lost amid a tidal wave of self-indulgence and excitement. It's an epiphany, an overwhelmingly decadent one that I want to last for the rest of my life. Becker Hunt has found me – not in the physical sense, but discovered me, unearthed who I am – a woman who thrives on excitement and holds her own. Someone confident and vivacious and set to take on the world. Someone daring and bold. Strange as it might sound when he's thrashing into me like a jackhammer on speed, but holy shit, the sense of raw abandon, the feeling of control when I haven't really got it, is bringing me to life.

Becker thrusts over and over, every pound harder than the last, every smack against my arse getting louder and louder. Reaching around to feel my breasts as they bounce and dance under the force he's subjecting me to, he clamps eager hands around each aching mound. 'How much does my filthy girl love my cock pounding her?'

'Oh God.' My stomach knots, twisting with exhilaration when the tell-tale pressure drops lower. My eyes close in preparation. It's coming. I'm going to scream. Loudly.

'How much?' he roars, twisting my nipples harshly.

My eyes snap open and my head bolts up, my fist pummelling the wall, hitting it hard, beating the ever-loving shit out of it. 'Don't ever stop!' I scream the words as stars start to form on the edges of my vision, drifting inward, clouding my sight.

'Oh, baby, we are going to be doing this a lot,' he shouts, and rams into me hard. It knocks what breath was remaining from my lungs, making me woozy. He doesn't relent, moving his hands back to my hips and holding me firm, like he senses the possibility of me collapsing to the floor. It's a very real possibility. My bones must have liquefied, disintegrated, shattered; I don't know what, but I'm suddenly incapable of holding myself up. 'Make it count, Eleanor.'

And I do, using my last scrap of sense and energy to seize the orgasm that's looming and letting it possess me like the devil himself, my whole body going up in wild flames.

I scream for as long as my lungs will allow, ignoring the scratching in my throat that feels like I'm swallowing nails. My arms are useless lumps of nothing braced against the wall, my head rolling and when I hear Becker take in a deep breath and hold it, I know he's about to tip over the edge, too. His sudden silence defies the brute force with which he's still taking me, smashing repeatedly against my bottom as he bangs every tiny piece of pleasure out of me. Then he releases his breath and seizes another long lungful, giving me no break from the attack my limp body is under. I'm spaced out, accepting, still riding out the release of a thousand accumulated orgasms.

His gasp for breath overrides the slapping sound of our sweaty bodies, and I'm jacked up on to him with very little effort. He moans and drops a level, now grinding forcefully. And I feel it. The swelling, the thundering of his heart, and the relief as he finds his release, mumbling incoherent words into the heavy air.

For the love of every Greek god in existence. Damn.

My orgasm has zapped me of the ability to feed instructions to my brain. It's stripped me of the ability to think, to speak, to move. He collapses against my back, and I fold to the floor, Becker following me down.

'Fuck me,' he heaves, rolling on to his back, leaving me a pile of sweaty uselessness beside him. 'That was better than . . .'

'What?' I pant, rolling on to my back too, kicking off my shoes when it registers they're still gracing my feet.

His chest rises and falls on long, strenuous breathes, his soaked face frowning. 'That was better than seeing Brent's face when he finds out he's spent fifty million on a lump of marble.'

Every other muscle has failed me, but that right there makes my face muscles twitch. Because I know how much Becker would enjoy that face. 'It was good.'

'Good?' He lets his head flop to the side until he finds my eyes, bringing his knee up to rest the sole of his foot on the floor, his palm on his rippling stomach. His hair is all mussed up, sexy as fucking hell. 'That wasn't good, princess. That just blew my fucking world in two.'

The twitching of my mouth transforms into a full-blown smile. I feel good. So, *so* bloody good, like I could run through London naked and not give a shit. Because I, Eleanor Cole, have just blown Becker Hunt's world in two – a man who I expect has been blown by half of London before he blew *their* world in two and fucked them stupid.

'Me and you have something pretty fucking phenomenal, princess.' It's like he knows I needed to hear that. Like he's telling me no other woman compares. Chemistry. He's talking about chemistry, and Becker and I have it by the bucket load. Tons of the stuff. The thought of anyone experiencing what I just had with him sticks in my throat like an old oak tree. A huge fucking oak tree. My nose wrinkles in revulsion.

'All right?' He rolls on to his side and cheekily pinches my nipple, snapping me from my uninvited thoughts.

'Very.'

He grins. 'Of course you are. You just hit a ten on the pleasure scale.'

I scoff and bat his hand away, earning a snarl and a harder tweak. 'Ouch.'

'Mine.' He raises his eyebrows, daring me to correct him. 'All of it.'

I don't argue. Wouldn't dream of it, because madly and quite unexpectedly, I want this cheeky maverick twat to take it all. So, I lie here and let him touch what he deems his. Me. And I hope beyond all hope, more than anything I've ever hoped for, that Becker might accept himself as mine. It's an alien prospect with a whole heap of complications attached to its arse. Me and Becker. Becker and Me. Secrets, Becker and me. The Haven, Becker and me. Here. Us. Working and screwing and . . . loving.

Loving?

'All right?' He asks the same question again, pressing the pad of his finger under my chin and lifting it, searching my eyes. His observation of my deep thinking disturbs me, and I find my cowardly arse shying away from the inquisitiveness in his stare *and*, more importantly, the direction of my thoughts.

Stupid thoughts.

'I'm fine,' I squeak. I sound like a startled cat.

'You sure?' He's suspicious. Understandably.

I decide it's probably wise to keep my mouth shut before I clue him in on any more of the silly thoughts that are stinging me like a swarm of jellyfish. Repeatedly. Over and over. Relentlessly. Ouch. 'Yes.'

'Good.' He lands a chaste, almost loving kiss, slap bang on my lips, biting down gently before he pulls away, dragging my bottom lip with him. He grins and releases, then rolls over swiftly and sends me cross-eyed when he stands slowly above me, like Poseidon breaking the waves of the sea and rising. He looks glorious. Powerful and strong. Lickable. Edible.

'Make yourself comfy. I'm going to use the bathroom.' He makes to turn but pauses, pouting his lips. 'You haven't seen my arse naked yet, have you?'

Becker's observation serves as a trigger and has me propping myself up on my elbows, interested, and likely to explode with delight when I get to see it. His arse. Bare. 'Nooooo.' I drag the word out for ever, dropping my eyes to his crotch, seeing straight past the beauty of his cock and imagining the beauty of his lovely arse. I've felt it naked. I've squeezed it. And it felt pretty damn good. I'm chewing the inside of my lip when I muster up the willpower to drag my eyes away.

His lip has curved at one corner. 'Enjoy,' he says brazenly, cockily and, with 100 per cent confidence that I will, he turns and wanders away.

Oh my, I do. My head tilts to the side in admiration, my lip worrying through my teeth as I fall into a trance. My eyes struggle to decide what to look at. His incredible arse, or that magnificent tattoo spanning his strong back. Surprisingly, given my love of his arse, my eyes fix on his back and that colossal tattoo. I squint, trying to figure out all the lines and shadows in the dim light, but he disappears into the bathroom before I can zoom in. I pout to myself and spend a few minutes getting my heartbeats back to a safe pace.

Injecting some life into my legs, I rise to my feet and glance around, wondering where I should make myself comfy. It's also an opportunity for me to take in the space. The greys and blacks are a common theme, even on the ceiling. If it wasn't for the tiny spotlights sprinkling the space in a dust of hazy light, it would be pitch black.

The area is small but perfectly equipped. It's an open-plan space with a zone sectioned off by a huge bookshelf serving as a room divider that distinguishes the bedroom from the rest of Becker's apartment. There's a kitchen, small but functional, and two oversized corner couches positioned to form a U-shape facing a colossal flat-screen TV that takes up most of one wall. Grey rugs are scattered, softening the feel of the sparkling marble floor and adding much-needed warmth. The Juliet balconies that can be seen from the courtyard are here, and I have a distinct memory of staring up at them on the first day I arrived at The Haven, wishing I could swing them open and stand in the morning sun.

I smile to myself, casting my eyes across the space to where Becker just disappeared. The bathroom walls are built with thick glass bricks, the light from inside basking the space in a soft glow. Wandering over to the bookshelf that separates the bedroom, I trail my eyes across the rows and rows of books, noting that many are biographies on various artists. I smile when I spot one on Michelangelo and pull the book from the shelf.

'Your arse is glowing.'

I turn and find Becker standing in the doorway of his bathroom, his shoulder resting against the frame, still naked. Gloriously naked. 'It's also tender.' There's no resentment in my statement. Quite the opposite, in fact. It feels warm and comforting, a reminder that he was there. A bit like between my thighs. I flick through the book casually, but snap it shut when something comes to me. 'The police,' I say, sliding the book back on to the shelf. 'I need to call them. Mind if I use your phone? You know, since I don't have one at the moment. Because someone destroyed it.'

His scowl is playful. 'I've called them already.'

'Oh. Shouldn't I have done that?'

'Well, you don't have a phone.' He shrugs, and I still get no apology for his outburst and the subsequent demise of my mobile. 'Anyway, it's not an emergency and nothing was taken, so they'll let me know when they can get an officer out.'

'Oh.'

He pushes off his shoulder and wanders over, having a quick

peek at the book I just replaced on the shelf. 'Reading up?'

'Just browsing.' He's standing close to my side, shoulder to shoulder, and my eyes are pulling in their sockets to get a glimpse of his back again, this time a close-up. I can see the crest of . . . I'm not sure what it is.

Becker looks out the corner of his eye and catches me frowning, but he ignores it, and I suspect it's because he knows exactly what I'm trying to look at. 'Let me show you something.' His warm palm slips across the top of my bare back until his arm is draped across my shoulders. A delightful warmth descends, engulfing my naked body. 'This way.' He keeps me close as he takes us to the far side of the room, where the glass wall stretches from one end to the other and from floor to ceiling. On our approach, all I can see is an old brick wall across open air, but as we near, the Grand Hall below begins to come into view until we're standing at the foot of the wall, staring down on the enormous treasure chest of antiques and art.

'Wow,' I breathe, taking it all it. I've been down there, been lost amid the organised chaos of wonderful furniture and treasures, but from up here it looks beyond incredible. I can see everything, with the exception of the section directly below that leads into the main building. This mezzanine floor is a late addition to this grand old building, and undoubtedly built to Becker's specification so he can guard what he deems his treasure. It's spectacular.

'Pretty cool, eh?'

'It really is,' I agree, reaching up and touching the glass to check it's there, feeling like I'm floating above the room. Looking down, I have a flashback and see myself fidgeting awkwardly among the priceless objects. I also see myself looking up to where I'm standing now and seeing the shadow of a man. The man standing next to me. 'How long were you watching me?' I gaze up at him to find he's already looking down on me, a hint of a smile gracing his lips.

'Every second.'

'Why?' I knew it. I'd felt it. It's the same delicious feeling I still get when he's close.

He considers my question for a moment, his lips pouting in contemplation, but his eyes never wavering from mine. He laughs under his breath and turns me in his arms, having a feel of my sexed-up red locks before scanning my face, thoughtful. Then his head tilts to the side a smidgen, telling me he's *really* thinking about this. 'I stand here,' he begins, eyes still roaming my face, 'and look down on my grand hall, often wondering how I could ever pick out the most beautiful thing in there.' His hazel eyes creep on to mine. 'I've never been able to. Nothing has ever stood out as being particularly more incredible than anything else.' His fingertip trances lightly over my eyebrow as he takes a deep inhale of air. 'Then one day I looked down and saw you.'

I breathe in and hold it, trying to remain still as his finger affectionately traces the contours of my face, not wanting to disturb his flow. Nothing could have prepared me for that. My heart just melted and my hopes just skyrocketed.

His touch shifts, slipping on to my nape, his other hand joining it there. I feel his fingers lace together, and then my head is tilted back and he closes the small gap between our torsos, bringing us together, sealing our skin. He looks at me with a determined stare and robs me of air, having me swallowing repeatedly to try and win it back. The sincerity shining in his eyes overwhelms me.

'You must have been surprised,' I say quietly.

'Oh, I was.' He laughs mildly. 'I know you don't believe in The Fates, but I hadn't stopped thinking about you and your annoyingly gorgeous face and blinding red hair since I first saw you on the street. Then you turned up here.'

'That's because I was stalking you.'

He smiles, and his lips drop to mine, swallowing me up in

a soft, adoring kiss, my eyes closing in contentment, my arms wrapping around his broad shoulders.

'Maybe I'm starting to believe in fate,' I say into his mouth. 'If you hadn't stolen my cab, I would've made it to my interview on time, and then maybe I would've got the job there.' I pull away, and he smiles, though it feels a little strained.

'Maybe,' he murmurs.

'Are you okay?'

'Super.' He dips and nibbles my lip. 'How could I not be with you in my haven? Everything is just about fucking perfect.'

I have no idea what to say. He's dazed me with his tender words. So I say nothing, but I think lots. Too much for me to try and unravel now. I need space and quiet, maybe even a listening ear. Lucy springs to mind first. I need to call her tomorrow.

'Let me show you where you'll be sleeping.' He dips and picks me up, draping me across both arms, and carries me into the bedroom. His arms locking me tightly to his chest offer me a sense of security that would be far too easy to get used to. My head falls limply on to his shoulder, suddenly too heavy to hold up, probably from the weight of everything on my mind.

When I'm placed on my feet, Becker stands back and lets me take in his bed. I'm sleeping in his bed. With him. More grey in the form of shimmering gunmetal bed sheets. I could get lost in this bed; it's humongous, but annoyingly the details of the bed are a fleeting thought. A lasting thought, however, and most nauseating, is how many women he's had in it. I cringe to myself. Plenty, I bet.

'Are you going to get in, or stand there all night and wonder how many women I've had in there?'

I look at him, bold and together. 'Well?' I can take it.

'Not as many as you think.' He motions to the bed, and I cock my head a little, surprised by his answer, though I don't press. Besides, do I want specifics?

Without a word, I slip between the soft sheets, and the smell of him hits me, embedded in the threads, mixed with a sweet-smelling washing power. It's intoxicating.

Becker crawls in beside me and sets about arranging his pillows just so, before he looks up and down my tense body a few times. He frowns. *What have I done?* He sighs and pushes me further away from him. 'Make sure you stay on your own side.'

I sink into the mattress, injured. 'Right,' I confirm, rolling over so my back is away from him, putting more distance between us. From the fuck of a lifetime to those spellbinding words to this? He jumps from one persona to another quicker than I expect his Ferrari gets from zero to sixty. 'Keep your hands to yourself,' I mutter.

I'm seized on a soft laugh and hauled back into his chest, being squeezed to a point I think my bones might crumble to dust under the pressure. 'You think I'll be able to keep my hands to myself while you're naked in my bed?' He chuckles, kissing the back of my head. 'Think again, princess.'

I have about as much fight in me as Eve did when that serpent offered her the tempting apple. Not a lot at all. If being held in Becker's arms is a lovely feeling, then being locked in his strong embrace under the sheets is dreamy. Every hard inch of him is pressed into my back, our bodies spooning delightfully. It adds a whole new dimension to gratification.

'Hmm,' he says, squeezing me to him. 'Naked cuddles.'

I smile, closing my eyes and savouring the feel of him. 'You should make up with your grandad,' I say quietly into my darkness. He was so upset, and time shouldn't be wasted on bad feelings when life is so precious. Becker should know that.

He's silent for a few moments, breathing low into my hair. 'Turn over,' he whispers, releasing me and pulling at my shoulder impatiently. I shuffle over until I'm facing him. His head is resting on the pillow, a palm under his cheek, and his hazel eyes are glimmering in the soft light. The sheets are pulled down my body a little until my breasts are exposed. He studies my nipples as his finger lightly swirls around the dark circle of one. They harden to bullets and he flicks me a cheeky grin. 'I told you, he'll get over it.'

I try to hide my doubt. He looked positively furious. 'And will Mrs Potts get over this?' I sway my finger between us casually. Suspicion made her twitch a little. Confirmation might see me faced with the Incredible Hulk.

He stops with his toying of my nipple and sighs, rolling on to his back. 'Probably not. I'm not a commitment person. I break hearts, Eleanor. Besides my job, it's what I'm best at.'

His admission stings like a bitch, making my brain swell with a barrage of doubt, the most worrying fighting its way to the front, refusing to be ignored. 'Will you break my heart?' I can't forget what his grandad bellowed at him. *Stop using women as therapy.* Does he see me as therapy?

His head drops to the side and he gazes at me. 'That depends if you're stupid enough to fall in love with me.' He almost winces at his brutal answer, shaking his head a touch and returning his attention to the dark ceiling. I'm eternally grateful, because now he can't see the hurt that's twisting my features. I roll on to my back and look up, considering the benefits of leaving before I let him worm his way into my heart any more. Tears pinch at the back of my eyes when I reluctantly accept that it's already too late.

'Don't fall in love with me, princess,' he whispers. 'Because I'd hate myself for ever if I hurt you.'

I clench my eyes shut to hold the tears that threaten to break free. 'You've nothing to worry about,' I assure him with feigned grit. His request is cowardly – like he's limiting damage control, assuring blame can't be placed at his door. He told me not to fall in love with him, so if I do, it's entirely my fault if he breaks my heart. The fact that his tender gestures and lovely words are helping me along the way to falling will not feature in Becker's mind, which begs the question why he's being so lovely. He told me not to dwell on the past and not to fear the future. He's a hypocrite. But I'm slowly figuring him out. I don't think he knows what he's doing, but he can't help doing it. Is his easy affection towards me coming naturally? Can't he stop it? Because if so, this could be ground-breaking for Becker. Would it be stupid of me to think I could be the one to change everything? He said it himself. This could be something fucking incredible.

'Have you ever loved a woman?' I ask outright.

'I loved my mother and my grandmother.'

'And no one else?'

'Nope,' he answers decisively. I believe him. 'Love is a waste of time.'

'You won't let anyone in,' I breathe on impulse, perplexed by my own automatic reply. He's scared to love – or to love again, even if it's a different kind of love. It's still attachment.

'Why would I?' he asks, an irritated edge to his words. It doesn't bode well, but then again, he's already let me in. He knows that. I don't have a chance to remind him, because he goes on, his irritation flaming by the second. 'I need no one. They only die on you when you become attached. Gramps had Nana, and she died. He was crushed. Hasn't been the same since. My dad had my mum, who died. Another man crushed. Then Dad died and practically finished Gramps off.' There's venom in his voice. Pure hatred.

The pieces of the puzzle are slotting into place. He hasn't said as much, but the losses his grandad and father experienced aren't his only motive for closing himself off from the potential of getting hurt. It's his own hurt too. Gramps lost his wife, but Becker lost his nana. Becker's dad lost his wife, but Becker lost his mum. And then Becker lost his dad, too. He's had his own fair share of losses. Too many for a man in his early thirties. And his security blanket, his self-preservation, is to cut off all feeling altogether. 'So you have a dog,' I mumble mindlessly, trying to gather my scattered thoughts.

He huffs a sarcastic puff of pissed-off laughter. 'Yeah, and even his loyalty stands for shit.' He gives me a filthy look, which I choose to ignore, given the delicacy of the conversation.

'And your gramps?' I say gingerly, looking for that tiny nugget that will seal the deal, slot everything into place.

'He'll die, break my heart, and then there will be no one else to leave me.'

Not even me? 'You'll be lonely,' I whisper.

He rolls on to his side and gives me a forced smile. I can see crystal clear there is too much pain following Becker Hunt around. 'I'll be safe from heartbreak, princess.'

Safe from heartbreak. Because his heart is locked away with his other treasures. This is his haven, but it's also his fortress.

He really is all for damage control.

I feel like I've hit the jackpot, except I don't feel fulfilled for having my suspicions confirmed. I feel crushed, because clarity has just smashed me in the face. He'll never love me because he won't allow himself to. He's broken my heart without even realising, and barely even trying. He thinks he's not a commitment type, but he's wrong. He's committed to finding that lost treasure with nothing holding him back. Like a family. Like a woman. Like love. No risk of getting caught up in an emotional or moral battle with himself. It's just him. Becker and his obsession with finding what three generations of his family failed to find. He wants to avoid the crippling guilt that so obviously weighs his grandfather down.

I'm devastated, but I give him an understanding nod, roll over and close my eyes. But I don't go to sleep. I lie awake for hours wondering if I have the strength and gumption to do this to myself. His words contradict themselves. But his heart never will. Have I made a terrible, terrible mistake?

Chapter 26

I mustn't fall in love with him.

I mustn't fall in love with him.

I must *not* fall in love with him.

I can smell him.

I can feel him.

I blink sleepily, feeling suffocated and disorientated. I'm on my back and he's spread all over me, trapping me beneath him. One of my hands is stuck to his arse, my other arm sprawled above my head, and my chin is resting on his shoulder. He's breathing deeply, his tattoo rising and rolling as he releases each breath. My eyes roam, trying to decipher what I'm looking at, and my finger gently rests lightly on his skin, tracing the path of a thick grey line curving around one of his shoulder blades. He flinches, and his breathing pattern changes.

'What is this?' I ask quietly, ghosting my fingertip across his skin.

'A tattoo,' he answers seriously, his voice gritty from sleep.

My finger pauses again, and I nudge him, feeling him smiling against my neck. 'Of what?'

'The world.'

I frown and tilt my head, trying to focus better. It's no good. The only times I've seen it he was too far away, and this morning he's too close. Intrigue gets the better of me, and I'm soon wriggling to free myself. I need a closer look.

Reluctantly, Becker rolls off me, on to his back, and gives

me tired eyes. 'I want to see,' I tell him, pulling at his shoulder. 'Turn over.'

He hesitates for a few moments, but does what he's told, lazily rolling on to his front. I notice he's tense when I straddle him and park myself on his perfect butt, his back muscles bunching as he brings his hands up and rests his cheek on the top of them.

The world.

My ability to breathe steadily deserts me.

A map of the world. I've seen it before.

My mouth drops open, my eyes darting across the expanse of his skin, absorbing it all. And there's a lot to absorb. Fine lines run into thick lines, curved lines are joined by straight lines, the edges of countries shaded deeper. My finger hovers over the details, tracing the millions of outlines without touching them, like I could smudge them and ruin it if I touch it. The detail isn't only in the physical drawing of the map. It's also in the wealth of information incorporated – a compass on his right shoulder, a grid shadowing his whole back over the map displays time zones, longitude, and latitude. Every country is labelled, every sea named, each continent titled. Every single piece of geographical information is noted somewhere on Becker's back, like a personal reference. Yet I know without question that he will know everything here without having to look it up. On his back *or* on the hidden map. Every intricate detail has been applied in various shades of grey, making it almost three-dimensional, and his skin beneath could be mistaken for aged paper, making the map appear antique. Just like the real thing. It's breathtaking. I could look at it for hours.

I worry my lip through my teeth, a million questions bombarding my mind. He doesn't know I've seen this map somewhere else. 'It's beautiful.'

'It's not finished yet,' he says quietly. 'A few more sessions to finish off Europe.'

I find Europe, seeing a huge space with missing countries. The same piece is missing on that ancient map I discovered by accident, but I know about *a* map. Fucking hell. When Becker said it was kept somewhere safe, he wasn't kidding. 'You could give the museum the map,' I say, my eyes still scanning the elaborate detail. 'You'd still have a copy.' It's not like he needs the original to find what he's looking for. And anyway, I bet he's photographed this for safekeeping.

'Call me possessive,' he mumbles quietly.

I smile, shaking my head in wonder as I study his back again. I touch this time, my finger travelling across the Atlantic to Canada. He needs the missing part of the map before he can finish his tattoo and find what he's looking for. 'Where's the missing part?' I ask.

He's quiet for a few moments, and I know it's because he doesn't know. The missing piece is part of Europe. Italy is in Europe. Michelangelo was Italian. The most important part of this map is missing, and I sense it's driving Becker insane.

'I don't know,' he says quietly. I watch his profile carefully, looking for the sadness on his face that will match his tone. 'But I'm getting close.'

'How close?' I ask, almost excited for him.

'Frighteningly close.'

'Why is it frightening?' I ask, frowning.

'Because it's taking me to places I never expected to go,' he whispers, as I continue to take it all in.

I smile at his wistfulness. 'Where am I?' I ask, drifting my finger down on to the States.

'America,' he answers immediately, smiling. 'Texas, to be precise.'

My mouth gapes. How the hell? 'Now?' I ask, running my touch through the Pacific Ocean.

'Hawaii.'

'Seriously?'

'Am I right?' He's cocky. He knows damn well he's right.

I venture a few inches to the right. 'How about now?'

'You're drowning, princess.' He laughs, and I gasp, looking down and seeing the tip of my finger is in the middle of the Pacific Ocean.

This time I remove my finger from his back, thinking maybe he can guestimate from the feel of my touch travelling across his skin. And I plonk it right on the edge of the clear flesh where part of Europe should be.

'Czech Republic,' he says simply, following up with a yawn. It's a fake yawn, one that tells me he's bored of this game.

Without that particular part of the map inked on his back, there's no solid evidence to confirm he's right, but I know he is. 'How?' I ask, staggered by his ability to identify any country from a touch of my finger.

He turns over beneath me, negotiating my body to allow his change of position before settling me on his groin. His cock isn't solid, but it isn't exactly soft either. I gulp down the inevitable heat that rises from my toes and settles in my tummy. 'I'm well travelled.'

'It's freaky,' I say, planting my palms on his stomach and stroking wide circles.

'Or a gift.' He seizes my hands, stopping their exploration of his sharp stomach.

I eye him carefully and try to move them, getting nowhere. He smirks, and I try again. Not even a dash of movement.

'Tell me how you feel,' he says, hesitant and regarding me closely.

'How I feel?'

'You've learned a lot about me.'

'Oh, you mean that there's more to you than being a holier-than-thou twat?'

He moves his hands to the tops of my thighs and squeezes playfully, making me grin. 'I'm holier than most,' he claims cockily. 'But not you, princess.' My smile widens, and he laughs a little, as if not quite believing he just said that. 'Tell me,' he pushes.

My answer comes naturally. 'I feel privileged.'

'Not frightened?'

I shake my head. I'm only frightened of what he can do to me. I go into my shell, looking away, unsure whether I should confirm beyond doubt what he must already know.

'I trust you, princess,' he breathes, knocking my leg to get my attention. I give it to him, but my mind is reeling, trying to figure out what he means by that. Does he trust me with his secrets? Or does he trust me not to fall in love with him?

'Why?' I ask instead.

He's silent for a beat, clearly thinking. 'My instinct is my best friend. I trust it.'

'You've never shared anything with anyone, have you?' I didn't lie. I really do feel privileged, even if I'm still a little stumped by his willingness to confide in me.

'Never.' His lips slope into a small, shy smile. 'You should think yourself lucky.'

My eye-roll is epic. 'And there's the holier-than-thou—'

'Shhhh . . .' His eyebrow arches and he takes my hands, constricting in warning.

'Well—'

'Shhhh . . .'

'Stop shushing me.' I try to yank my hands free, but before I can fathom what I'll do if I win them back, they're behind me and I'm on my front, Becker straddling my arse. My cheek is squished into the pillow. I'm helpless.

He transfers both of my wrists into one of his hands and strokes a teasing path down my spine with his palm, coming to rest on my bum. I stiffen. 'Still glowing,' he muses, blowing a cool stream of air into my ear. I clench my eyes tightly shut and brace myself. 'But not red enough.' His palm comes down and collides with my left cheek, smooth and sharp.

'Youch.'

He laughs and frees me, spinning me over and planting a forceful kiss on my lips. 'I have a meeting,' he whispers, and it's all I can do not to grab him and cling on so he can't escape. 'Have the McDonald file on my desk by noon.'

'Okay,' I breathe, and he grins, all wolfish. He can see my struggle.

'Super. I'll see you later, princess.' After a playful tug of my hair and a chaste kiss on my forehead, he jumps up and struts off to the shower. My eyes drop to his butt.

'Stop looking at my arse,' he calls as he disappears into his bathroom.

I smile and sink into the bed. Another ten minutes. I can have another ten minutes.

Chapter 27

'Eleanor.' My name is a distant call, rousing me from my slumber. 'Eleanor, wake up.'

'Ten minutes,' I mumble sleepily, rolling on to my tummy.

'You've had an hour, dear.'

I frown into my darkness, replaying that last word. *Dear?* My eyes blink open, and I roll back over to find Mrs Potts leaning over my sprawled body. The one that's all comfy in Becker's bed. Naked.

'Oh dear,' she says, her face creased with disappointment.

Oh shit.

Her stern look is like a foghorn has been held to my ear and evilly blasted to wake me. I'm not wriggling my way out of this one. 'Morning,' I croak awkwardly, gathering the covers up to my chin to hide as much of me as possible.

'Oh dear,' she repeats. 'Oh deary, deary me.'

I don't mean to be disrespectful, but I've just about had enough of the *'oh deary me'*s I sigh and roll my eyes. 'I'm sorry for misleading you, Mrs Potts,' I mutter, watching as she slides a tray on to the cabinet next to the bed. I may as well get the inevitable telling-off out of the way.

'You mean fibbing, dear.' She rests her hands on her plump hips.

I cringe beneath the sheets, wishing they'd miraculously transform into an invisible blanket and help me escape her disapproval. 'And that,' I concede, spotting a vibrant fruit salad on the tray, accompanied by a mug of coffee. My mouth begins to water.

'Becker sent me to wake you.' She brushes her hands off and passes me the coffee.

'He did?' I sit up and strategically tuck the sheets under my arms to cover my dignity before I accept the mug. *He told her?*

'Yes.' Her double chin hits her chest and she looks down at me, lips straight. Her violet hair is glowing, making me squint. It's particularly bright today, indicating a recent trip to the salon. 'Said you might have accidentally fallen into his bed. He had a grin on that handsome face when he mentioned it.'

I flame red, looking away. 'Okay,' I squeak, tipping the coffee to my mouth for something to do other than sit like an idiot, waiting for more judgement. I can imagine that grin. I'm also jumping all over the fact that Mrs Potts is at least speaking to Becker after last night's showdown. What about Mr H? Is he speaking to Becker now? Or, more worryingly, does he know where I can be found this morning?

'Sorry to hear your terrible news.'

Terrible news? What terrible news? I don't get a chance to ask her to elaborate on that. She must catch me staring blankly into my coffee mug.

'About the break-in at your flat, dear.'

'Oh,' I say. 'Yes, of course. Becker's called the police. Nothing was taken, not even my laptop. I think we must have disturbed them.'

'The world we live in,' she muses, dismay and genuine sadness creeping on to her old face. 'How thoughtful of Becker to sacrifice his bed for you.' She eyes my static form, a knowing look on her old face. 'And put you in there naked, too.'

I want to dive into my coffee and drown myself. 'Hmm,' I hum, because I have nothing to say, and she wouldn't want to hear it if I did. It's game over.

'About yesterday,' she begins. 'I'm sure you appreciate the need for discretion.'

'I understand,' I say without hesitation, smiling a little. I won't mention the NDA.

'I have to admit, I'm surprised he's willingly exposed that side of himself to you.'

She means his vulnerability. His hurt. 'Me too,' I agree. Maybe I *am* different. I know she also means the fact that Becker has put me in the middle of the Hunt family history. He's not just exposed himself, he's exposed his secrets.

She sighs and turns to leave, while I drift into a daydream, finally giving my *other* situation the attention it deserves. I need to make time this morning to check my flat. And collect my new phone. 'Mrs Potts,' I call, placing my mug on the tray. I need to make sure she's okay with me. I'd go to her, be a brave girl and face her up close so she can see my sincerity ... if I wasn't butt naked under Becker's bedding.

She stops at the door but doesn't turn around. 'No need, dear,' she tells me, not really giving me anything but giving me everything with those three small words. 'Just ... be careful.' Another three, except these are overflowing with genuine concern. 'Your bag is in the bathroom, dear.' She leaves.

Be careful. Easier said than done with Saint Becker Boy Hunt.

I collapse on my back and try to form any kind of sense out of the break-in. But I'm struggling. I've been violated again, but not in a delicious way.

I feel my way down the stone steps, unable to find a light switch to help me out. What is it with dark corridors and alleyways in this place? I'm taking my life into my own hands just wearing heels around here. And today they are particularly high. My cropped trousers skim my ankles and a super-fluffy cream jumper is keeping my body warm.

When I get to the bottom, I make my way to the library to grab the McDonald file. And once again, my eyes are pulled to the secret compartment where I know that map is hidden, except now I know the significance of it. I stare at the section of bookcase, wondering where the missing piece could be. Becker said he's close. I bite my lip as a surge of excitement springs from nowhere. A treasure map. A treasure hunter. I shake my head in wonder and force myself away from the bookcase with the hidden compartment, grabbing the McDonald file and heading for the door. I'm pulled to a stop when I hear a phone ring, and a quick scan of the room shows Becker's mobile on the couch. I rush to answer, seeing Paula's name greeting me. 'Hi, Paula. It's Eleanor. Becker must've left his phone in the library.'

'Eleanor, how are you?'

'I'm well, thank you. Anything I can help you with?'

'Oh no, it's nothing important. I heard Becker got himself into a bit of a bidding war with Brent Wilson. Just wondering how the injured soldier is after losing.'

'Oh, *Head of a Faun.*' I laugh. 'News travels fast. He's taken it quite well. Left Countryscape with a smile on his face.' Shit. I immediately berate myself. I shouldn't have said that. 'I mean, I think it was forced, but—'

'He took you with him?'

I frown down the line. 'Yes.' There's silence for a few moments, and after Paula hasn't come back with anything, I feel compelled to ask her something, if only to kill the painful quiet. 'You deal in art?' I ask casually.

'No,' she answers coolly. 'I'm just an Italian Renaissance enthusiast. That's all. Have Becker call me, would you?'

'Sure.'

She hangs up, and I stare at Becker's phone. Well, that was strange, but I don't spend too much time dissecting the call. I have work to do.

When I leave the library, I head straight for the kitchen. I need more coffee.

'Hey, boy,' I say, spotting Winston in his dog bed in the corner. He's up like lightning and sprinting towards me excitedly. I laugh and crouch, opening my arms to him. But he skids to a stop a foot away from me. He might be a dog, but I can see clear as day that he's looking at me suspiciously. 'C'mon, boy,' I encourage him on a laugh, patting my thighs.

He cranes his neck forward, keeping his paws grounded, stretching his neck to reach me. I can only watch, baffled by his sudden cool approach to me. He sniffs me. Then he snorts. He bloody snorts, spraying my outstretch hand with sticky doggy drool. 'Eww.' I shake it off, and Winston turns on his bear paws, sticks his arse in my face, and trots away, the whole back end of him swaying haughtily.

Rip-roaring laughter fills the air, and I glance up, finding Mr H at the table eating poached eggs. 'Oh.' He chuckles, shoulders jigging. 'Oh, that's tickled me.'

I let the old boy have his moment and move across the kitchen to wash my hands. 'I don't know what's got into him,' I mutter, squeezing some soap on to my palm.

'He can smell something on you,' the old man informs me, straightening his thin lips when I look at him questioningly. 'Or *someone*.'

Bugger.

I can't lie, and now I know for sure that Mrs Potts has filled in Mr H on what she found in Becker's bed this morning. 'No *oh dears*, please,' I beg, rinsing my hands. I can't even find the will to blush scarlet. It is what it is, and it's exactly what Mrs Potts and Mr H predicted it to be. I look to Winston, who's now settling back in his basket. I've showered. Surely he can't smell Becker on me.

'I'm saying nothing.' Becker's grandad watches me rinsing my hands and slips some egg past his lips, like he's filling his mouth to make it impossible to speak. Maybe he can't trust himself, because I'd put my life on him having far more to say.

I grab the tea towel and lean my arse against the worktop while I dry my hands, flinching when my tender skin comes to rest on the hard surface. Then I remember the vow I made to myself yesterday. 'I'm going to take you for lunch,' I declare, strolling over and sitting opposite him.

He stops chewing and is looking at me like I asked for the secret to eternal youth. 'Pardon me?'

'You and me,' I say, putting the tea towel down and passing Mr H a napkin when I spot a bit of egg yolk on the corner of his mouth. 'Together. Anywhere you want.'

He accepts the napkin gingerly and wipes at his mouth, eyeing me with doubt. I smile back at him, amused by his wariness. 'Whatever for?'

'Just . . . because.'

'Because what?'

'Because I want to.'

'Are you going to pick my brains about my dumb maverick grandson? Because if so, I'm not sure it's such a good idea.' He returns his attention to his plate and cuts into another egg, shaking his head to back up his dismissal.

I retreat in my chair on Becker's behalf, because I'm certain that would sting him like hell if he was here. Obviously, they haven't cleared the air yet. Mr H can't seem to even *think* about his grandson without looking like he's sucking on a lemon. He's well and truly miffed. But maybe I can fix that. I open my mouth to speak, but he interrupts my intended fix-it speech.

'And he's just made things worse by casting you under his spell. I thought you were smarter than that, Eleanor. Not like the rest of the brainless tarts.' Mr H huffs disgustedly, and I withdraw again. Is he calling me a brainless tart? Ouch. 'Sorry about your apartment, by the way.' He waves a fork in the air, keeping his attention on his eggs. I keep my mouth firmly shut. I'm dealing with two very anti-Becker people. After the head-to-head last night, I know that the revelations of this morning – namely, me in Becker's bed – have only added to the sour feelings. But he's right. I am under Becker's spell. I'm a baffling mixture of confused and excited by it. And I'm a whole lot of feeble, too. But fighting something that feels so incredibly right is fucking hard, even if you know it's wrong. I should cut myself some slack. It's a powerful spell. 'Man thinks with his penis,' Mr H barks to himself.

I cough in surprise, not that it's noted. Then I lean across the table to assure him I know what I'm doing, even if I haven't a clue. I just want to try and ease his worry, but I get no further than opening my mouth before he's off again.

'Let me enlighten you on something, Eleanor.'

I sit back again, wary, and he sighs.

'My Mags, that's Becker's grandmother, fell ill while I was away looking for that damn missing piece of the map. Cancer. Given weeks, but she didn't tell me. She left me gallivanting around the world while she suffered alone at home.' He shakes his head sadly, looking off into the distance. My heart breaks for him. 'I got home and found half the woman I left. It had only been weeks. Aggressive, it was. Ravaged my beautiful girl.' His voice breaks. I have to swallow down the lump in my throat, thinking about my father. Just like Mr H's wife, my father kept his suffering from us until it was too late.

'I'm so sorry.'

'So am I,' he murmurs. 'I'm sorry I made her believe that my search for that blessed map and sculpture was more important than she was.'

'I'm sure she didn't think that,' I offer, anything to ease the crippling guilt he clearly lives with.

He forces out a laugh. 'Thank you for your compassion, however wasted it is. I'll never forgive myself for squandering precious time looking for that damn map. Let me tell you this, Eleanor. Becker won't allow himself to get attached to anyone.'

'He doesn't want anyone holding him back?'

'Or breaking his heart. He has no sentimentality when it comes to living, breathing things, Eleanor. Hasn't allowed himself to since he lost so many people important to him. Heck, he barely shows me any affection any more. He's obsessed with finding that sculpture and won't get himself attached to anything that will hamper his search.' I deflate, and I know he sees it. Love is an inconvenience that Becker neither needs nor wants. It'll just add a risk of guilt to his mission, guilt like his grandad is living with. If Becker is on his own, he doesn't need to worry about the needs and wants of another person. 'So, dear girl, the only way this thing between you and my grandson can end is badly. He's a lone ranger, sweetheart. You'd be silly to think you can change that.'

'Thanks for the advice,' I whisper dejectedly, my stomach turning.

'I love my Becker boy with all my heart, but when it comes to women, the man is an arsehole. Emotionally incapable. I like you, Eleanor. I'd hate to see you turn into a desperate, bunny-boiling fruitcake. Don't think you can make him feel as strongly for you as he does for his treasure.'

Jesus, please stop. 'I don't think that.' I drop my eyes to the table. I'm aware of the lack of buoyancy in my tone. I'm also aware that this dear old man's grandson has already sent me somewhere close to crazy. He must have. I'm still here, tumbling deeper into his world. But I can't seem to stop myself. Becker has a strong hold. Not that I'm exactly fighting him off.

I frantically search my twisted mind for something to say, anything to try and reassure the old man, but the kitchen door opens and we're both distracted by who enters.

The prodigy himself.

Becker's eyes flick between me and his grandad. Mr H doesn't bless his grandson with his attention for long, sniffing and returning to his breakfast, whereas I, despite the crushing conversation I've just had, can't help but fall into a pathetic daydream, my elbows meeting the table and my chin resting on them. He looks buff, not a word I'd usually use, but with worn jeans and a black T-shirt that hugs in all the right places – and there are a lot of right places – Becker looks drool-worthy, as per usual, but in a different way. And instead of the usual dress shoes, he has boots on. Sturdy, brown leather boots, and his jeans are caught in the tops haphazardly. Not intended, which just makes his whole scruffy outfit that little bit extra sexy. Don't get me started on the glasses. Or the stubble. *Shit, I'm in deep, complicated shit.*

'Gramps,' Becker greets formally, face straight, lips pursed.

'Becker,' Mr H replies, perfectly polite but as huffy as can be.

Oh dear. I want to hide under the table. 'Morning,' I sing, earning doubtful looks from both men in the room.

Becker sighs his exasperation. It fills me with hope, but that's dashed when he marches over to me and grabs the file and his phone before marching right on out. 'In my office, princess.' The door slams, making me jump, and Mr H's wrinkled forehead wrinkles further.

'Princess?' he asks in question.

My cheeks heat. 'I hate him calling me that.'

Mr H looks serious. And very unhappy. 'You've been summoned, *princess.*'

'So, lunch?' I ask, ignoring his obvious scorn and moving things along.

The suspicious eyes are fixed. It bothers me, but I brave their scrutiny in the hope of his acceptance. I want to talk Mr H around, to encourage him to make peace with his grandson, since Becker is a stubborn twat. Problem is, Becker gets that stubbornness from someone, and I'm quite sure I'm looking at him.

'Go on, Mr H. Let me take you out.'

'I don't think so, Eleanor, but thank you for offering.'

I suspect he's not only avoiding it because he thinks I'll pick his brain on Becker, but because he feels like I'm offering out of sympathy. He feels like a burden. The fact that I would love to hear his tales of times gone by when he trekked the world won't appeal to Mr H. I suspect reminiscing brings back regret and heartache.

The door swings open again, and Becker appears, impatience bubbling from every pore of his face, making his young, boyish handsomeness appear rugged and worn in. He gives me an expectant look and points down the corridor. 'Work.'

'I'm coming,' I say. 'See you later, Mr H.' I hope he doesn't think this is the end of it. I'll get him out for lunch if it kills me. I would love to pick his brain, but not about his grandson. I didn't finish my university degree, but history is still my passion, and I'm sure Mr H would be an excellent teacher.

Becker glowers at me, unhappy, as I rise from my chair. 'This isn't a social club,' he mutters.

I ignore him, because I'm at work and I need to get that even balance, which means occasionally letting his arsehole attitude slide off my back like oil. Right now, I'm giving him the benefit of the doubt, due to the family feud.

Mr H, however, bites. 'It's also not a knocking shop,' he mumbles under his breath, but loud enough for his grandson to hear.

I wince, but not because his grandad insulted me. He's just reminded me of the numerous women who might have come before me. *Might?* I don't know who on earth I'm trying to kid. Definitely is *definitely* the right word.

How do I look past this? How do I look past the lack of respect from Mrs Potts and Mr H? *I thought you were smarter than that, Eleanor. Not like the rest of the brainless tarts.* Yeah, I thought so too, Mr H. But I can hope. It's all I have, but at what point do I admit defeat? Will I need to admit defeat? Can I change him, prove them all wrong? *Hope.* I know I'm grappling here, but surely I can cling to his words last night, when he pleaded with me to believe in him.

I want to talk to you, watch you, share my love for my treasure with you. I hope you see my determination to prove to you that I'm a better man than you think.

I have to try. He *begged* me to try.

I sense the bad vibes bouncing between grandfather and grandson, not daring to squeak a word for fear of tipping either one over the edge. Becker looks a little lost, his mouth flapping open repeatedly like a goldfish, clearly stumped for what to say. I can't help feeling sorry for him. 'Work,' he barks finally, focusing his grievances on me. I'll let him off, just this once. I didn't sign anything that gave him the okay to use me as his verbal punching bag.

I pass him, trying to get a sense of how pissed off he really is. It takes a nanosecond. He's livid. I wander down the corridor, feeling vulnerable with him stalking behind me. I'm torn. I know it's not my place to say, but what I really want to do is tell him to snap out of it and make peace with his gramps, but just when I think I might brave broaching the subject, Becker slides his hand on to my nape and fists my hair. It's the sexiest threat ever. 'I think we need a repeat of last night very soon,' he whispers in my ear.

My thoughts scatter, leaving only one remaining in my head. *Fuck, yes.*

But I don't say that. Instead, I gather my wits and detach his hand from my neck. 'Work,' I say as stably as possible, which isn't very stable at all.

This balance might be tricky.

I let myself into his office, my legs shaking, and come to a screaming stop when I spot Brent sitting patiently at Becker's desk. My shaking takes on new heights, and I start retreating, panic beginning to flare. What the hell? I back into Becker, and he nudges me into the room. I flinch when the door slams behind me. The bastard. I feel like I have a big fat sign on my chest saying, '*Becker's conned your arse.*'

Holy shit, does he know that already? Is that why he's here?

'Eleanor.' Brent's chirpy greeting and wide smile tell me no, but it doesn't stop me shifting from foot to foot like my feet are on fire.

'Hi.' My voice is high and pained. I cannot believe Becker is doing this to me. 'Tea?' My instinct is kicking in and plotting my escape. Now I know the history of the rivalry, I feel even more uncomfortable in their joint presence.

'No, thank you. Becker told me about your flat.' He stands and approaches me, shaking his head in disgust. 'How awful for you.'

'She's staying here for the interim,' Becker says, placing a hand on my shoulder. 'I have to ensure the safety of my staff.'

'Of course,' Brent agrees.

I feel Becker's fingers flexing on my shoulder, like he's preparing to grip harder if need be. I hope need *not* be. His hold is already pretty firm. And he should use the term *staff* very loosely. I'm not sure what we should call me now. In-house fuck? Or in-house mindfuck? The latter for sure. Especially after last night. And his grandfather's words are rolling through my mind relentlessly. They're still stinging.

Don't give up on me, princess.

Brent's looking at Becker's hand on my shoulder with a small smile on his face. 'Diabolical world we live in, when a *single* woman can't even stay in her home and feel safe.'

Single. There was definitely emphasis on that one word. Why is he here? To gloat about his acquisition? To rub Becker's nose in it? What a waste of time.

Becker's fingers flex, and I suck in a hiss of pain, dipping out of his hold. He's being possessive. Marking his territory. And why the fuck is Brent even here?

I try to call on my sass and the fire in my belly, but when I need them most, they've deserted me and nerves have taken hold. A combination of Mr H's harsh reality check and the nasty history between the Wilsons and the Hunts that I now know about has me in a fluster. What do I say? What do I do?

'Congratulations.' I startle myself with my enthusiastic grace. I have no idea where that came from, and I certainly don't know if I should be making any mention of Brent's winning bid and the subsequent acquisition of a forged treasure. And when he frowns at me, confused, I realise that my one-word outburst wasn't very specific. '*Head of a Faun*,' I say more calmly, tensing, wishing I'd kept my mouth shut. It's Becker's fault. I'm talking for the sake of it, and talking about stuff I really shouldn't be talking about.

'Ah.' Brent laughs, giving Becker a smug look. It won't ruffle my boss's feathers. He's got the upper hand. He's a point ahead, even if Brent Wilson doesn't know it. 'Yes, quite. Unfortunately, my celebrations were cut short when I found a scratch on the bonnet of my Bentley.'

I burst into flames. Literally. Every trace of skin on my body matches my hair within a second. 'Oh no,' I gush, hearing Becker laughing in my mind, howling, rolling around on the floor. I, however, want to dive out of the window. 'That's shocking,' I exclaim, thinking I need to shut up right now. 'Terrible.' But I don't. 'It's a travesty. Diabolical.' I shake my head, rambling on. 'And to such a beautiful car.' I morph my face into something close to disgust. 'I don't know what the world is coming to.' I jolt forward as a result of a sharp nudge in my back, courtesy of Becker, and I start to laugh nervously, doing my best to style out my stumble with a shift of position, transferring my weight on to my right hip casually. He's telling me to zip it. Of course, I don't. 'Who would do such a mindless thing?' Just give me the lethal injection and be done with it.

'I wondered the same thing.' Brent's distrustful eyes watch

me, waiting for me to cut to the chase and spill the beans. I feel like I virtually have already.

'Vandals,' Becker breathes, sliding his hands into his pockets and sighing. 'It's enough to make you want to kill.'

'Indeed,' Brent says quietly, locking stares with Becker. Good God, the animosity in this room is potent. Enough to make you want to kill? Jesus. 'Eleanor.' Brent turns back to me. 'About that lunch.'

What?

My eyes go round and all saliva dries from my mouth. What on earth? I tilt my head with a lack of words coming to me as Brent looks down at his watch.

'I have a spare couple of hours before I head back across town to The Staton.' What's his game? He must know Becker and I are ... involved? If he doesn't, then he's quite dim, and if he does, then it's clearly of no consequence. I'm not sure which irritates me most, and that sass and fire I was looking for suddenly finds me. But Becker speaks up before I can unleash it.

'I'm sorry,' Becker says, all casual and unperturbed. 'Hunt Corporation employee contracts state no client–employee socialising.'

'I'm not a client,' Brent retorts, a glimmer of a cunning smile on his face.

Becker's teeth clench, and he virtually snarls, but he doesn't counter because he can't. Brent really isn't a client. He's the enemy.

I look back and forth between the two men, my anger growing. They may as well have one of my arms each and be playing tug of fucking war with me. *Boys!*

'Thank you for the offer, Brent,' I say on a sweet smile, getting a sharp poke in my back, courtesy of my boss. I ignore it and step out of his reach. He's being *so* possessive, and I'm not taking much pleasure from it. What the hell am I involved in? Then my bottom rubs on the material of my trousers, making me wince. Becker. I'm involved with Becker Hunt, his filthy fucking, and his filthy business dealings.

He's bristling like a bear with a sore head next to me, and Brent is loving every second of it. Does he really think I want to date him? The prick. But at the same time, I'm furious with Becker for putting me in this situation.

'But it's a no.' I turn and walk away, hearing Becker chuckle. Oh, he's pushing my buttons. I stop and turn. 'Not today, anyway. Maybe tomorrow?' I raise my eyebrows, and Brent smiles, victorious. Becker, however, looks like his head might pop off with shock. Take that, Hunt. Two can play your game.

'Tomorrow,' Brent says on a huge smile that I'm dying to slap away.

I grit my teeth. 'Fabulous.' I slam the door behind me, and march to the kitchen. Mr H is gone, and I ignore the stab of guilt I feel for being grateful I'm alone. I need to pull myself together.

I spend five minutes pacing the kitchen, trying to cool off, at the same time playing over my senseless rambling about Brent's car, worrying whether I've planted any seeds of suspicion in his head. Maybe I have where his car is concerned, but I couldn't have possibly given any reason for him to believe the sculpture is a fake.

I pull my jumper away from my chest, coming over all sweaty. Bloody hell, I can feel myself going into meltdown. I wasn't told deception would be part of my job. Or willpower to resist my boss. I'm crap at both.

Winston looks up at me, his doggy brain probably wondering what has got into me. Yesterday, I'm sure he would've come to comfort me, but he simply watches me from his basket today, sleepily. He even pokes his nose out a little, trying to get a whiff of me without having to drag himself from his bed to find out if I'm still sleeping with the enemy. 'I still smell of him,' I snap.

'Who are you talking to?'

I whirl around and there's Becker regarding me with slight concern.

I'm talking to myself, marching doggedly around the big kitchen, pulling at my clothes to try and relieve the claustrophobic feeling and anger. 'You've got a nerve, Hunt,' I yell, and he laughs, but it is 100 per cent sarcastic.

'So do you.' His face deadpans quickly, all amusement gone.

'Why was he here?'

'To ask you out, obviously.'

'And you let him in?'

'Yes,' he answers simply, stunning me further. 'I couldn't resist seeing you turn him down.' His face twists dangerously.

Good. His plan backfired. What was he trying to prove, anyway? 'Well, sorry you're disappointed.'

'I'm not disappointed, because you're not going. I know you're only trying to get a rise out of me, but it won't work. You've had *this*.' He indicates down his front, pointing out the perfection of it all. 'Why would you want anything else?'

The arrogant bastard. And I'm not getting a rise out of him? Sure. 'Excuse me. I need to call someone to confirm a date.' I make to move and get intercepted before my feet leave the ground.

'Whoa.' He laughs, but there's a nervous edge to it. It fills me with all kinds of smug satisfaction. 'Don't be spiteful.'

'I'm not.' I move to the left, knowing damn well he'll do the same. He always does. It's like he's wired to my brain, knows every move I'm going to make. It's not a good thing. I look up and give him a rebellious stare. 'You're in my way.'

Becker's hackles rise, his boots bringing him a step towards me. 'And?'

His aggravation makes me smile. 'You okay?' I ask, watching him bubble with annoyance.

'Never better.'

'You sure?'

'Yes, absolutely.' He waves a hand indifferently in the air but fails to rid his face of the tight scowl.

'That's good then.'

'You're not going for lunch with him!'

I burst into a fit of giggles. 'I'm not getting a rise out of you?'

'You fucking infuriate me.'

'Join the club, *boss*,' I snipe, poking him in the shoulder. 'I'd rather be trapped in a tomb with a million rats than go on a date with Brent Wilson, but don't you ever put me in that situation ever again.'

He settles immediately, pouting. 'Sorry,' he more or less grunts.

'And I don't just mean the possessive bullshit, either. You shouldn't have tossed me in with the lions. I could have dropped you in it about the car or the sculpture. I wasn't prepared.'

Becker rolls his eyes condescendingly, walking over to the fridge. I know what he's doing. He opens the door and closes it quickly, facing me with an apple poised at his mouth. 'Wilson knows who scratched his car.' He takes a big bite, making a long, drawn-out affair of munching his way through. My stomach clenches. The nerves of my core tingle. I just can't stop them, and I'm not under any illusion that every muscle in my body solidifying will rein them in. Becker catches my sudden stiffness, his glimmering eyes dropping to my crotch. I furiously fight to ignore him. 'You handled yourself just fine,' he says on a secret smile.

Did he hear my rambling? 'I need to get on.'

He finishes chewing and swallows, heading for the door. 'Yes, are you actually going to do some work today?'

I scowl at his back as I follow him to his office, taking a seat opposite his desk. 'Have you heard from the police?'

He falters as he lowers to his chair. 'No.'

I deflate. There's nothing like a bit of urgency. 'Well, I suppose I should be grateful it wasn't worse.'

Becker removes his glasses and starts cleaning the lenses with the bottom of his T-shirt. 'I've made arrangements for a locksmith to fit some extra security.'

'Oh,' I murmur. That's very good of him. 'Like what?'

'Better window locks, for a start.' He gives me an accusing look, like it's my fault the window locks aren't up to scratch. Replacing his glasses, he then takes a pen and starts making a few notes on a pad. 'Now, let's get on with this list of things to do,' he says, all businesslike, getting up and wandering over to the replica of the Shepherd Gate Clock, looking up at the hands. 'I need the Cashwell file so I can go over it before my meeting next week.'

I cross one leg over the other, and with a lack of a mobile to make notes on, I grab a pad and rest it on my knee, starting to scribble.

'Have the Constable ready in the viewing room at two fifteen on Thursday. Lord Demontford wants it.' He reaches up to the clock face and glides his finger across the thick black rim. 'This needs cleaning. Make arrangements.'

My hand works quickly, writing down his instructions. 'Oh,' I say, something coming to me. 'Paula called.'

'She did?'

'Yes, asked how you got on at Countryscape. She sounded surprised when I told her I went with you.'

'I bet.' He laughs under his breath. 'She'll love that.'

'Why?'

'Stepping stones, not leaps,' he says to himself, drifting off somewhere.

'What?'

'I refused to take her. She's a keen historian. Loves all things Italian and old.'

'Who is she?'

'My therapist.'

I go rigid in my chair. 'Your therapist?' I'm shocked, for two reasons. One, I've unwittingly chatted with her on the phone a few times, and one of those times Becker had me answer the call. He basically set that conversation up. What was the purpose? So she could try to figure me out? Do her research? I feel violated again, and, *again,* not in a delicious way. The second reason I'm sitting here all quiet is because Becker just told me himself that he's in therapy, and I don't know how to react. Yes, I knew, but he doesn't know that. 'What are you in therapy for?'

A tired look is pointed at me. 'Really, princess?'

'Well, I don't know what else to say,' I exclaim, exasperated.

'*We* say nothing. That's why I'm in therapy. To talk.' He rolls his eyes. 'Waste of fucking time, anyway.'

Oh? So that's why he made an emergency call to her the other day, is it? I can't help wonder what I might say to Paula next time I happen to take her call. Ask her what the verdict is on Becker and me? Does she have an opinion? I inwardly laugh. Of course she does. But she's not likely to tell me. God, what I'd do to be a fly on the wall during one of their sessions.

'Oh.' Becker turns to face me, and I quickly wipe away any traces of my curious mind spinning. 'Call Sotheby's. There's whispers of a few Picasso pieces coming to market.'

'Sure, I'll get . . .' I fade off. 'Crap.'

'What?'

'My new phone is being delivered today, and I'm not there.'

Wandering across to his desk, Becker pulls a drawer open. 'Hunt saves the day.' He slides an iPhone across the table. 'I've had your new SIM programmed with your details, so you still have the same number and all your contacts from when you last backed up your phone.'

I stare at it for a few moments, a bit taken aback. 'You replaced my phone?'

'Yes.' His answer is quick and dismissive, but I *still* don't receive an apology for him smashing my old one to pieces. 'It's all set and ready to go.'

'How?' I ask, looking up at him. 'You'd need my password to transfer all the data.'

'I have my ways.'

'Percy,' I breathe. 'He hacked my account.'

'Accessed.'

'He hacked, Becker. Unlawfully.' He really is a whizz kid. For the love of God. I pick up the phone on a sigh and scroll through. I haven't called my mum for a few days. I need to do that. But, again, he hacked my damn account?

'Who's David?'

My thumb pauses on the screen at the mention of my ex-boyfriend, and I look up at Becker, finding an apprehensive face. 'You went *through* my phone, too?' I ask, horrified. Oh my God. The texts? Can he see the text messages?

'He sounds sorry.'

That answers my question. 'Of course he's sorry,' I spit. 'He got caught with his trousers around his ankles with my best friend.' The moment I see pity on his face, I regret telling him. I don't need his pity. I don't need *anyone's* pity.

'She sounds sorry, too.'

I recoil. 'Did you read *all* of my messages?'

'He sounds like a prick.'

'He is.'

'He doesn't know where you are?'

'No,' I snap. The mention of his name has me fired up. I start hammering away at my phone, trying to expel some of my rage, as I power through, deleting messages and contacts. I don't know why I didn't do this before. It's long overdue. But as I'm scrolling through my phonebook, I notice something. I look up at him in disbelief. 'You deleted Brent's number?'

'And blocked him.' He shows complete indifference. I'm staggered.

'This is taking things a bit too far.'

'You don't need his contact details.'

'That's not the point. You've violated my privacy.'

'I bought that phone, so technically it's a work perk. Which means I'm perfectly within my right, as your *employer*, to monitor activity. I'll remind you of the NDA.' His straight face is hovering on the edge of humour, and my eyes bug at his cheek. There's nothing funny about this. This is being much too controlling. 'And if we're going to talk about violating—'

'No.' I hold up a hand before he can head down that road. 'Is that all?'

'No. I'll need my tux dry-cleaned for the Andelesea Gala. Make arrangements with Giles at Fosters.'

The Andelesea Gala. It's one of the biggest annual events in the art world. It's always held at Countryscape, and usually exhibits some spectacular piece of art or treasure. I nod and draw a line under my list. 'Got it.'

'Good.' Becker takes off his glasses, rubbing at his eyes. He looks troubled all of a sudden, like the weight of a thousand elephants is on his mind. I inwardly laugh. Join the club. I open my mouth to ask if he's okay but pull up when I remember that I'm on work time. The balance. I mentally yell at myself, and at Becker, too. I don't know how to approach this situation; don't know how he wants me to be. I need help.

'Mr Hunt,' I begin, and he looks up at me, startled. I've just interrupted some deep thoughts. I hope he's worrying about the same things I am. Like how we proceed. What happens next? Are we crazy?

'*Mr Hunt?*' he says. 'Really, princess?'

'Well that's just it, isn't it?' I flop back in my chair, exasperated and exhausted from the weight of my worries.

'What is?'

'This' – I wave my pen between us – 'after yesterday, last night . . . all of the . . . and the . . . with my job . . . and the thing that happened.' I give up, struggling to articulate my issue. He's not stupid. He must understand.

Becker flops back in his chair, too, exhausted by my nonsens-ical blabbering. 'Yeah,' he says quietly, sliding a palm on to his nape and massaging. 'It's screwing with my head too.'

Oh, thank God. I'm all kinds of relieved, and the air that gushes past my lips is proof. 'You need to set some boundaries,' I say. This is a stupid request. The boundaries since I've been here have always been blurred.

'We have this.' He looks a bit too pleased with himself when he raises the NDA above his head before slipping his glasses on and glancing down at it. 'Maybe we could add a few more things.'

My jaw hits the notepad on my knee. 'Are you serious?'

He grins down at the paper. 'Totally.'

'Seriously, Becker. We need to draw lines. Big fat black ones that are as clear as day.'

'Probably wise,' he agrees, placing the NDA in front of him. 'What would you like to add to clause three?' He arms himself with a pen and looks at me expectantly. He really is serious. 'Oh' – he takes his pen to the paper – 'no . . . flirting . . . with . . . the . . . enemy.' A dramatic full stop is added when he stabs the paper with the nib of the pen.

'Then stop letting him in The Haven.' I basically sigh my way through my words. 'And so we're clear, where it says in the NDA that there should be no client–employee re-lations, do you mean on the whole or just Brent Wilson specifically?'

'Brent isn't a client,' Becker breathes tiredly.

'Oh, yes. Of course. He's the enemy. In that case,' I go on, well aware that my next words might push a dangerous button, 'do you mean no flirting with *any* enemies, or just Brent in particular? And if it's the former, can you confirm if any other enemies you might have are as hot as Brent, because if that's the case I might have to quit.'

I was wrong. I didn't just push a button, I whacked it. Becker's nostrils flare, his features going sharp. He looks murderous. 'Don't even think about it,' he warns.

There it is again. Possessiveness. Becker scowls, and I grin. I can't deny it, I get a really big kick out of it, especially since I know Becker Hunt isn't possessive about anything other than his treasure. So, really, doesn't that make me different already? 'Okay,' I sigh. 'No cavorting with *any* enemies. What about cavorting with co-workers?' I ask.

'You want to get familiar with Mrs Potts?'

I purse my lips. 'What about cavorting with my boss?'

'Oh.' He feigns realisation, grinning. 'That's allowed.'

'Of course it is.' I roll my eyes and try to get us back on serious ground. 'We need ground rules.'

He pushes the NDA aside and rests his forearms on the desk, leaning over. He cocks his head for me to come closer, so I pull my chair in and mirror him. 'It's simple, princess.' He reaches forward and brushes a strand of hair from my face, and I look, wondering what's so simple in this heap of complexity. 'Now I own you professionally *and* personally.'

'What?' I stammer. 'You don't own me.'

A hint of a smile breaks through, and he slowly comes closer, closing the gap between our mouths, rising from his chair as he does and bracing his hands on his desk. He's looming over me, and I'm looking up at him like the worthy god he is, waiting patiently. Tenderly, his lips meet mine, and I'm blindsided with the most worshipful kiss in the history of kisses. Every woe and worry pales into insignificance under the gentle attention of his mouth. The feud with Brent vanishes from my mind and his grandad's warnings evaporate. 'Kissing the boss, princess?' he mumbles into my mouth, slowing down our kiss until our lips are simply touching. 'And during working hours?' He pulls back and gives me a genuine disapproving look that snaps me back to life. He sits, takes his phone and dials someone. 'I own you,' he asserts confidently.

The call connects, and I hear a familiar voice greet him. *Paula*. His therapist. I might need a therapist myself soon, because my mind is becoming increasingly fucked. He can't be real. But, scarily, he is. Very real.

Narrowing my eyes at him, I rise from my chair and gather my pad and new phone, then walk quietly around to Becker's side of the desk. I bend and get my face close to his, close enough for Paula to hear. 'You don't own me, Hunt.' Let's see what his therapist makes of that. 'Never will.' I walk away with my shoulders straight, my chin high, turning as I'm pulling the door closed behind me. His smile is back, and his eyes are dark, hooded, full of sex, and nailed to my arse.

Who owns who, Hunt?

Chapter 28

Over the next few days, Becker proves his point. He really does own me. The notion doesn't disgust me, more thrills me. But he's delusional if he thinks he's in full control here.

When the working day is done, I'm carried up those stone steps to heaven. I'm lost in the clouds. His smiles, his words, his need to ravish me, it's all making me tumble harder. The grey areas have never been so grey. But grey has also never been so bright and alive. Yeah, he owns me. But I'll never admit it to the egotistical arsehole. I'll just keep telling him that he doesn't. And he'll just keep smiling in return.

On Thursday, after I escorted Lord Demontford, a middle-aged, stuffy, portly man with a roving eye, into the showing room, Becker greeted him with a firm handshake and proceeded to stand by silently while he gushed and swooned over the magnificent Constable that depicts the beautiful English countryside. The look on that man's face when he clapped eyes on it can only be described as pure ecstasy. Within two seconds, he was asking Becker to name his price. I quietly made my way to the door to leave him to business, but Becker flicked me a look, one that told me he wanted me to stay. I did, and as I stood there watching him, I might have fallen deeper. Becker Hunt is a sexy bastard under normal circumstances; when he's selling one of his treasures, he's deadly. He was calm, cool and collected, just like he was at Countryscape, whereas Lord Demontford couldn't contain his excitement. It gave Becker the ammo he needed. There was no back and forth or meeting in the middle on a mutually agreeable sum. Becker named his price and made it clear it wasn't up for negotiation. 'I'll give Sotheby's a call,' he'd said when Demontford decided he was going to try his arm. Of course, that call never happened, and it was never going to.

I fell into a quiet trance, my eyes unprepared to leave Becker, and when he ghosted a finger across the painting with an admiring smile on his face, I literally lost my breath. I know how it feels to be the focus of his devoted attention. At that moment in time, I was jealous of the painting. And then I left because being envious of a painting is ludicrous, and I'm sane enough to acknowledge that.

By Friday evening, I'm beat after a long, non-stop week. My constantly spinning mind has no doubt contributed to my exhaustion. With the monumental turn of events, the continued unease between Becker and his grandfather, the total mindfuck that is my relationship with a crooked antiques dealer, the crazy amount of sex, and the frightening fact that I'm falling in love with my boss, I feel trapped but free. Excited but apprehensive. Positive but unsure.

I make my way to the library to check in with Lucy after promising via text to do so all week. Her chirpy voice when she answers goes some way to restoring some stability in my shaking world. 'I'm beginning to get a complex,' she says as I settle on the couch.

'I'm sorry,' I sigh. 'I've been so busy, and I don't know my arse from my head at the moment.' That's an ironic figure of speech, since my arse is stinging after another spanking session last night – telling me exactly where *it* is – and my head is pounding, too, so I definitely know where *that* is.

'Don't say any more,' she orders, and I hear the slamming of a door followed by a few scuffles in the background. 'I've just got in from work. Let me get comfy.'

'Late night in the office?' I ask, sarcasm spilling out of me. 'Or late night in the printing room?'

'You're hilarious, Eleanor,' she says. 'Have you heard from the police yet?'

'No. Nothing was missing, and it's not an emergency. Becker chased them up yesterday. But that's not why I called.'

'Oh? Interesting. Do I need wine for this?'

'Yes,' I confess. 'I'm fucked.'

'In the physical sense or the mental sense?'

'Both.'

She gasps over the clashing of glass on glass. 'Oh, sod it. I'll drink out of the bottle. This better be juicy. I'm skipping *Coronation Street* for this.'

Juicy? Christ, she has *no* idea. I close my eyes and think hard about what I can share, the NDA materialising in my darkness, like it's reminding me of its existence. Blinking my lids open, I think of the library and the bookshelf where I found the secret compartment. Where the map is. Or most of it. 'He's violating me in the most delicious ways imaginable.'

'Eek.'

'And he's having extra security fitted at my flat.'

'That's good of him.'

'But I keep asking him if it's been done, and he keeps saying they're busy.'

Lucy laughs. 'Even I know you can get a locksmith within the hour.'

'Exactly. So what does that mean?'

'It isn't hard. It means he's fucking you and clearly enjoying it so wants you to stay.'

I shake my head. 'I was hoping you'd say something else.'

'What, like he must be in love with you?' There's amusement in her tone that fucking hurts, and I cringe as silence falls. Until Lucy breaks it. 'Oh,' she breathes.

'I have a problem,' I admit. Fixing a problem means

acknowledging that there *is* a problem. I have a very big problem. 'I think I'm falling for him, Lucy.'

There's quiet for a few seconds. Quiet that drives me a little mad. I hear Lucy gulp hard, and a mental image of her holding the wine bottle at her lips invades my mind. 'Say it,' I push. 'Whatever you're thinking, Lucy, just say it.'

The connection muffles with her exhale of breath. 'He's dangerously good-looking, Eleanor.'

'Do you think I haven't noticed that, Lucy? What are you trying to say? That I'm punching above my weight?' I bubble with resentment.

'No.' Her gasp of defence doesn't lessen my annoyance. 'If you'll let me finish, I'm saying that you can tell a lot from a man's looks and how he carries them. Your boss carries his looks like a weapon.'

'What are you talking about?' I snap, fully aware that my reaction is over the top. Especially as I know she's right.

'He's a womaniser, Eleanor. You said so yourself. I'm all for you taking what you can and enjoying it, even if it's on the risky side, but hey, risky is exciting. You just have to go in with your eyes wide open.'

I laugh. Oh, my eyes are so wide open they're being blinded. Literally. 'I know exactly what I'm walking into.'

'Does he?'

I snap my mouth closed. I can't mention the NDA. And she'd laugh if I told her, anyway. But what she doesn't know, what she hasn't been privy to, is how Becker and Mr H very clearly communicated that Becker Hunt's only love will be his passion for treasure. I can't ignore Mr H's words about Becker: he won't allow himself to get attached to anyone and has no sentimentality when it comes to living, breathing things.

Don't think you can make him feel as strongly for you as he does for his treasure.

But I don't know how to explain that to Lucy. 'He's said he's not seeing anyone else.'

'Oh, that's nice of him.'

I roll my eyes. I totally understand Lucy's sarcasm, and even though Becker assured me he didn't want other women, I can't in all honesty wipe that fear from my mind.

You're not like the other women, Eleanor Cole. You, I need to keep close. You, I want to see every day. I'm hungry for your smiles.

'He's opened up to me about so much, and according to his grandfather, that's never happened before.'

'Opened up about what?'

I'm fucking addicted to you.

I wriggle on the couch, biting my lip. 'Lots. I'll tell you when I see you. We need to go for a drink sometime.'

'We do,' she agrees. 'This weekend?'

'I'll call you.'

We say our goodbyes and I rest my head back, telling myself I'll have a quiet five minutes before I finish off cataloguing the rest of the files. Becker's not back until later. I suspect he's seeing his therapist, though he didn't confirm it. My job has many different aspects to it, but as I don't manage Becker's calendar per se, I'm not always aware of his daily movements.

I close my eyes and try to clear my speeding mind of the thoughts swamping it, having my own little therapy session.

I can feel myself moving. The notion of swaying gently would probably rock me to sleep if I wasn't snoozing already. My eyes blink open and adjust to the soft light surrounding me, homing in on his face close to mine. He's looking straight ahead, unaware that I've woken. I'm draped across his arms as he strides through the corridor, my hands looped around his neck, my body reacting and holding on to something it loves without my mind telling it to.

'Becker boy?' Mrs Potts's hushed whisper reaches my ears,

and I shamelessly close my eyes again and pretend I'm asleep. I don't want to endure another disapproving look or be caught up in another disagreement. Being asleep in Becker's arms is the perfect way to pretend I'm not here.

I feel him gently turn towards her voice. 'Found her in the library,' he says softly, almost on a whisper. 'I'll take her up then I'll be in my office.'

'Okay,' she says, without any suggestion that she thinks it might be a bad idea, which I know she does. I've seen Mrs Potts's and Mr H's silent disapproval every time they've found me sneaking up to Becker's apartment, or sneaking back down in the morning. 'Would you like me to get her pyjamas on?'

And there it is. Subtle, but it's there. If I could see her, her eyebrows would be blending with her violet hairline.

'I think I'll manage,' Becker says quietly, laughter in his tone. 'Don't worry. I'll close my eyes when I undress her.'

'Oh, stop it,' she whispers on a hiss, and Becker starts to jig under me, chuckling. It takes everything in me not to crack a smile. 'Becker boy, she fits in well here. Your gramps loves her. I love her.' She pauses, and I smile like crazy on the inside, feeling warm and an intense sense of belonging. The feeling is mutual. I love them both, too. Mrs Potts sighs, almost despondently. 'Don't break her heart.'

My secret smile fades, and I wait with bated breath for Becker's reply. His heart is thumping against me, strong and steady. 'I'm going to try my hardest not to,' he eventually says, his voice almost shaky. 'I love having her around, too.'

'Guess I can only ask that much of you.'

I feel Becker's nod, before I'm jerking mildly in his arms as he turns, taking the steps to his apartment as I wonder *how* hard he'll try. I bet he tries harder than hard. But Mrs Potts is right. That's as much as any of us could ask.

The whole way up, I'm pretending to be asleep, my mind full. Becker lays me on the bed and gently pulls off my shoes, and then he reaches for the top of my trousers. This is going to be torture.

'This is going to be torture.' He voices my thoughts, and my lips twitch in amusement. 'Why do you insist on making my life so difficult?' he asks me, sounding like he expects an answer from my supposedly unconscious form. He starts to gently tug my trousers down my legs, and I fall apart on the inside when he growls under his breath. 'Even when you're asleep I want to fucking strangle you.' I'm suddenly free from my trousers and having my arms lightly fed through my sleeves. 'And ravish you.' My thighs shudder. 'But that would be wrong.' He starts on the other arm, and I just about stop myself from yelling, '*I won't hold it against you.*'

Once he's removed my arms, he gently tugs me up, and I continue to imitate a dead fish. 'And I don't know why Gramps and Dorothy love you so much.' He grunts a few times as he fights to manipulate my floppy body, holding me to his front while lifting my jumper up over my head. When he's done, he just holds me to his chest for a long while, breathing deeply. 'Or maybe I do,' he whispers, dropping a gentle kiss into my hair. The smell of him, the hardness of him as he squeezes me against him, those words. It overwhelms me, and I swallow repeatedly to clear my throat of the emotion that's sprung up on me.

I've already fallen in love with him.

His charm, his maverick ways, his passion for *everything* he does. He's pushed me way past my boundaries and normal behaviour. And I'm starting to see that perhaps he pushes because he believes in me to handle whatever is thrown at me. And I can almost take comfort in that. Becker found me, injected me with an unrelenting zest for life, and at the same time he's crept into my heart and taken a solid hold. I love him. I love everything there is to love about him, and there's a lot.

Oh, God, how did this even happen?

I remain still in Becker's arms, praying he releases me soon so I can commence my panic attack. My body is feeling heavy in his hold, and I'm certain he must feel my shallow breathing.

When he finally lets me go, he lowers me to the bed, tucking me in tightly. He rests his lips on my cheek and holds them there for the longest time, gently caressing my head. 'Don't fall in love with me, Eleanor,' Becker murmurs. 'Please.' He gets up and leaves the room.

I hear the door close, and I lie in the dark for an age, trying to come to terms with my situation. I heard nothing but pain in his words just then. I'm not completely naïve. I believe I'll always hold Becker's attention, but I am more aware that his love of his art could be our undoing. And yes, I can see the irony that one of the things I most admire about him, that we share, could be the thing that causes the sharpest wedge.

He's a lone ranger, sweetheart. You'd be silly to think you can change that.

I can ponder the hurt he can inflict, imagine and evaluate the consequences, but I'll never truly grasp the damage he can cause until I experience it for myself. Am I going to hang around and wait for that to happen? *Will* it happen?

I'm stumbling willingly into the unknown, and although every scrap of sense I have is warning me against it, I have no desire to stop myself. I rewind a few paces. No, this isn't the unknown. What I'm actually doing is walking into the known. I know exactly where I'm headed. I now know what he's capable of in business, but more daunting than that, I know he's capable of breaking my heart. Heartbreak is devastating. It's agony. But you need to be able to feel your heart for it to hurt. You need to know it's there, beating in your chest. My heart is currently thundering, smashing against my ribcage like a monster trying to escape. My problem is, I have no idea if that is because it's desperately trying to escape the pain I'm willing to inflict on it, or whether it's just so happy to be feeling again after being dead for so long.

Looking up to the ceiling, like the thin air might offer me the answer, I fold my arms around my body and hug myself. It's a lame effort to try and physically hold myself together. I get out of bed and go in search of my phone. I need to call Lucy back. I hope she can give me some advice on my sorry situation.

She answers after two rings. 'I love him, Lucy,' I confess. 'And now I'm scared because I'm not sure he's capable of loving me.'

'The King's Head? Half an hour?'

I smile. 'I'm on my way.' I hang up and quickly get myself dressed before rushing down the stone steps from Becker's apartment. Space. I need some space away from here, if only for a few hours with my friend to talk, to spill my heart out. To try and get some perspective. To feel like me again.

Pausing at the bottom, I wonder whether I should at least tell him I'm going out. Not *why*, but I should tell him I'm going to see Lucy. I don't want him to worry.

My feet take me towards his office, but my pace slows when I hear him talking. 'I don't know, Paula.' Becker's words are frustrated, strained. He's talking to his therapist? 'Part of me desperately doesn't want to fuck this up,' he goes on, now sounding despondent. 'But the other part knows I will.'

I rest my hand on the wall and close my eyes, breathing in a shaky breath. *Please don't, Becker.* But if he has no faith in himself, how can I have faith in him?

'I've already told her too much,' he goes on, his words pained. 'I keep telling myself to keep my mouth shut, yet when I'm with her shit flies out without any thought for the consequences.' There's silence, and then he laughs. 'Instinct? No, Paula. I'd call it stupidity.'

I flinch and swallow, silently begging myself to leave. Go. Before I hear any more words that will fracture my heart.

More silence. And then more brutal truths. 'I'm not falling in love with her.' Another laugh, though this time it's half-hearted. Pathetic. Every reason for my anxiousness is there. And now

I'm even more panicked. Because if he feels like I do, he will never admit it. Because love is an obstruction to him. A bind he'll never want or need.

I put one foot in front of the other, my legs shaky, and my throat shrinking each time I swallow down my emotion. I reach for my key card with trembling hands as I approach the door to the Grand Hall and then freeze. A familiar electricity crackles in the air around me. He's near. I can sense him. That's how connected I feel to him. That's how much trouble I'm in.

I hear his office door close. 'Where are you going?' He sounds anxious.

My heart is suddenly lead, weighing me down. I turn to face him. He looks the most uncertain I've ever seen him, and I know it's because he knows I heard him. 'Just to see Lucy.'

'Without telling me?'

I bite down on my lip, glancing away, looking as guilty as I am. Too long passes with no words, and I eventually risk a peek at him. The nostrils of his perfect nose flare, his shoulders rising and falling from his heavy breaths.

'You heard me,' he says, taking one step forward, like he's preparing to chase me down when I bolt.

I shake my head, not willing to admit what he knows. 'Heard what?'

Becker eyes me doubtfully. 'What's wrong?'

I love you, and you will never let yourself love me. 'Nothing,' I say quietly, furiously ignoring the part of me that's demanding I confess my feelings. His pathetic warning not to fall in love with him is horseshit. He must know that.

His Adam's apple protrudes on a harsh swallow, the muscles in his jaw ticking as he continues to move forward. 'You're lying.' He reaches me, encroaching on my much-needed personal space. 'You're not fine.'

I don't mean to, but I find myself stepping back, away from him.

He ignores my attempt to escape him and carries on coming at me, and I continue to reverse my steps until my back is pinned against the wall and I have no more retreating space. I'm shaking, my despair taking a firmer hold now that he's before me, and he hasn't missed it. My bag and phone drop from my lifeless hands and hit the floor with collective thuds. He's looming over me, looking threatening and subservient all at once. His body screams power. But his eyes are flooded with weakness. I'm the source of that weakness, I know that beyond a doubt, and I'm fast figuring out that it scares him. *I* scare him.

Resting flat palms on the wall behind me, he leans in, scanning my face. He has a habit of doing this. Trapping me. I close my eyes, attempting to shut off my other senses.

His fingertip meets my arm and trails up my skin, on to my shoulder, and then my neck. It leaves a path of flames in its wake. The cool blood in my veins explodes into dangerous flames. And my heart explodes into hopeless shards of love.

I plant my hands on his chest and gather every scrap of strength to push him away. He jolts, but that's about it. A second later, my wrists are seized and pinned against the wall behind me. 'Becker, stop, please. Leave me alone.'

His face comes down to mine, close as can be without touching, his breaths forced into a steady pace. 'You look me in the eye and say that again,' he orders softly. 'If you truly want that, you'll look me in the eye and say it.' My cheeks are grabbed and my face directed to his. He's forceful but gentle with me. I'm made to confront profound magnificence. My eyes brim with tears, my stomach flutters with butterflies, and my skin tingles with need. His hazel eyes are the darkest I've ever seen them. 'Tell me.'

The words collect on my tongue but refuse to leave my mouth.

'Tell me to leave you alone, Eleanor. Tell me to fuck off and never bother you again. Tell me you don't want my body over yours. Our skin touching, our mouths touching, our fucking souls touching. Say it,' he whispers.

'I can't,' I whimper, trembling. The very thought of those things never happening again feels like a knife plunging repeatedly into my stomach, being twisted each and every time. I look into his eyes and let him see what's harbouring in mine. Fear. Love. Hope. 'I can't. Just like you could never let yourself love me.'

My words seem to anger him, the flash of rage in his eyes confirming it, but I know for sure he's angry with himself. Not me. He's angry because I am right. 'Do you want to leave?'

I feel my jaw tighten. 'Yes. But I can't, can I? Because you won't let me leave with your secrets.'

'It has nothing to do with my fucking secrets and everything to do with the fact that I don't want you to go. Understand?'

We stare at each other; his hazel eyes are balls of fire burning into mine.

'Understand?' he asks gently.

'No,' I admit. 'I don't understand anything.'

'Then maybe you'll understand this.' He's on me like a lion, fast and ferocious, pulling at my clothes as if they're the enemy. And I'm with him. I'm angry and confused, but I'm with him.

Our kiss is wild and crazy, desperate and passionate. His arousal is iron, pressing into my stomach, causing me to swivel my hips to ease the throb that's hijacked every single piece of me. My body is acting on instinct. My mind is focused on accepting his punishing attack. I don't know what to do. I don't know what to think.

So I do the only thing I have left – the only thing I'm capable of with Becker.

I surrender.

My clothes are being ripped from my body, his hands working fast while he maintains our manic kiss. 'Skin,' he pleads, sending my hands on a mission to remove his clothes. His

T-shirt is gone first, my arms yanking it above his head, taking his glasses off with it. He doesn't care. He kicks off his boots while pulling at the zip on my trousers, and I start on his jeans.

It's fast and it's clumsy.

It's desperate and it's hectic.

Hands are a blur of movement, and our mouths are greedy and unruly. I need to experience this disorder for longer, stretch it out and soak up the pleasure of his craving for me, because it feels so good to feel his need. But my own need is running away with me, the pressure in my groin increasing by the second. Patience isn't featuring in either of our plans. I need him inside me, I need him moving and making me feel good.

'Becker,' I pant, biting at his rough cheek, pushing at the waistband of his boxers to find my target. I wrap my hand around his cock and squeeze.

'Fuck.' His curse is strangled and weak, and my bra is cast aside, exposing my breasts to the cool air. My nipples are hard and ready, and his mouth abandons mine, encasing my soft flesh, his tongue swirling fast. 'You taste like nothing else.' He nips my nipple, and I yelp, tossing my head back and dropping his cock in favour of his hair. I roughly pull at it, then push his head to my chest, pull and push.

'I need to fuck you, princess.' He bites down hard and kisses his way to my mouth. 'I need to fuck you so hard, you never forget I was here.' He pushes two fingers into me, groaning at the wetness.

My greedy muscles grab and hold on, making it as difficult as possible for him to withdraw. 'Please,' I stutter. 'Please, please, please.'

'Shhhh, baby.'

I gasp into his mouth.

He bites my lip.

'You ready?' he asks urgently, taking my shoulders and turning me to face the wall. I nod, because speech has abandoned me. 'Hands on the wall.' He takes them for me and places them where he wants, before sliding soft palms down to my hips. I shudder. 'Back,' he says softly, tugging at my waist.

My forehead meets the wall when he paints a perfect line down my spine, tracing the crease of my bum. 'Perfect,' he muses. 'My filthy little princess wants me badly.' He pushes the pulsing head of his erection to my opening, driving me wild, and I begin mumbling nonsensical prayers to the floor, rolling my forehead from side to side. 'How badly do you want me, Eleanor? Tell me how badly you want me inside you.' My arse flies back in answer, earning a sharp slap.

'Ahhhh.'

'Fucking tell me.'

'Fuck me,' I plead, my voice desperate and broken. 'Please, fuck me.'

His growl is pure, raw and aching. 'That bad, huh? So bad you'll resort to begging?' He kicks my ankles apart and pushes halfway into me. I cry out, thrusting back to try and attain full penetration. I get denied the friction I so urgently need. I could cry – cry with frustration, cry with delight. He's depriving me, making me comprehend exactly how much I need it. How much I need *him*. It's coming. The penetration I need; I know it's coming, but the long, drawn-out affair he's making of this, intentionally fucking with my mind and senses, is making me hysterical. Irrational.

'Who owns you?' he yells. 'Who fucking owns you?'

'You,' I scream.

He shakes uncontrollably, and like a man possessed, he impales me on a pain-filled roar. I choke, my eyes flying open in shock, as he pants, withdrawing from me and re-entering on a deliberate, hard thrust. My mind begins to spin wildly. Then he's sliding out again, stroking my internal walls deliciously, and drives back into me forcefully. I gasp, pushing my hips back on to him in acceptance as he yells in appreciation and repeats his powerful drive again.

I could sob, overwhelmed by my feelings. My emotions are taking over, my body vibrating in bliss. He's unforgiving, punishing, but my body is welcoming him, craving him.

He slows down and circles meticulously, spreading my pleasure. The fullness is incredible, deep and satisfying. 'Just remember one thing.' He glides out smoothly and rolls back in slowly, and I whimper, desolate yet alive. 'No other woman has ever made me this crazy with want.' In one rapid action, he withdraws and strikes home, and I scream, my breath robbed by the brutal move. My hands slide across the wall, searching for anything to hold on to, but finding nothing. His pace increases, slamming into me, hitting me as deep as possible every time. Our bodies are wet, riddled with sweat, and clashing together frenziedly. 'No other woman, Eleanor. It's all about you.'

I'm about to splinter into a thousand pieces. My climax is charging forward ruthlessly, taking over my body, jumbling my mind further.

'Are you there?' he gasps, flexing his fingers and then drawing a long, deep breath.

'Yes,' I yell, sinking my teeth into my lip. Becker moans as he exhales, the sound of pure euphoria stretching on for an age.

'Can you wait for me?' he shouts, pounding harder still.

I cry out, clamping my muscles around his relentless cock to try and delay the orgasm from steaming forward.

'Oh fuck, you're clenching.' He hits me hard with his hips and starts shouting mindless words.

I can't hold off any more. I might lose my climax, and that will send me into psychosis. I can't risk it. I need this. I need to scream, make my throat sore, make my body shake from the pleasure it'll bring me. I burst, tossing my head back.

No other woman, Eleanor. It's all about you.

My body pulses, waves of pleasure ripping through me, my muscles starting to relax from exhaustion and relief.

But then I think of something and I tense up.

'Condom,' I gasp, trying to move.

'I'll pull out,' he barks, hammering on.

He's still mindless with pleasure behind me, thrusting madly in search of his own release. Then it happens, that last exhale of air on a long moan, and true to his word, he slips out and rests his cock in the crease of my arse, slowly thrusting, his fingers flexing on my hips.

'Oh God, help me,' he breathes, twitching and jerking behind me. His release hits my bare back, coating me wide and high, the warmth symbolic of how I'm feeling inside.

He slows his thrusts until he comes to a stop and collapses against me, but I can't stay upright any more. My legs are boneless. I fold to the floor, taking Becker with me, and he shifts just in time to cushion my landing, rolling to his back and pulling me on to his chest.

'Naked cuddles,' he murmurs. 'I need a naked cuddle.'

Of course. He may never love me, but he needs me.

My eyes close and I drift off, exhausted, sated . . . and helplessly in love.

Chapter 29

I'm woken by a gentle nudge to my ribs, and I come to, spread over Becker's chest, his wet skin still slipping with mine. 'Your phone, princess,' he mumbles sleepily. 'Make it stop.'

I scramble from his body and crawl up the corridor a little, finding my phone where I dropped it earlier. I brush my wild hair out of my face, all fingers and thumbs, trying to turn it up the right way to see who's calling me. 'Oh shit.' Lucy's name glows on the screen, almost menacingly. I look at the time in the corner, seeing it's nearly nine. I should have been at the King's Head over half an hour ago. *Shit, shit, shit.* 'Hello.' My shoulders skim my earlobes as I answer, my face screwing up.

'Are you okay?' she blurts.

'Yes,' I squeak.

'You sure? You sound . . . breathless.'

I actually am, an hour after being pummelled like a rag doll by Becker. And my heart's still going like the clappers. I shuffle to my arse and sit up against the wall, stark naked . . . in the corridor of The Haven. 'I'm fine.' I drop my voice. 'I need to talk to you.'

'Well, yeah. Weren't you on your way over an hour ago?'

'Something came up.'

She coughs and splutters. 'Something came up, or something *went* up?'

'Lucy,' I gasp, looking over to Becker's naked body sprawled across the corridor. He's on his back, arms spread wide, eyes lightly closed in a peaceful slumber. He looks like a fucking angel – a delicious, tempting, dangerous angel.

'Still wanna talk?'

'Yes,' I croak, my throat closing up on me once again. I need a friend to help me unravel my tangled mind, to understand and tell me it's going to be okay, to listen and not judge me.

'I'll meet you at my apartment,' Lucy sighs. 'I've been sitting in the pub on my own for half an hour. I'm sure everyone here thinks I've been stood up by a date.'

'Okay. See you there.'

We hang up, and my phone slides from my hand, thudding on the floor by my side. I sit for a few minutes, chewing my lip as I study my naked boss. 'Bastard,' I mumble, dragging myself to my feet. My muscles scream in protest as I straighten up, every part of me stiff and tight. I feel like I've run a marathon with no training. And my arse. That's still sore too. 'Why do I let you do it to me?' I ask his sleeping form. This feeling – emotionally and physically, because I'm hurting everywhere – is like I have the hangover from hell and I'm not sure whether the sensational night that's responsible for it was worth the agonising aftermath.

Becker stirs on a cute moan, his eyes fluttering open. He frowns at me standing above him, then looks around. 'This isn't my bed.'

I gather up my knickers and slip them on. 'I'm going out.'

The top half of his body is up and propped on his elbows in a second, his face anxious. 'Where?'

'I was supposed to meet Lucy at the pub half an hour ago.'

'Oh.' He deflates before my eyes with disappointment. 'I thought, well, I thought . . .'

'I'll be back,' I assure him, because I know I will. Despite everything I've heard and the constant sway from elated to sad, I'll be back. My reason for this is simple: hope. Hope amid my chaos. Hope that Becker Hunt lets himself go, lets himself fall in love with me.

I hesitate when I go to pull my trousers on, thinking I could really do with a shower after Becker's had his way with me and emptied himself all over my back. But I haven't time. I shudder on a little grimace as I root through my bag for a tissue and reach around my back to wipe the remnants of him away.

I pull on my trousers, followed by my bra and jumper. Then I reach into my bag again and spray myself stupid with perfume. When I'm done, Becker's still on the floor, staring up at the ceiling. 'Becker?'

He looks at me, and I see true worry in those angel eyes. 'I'm going to try my hardest not to break your heart, princess.' He pushes himself to his feet and rests his palm over his heart. I smile at his sweet gesture. 'I swear, I don't want to hurt you.'

I nod and approach him, reaching up on my tiptoes and coiling my arms around his neck. He returns my embrace, holding the back of my head and pushing me into his shoulder. 'I'll see you later,' I say quietly.

He squeezes me hard before abruptly letting me, like he's ripping a plaster off, rather than peeling it away and prolonging the pain. 'How long will you be?'

'A couple of hours, I suppose.' Depends how long it takes Lucy to convince me I'm not mad . . . if she can.

He gives me a strained smile, his dimple deep. 'Okay.'

'Okay,' I mimic, returning his smile and head quickly for the courtyard before I can convince myself to stay.

He looks truly lost, and I hate it.

I make it to Lucy's in record time and find her holding a glass of wine out to me when she answers the door. My hello is a quick raise of my glass in thanks and then a long glug of the sweet stuff. I follow it up with a satisfied gasp.

'This doesn't bode well.' She watches me drop to the couch. 'That bad?'

'Yes ... no ...' My head drops back. 'I don't know what's happening, Lucy.'

'Catch up, Eleanor. You've fallen in love.'

I don't feel like I've fallen. I feel like I've crashed-landed. He's bamboozled me. Knocked me on my unexpected arse. Consumed me with the passion he injects into everything he does, even testing my patience. 'I love my job. I would with or without Becker in the equation.'

'But he is in the equation,' she points out, joining me on the couch.

I nod in silent agreement. 'I need to see where this could take me, Lucy. If I walk away now, I'll never know. He's special. Funny. Exciting. So passionate and energetic.' I leave out immoral, cunning, and an arse-spanker. I can tell myself I can walk away until I'm blue in the face, but I'd be lying. I can't. Not until I really need to, and I'm not there yet. It's that simple. I'm in now. I can't turn back time.

Her hand takes mine, squeezing in reassurance. 'I'll be here. Whatever happens, I'll be here for you.'

'Thank you.' I'm so grateful for her crazy arse.

'Welcome.' She drops my hand. 'Besides, I'm counting on you doing the same for me.'

'Oh? What's happened?'

She grimaces at her glass. 'Nothing, but you know when you get the feeling that it might?'

I almost laugh. Has she listened to a word I've said? 'Um ... yeah.'

She doesn't appreciate my sarcasm, dipping a finger into her wine and flicking it in my face. 'Printer-room girl's been sniffing around.'

'Oh ...' I deflate on Lucy's behalf.

'Dirty slapper,' she mutters, giving her wine a filthy look before downing the rest. Glancing up at me, she catches my doubtful face before I can hide it.

'Why is she a dirty slapper?' I don't need to remind Lucy the dirty slapper wasn't in the printing room alone, but just in case she's forgotten, my subtle question serves as a good reminder. I half-smile and fall back on the couch when Lucy looks at me, outraged.

'I've been on four dates with Mark. I think I've earned the right to label any woman he's slept with before me a slapper.'

'Okay,' I relent, grinning. 'And how did you feel when you caught her on the prowl?'

Lucy's hackles rise, and I know she is in trouble herself. 'Like I wanted to hold her face on the copy machine, smash the lid down, take a copy, and then deface it with warts and a moustache.'

A sharp shot of laughter erupts, making me cough in quick succession.

'Yes, like that.' She drops her forehead to my shoulder. 'I don't do jealous. It's an ugly quality.'

'You do now.'

'For fuck's sake,' she mumbles, sighing dramatically. 'You staying with him tonight?'

'At Becker's? Yes.'

The intercom dings, and Lucy springs from my shoulder and rushes to the phone hanging by her door. 'Mark,' she says, throwing wide eyes across the room to me. 'Yes, come up.' The phone gets slammed against the wall, and her hands go straight to her blond bob. 'Shit, how do I look? Damn, I need to shave my pits and bits.'

I laugh out loud, just as she swings the door open. Mark appears, a smile on his face, but it falls slightly when he clocks me. 'Oh, hi.' An awkward hand comes up in greeting. 'Thought you were shacked up with your boss.'

My jaw goes slack, my round eyes turning to my blunt friend. Lucy's too busy patting her hair down to notice my offended state. 'I'm not shacked up,' I say through gritted teeth, turning a tight smile towards Mark.

'Of course.' He shifts from foot to foot, twiddling with his car keys. 'I didn't mean to ... I wasn't suggesting ...'

'It's fine.' I put him out of his embarrassed misery. Besides, I kind of am shacked up. It isn't his fault Lucy is brutally blunt.

He smiles awkwardly and finally looks at Lucy. She quickly falls into a cool, unaffected persona. 'All right?' she asks.

'I'm great. Fancy a drink?'

'Oh, I'd love to, but Eleanor and I are having a bit of a heart-to-heart.' She looks across at me with a coy smile. 'I can't leave my friend right now.'

God love her. She'd stay if I really needed her to, but I don't. 'No, you go.' I finish my wine and pull myself up from the couch. 'I'll call you in the morning.'

Her little face lights up. 'You sure?'

'Positive.'

Lucy immediately grabs her coat and shoves her feet into her boots, following me out into the corridor. Mark smiles a goodbye to me and starts towards the stairs, leaving Lucy and me behind. She pulls her coat on, smiling at my grinning face. 'I'm glad we both chose London,' she muses quietly, throwing her arms around me. 'I know our heads are a bit fucked up right now, but I'm still glad we're here.'

'Me too.' I snuggle into her, thankful for my crazy friend. I really am glad I chose London. When I pull away, I spot something poking out from under my front door. 'I need to get a few things from my flat. Go and have fun,' I say as I pull my keys from my bag.

'I will. Call you tomorrow.' She dances off, and I let myself into my flat, kneeling and collecting the card. It's a 'sorry we missed you' card. 'My phone,' I say to myself, slipping it into my bag and making a mental note to call and rearrange delivery in the morning. Not that I now need a new phone.

Deciding to take a few more things to Becker's, since I have no idea how long I'm staying, I pull my rucksack from under my bed and collect some clothes before heading to the bathroom to grab some other bits. I rifle through the basket under my sink to find a new blade for my razor, and as I stand, something catches my eye in the reflection of the mirror that hangs over my sink.

The window in my lounge.

It's open.

With my heart beating its way up to my throat, I drop my bag and slowly turn, seeing straight through to my flat. I tentatively creep forward, cautious and fretful. My eyes are darting wildly, taking in my small space. It's suddenly so cold. Freezing. But that's only a tiny reason why I'm shuddering. Every hair on my body is standing to attention, warning me, telling me to be on my guard.

I try to conjure up an obvious reason why it would be open. I can't. Even with the broken lock, it wouldn't be wide open. Unless someone actually opened it.

Feeling vulnerable and panicked, I rush back to the bathroom and grab my bag, but I don't make it back out. The door shifts when I clumsily bump into it in my frantic state, and I look up to the mirror, seeing it moving a fraction.

Only a tiny bit.

But enough to see that there's someone behind it.

The blood drains from my head and I swing around, backing up until I bump into the sink and send bottles and cans crashing to the floor. 'Oh my God,' I gasp, my mind screaming, confusing me with two conflicting instructions.

Fight.

Or flee.

Instinct takes over before I can decide, having me snatching my bag from the floor and hauling it with brute force across the space. It collides with the door, pushing it back, concealing whoever is there for a split second before it bounces off their body harshly and then slams shut. I back up until my backside hits the wall, my blood running cold.

My rash decision now has me shut in my bathroom staring at the intruder, who's clothed from head to toe in black – black combat trousers, black roll-neck sweater, black gloves, black boots . . .

And a black balaclava.

Terror grips me, takes me in its evil clutches and constricts until it feels like my bones could break. I can't breathe. Can't think. Can't move. I'm staring at his ominous frame, just staring, waiting for him to attack me.

But he doesn't move a muscle. He stands motionless. The only evidence of life is the slight rise and fall of his chest. He's by the door. He knows he has me trapped. My eyes flick continuously from his tall, menacing physique to my only means of escape.

Then he moves. It's sudden and jerky, and it shocks me back to life. I pelt for the door and grapple with the handle, but my body, my hands, everything is shaking too much for me to control my movements and take a firm grip of the handle. He grabs my arm.

'No,' I scream, swinging around with flailing limbs. The back of my hand collides with the side of his head with a force I never thought I was capable of, sending his head cracking to the side. He growls, and I back up, shocked by my own strength. His body reeks power, the outlines of taut muscles clear under the tight material of his sweater. I'll never fight him off. He'll crush me.

But my survival instinct is strong. I grab anything I can lay my hands on and start launching things at his head, hoping to daze him and buy myself enough time to escape. He just steams straight through the objects flying through the air towards him and seizes me, wrapping a forearm around my chest and opening the door. 'No,' I cry, fighting with everything I have, screaming as he wrestles with my bucking body, grunting each time I kick a leg out and catch him. I'm uncoordinated, thrashing aimlessly, pulling and ripping at his sweater as he tries to grab my hands. I won't let him. I can't let him. 'Get off me,' I scream, throwing my head back when he wraps an arm around my waist and hauls me up. The pain that sears through my head is like nothing I've felt before, making my brain throb instantly. But the loud hiss of pain that comes from behind tells me he didn't dodge my thrashing head, and that injects more determination into me. Gathering every scrap of strength and energy I have left, I claw at his hands and throw my heel back, catching him cleanly in the shin.

He gasps and we're crashing to the floor a second later, my head skimming the edge of the sink. The impact is brutal, and I grunt as my back hits the floor, knocking every bit of air from my lungs. My eyes blink over and over, trying to keep their focus. My vision has gone blurry, but my hands still work. I reach and sink my nails into his back and yank, tearing at his sweater and spiking a low grunt of pain. He grabs my hands harshly and shoves them to the floor above my head.

And then I'm helpless. My hands have been captured, and he's lying across me, effectively pinning me to the bathroom floor. Bursts of his angry breaths saturate the air, and he shifts to get a better hold on me, his head hung low near my shoulder, his hard muscles cutting into my flesh. I whimper, the terrified tears that have been held back by pure adrenalin now charging forward and pouring from my eyes.

'Please don't hurt me,' I sob. 'Please, I don't know what you want.'

He doesn't move for a painfully long time, probably feeding off the fear he's evoked. Then he slowly brings his head up, keeping his face away, and my distress amplifies, just from the close-up view of the menacing black balaclava.

My stomach twists, my vision blurring as my tears build and build, and I tremble beneath him, terrified. My hands are becoming numb from his tight hold of my wrists, but the rest of my body is physically pulsing from the blood rushing through my veins. 'Please,' I murmur weakly, my plea trickling past my lips on a shaky breath.

I close my eyes and pray. *Please, please, please.* I repeat my silent prayers over and over, turning my head away when I feel him staring down at me, watching me hide from my fate.

My breathing slows, and I relax. My mind is giving up. Everything is giving up. Then the sense of freedom engulfs me, my body becoming weightless. It takes a while to figure out why.

My eyes snap open. My arms are free. He moves fast, lifting himself from my body and lunging for the bathroom door. Life powers through me and I scramble to my feet quickly, seeing the bathroom door slam. Instinct kicks in. I dash for the door and yank it open, my legs miraculously working. I can't feel them. I can't feel anything. But I can see. He's at the window. I stutter to a stop and watch him climb up on to the windowsill, and then in the blink of an eye, he's gone.

The adrenalin suddenly drains from my body and I release a sob, my body starting to convulse as I lose control of my emotions. I grab the doorframe to steady myself, every muscle going slack, and I start to drag in long breaths, knowing I need to get some air into my lungs. *My phone.* I dash into the bathroom and rummage through my bag, yelling my frustration when I don't find it. Then I remember it dropping to the floor in the corridor at The Haven after I took Lucy's call. 'No,' I shout, slamming my bag on the sink. I need to get out of here. Gathering my things, I fly out of my apartment like a gust of wind.

I stumble down the stairs clumsily, out into the cold like a madwoman. My head is spinning, my heart racing, and in an act of pure impulse and desperation, I rifle through my bag, finding my purse and pulling out the tattered old picture of Dad and me. It doesn't give me a scrap of comfort. His face laughing up at me doesn't help calm my nerves. I sob into the cold night-time air as I take off down the street to the Tube station, my impulse sending me to the place I've made my sanctuary and to the man who has my heart.

Chapter 30

The sight of the courtyard at The Haven doesn't capture me like it usually does. The peaceful atmosphere that engulfs this space doesn't settle me. I don't have the usual warmth coursing through me. I thought it would help calm me but it hasn't. But I know Becker will.

Dashing across the cobbled stones and into the Grand Hall, I stumble through the space carelessly, more than once hearing the precarious shift of something as I steam past. I swipe my card, and I'm out of there before my mind has caught up with my body. Then I'm standing at the mouth of the corridor, trying to catch my breath.

I deliberate my next move, wondering where he could be. 'Becker,' I yell, but I get no response. I don't know where to look, his office, the kitchen, the library. My frantic state is making it impossible to calm down. But then I'm racing up the stone steps like a bat out of hell. My key card grants me access to Becker's apartment, and when the door closes behind me, I drop my bag and force myself to be still, listening for any sounds. My breathing is hampering me. It's loud and chaotic. Blood is whooshing around my head, invading my hearing, making me dizzy. I'm moving towards the glass-bricked wall before any senses kick in, something drawing me there, telling me what I'm seeking can be found beyond the shimmering bricks. The sound of rushing water starts low and quiet until I'm at the door and it becomes loud and harsh. I can't see a thing. Becker's bathroom is engulfed in steam, the hot air clinging to me, making me instantly damp. I need him to hold me, tell me everything is okay.

'Becker.' His name on my lips is a whimper.

The water shuts off immediately. Now the only sound is my chaotic gasps for breath. He appears, like a mirage, making my legs wobble. He looks grave, his naked body dripping wet and oozing wariness. 'Eleanor?' He grabs a towel and wraps it around his waist, coming towards me. 'Shit, baby, what happened?'

I stagger forward on a meek cry, and he catches me, pulling me up to his body. 'Fucking hell,' he curses, crushing me to him and lifting me from my feet, carrying me out of the bathroom. Settling on the edge of his bed, he negotiates my body until I'm cradled in his lap and he's whispering comforting words in my ear. 'Shhhh.' He cups my head in his big hand and rocks me. 'Eleanor, princess, tell me what happened.'

'Someone.' I hiccup over my words, clutching his naked chest like a comfort blanket. 'Someone was in my flat again.'

His hold of me constricts some more, his chest heaving. 'You went back?' He asks it as a question, despite already knowing the answer.

I nod into his chest. 'To get some clean knickers,' I tell him.

'Shit, Eleanor. Why did you go there? For fuck's sake.' He's really mad, and through my fright I manage to wonder why.

I pull away from his chest and find him regarding me carefully. 'Why are you so mad with me?'

He removes me from his lap, placing me on my still unstable feet, and backs away from me, dragging his hand through his wet hair. 'You shouldn't have gone back.'

'Why?' I don't like his stricken expression. At all.

'It's not safe.'

'Why?' I demand again, focusing on his stressed features, seeing a torn soul before me. He's behaving oddly. What does he know? Is he hiding something?

'It's just not safe,' he shouts, snatching up some grey lounge pants and yanking them on. 'Never go back there, do you hear me?' He gives me a determined stare, effectively pinning me in place.

'Why?' I whisper. It's all I have. Why is he so angry, so stressed? What does he know?

He looks at me like the weight of the world is on his shoulders, his expression wavering between strength and defeat. He clenches his eyes shut for a few moments, gathering some fortitude, then he approaches me carefully, like someone might approach a frightened animal. He takes my shoulders and the warmth of his hold through my clothes makes everything so much better. He pushes his lips to my forehead, breathing in. 'Trust me,' he whispers hoarsely. His forearms wrap around my neck and pull me in, his chin resting on the top of my head. 'Calm down,' he soothes. 'Just calm down, and I'll explain.' He holds me tight to his body like he never intends on letting me go.

'I'm okay,' I lie, wriggling a little until he eases up on his grip, releasing me.

My hands drag across the hot flesh of his back as I pull away. 'You're all wet,' I say meekly, bringing my hands around, showing him my damp palms.

Becker gasps, his face drops, and he steps back, staring at my hands.

I frown and look down.

And stagger back.

Blood.

'Eleanor . . .' He barely whispers as my eyes snap to his. Why is he distancing himself? His mouth opens again, but nothing comes out. He's just staring at my hands that are coated in a diluted mix of blood and water.

'I don't unders—' My words fade to nothing, my gaze dropping to my palms again as something so unbelievable slams into my brain like a bullet, so hard it can't be ignored. I shoot my eyes up and lunge forward, grabbing Becker's shoulders and wrenching his body around. He puts up a fight, his face twisting, but I'm determined. 'Turn around!'

I lose sight of his frightened hazel eyes when he squeezes them shut, and he sluggishly turns away from me, his tattoo slowly revealing itself. The lines, the grey, the shadows, the figures, and labels, they're all there. The map is dominating his back.

But nestled between the beauty of his mammoth tattoo is something else. Something new. My lungs shrink to nothing. Lacerations. Four long slashes, weeping with blood. Four long grazes stretching from his shoulder to the middle of his back.

Scratches from fingernails.

Oh fuck.

No. Please, no

My fingernails.

I flash back to a memory of me clawing at my attacker's back, ripping at his sweater. 'No.' I shove him away, retreating until my calves hit his mattress and I lose my footing. I land on the bed clumsily and instinctively start scrambling back. Becker slowly turns, and his face tells me everything I need to know. I'm not imagining this. 'No.' I shake my head, like I can shake myself away from here.

'Eleanor, listen to me.'

'No.' My back hits the headboard. 'No.' If I shout it loud enough for long enough, I might snap out of my nightmare. This has to be a nightmare.

'It's not what you think.' Becker approaches warily, his hands held up in a sign of surrender. 'Please, just listen to me.' His chest is heaving. The laboured breaths that I thought were a result of anger are actually a result of exertion. He's been running. Running from his secret underground garage after racing across town in one of his many cars. To try and beat me. To try and pretend he was here the whole time.

My body fuses to the wood behind me, my feet pushing into the mattress, like if I put enough effort into it, the wall behind me might swallow me up and take me away from this bad dream. 'Was it you?' I choke the question out and hold my breath, stupidly hoping for a miracle. I don't know why I'm asking. I've seen the scratches on his back, the scratches I put there, and I'm analysing his persona, his reaction to my clarity. He looks traumatised. Totally broken.

Guilty.

He stops at the foot of the bed. His bare chest is quivering, and his hands drop to his sides. What I'm looking at right now is true surrender. 'It was me,' he murmurs, keeping his eyes on my shaking form. 'You said you were meeting Lucy at the pub. You weren't supposed to be there.'

Air leaves my lungs on a desolate cry, and I'm off the bed like a rocket, grabbing my bag and flying through the door. I needed him to admit it, to say it out loud, and now I need to escape. My poor heart struggles under my shock, and my legs lose all feeling as they pelt down the stairs.

'Eleanor.' The slap of bare feet on the stone echoes around me, banging in my head, making me dizzy and freaked. 'For fuck's sake. Eleanor.'

My shoulder crashes with the wall on the corner of the stairs, the force sending me hurtling into the wall at the bottom. My palms slap the plaster, but the sting burning my skin as a result doesn't even touch the agony of my breaking heart. I'm off down the corridor, mad and deranged, my mind being flooded with too much to unravel.

I see my mobile lying on the floor and collect it as I pass, reaching the Grand Hall door. I fumble to swipe my card and open it, then I run like my life depends on it to the courtyard. I could navigate the dark alleyway with my eyes closed now, but I home in on the switch at the entrance and give myself the benefit of light, hoping it will get me out of here faster.

He's coming. I can hear his feet pounding on the concrete behind me, but he won't stop me this time. I swipe my card and stumble on to the main street, relieved when I land on the busy pavement. No one takes any notice of me; they just dodge my body as I spin on the spot, trying to gather my bearings. It's dark, it's cold, and I have no idea where to run.

'Eleanor!' Becker's roar echoes loudly, spilling from the entrance of the alleyway.

I turn around and come face to face with him as he skids to a stop. His expression is tight, his bare chest pulsing. 'Eleanor.' He reaches for my arm, but I dodge him and move away.

'Why were you there?'

He closes his eyes, his cheeks hollow from his gritted teeth.

'Tell me why,' I scream.

'Fuck!' He swings around and throws his fist into the wall, roaring his way through the pain he spikes. I jump, startled by his fury.

He shakes his hand as he comes close, taking one small, cautious step at a time until he's breathing down on me. His closeness, it doesn't have the usual effect. I'm not breathing heavily with lust or desire or need for this man. Now my deep breathing is fuelled solely by fear. I'm frightened of him. 'You bastard.' My voice quivers with emotion, and my arm flies forward, my palm landing a brutal slap to his face. His head snaps to the side, his jaw tensing. 'Stay away from me.'

'Trust me, Eleanor. Please, you need to trust me.'

'You attacked me,' I scream, backing away.

'I didn't fucking attack you,' he bellows back, grabbing my shoulders and pushing me into the wall. The impact shocks me still. 'I was restraining you.' He looks panicked. 'Please, for fuck's sake, please, just trust me.'

'That's just it, Becker. I did. I did fucking trust you. And you destroyed it.' I barely get the words out through the ache crippling me. 'Don't try to find me.' I use all my force to shove him away and sprint across the road, being stupidly reckless, not checking for traffic. I make it to the other side, ignoring the loud screeching of annoyed car horns.

'Eleanor!' Becker shouts repeatedly, desperately.

I swing around and see him on the other side of the road, bare-chested, his eyes frantically trying to keep me in view while he dives between cars, smacking bonnets and yelling for people to stop. But his shouts fade to nothing when a bus comes between us and I disappear down a side street. I don't know where I'm going. Have no idea what to do.

My new start, my new life free from grief, guilt, pain and betrayal has been stolen.

Becker Hunt stole my heart.

Ripped it from my chest.

How is it possible that my heaven has transformed into the worst kind of hell?

Betrayal.

How could my spirit be unearthed and then lost again?

Stolen.

His angel eyes have danger looming behind their beauty.

Grief.

My saint really is a sinner.

I will *never* get over this.

Agony.

Acknowledgements

This book has been a long time coming. Not because the idea has been floating around in my mind for a few years, but because this book has actually been written for a few years. Five years, to be precise. I wrote Becker and Eleanor's story straight after *One Night*, and then the universe happened and it got banked. Each year, I've had every intention of giving you Artful Lies, and for one reason or another, it hasn't happened. Trust me, it's killed me. But now, as I write this, I'm reminding myself that everything happens for a reason. Becker Hunt is a wonderful mix of a man. If I was asked to describe *Artful Lies* in one sentence, it would be: *This Man* meets *The Thomas Crown Affair*. And there is probably your reason. I honestly don't think you could have handled Becker Hunt so close off the back of Jesse Ward. He is pure and utter fire, alpha but loveable, dangerous but safe, and he has an unrelenting passion for adventure. With Eleanor, you are about to be taken on an journey into his corrupt, thrilling, secret world of art and antiques. Try not to fall in love with him. I dare you.

As ever, thank you to my kick-arse agent, Andrea, for guiding me and being my soundboard for the past seven years. Finally, Becker is out there! To my editor at Orion, Victoria, your passion for my stories and characters makes me smile so much. It's been a pleasure working on Artful Lies with you. To Marion Archer, your input on my stories is invaluable. Thank you for navigating the world of Becker with me. To Nina at SBPR, I know I drive you to insanity with my cluelessness. I just wanna write! Thank you for being patient with me and giving me the kick up the arse I sometimes need to get sh!t done.

And to my readers, thank you for . . . everything. I can't tell you how relieved I am to finally get Becker in your hands. Because I know, beyond anything I know, that you're going to fall in love. I'm sorry for making you wait so long for him, even if you didn't really know you were waiting.

JEM x

Credits

Jodi Ellen Malpas and Orion Fiction would like to thank everyone at Orion who worked on the publication of *Artful Lies* in the UK.

Editorial
Victoria Oundjian
Olivia Barber

Copy editor
Justine Taylor

Proof reader
Jane Howard

Audio
Paul Stark
Amber Bates

Contracts
Anne Goddard
Paul Bulos
Jake Alderson

Design
Rabab Adams
Joanna Ridley

Nick May
Helen Ewing

Editorial Management
Charlie Panayiotou
Jane Hughes
Alice Davis

Finance
Jasdip Nandra
Afeera Ahmed
Elizabeth Beaumont
Sue Baker

Marketing
Jennifer McMenemy

Production
Ruth Sharvell

Publicity
Alainna Hadjigeorgiou

Sales
Laura Fletcher
Esther Waters
Victoria Laws
Rachael Hum
Ellie Kyrke-Smith
Frances Doyle
Georgina Cutler

Operations
Jo Jacobs
Sharon Willis
Lisa Pryde
Lucy Brem

**A desperate passion. A dangerous love story.
Becker is back . . .**

Truths

Eleanor Cole had no idea that when she met the charmingly
irresistible Becker Hunt, she was putting her life on the line.
So when she discovers his secrets, escape seems to be her only
option – but Becker isn't ready to let Eleanor go.

She knows better than to fall into his corrupt world again, but
how long can she resist when he's stolen her heart?

Eleanor must make a choice, to stay and follow Becker into
the heart of the danger . . . or risk losing him forever.

**If you loved *Artful Lies*, don't miss the sizzling new novel
from international bestseller Jodi Ellen Malpas**

Available to pre-order now